She was a spoiled and willful young beauty — and no match for a man with . . .

Hamilton's eyes were closed, the lids flickering sporadically. The thick, wide bandage that was wrapped around his midsection was tinged with blood.

Catherine moistened her lips, uncertain of whether to stay or go.

It took several seconds for recognition to break through the glaze of pain. "Catherine?" he gasped.

"Hamilton," she sobbed in a whisper. "Oh, Hamilton, what have I done to you?"

"You've nothing to blame yourself for, Catherine. It was my contest. I lost it. He proved himself the better man."

"No, Hamilton! No! He's vile and brutal and cold-hearted — I had no choice, Hamilton! Father forced me to do it. He was in a rage, he threatened to throw me out into the night — "

"You *married* him?"

. . . THE PRIDE OF LIONS

THE PRIDE OF LIONS

MARSHA CANHAM

PaperJacks LTD.

TORONTO   NEW YORK

AN ORIGINAL

PaperJacks

THE PRIDE OF LIONS

PaperJacks LTD

330 STEELCASE RD. E., MARKHAM, ONT. L3R 2M1
210 FIFTH AVE., NEW YORK, N.Y. 10010

First edition published March 1988

This is a work of fiction in its entirety. Any resemblance to actual people, places or events is purely coincidental.

CDN ISBN 0-7701-0867-9
US ISBN 0-7701-0792-3
Copyright © 1988 by Marsha Canham
All rights reserved
Printed in the USA

To Peter, my mainstay, who puts up with the insomnia, the forgotten meals, the constant doubts and biweekly threats to heave the typewriter through the window . . . any window . . .

To Lesley, who says she has yet to see her name in any of my books, and to Suzie and Lindsay, whose mother insists they be twenty-one before they *find out* if they are in any of my books.

To the various friends and acquaintances who step lively through these pages, I hope they realize they do so out of affection.

And to my son, Jeffrey, who was just a little boy the last time I looked up from my desk and now, well, *he* calls *me* Shorty.

GENEALOGICAL TABLE

Stuarts and Hanovers

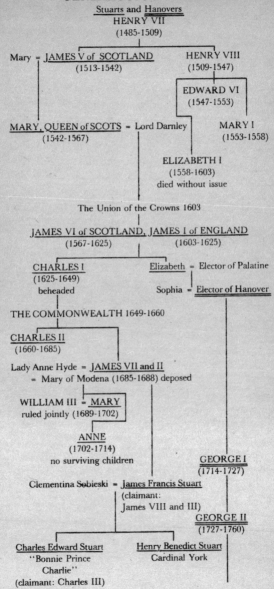

HENRY VII
(1485-1509)

Mary = JAMES V of SCOTLAND
(1513-1542)

HENRY VIII
(1509-1547)

EDWARD VI
(1547-1553)

MARY, QUEEN of SCOTS = Lord Darnley
(1542-1567)

MARY I
(1553-1558)

ELIZABETH I
(1558-1603)
died without issue

The Union of the Crowns 1603

JAMES VI of SCOTLAND, JAMES I of ENGLAND
(1567-1625)   (1603-1625)

CHARLES I
(1625-1649)
beheaded

Elizabeth = Elector of Palatine

Sophia = Elector of Hanover

THE COMMONWEALTH 1649-1660

CHARLES II
(1660-1685)

Lady Anne Hyde = JAMES VII and II
= Mary of Modena (1685-1688) deposed

WILLIAM III = MARY
ruled jointly (1689-1702)

ANNE
(1702-1714)
no surviving children

GEORGE I
(1714-1727)

Clementina Sobieski = James Francis Stuart
(claimant:
James VIII and III)

GEORGE II
(1727-1760)

Charles Edward Stuart
"Bonnie Prince
Charlie"
(claimant: Charles III)

Henry Benedict Stuart
Cardinal York

DERBY: July 1745

Chapter One

Catherine reined in her horse at the top of the forested knoll and waited, her eyes sparkling, her heart pounding within her breast. She could detect no signs of pursuit through the deeply wooded grove, but to be doubly sure she urged the roan down into a hollow and cantered behind a dense copse of fir trees. Sitting there, panting to catch her breath, her cheeks flushed pink from excitement, she wished she had never outgrown childhood, never entered the world of whalebone stays and stiff linen stomachers.

In the next moment, however, she knew she was deliciously happy to be Catherine Augustine Ashbrooke, the toast of three counties — admittedly beautiful, admittedly pampered, and admittedly spoiled. She was happy to be home in Derby, now that the season in London was over, and although it had been as exhilarating and stimulating and madly scandalous as always, she was looking forward to an entirely different season in the country — more melodic, far more relaxed. Here there were quiet, starlit evenings, days drenched in sunlight and pungent with the perfume of roses and lilacs. There were also brisk morning chases — as there had been today — when the fox only appeared to be the true quarry.

Laughing, she dismissed the feeble efforts of the two-legged bloodhounds and with a smug twinkle in her violet-blue eyes, she spoke gently to the roan again.

"Well done, my beauty. I should think this calls for a sweet reward."

There was a stream a few hundred yards ahead, if she remembered correctly, one that ran cold and clear and tasted faintly of soft green moss and black peat.

"We could both use a cool drink, now couldn't we? Let the hounds wander in circles as they may."

The mare nickered softly in response and pulled against the bit. Catherine gave her her head, trusting the animal's instinct to choose the correct path. She felt safe enough, knowing she was well within the boundaries of the Ashbrooke estate, knowing also that if she simply gave the order, the mare could easily carry them back to Rosewood Hall.

She ducked her head to avoid a low branch and pursed her lips in a quiet, "Whoa."

Patting the gleaming neck, she slipped soundlessly to the carpeted forest floor. In the distance, she could hear the braying of the dogs and the eerie, hollow echo of the trumpet calling the riders to formation. She ignored the sound, preferring instead to remove her tall, veiled hat and tug at the webbed snood that bound her hair in a restrictive knot at the nape of her neck. She shook the thick golden cascade free as she walked, her attention divided equally between observing the riot of new saplings thrusting their heads up through the bed of withered leaves, and listening for footfalls that might be hidden by the musky covering.

Since she was alone and had every intention of remaining so, she removed her fine gray kidskin gloves and unfastened the cameo broach that held the collar of her white silk blouse closed at her thoat. The buttons of her dark blue velvet riding habit were loosened next, along with the pearl closures of the fitted satin waistcoat. Halted abruptly by a branch that had snagged the hem of her long, pleated skirt, she was leaning over to free it when she felt an unaccountable prickle of alarm skitter down her spine.

Her first thought was that she had been found out, and she whirled around, fully expecting to see the grinning visage of a scarlet-coated hunter. Only the trees, however, green and sparkling in the filtered sunlight, met her alarmed gaze. Listening intently, she could hear the soft gurgling of the stream just up ahead, the birds bickering in the high branches, squirrels and other ground animals rustling in the dense undergrowth all around her. She tilted her head up to catch the secretive whisper of a breeze chasing through the silver-backed leaves, and she felt the warmth of a sunbeam dancing through a break in the trees. She smiled inwardly and even imagined she could hear the crackling voice of her old governess reaching out through the tunnel of time: *Never go out walking alone, Young Missy, it's a sure invitation to trouble. The woods are full of gap-toothed boar hunters who'd as soon ruin a fine young lady as stop to ask the time of day.*

Dear old Miss Phoebe. As stern as a yardstick, as pinched as a prune. She'd had her hands full trying to turn Sir Alfred Ashbrooke's daughter into a Fine Young Lady Whose Sterling Reputation No One Could Question!

Catherine's smile was a little sad as she continued walking, for Miss Phoebe had died of the fever two summers before. As stern and as uncompromising as she had been, at least the governess had genuinely cared for her charge. The same could hardly be said of Lady Caroline Ashbrooke, the cool and untouchable mistress of Rosewood Hall, or Sir Alfred, a recently elected member of Parliament who rarely spared more than a quick, passing thought for anyone in his family, let alone a daughter who seemed determined to challenge him into early gray hairs. Catherine had only her brother, Damien, to turn to for advice or comfort, and even he was distancing himself more and more these days. He had established a law practice in London and rarely found time to commute to Derby. He was here now, for a fortnight, but only because she had practically threatened him at gunpoint.

It wasn't every day a girl turned eighteen, nor was it every girl who could boast of fourteen proposals of marriage in the twenty-four months since her "coming out". To that end, Catherine had grand plans for the stroke of midnight. Thoughts of them made her skin tingle and her pulse race and her footsteps turn swift and light as she rounded a thatch of tall junipers. There, she stopped so suddenly her blue velvet skirt creamed against her ankles like the backwash of a ship.

The stream was directly ahead of her, a shiny ribbon of water slicing neatly through a wide clearing of moss-covered earth. The sunbeams, bolder and broader here, fogged with the mist of evaporating dew, lit the brilliant greens of the leaves and moss, silvered the surface of the bubbling water, and immodestly outlined the naked torso of a man kneeling by the stream.

Jolted by the unexpected sight, Catherine stood absolutely still. She had no idea who he was, as his back was to her, the muscles rippling with the motion of his hands as they splashed water on his face. A poacher? She thought not; from what she could see, he did not have the ragged, hungry look of a thief about him. His breeches were clean and well tailored to his long, powerful legs; his high boots were fashioned from expensive leather and polished to a mirror gloss. A shirt and coat lay nearby on the moss, the shirt of fine white linen, the jacket of rich, claret-coloured wool.

His black hair curled down his neck, dripping water on shoulders that were broad and gleaming like newly sculpted bronze. Raking his hair back with impatient fingers, he flicked the water from himself in a bright shower of droplets. The question of why he had stopped in the clearing was apparent; the question of how he had come to be there was partially answered by a shrill whinny from the opposite side of the stream. An immense black stallion stood there, ears pricked warily upright, nostrils tautly flared to catch the scent of the intruder. Catherine had not seen the beast at first because of the haze of sunbeams, but the animal had obviously seen her. And the man, hearing the alarm from the horse, pivoted swiftly, his hand a blur of motion as it stretched out for the pistol that lay hidden beneath the folds of his jacket. The sight of the gun, and the speed with which he palmed it, startled a cry from Catherine's lips. She dropped her hat and gloves and her hands flew up to cover her mouth.

For a moment, the two stared at each other without further sound or movement. His eyes commanded all of her attention; they were as black as his shaggy mane of hair, as dangerous and riveting as the barrel of the pistol he held pointed unwaveringly toward her breast. He blinked once, as if to confirm what his eyes were seeing, then quickly lowered the gun.

"Has no one ever warned you against sneaking up on a man when his back is turned?" His voice was harsh with anger, a deep masculine baritone that sent a strange, warm thrill through her limbs.

"Has no one told you, sir, that it is singularly unhealthy to trespass on private property?"

He blinked again and some of the wild, savage look went out of his eyes. "I beg your pardon?"

"This is private property," she repeated tersely. "And you are trespassing. If I were a gameskeeper, or if I were armed, I could have shot you out of hand."

"Then I should count myself lucky that you are neither," he mused, the dark eyes narrowing. "May I ask what you are doing out here in the middle of nowhere?"

"You may not!" she retorted indignantly. "What you may do, however, is gather your belongings and leave here at once! This land belongs to Sir Alfred Ashbrooke, a man who does not take kindly to strangers . . . or *poachers*."

The man studied her a moment longer, then slowly stood up, straightening to an impressive height of well over six feet.

"It's been a long time since anyone has accused me of poaching" — He smiled faintly — "and lived."

Catherine's temper flared. Not entirely certain of how to react to his bold stare, she had no hesitation whatsoever in responding to his insolent humour.

"There are forty men riding within the sound of my voice. A single scream and —"

"At least you have sense enough to be frightened," he interrupted, his grin broadening. It changed the entire composition of his face, lending him a rakish, almost aristocratic bearing. "I think you should have listened to your nanny years ago when she warned you against walking alone in the forest."

Catherine's eyes widened. "How did you know —"

"Doesn't every nanny worth her vinegar warn her charges of the perils of walking in the woods?" He gave his wrists a final flick to clear his hands of excess water, then leaned over to pluck his shirt off the ground. "In your case, you should consider yourself lucky you didn't run across someone less scrupulous than myself, someone who might not be deterred by a sharp tongue and an equally sharp disposition."

"Someone less scrupulous? You flatter yourself, sir. And what do you mean, sharp disposition? My disposition is perfectly fine."

The calm, unnerving stare pinioned her again, holding her without evasion, long enough for a flush to deepen and spread down her throat. His gaze followed, lingering on the parted edges of her collar before descending to where the fabric molded attractively over her breasts. As if that was not indecent enough, he showed his teeth again in another wolfish grin.

"My first guess tells me you might be related in some way to this . . . Sir Alfred Ashbrooke?"

"I am his daughter. What of it?"

"His daughter." She was aware of his taking slow, measured steps closer, but her feet would not respond to an inner command to turn and run. Her roan sensed her sudden nervousness, however, and snorted a warning, which instantly challenged the enormous black stallion into thundering several paces across the clearing.

"Shadow!" the man said sharply, not taking his eyes away from Catherine's face. "Stand!"

She glanced past his shoulder and saw the stallion skid to a halt at once. He stood, sable head held erect, eyes like smoldering coals, the gleaming flanks trembling with the desire to attack. Catherine's astonishment was made complete when she realized the diversion had allowed the stranger to come within arm's reach. His attention was no longer on her, but on the roan, and he was going so far as to extend a hand toward the velvet-soft muzzle.

"She'll tear your fingers off!" Catherine cautioned.

The hand hesitated, but only fractionally, before continuing toward the smooth muzzle. The roan's nostrils flared, her eyes widened with hostility, but she made no overt move to stop the long, tanned fingers from stroking the tapered snout. The stranger had donned his shirt, but it hung carelessly open and Catherine had nowhere to look but at the wall of his chest, at the cloud of dark curling hairs that did little to conceal the powerful planes and contours of the muscles beneath. She lifted her eyes slowly, settling first on the lean, square jaw, the mouth that was neither full nor thin, the nose that was straight and prominent. At this close proximity his eyes were obsidian, but when they came into contact with a stray sunbeam, the light was absorbed and they became a vibrant, glowing midnight blue, at once full of secrets and hinting at dark passions. Arched above were eyebrows the colour of a raven's wings, one of them slashed through with a thin white scar — a dueling scar? — to give his arrogant features an added sardonic twist.

His arm accidentally brushed against her shoulder as he

stroked the roan, and Catherine flinched as if touched by fire.

"Excuse me," she said tartly, "but this is my horse. It is, in effect, my clearing as well. So if you don't mind, I would prefer that you leave here at once."

Bemused, he raised an eyebrow. "And if I said I preferred to stay?"

Catherine's mouth gaped at his audacity. "You, sir, are a nuisance and a trespasser, as impudent and shameless as any man I have ever had the misfortune to meet, and one who no doubt has thoughts of poaching, even if he has not done so already."

He edged closer and Catherine felt the sudden burst of courage desert her as the midnight eyes raked her again.

"Oh, I am beginning to have thoughts, Mistress Ashbrooke," he murmured. "But not of poaching."

Catherine stumbled back and came up hard against the roan's warm flesh. The stranger moved with her, placing his hands on the horse's neck, effectively trapping her between them. He was near enough now that she could smell the sunshine and saddle leather on his skin; she could see the beads of water glittering in his hair, dropping onto the white linen shirt, dampening it so that it clung to the broad shoulders. The top of her head barely reached his chin. She felt small and insignificant and terribly vulnerable in the lee of his imposing frame.

"I . . . I think I should return to the others," she whispered, shocked by her total lack of control over the situation. There was hardly a man in Derby who would dare accost her in such a way, and certainly no gentleman would ever speak to a lady the way this creature was speaking. For that matter, she was unaccustomed to dealing with anyone not instantly overwhelmed by her position, wealth, and beauty. She was the squire's daughter, not some coltish serving wench to be waylaid and frightened into submission!

And yet, a glance up into the dark eyes warned her that despite his fine clothes and genteel bearing, this was no well-bred gentleman who would adhere to proprieties, or follow any rules other than those of his own making. There was something raw and primitive about him, something that made her heart pound and the blood sing through her veins.

She swallowed with difficulty. "If it's m-money you want, I'm afraid I have nothing of value on me."

She saw the flash of white teeth, felt the heat of his breath on her temple.

"So now I'm a highwayman rather than a poacher? I don't know if I should be flattered or insulted."

"P-please, I —"

"As for you possessing nothing of value" — he shifted even closer and Catherine's heart throbbed up into her throat — "you underestimate the temptation of a silent forest, a bed of soft pine needles, and a fresh young minx sorely in need of a hard lesson in reality."

"A lesson which you, of course, feel capable of delivering?" The aura of indisputable mastery that emanated from him, his ease with it, his casual acceptance of it infuriated her, but she was strangely helpless to undermine it. Her swift rebuttal only brought a smile and a deepening of the roguish cleft that divided his chin.

"My services are yours to command, Mistress Ashbrooke."

A golden tendril of her hair stirred against her throat and Catherine realized with a start that his long fingers were toying with several shiny strands. She tried to pull away again but his hand was suddenly cupping her chin, tilting her face abruptly up to his. His eyes held a shuttered watchfulness as he surveyed the play of sunlight on her skin and hair, and their intensity, combined with the contact of his hand on her chin, sent a shiver of excitement trickling down her limbs like water melting down an icicle.

The stranger felt the tremors racing beneath his fingertips and was disturbed by the response seeping into his own loins. With her scattered yellow hair and her blush-kissed cheeks she looked far too young to be inducing the kind of thoughts that were possessing him. Unlike so many of the painted and preening women who had intruded on his conscience of late, this raw beauty needed no gimmickry to enhance the pearly sheen of her complexion. Flawless and smooth, her skin rivalled the look and feel of warm satin. Her mouth was a luscious invitation to trouble, her nose a pert confirmation of the refined, upper-class society to which she belonged. Her eyes defied description. Their colour, he thought, might well put a bouquet of wild heather to shame; their brightness more than suggested a passion waiting to be unleashed.

His gaze dropped to the opened collar of her blouse and Catherine felt as if the layers of silk, linen, and lace had been stripped away by their probing until there was nothing shielding her aching flesh. She could not move, could not even close her eyes to escape the penetrating stare — a curiously alarming predicament since every inbred instinct was telling her to run. With an abstract, almost indifferent kind of logic, she knew he was about to kiss her. He was as still as a rock, even his breathing suspended, and though she continued to fight against the shocking, melting sensation, she also knew beyond a doubt that she wanted nothing more than to feel those wide, sensual lips setting hers aflame. They were alone in the forest. Who would know of her impropriety aside from the trees, the birds, the shadow-drenched silence?

His hands descended to the narrow indent of her waist and Catherine swayed forward. Her mouth went slack as the pressure from his hands increased and he began to lift her. He drew her against him as he did so, and she nearly cried out as her breasts were brought crushingly close to his chest. Her fingertips brushed the warm teak of his skin, her heart thudded and pounded in her ears as she angled her mouth up to his.

But instead of ravaging her as she so fully expected him to do, he continued to lift her until she was high above his shoulders. With a sardonic twist of his lips, he plumped her unceremoniously onto the roan's saddle and handed the reins up.

"I am truly sorry to have to disappoint you, but I am a little pressed for time today. Should we meet again, however, and should you still want a kissing so desperately, I dare say I could rouse the inclination to oblige."

Catherine's jaw dropped. "Why you — !"

He laughed and slapped his hand across the roan's flanks. Catherine jerked back in the saddle, her hair flying, her skirts flaring up in a froth of lace petticoats as the mare spirited away from the clearing. Her cheeks were on fire, her hands trembling as she sought to grasp the reins and steer her way clear of the overhanging boughs. She could hear the deep resonance of his laughter following her into the forest and for the first time in many long years, her eyes flooded with tears of mortification. Too late she remembered she had left her hat and gloves behind, but she was not about to turn around and go back. If she'd had a gun, she would have certainly gone back. In fact, if she'd had any weapon more threatening than a short leather riding crop, she would have gone back and used it with the greatest of pleasure!

Catherine rode into the courtyard of Rosewood Hall, the roan's hooves beating an angry tattoo on the cobbled stones. A groom, alerted by the sound, came rushing out of the stables and arrived by her side in time to catch the tossed reins.

"See that she is given a ration of oats," Catherine ordered. "And walk her well: She has had a hard run."

Still suffering the effects of her chance meeting in the woods, she barely heard or cared for the groom's muttered response as she strode toward the main house. Her cheeks were flushed, her eyes as bright and keen as a rapier's edge and would have proved twice as deadly had anyone dared to stop and challenge her. Her hands, normally as pale and delicate as fine china, were red and chafed from handling the reins without gloves, and her windblown blonde hair tumbled across the vibrant blue of her jacket like a painted starburst.

No one treated Catherine Ashbrooke like a truant child —
no one! Certainly no one had ever dared laugh at her to her
face or threatened to tumble her in the moss — or, worse
still, pleaded a disinclination to tumble her! Men were usually
reduced to slavering schoolboys around her. She had come to
expect nothing less than the devoted homage of every eligible
male with whom she came into contact. The impudence of
the lout! The arrogance, the *conceit* of the oaf to suggest she
wanted or needed lessons in handling a man. She *should* have
screamed for help. She should have dispatched all forty men
back into the forest with muskets in hand and vengeance in
their hearts.

Catherine's furious pace slowed as she followed the cobbled
drive around to the front of the house. Rosewood Hall, built
in the Elizabethan style, was a two-storied, horseshoe-shaped
manor with three sides facing in to an enormous central
courtyard. The red clay brickwork contrasted pleasantly
with the pure white plaster of the cornices and pilasters that
accentuated the rows of tall, multipaned windows. Columns
of ivy and lichen clung to the lower story, their thin, spidery
fingers pointing upward to the sloping, gray slate roof.
There was no porch or terrace leading to the front entrance,
but the double doors were housed between two massive turrets consisting of floor-to-ceiling bay windows. The pedi-
ment over the doorway was engraved with the Ashbrooke
family crest, a testament that the family had been in
residence for more than one hundred years.

The Hall itself was nestled in the midst of a thousand acres
of formal gardens, fruit orchards, and swan-filled reflecting
pools. Willow trees wept gracefully over immaculately
groomed lawns. Box hedges and lavender bushes were
trimmed and trained to ornamental shapes, beds of herbs
were grown in manicured patterns to resemble the signs of
the zodiac. It could take many hours to stroll the winding
pathways, especially if the company were amiable.

The transition each season from the bustling streets and
elegant row houses of London to Rosewood Hall, considered
a modest home by country standards, normally took the

Ashbrooke family several weeks of adjustment. The peaceful tranquility of the country was a shocking change from the endless rounds of balls, masquerades, and cotillions that kept a young woman dancing and laughing gaily through each London night. There were horse races and gaming parties, crowded coffee houses, theatres, operas . . . . For three months Catherine had been wined and dined, had entertained the earnest flirtations of so many eager new suitors that their faces, after a time, had begun to run together. She hadn't had the heart to tell them their efforts had all been in vain. She had already made her choice, and that choice was garrisoned right here in Derby.

Lieutenant Hamilton Garner was tall and heartbreakingly handsome. He had the lean and sinewy body of a fencer, and, indeed, was Master of the Sword for his regiment of the King's Royal Dragoons. He was twenty-eight, the son of a London banker, and from the moment Catherine had first set eyes upon him, she had known he was the man worthy of her affections. The fact that he never lacked for beautiful and willing companions did not discourage her, nor did the reputation he had brought with him from the Continent. The rumours of his quick temper, of his duelling escapades, and many scandalous affairs only made the challenge of bringing him to heel all the more intriguing as far as Catherine was concerned. His very nature dictated that he seek the most popular, most sought-after heiress in Derby for his own, just as her nature demanded a conquest of equal proportions. Their three-month separation had added just the right amount of spice to their relationship — he was fairly champing at the bit to stake his claim.

Smiling, Catherine neared the porticoed entrance of Rosewood Hall. The door swung open just as she was about to reach for the latch, and her brother stepped out into the sunlight, his trim form looking especially dapper in a chocolate-brown broadcloth coat and fawn breeches.

"Whoa up, there. You seem to be in quite a hurry — has the hunt run the course already?"

"No it has not," she replied sweetly. "I simply decided

I'd had enough. You know full well I detest hunts. The sound of braying dogs leaves me with a migraine, as does the sight of grown men cheering while a pack of blood-crazed hounds tear apart a cornered fox.''

''My sister the humanitarian,'' he chided wryly. ''The same one who goes quail hunting and shoots charming little feathered creatures full of buckshot?''

''Those charming little feathered creatures provide us with dinner, brother mine, while hapless little foxes only provide bloodthirsty men with a morning's diversion. If you are so defensive of the sport, why are you not in your scarlets instead of lounging about the house like a vapid schoolboy? Has Harriet Chalmers had the good sense to snub you again?''

Damien Ashbrooke smiled easily. He was of medium height, not much taller than Catherine, with a shock of wavy chestnut hair tied and neatly clubbed together at the nape of his neck.

''No, the lovely Mistress Chalmers has not snubbed me. If anything, it is her smothering good intentions that make hearth and home the more appealing thought today.''

Catherine's violet eyes narrowed. ''She'll have you wed, regardless of how you try to hide from her, you know. Once we women have set our bonnets at a man, he rarely has a chance of reprieve.''

''Is that so? Well, unless I have missed something along the way, propriety still dictates that a man must do the proposing, not the woman.''

She stuck out her tongue and pertly misquoted, ''Thou dost protest too much, methinks. I've seen the way you ogle Harriet: like a wide-eyed lap dog, oblivious to everything but the wealth of charms that pour over the top of her bodice.''

''True enough,'' he murmured and followed Catherine into the dim light of the foyer. ''Perhaps you should consider a visit to her dressmaker to see if something equally artful could be done for you.''

"Swine."

"Tut, tut. Jealousy does not become you, little sister."

Halting, Catherine took a deep breath, turned, and met her brother's gaze directly. "And just what should I be jealous of? The way her bosoms threaten to spill out of her gowns . . . or the fact that they probably have already, and no doubt into your more than willing hands?"

Damien could not contain the flush that crept up his throat to stain his cheeks a dark crimson. Catherine laughed smugly.

"There, you see? And you still insist you have some control over your fate? A month, brother dear, and five gold sovereigns say she'll have you so frustrated you will be dragging her to the altar."

"You're on," he murmured. "But only if we can set the same time limit and stakes on your conquest of Lieutenant Garner."

"Have your money ready," she said tartly and glanced around the deserted hallway, "because he has already proposed. He intends to speak to Father tonight at the party so we can make an official announcement."

"Well, I'll be damned," he said, genuinely impressed. "I thought for sure he was only playing at courtship."

"Only because you sadly underestimate the extent of my own charms — copiously displayed or not!"

"Does Mother know?"

Catherine's smile turned bitter. "What on earth does she have to do with *my* marriage?"

"Nothing, I suppose. Just that both she and Father have been conspiring to marry you off to Pelham-Whyatt for the past three years."

"Him!" Catherine wrinkled her delicate nose in distaste. "He's boring. He wears clothes ten sizes too big and ten years out of date. He speaks with a lisp, and he smells suspiciously as if he hasn't bathed since I pushed him in the duck pond when we were children."

"He is also in line to inherit the land that borders ours. He is rich, he is not too dreadfully ugly — "

"Not ugly!" she exclaimed. "He's missing most of his teeth and his skin is so badly pocked it's a wonder he can shave it. His bones stick out everywhere on his body, and the last time he rode to hounds, he fell headlong into the pack of dogs — they started to chew on him because they mistook him for the fox! Marry him? I would sooner marry myself to a convent, thank you very much."

"You should never speak in haste, darling Kitty. Father has promised that and much more besides if you dare involve the good family name in any further scandal."

"Scandal? It is usually considered an honour when one man duels another for the sake of his lady's reputation."

"Not when her champion gives the distinct impression he enjoys running a man through with his sabre."

"Good Lord, you talk as if Hamilton *killed* Charles Wade. The fool isn't dead, he merely suffered a scraped cheek."

"Only because Lieutenant Garner knew a novice when he saw one and had no desire to face a charge of murder — which it could easily have become."

"Charles challenged Hamilton. What choice did he have?"

"He could have waited until the boy sobered up and realized the gravity of his error."

"His error was to offer me an insult within Hamilton's hearing," she countered primly.

"Brought on by your trying to make the good lieutenant jealous. Well it worked. And even though I know you are suitably repentant, I shall still warn you to be deuced careful around Father until you are safely wed and away from his parliamentary eye."

"Are you quite finished lecturing me for the day?" Catherine demanded, her anger rising swiftly again, as it usually did when she was caught at fault and boxed into a corner. "Since you seem to show such concern for my well-being, perhaps it would interest you to know that I was accosted in the woods today. *That* is why I am home from the hunt so early."

"Accosted?" Damien's easy features hardened instantly. "By who?"

"By *whom*, my Oxford-graduate brother. By a poacher, that's who. A vagrant. A trespasser . . . undoubtably a cut-purse in hiding."

Damien relaxed slightly. He knew his sister well enough to recognize the bright flecks of fire in the violet eyes. She'd met someone, all right. More than likely someone she had not been able to wrap around her little finger in ten words or less. Now she would be righteously indignant until she could vent her frustration on some other poor, hapless victim. It explained the cutting edge to her wit and the sharp remarks about Harriet Chalmers — Catherine's best friend since early childhood.

"He sounds interesting. Anyone I know?"

"I wouldn't doubt it for a moment," she retorted. "He looked the exact type who would keep you company in gaming houses and . . . and other places a lady would be no lady if she mentioned. On further consideration" — her eyes slitted vindictively — "I believe five gold sovereigns would be a small price to pay to save Harriet from committing a horrendous error in judgement. I shall speak to her the instant she returns from the hunt. By tonight, Damien Ashbrooke, you will be able to count yourself among the fortunate if she so much as glances your way."

With a toss of her long blonde hair, Catherine turned and began mounting the wide, massive wooden stairway to the upper floor. Damien walked to the bottom step and rested his hand on the carved mahogany newel post, his thoughtful blue eyes following the agitated swing of her slender hips. He had no fear of Catherine's threat coming to pass — she had schemed too long and too hard to make him awaken to the fact that Harriet had outgrown her braids and pinafores and developed into a beautiful young woman. What Catherine did not know was that his and Harriet's commitment to each other had gone well beyond the stage of casual flirtation. And she could not know how truly frustrated he was that, although Harriet was staying under the same roof, because there were so many other houseguests she was forced to share Catherine's bed, not his. A moment here and there had been all they had managed to steal so far, and with everything happening so fast . . .

"Kitty?" he called up softly, half expecting her to ignore him and keep climbing. But she didn't. She stopped on the first landing and glared down at him over the dog-gate as one would glare at an insect under glass.

"I was just thinking" — he hesitated and offered her the smile she knew was reserved for her and her alone — "We could make it a double announcement tonight. I think I could scrape up ten gold sovereigns from somewhere."

Catherine stared at her brother's handsome face. She knew he didn't truly approve of Hamilton Garner — what brother would? He considered the lieutenant pompous and overbearing, cruel to his junior officers, malicious to anyone who crossed him. Be that as it may, Hamilton kept his duty strictly separated from his personal life, and had never been anything but warm and gallant to Catherine. She knew Damien loved her dearly, and, more than just a brother to her, he'd been father, confessor, adviser, and friend when it seemed as though she was growing up all alone in this vast, empty house. Damien wanted her to be happy, and if winning Hamilton Garner, if becoming Mrs. Hamilton Garner would make her so, then he would support her choice all the way.

Catherine took a deep breath and, releasing it, gave Damien a wistful smile. "That would be wonderful, a double announcement. I couldn't wish for a happier way to welcome in my eighteenth birthday."

"Then you shall have it," he whispered. "Happy birthday."

Chapter Two

The festivities at Rosewood Hall progressed through an afternoon of croquet games and archery contests. The younger ladies squealed with delight and vied for attention as their chosen champions displayed their skills. Heavily corseted and far from comfortable in the July heat, matrons and chaperones followed like a swarm of blackbirds, for although scarcely able to breathe without the ominous creaking of whalebone ribs, they would sooner be dead from suffocation than miss a single word of gossip.

By four o'clock the bustle moved indoors, where massive preparations began for the evening ahead. Corsets and stomachers were loosened to permit a few hours of normal respiration. Huge vats of water were supplied for the dozens of slender hands that needed to dip and splash away the effects of the day's heat. Cosmetics were applied by skilled artisans, removing years of wear from the faces of some and adding the suggestion of years of experience to others. Hair was crimped and curled and tortured into elaborate pilings.

Some added enormous wire contraptions to existing coiffures and then had false curls of horsehair pinned and woven in place before clouds of flying white rice powder were applied to the whole. Artful additions of flowers, ribbons, jewels, even small artificial birds and animals, were set to roost in the heights, making the ability to balance her headdress an essential skill for a young woman of substance and fashion.

Belowstairs, the final touches were being added to the great hall. Multi-tiered chandeliers were lit, their prisms sparkling like flashes of white fire, their candles spilling fountains of glittering light over banquet tables that sagged beneath platters of food and drink. Waiters stood in long straight lines, their livery starched to perfection, their gloved hands held rigidly by their sides. There was seating for eighty guests, and at every place setting the silver gleamed, the porcelain shone, the crystal sparkled in anticipation of the feast to come.

Such a feast it was! Roasted and stuffed quail, ptarmigan, and guinea fowls were presented on platters surrounded by fresh pink prawns and swan's liver. Salmon was delivered up on beds of steaming leeks, dripping with butter, piquant with lemon sauce. Jellies, tarts, and crumbly venison pastries followed dishes of frozen sorbet, in turn paving the way for huge joints of roast lamb. Glasses were filled and emptied with laughing abandon. The knives and forks at each setting dwindled in number as each course was served and carried away, until there remained only the dessert cutlery.

Cakes foaming with icing, tarts melting with fruit and syrup, puddings, pastries, and sweet syllabubs were marched out from behind the serving screens, in good company with wedges of cheeses and fresh fruit. Corsets groaned en masse as each delicacy was sampled and judged superior to any tasted before. Plates were emptied to their last crumb and whisked away, glasses were drained of their fourth — or fifth? — variety of wine and cleared from the table as Lady

Caroline Ashbrooke stood and signaled for the ladies to retreat to the retiring room.

Almost immediately, the lower compartment doors of the sideboards were opened for the men to take advantage of the concealed chamberpots. Thus relieved of their discomfort and pinched expressions, they could once again relax in their chairs and enjoy the fragrant cigars Sir Alfred genially distributed. For the women, the process was not quite as facile. There was a flurry of activity at each *garde-robe* as maids helped hoist skirts and petticoats, as drawers were unlaced, shimmies raised and bared bottoms sought blindly for comfort without crumpling, wrinkling, or disturbing a flounce or feather.

With appetites assuaged and minor repairs effected to face and figure, the ladies waited patiently for the men to rejoin them. Sounds of the harpsichord and violin filtered down from the main ballroom as the fifteen-piece orchestra tuned their instruments. On a signal from Sir Alfred, the gleaming double doors were opened and the celebrations began in earnest.

Catherine took her sweet time in the upper chambers, adjusting curls that required no adjustment, fussing over a smudge of rouge or a faded line of khol. She had been moderately pleased to see that no one had dared attend her birthday party in a gown anywhere near as sumptuous as her own. The rose-coloured watered silk was cut in the latest Paris fashion, molded snugly to her narrow waist and pushing her breasts high so that they mounded impressively over the bodice. The sleeves were tapered to the elbow, and from there flared to allow the falling cuffs of her chemise to spill forth in a delicate profusion of creamy lace. The skirt was full and bell-shaped, spreading its width sideways in scalloped panniers while the front and back panels fell in straight folds to the floor. The skirt was pinned open to display the richly embroidered petticoats beneath — more tiers of exquisitely delicate French lace.

She had chosen to wear few adornments to detract from the effect of the shimmering pink silk. Only a necklace of blazing white brilliants caressed the plunging expanse of exposed flesh. Clean and fragrant and free of stiff horsehair curls or powders her hair seemed to shimmer with silver threads in the glow of the candlelight. Studying it critically, she was almost thankful for the allergy she had toward the grainy rice powder; even the lightest dusting had her sniffling and sneezing and — horror of horrors — breaking out into a mass of little red lumps.

"Lieutenant Hamilton Garner should be honoured I am even considering his proposal," she murmured, giving her ostrich feather fan one last flick to gauge the effect. Satisfied, she tucked her hand through Harriet Chalmers's arm and walked with her to the chamber door.

"Considering?" Harriet said. "Whatever do you mean, considering? I thought you had already accepted."

"A girl can have second thoughts. Or thirds, or fourths."

Harriet's soft brown eyes grew rounder. She did not possess Catherine's classic beauty; her eyes were overly large in a rather plump face, her mouth a shade too generous, and there was a definite spattering of freckles across the bridge of her nose despite the mercury wash she used day and night to bleach them away. All of her features combined to produce a cherubic countenance, one that contrasted dramatically with the luscious, hour-glass shape of the woman's body that fairly burst from the confines of her bodice. Men ogled her with the aplomb of guttersnipes, but for the most part she was oblivious. She had been enamoured of Damien Ashbrooke from the tender age of three, and it was just as well. She and Catherine could never have been friends otherwise; she would have been too much of a rival.

"On the other hand," Catherine said, pausing at the top of the staircase, "he hasn't exactly put his proposal into so many words."

Harriet, in the middle of descending a step, reached out and clutched the balustrade in an effort to maintain her balance. "What? *What did you just say?*"

"You heard me," Catherine hissed, glancing about to see if anyone had noted the startled outburst. "For heavens sake, keep your voice down. Of course he has asked me. I mean, he has hinted broadly enough, it's just that —"

"He hasn't . . . actually . . . *proposed?*"

"I'm sure he is only waiting for the opportune moment. Tonight, for instance. What better way to wish me happy birthday than to offer me a pledge of undying devotion?"

"But you told Damien —"

"Hush!" Catherine pinched her arm savagely as a couple strolled down the stairs past them. Harriet waited till they were out of earshot although she was nearly exploding with impatience.

"You told Damien that Hamilton was going to ask your father's permission tonight. You told him you were going to announce your engagement tonight!"

"Well . . . he was baiting me. He was being a perfect brute and teasing me and . . . and I simply said the first thing that came to mind. I wasn't *lying*. Not completely. Hamilton *does* want to marry me; everyone in Derby knows that. And he'd be a proper fool if he let someone else steal away my affections, now wouldn't he?"

"Well, yes, but —"

"He could not make a better marriage for himself if he courted one of King George's fat old daughters."

"Catherine!"

"Well it's true. I have the dowry my grandmother Augustine left me. I have *some* social graces, and now that Father has been elected to Parliament, there's no telling what influential friends he might acquire. A young, healthy rising star in the army could do a good deal worse than to marry me, and if he does not make a move soon, I may just leave him to it."

"You don't mean that," Harriet breathed.

"I certainly do. Tell me I couldn't walk into that room this very instant and receive a dozen proposals within an equal number of minutes if it became known that Hamilton Garner was out of favour."

"I'm not saying you couldn't. I'm just saying . . . well, perhaps Hamilton would resent being the subject of such a wager. He is rather . . . strong-minded."

"Content in his bachelorhood, you mean? Well it's time he opened his eyes. This is 1745, and there are simply not enough bachelors in England, not with everyone breeding daughters like rabbits."

"Catherine," Harriet gasped and blanched beneath the mercury wash. "Where do you hear such things?"

"In the finest London drawing rooms," Catherine replied absently, her eyes searching the foyer below. Harriet had to lay a gloved hand on her arm to draw her attention back to the present crisis.

"What if Hamilton hears about the wager? I mean, what if Damien offers a toast or tries to congratulate him?"

"He won't," Catherine insisted. "Not until midnight anyway. When he plays, he plays fair."

"But this isn't a game," the voice of doom persisted. "What if Hamilton simply smiles and says happy birthday to you at midnight with a bouquet of periwinkles?"

"Then he shall wear them emblazoned on his forehead the rest of his sorry life. But he wouldn't dare. And he wouldn't have continued courting me after the duel with Charles Wade if he had no intentions of doing the honourable thing. Why else does one gentleman fight another, if not to claim the lady's hand for himself?"

"If that were true, he should have a score of wives by now," Harriet murmured, and instantly regretted the words as she saw Catherine's mouth compress into a thin white line. "Well, you cannot deny he has earned himself quite the reputation as a lady's champion. Some even say — "

"I don't want to hear what *some* say," Catherine interrupted coldly. "They are most likely jealous old cows who have nothing better to gossip about. Now, are you on my side in this or not?"

"Of course I am," Harriet said quickly. "But what can I do?"

"You can keep Damien occupied elsewhere until I give you some sort of a signal."

"A signal?"

"Yes. Just before midnight, I shall invite Hamilton out onto the terrace for a breath of fresh air. If all goes well, when I return I shall be carrying . . . a rose." She paused and smiled conspiratorily. "I wagered ten sovereigns with Damien this afternoon. I am prepared to give you half as much again if Hamilton does not pluck the rose and hand it to me himself."

Marveling at the confidence and determination mirrored in the violet eyes, Harriet could not help but return the smile. "By midnight?"

"Midnight," Catherine agreed.

"It's nearly eleven now. You are not giving yourself much time."

"I don't need much time," Catherine declared, her mouth curving slyly as she mulled over the various strategies at her disposal. "After all, he is only a man."

Only a man: Harriet mouthed the words silently as she watched her best friend in the world — and her future sister-in-law — descend the rest of the way down the stairs. She knew it would do no good to try to dissuade Catherine from going ahead with her scheme. It would also do no good to caution her against leaping into this union with Hamilton Garner. She'd known the lieutenant less than a year, since he and his regiment had been sent to fortify the Derby militia. His reputation with women was not even Harriet's prime concern — most men, married or not, regarded it as a sacred right and privilege to keep a separate household for their mistress of choice, sometimes changing them as often as sheets on a bed. Women had affairs too, of course, but theirs were more discreet and usually the result of neglect in the marriage bed.

What Catherine said was true, she would bring Lieutenant Garner a considerable dowry, prestige, and social presence, but had she thought of what he would bring to her? Harriet doubted very much if the handsome lieutenant would give up his philandering ways — protected by marriage, he might even be encouraged to roam farther afield. Catherine was too stubborn and strong-willed herself to share any man with another woman. What would happen when she discovered the bloom was off the rose?

Thinking of roses, Harriet saw that Catherine had reached the bottom of the stairs. She hurried to catch up, hoisting her butter-yellow skirts in both hands so that the satin billowed out behind her like a sail in the wind.

Catherine's pulse quickened as she approached the doors of the ballroom. She had no doubt but that she would have the rose in her hand by midnight. Hamilton was fiercely protective of his bachelorhood, as all strutting cocks were, but the time was ripe for mending his ways. It *was* a perfect match, for both of them. Just the thought of the commotion it would cause when their engagement was announced sent a delicious thrill down Catherine's spine. Her peers would be writhing with envy. Each and every one of them had watched and waited, hoping she would fail as they so miserably had. Jealous, the lot of them. Jealous because they couldn't have him. Jealous because they knew there wasn't a man alive who could escape a net as fine as the one she had woven for Lieutenant Garner.

She spied him instantly, even though the room was awash with crimson tunics, bewigged heads, and a butterfly collection of multicoloured gowns. He was standing with Sir Alfred, a short gentleman with a profusion of chins and a girth almost equal in width to his height.

"Good," she murmured in a voice too low for anyone but Harriet to hear. "He is ingratiating himself with his future father-in-law. Sweet merciful heavens, but doesn't he look magnificent?''

If ever there was a man suited to wear a uniform, Catherine decided, it was Hamilton Garner. His shoulders filled the scarlet tunic with a power and grace that rippled clearly from every taut inch of muscle. He was exceedingly handsome — *indecently* handsome, with a lean, angular jaw and large seductive eyes the colour of jade. He had seen service with King George's brother, the Duke of Cumberland, and had returned from Fontenoy a hero, having intercepted a shot intended for the Duke's back. As a reward, he had been given his own company of dragoons and was expecting a full captaincy any day now.

Standing with Hamilton and her father were several other wigged and powdered gentlemen, among them Colonel Lawrence Halfyard, a short-tempered, gruff man who spoke in staccato sentences that sounded like gunfire. Hamilton was his protégé and as such was sure to be receiving every encouragement toward a union with his niece.

William Merriweather, a neighbour and friend of the family, seemed a little out of place beside the two festooned officers. He had few redeeming features other than a quick, dry wit, and had one very glaring fault: He liked to play devil's advocate, argue for the sake of arguing, and when William and her father were together for any length of time, the usual topic of conversation was politics. Luckily there were several other men in the group who might be able to keep the discussion on neutral ground.

''Now remember,'' Catherine said, nudging Harriet to gain her full attention, ''you must keep Damien away from Hamilton until I give you the signal.''

''I'll try,'' Harriet whispered, her eyes already meeting Damien's through the milling crowd. ''Good heavens, he is talking to Hamilton now. You don't suppose — ''

''Smile,'' Catherine ordered, ''and act as if you couldn't care less who we want to stand with.''

Smiling, nodding, pausing to exchange pleasantries with

several of the guests in their path, they strolled without apparent purpose toward the group of men. Catherine was, indeed, anxious to reach Hamilton's side, but she did not wish to appear so, not even to Harriet.

"Oh good Lord," she muttered. "They *are* talking politics. Look at Father. His wig is shaking so hard it's about to topple off his head."

"The Stuart line is finished," Sir Alfred was saying loudly, trumpeting his nose into a linen handkerchief. "Why the deuce these papists cannot seem to grasp the idea, I do not know. Y'd think they would be tired of fighting a losing battle, tired of defending a cause that has nowhere to go but the bottom of the sea. England is not going to stand for another Catholic king on the throne, certainly not one who speaks with a Highland brogue."

"Ek-tually," Merriweather said, arching his eyebrows, "James Francis speaks as clearly as you or I. If anything, he leans more toward an Italian influence, having spent nearly forty years there now."

"Papists," Colonel Halfyard snorted. "The Old Pretender's an old fool, maintaining a royal court in Rome. Who does he think he is?"

"The rightful heir and king of England, Scotland, and Ireland," Merriweather drawled wanly. "Ousted from his throne by a German usurper."

"King George is a direct descendant of James I."

"Through the daughter's succession, not the son's."

"James III is a fool, like his father before him," Sir Alfred insisted. "He should be thankful he was only exiled and not beheaded for his papist spoutings like Charles. Smartest thing Cromwell ever did, you ask me. A pity we don't have generals like him today . . . er, present company excepted, naturally. At any rate, why these Jacobites persist in threatening the stability of our government is beyond me. Only last month they arrested one of them, right in the Commons!"

"Cheek of them," the colonel pronounced. "Cropping up

everywhere. Can't be trusted. Don't know who your friends are anymore.''

"One thing we do know is that Louis will never mount another invasion fleet,'' Sir Alfred said. "Not after that sorry fiasco last year.''

"Lunacy,'' Colonel Halfyard agreed. "Launching a fleet in February. Crossing the Channel in the dead of winter Eleven good ships lost. Hundreds . . . thousands of stout lives lost or forfeit. Hope whoever planned that one bought the guillotine.''

"A pity Charles Edward Stuart did not go down with the others.''

"Yaas.'' Merriweather nodded. "The insolent pup. Imagine him declaring to all and sundry that he will not rest until he has returned victorious to England and won the throne in his father's name. Such impudence deserves a watery grave, what?''

Sir Alfred harrumphed emphatically to show agreement. His complexion was ruddier than normal, an indication that he had been enjoying a liberal quantity of Spanish Madeira. The lace that was gathered around his throat and cuffs was sprinkled generously with crumbs from the hors d'oeuvres he'd been sampling, some of which parted company with the cloth as he gestured angrily with one hand.

"I say we should hang all the blasted Jacobites we can lay a hand to. The deader the better.''

"Such a plan would involve laying waste to most of the Scottish Highlands,'' Hamilton Garner suggested blithely, "since most of the Pretender's support comes from that quarter.''

"Nothing but savages,'' Sir Alfred sputtered. "We should have driven them all into the sea when we thrashed them raw back in '15, but what did we do instead? We gave 'em amnesty, that's what we did. We gave 'em back their land and built them military roads better than our own. All of Scotland was to have been disarmed and subdued thirty years ago, but tell me, can you walk anywhere in that God-forsaken land and not find one of their skirted warlords brandishing a bloody great broadsword across your face? Especially now that they've found themselves an idiot who actually believes he can stir them into conquering the world.''

"Not all of Scotland is eager to fight for a Stuart king, Father,'' Damien said cautiously. "Most of the population is as wary of stirring up old feelings as we are. As for their being savages, I dare say there were as many Scots at Cambridge and Oxford as there were Englishman.''

"Bah! Is that why I sent you to law school, boy?'' Sir Alfred demanded. "To sound like a lawyer? Where's your passion? You lost a grandfather and an uncle in the last Jacobite uprising, and I'm not ashamed to admit you damned near lost your father from sheer terror. Not savages, eh? They live in the mountains and dress like wildmen. They walk about in woolen petticoats which they are not in the least modest about casting aside when they need their sword arms free. Dash me, can you even begin to imagine the sight of a horde of naked, hairy-legged creatures charging at you across a battlefield like bloody fiends out of hell — screaming and flailing those great bloody swords and axes of theirs like scythes. Not savages? They hardly know an intelligible word of the king's English, for pity's sake, and spend all their waking moments plotting thievery and murder on their neighbours.''

"We should recall the army from Austria, I say,'' a gentleman on the outskirts of the group interjected. "If law and loyalty cannot be brought to them by persuasion and logic, then by God we should carry it there by musket, bayonet, and gibbet.''

"Here here,'' came the general consensus.

"Actually'' — a small, thin, nervous-looking gentleman adjusted his pince-nez and thrust a finger forward to interject a comment — "the clans are quite ferocious in their loyalty and strictly law-abiding within their own sects. They regard their chief as father, magistrate, juror, even somewhat of a king with inherited rights and powers that the lowest of the tacksmen would not dream of disobeying.''

"What the deuce are you on about, Faversham? You consider yourself an authority because you have spent some months up there plotting maps?''

"Good gracious no, not an authority. It would require a born-and-bred Scotsman to fully understand the way a fellow Scotsman thinks, but I must confess my opinions of them in general were forced to change somewhat after having travelled the length and breadth of the country.''

"And now you mean to convince us they are amiable, honourable hosts?''

The sarcasm caused the little man to adjust his spectacles fastidiously again. "Actually, they were most hospitable, once it was determined that I had no intentions of doing injury to their persons. As to their honour, I made the unknowing error of intimating to one particular chief that some of his people had not behaved toward me with the civility I had come to expect. Damme if he didn't clap a hand to his sword and say that, if I required it, he would send me two or three of their heads for the insult. I laughed, thinking it a jest, but the chief insisted he was a man of his word, and . . . faith . . . I believe he would have done it.''

"You use this as an example to demonstrate their degree of civility?'' Lieutenant Garner's mouth curved sardonically. "I should think it better illustrates their baser instincts to be so ready to sever a man's head from his shoulders.''

"Perhaps I have explained it poorly then,'' Faversham said in defense. "I meant only to show that to a Scotsman — and to a Highlander in particular — honour is everything.''

"Show me a Highlander,'' Lieutenant Garner countered dryly, "and I'll show you a thief.''

"I do not recall that I ever lost anything among them but a pair of doeskin gloves — and that I owed to my own carelessness."

"You sound as though you harbour some respect for them, sir."

"Respect, Lieutenant? Indeed, I find it prudent to respect that which is so simple and basic it cannot be ignored."

"Hah!" Colonel Halfyard bellowed. "There you have it — simpletons! And by your own admission."

Faversham looked calmly at the colonel. "I meant 'simple' in its purest and strictest sense. Honour, to a Highlander, is honour. There are no wherewithalls, no provisions for exception. They swear their oaths before God and man, sealing them with their lips placed upon a dirk. Should they ever be found perjured, they accept the fact that they forfeit their lives to the steel of that same knife. How can one not respect such faith?"

"Are you implying, sir, that because they kiss knives and show a willingness to have their hearts impaled for telling little white lies" — Garner's voice dripped contempt — "that all of England should quake and tremble at the thought of them swarming across our borders?"

Faversham reddened painfully under the gust of laughter. "I only meant to imply — "

"I know what you meant to *imply*," the lieutenant cut in sharply. "But I state plainly and clearly that the whole of the Scottish rabble assembled together could not pose enough of a threat to dampen my collar. They have no regular army, no guns, no artillery, no navy . . . only swords and bagpipes to send against the most powerful, well-equipped military nation the world has known."

Saying this, the lieutenant turned his back on Mr. Faversham, rudely and perfunctorily dismissing him as a nuisance. The diminutive gentleman shaded to a throbbing crimson as he scanned the circle of hostile faces, as surprised as the rest of the company to hear a voice come to his defense.

"I myself have always been of the opinion that it is

healthier to take precautions against an enemy than to underestimate him completely.''

In the sudden silence, Hamilton turned slowly to confront this new, quietly spoken challenge. Other than his being an acquaintance of Damien Ashbrooke's from London, the speaker was unknown to him.

"Montgomery, isn't it?"

"Raefer Montgomery," the gentleman acknowledged with a slight bow.

"And you agree with Faversham's opinion that the Scots pose a threat of some kind?"

"The opinion I share is that I would not want to be too hasty in dismissing them as inept savages. They have, after all, managed to keep their own borders relatively sacrosanct for the past thousand years.''

"Possibly because there was nothing within their borders to merit conquest," Garner said evenly. "The land is barren, the weather unpredictable. You would likely have to be a thick-skinned savage to survive up there.''

Montgomery smiled. "Yet we pay prime prices for their beef, mutton, and wool, not to mention the thriving black-market dealing in their finer spirits. Unless my palate has grown rusty of late, I detected a distinct Caledonian musk to the whisky we enjoyed with our cigars.''

Sir Alfred cleared his throat noisily. "Yes, well, a gift of a few barrels came into my hands recently . . .'' His muttered words dwindled off to faint grumblings, but no one was paying heed. They were intent on the conversation between Montgomery and Hamilton Garner.

"May I ask your business, sir? And if I may be bolder still, your accent eludes me.''

"I grew up on the Continent, Lieutenant: France, Italy, Spain, but my place of birth was England, I'm afraid. The first impressionable years were spent on the banks of the Thames. As to my business, it is import and export, and to that end, I travel around the world in search of interesting and profitable acquisitions. As to my politics — assuming that to be your next question — I have none. Like Mr. Merriweather I enjoy examining both sides of an argument . . . and like Mr. Faversham, I am able to keep a relatively open mind about such things.''

Lieutenant Garner studied Montgomery as closely as one would size up an imminent opponent. The exquisite cut of his indigo-blue frock coat, together with the silvered blue waistcoat and breeches, reeked of money and easy living, but there was nothing soft or negligent in the strong, tapered hands or the broad, powerful shoulders.

''Accepting your declaration of neutrality for the moment,'' Hamilton mused, ''and acknowledging that your interests are purely financial, you must agree a stable government would be more to a *merchant's* liking.''

Montgomery absorbed the thinly veiled insult with a slight deepening of his smile. ''On the contrary. If I were strictly a profiteer — hypothetically speaking of course — I would be most anxious to see the collapse of one government and the instigation of another. There are always incredible amounts of money to be made in chaotic situations, just as wars provide grand opportunities for an ordinary, mundane soldier to spring into the public's eye.''

Hamilton Garner stiffened visibly. His hand slid up to rest on the silvered hilt of his dress sabre, and the skin across his cheeks and over the finely chiselled flare of his nostrils seemed to become more tightly drawn.

''Are you intimating, sir, that there are no genuine heroes in battle?''

''I'm sure there are. But there are no battles without wars, Lieutenant, and without wars there can be no glory — for soldiers or merchants.''

Garner's jade eyes bored into Montgomery with a rising fury. ''I would hardly equate the two professions, since the one exists to defend life and liberty and, the other was created by carrion to feed on the spoils of our labours.''

Damien Ashbrooke held his breath and glanced sidelong at Raefer Montgomery. He expected an explosion — they all did — at this outright affront. But whether or not the dangerous calm he sensed behind the dark, hooded eyes, would have resulted in a demand for satisfaction, they were not to know. An explosion of a very different kind burst into their midst with a swirl of coloured silk.

"There you are, you naughty boys," Catherine scolded prettily. "The handsomest men at my party and you're all huddled together behind a potted palm tree. No doubt you are arguing politics again while we ladies amuse ourselves by dancing with shadows."

"Mistress Ashbrooke!" William Merriweather bowed flamboyantly over her hand. "And Mistress Chalmers. What a perfectly timely observation. Have you truly been languishing for male company, or do you say it simply to tease these poor ravished heartstrings?"

"We're positively perishing," Catherine cooed from behind her fan. "And for that charming bit of gallantry, you may claim the first dance."

Her violet eyes flashed toward Hamilton to mark his reaction at being passed over for the honour — but her gaze never made it past the gentleman standing beside Damien. His face had been partially hidden by the potted palm, but at the sound of her voice he had turned, and at the first glimpse of those dark, penetrating eyes, her breath became trapped somewhere between her throat and her lungs.

There was no mistaking him. Despite the formal attire and the neatly combed and bound periwig, it was the same rogue who had accosted her in the forest that morning.

Chapter Three

Catherine stared at the dark stranger for what seemed like half an eternity. Her reaction did not go entirely unnoticed: Damien, for one, saw the flush ebb and flow into her cheeks and the violet of her eyes flare with tiny sparks of outrage. If he had not known better, if he had not known that Raefer had arrived from London only that afternoon and had never met any of the Ashbrooke family before, he would have sworn his sister was regarding him exactly as she would a lifelong enemy.

Acutely aware of the strained relations between Montgomery and Hamilton Garner, Damien attempted to cover the awkward silence with introductions.

"Raefer Montgomery, I don't believe you've had the pleasure of meeting my sister, Catherine."

Catherine's gaze was brittle and challenging as he stepped forward and bowed politely over her hand.

"A very great pleasure indeed, Mistress Ashbrooke," he murmured as he straightened. "And my warmest felicitations on your birthday. Damien was kind enough to invite me, although he neglected to mention he had such a lovely sister.''

"I'm so glad you could join us," she said frostily, her eyes flicking to Damien with a look that said: I'm going to have something to say to *you* later.

"Er . . . Mistress Harriet Chalmers," Damien proceeded lamely. "Mr. Raefer Montgomery."

Montgomery's smile widened and changed from one of amusement to one of genuine pleasure. "Mistress Chalmers. I have indeed looked forward to meeting you. Damien has spoken of you many times, but if I might be allowed to say so, his descriptions have not done you justice."

"Why thank you, Mr. Montgomery," Harriet demurred and blushed furiously, conscious of Catherine's rising agitation, yet puzzled as to the reason for it.

Catherine was fighting hard to control the fury pounding within her. She was perilously close to slapping the sly grin off Montgomery's saturnine face, and certainly would have if not for the presence of her father and Colonel Halfyard. There was a small warning voice at the back of her mind extolling caution: She could not afford a scene tonight, of all nights. As much as she savoured the image of Hamilton Garner exacting revenge for her honour, she knew the punishment would have to take a different tack.

"I do not recall my brother ever mentioning your name, Mr. Montgomery. But then I suppose some lawyers prefer to keep their, um, less palatable clients incognito. You aren't by chance a murderer or a highwayman?"

Damien was horrified but Montgomery only laughed — the same deep, resonating sound she had heard following her out of the clearing.

"Rest assured, Mistress Ashbrooke, I call upon your brother's expertise for purely financial matters."

"Raefer owns a small shipping venture out of London," Damien explained quickly.

"Slaves or black market?" she asked sweetly.

"At the moment . . . ladies' petticoats," Montgomery replied, not in the least perturbed. "The market is extremely genial in the present climate for anyone able to carry cargoes of silk, lace, and brocade. With trade to France cut off, goods from the Orient command top prices."

"How interesting," Catherine declared with a bored snap of her fan. She turned to William Merriweather and favoured him with a devastating smile. "I believe I hear the orchestra tuning for a minuet."

"By all means," Merriweather cried and offered his arm. Catherine glanced briefly at Lieutenant Garner, fully expecting him to intercede, but to her annoyance, all of his attention was fixed on Raefer Montgomery.

With a sweep of her wide skirts, she accompanied Merriweather to the dance floor, where other partners were forming two long lines. The music was slow and stately, the steps executed with precision and grace. Catherine determinedly avoided looking in the direction of the group by the potted palm, although she could not resist a few casual questions of her partner each time they approached to bow or turn a pirouette.

"Who is that odious man? Ladies petticoats, indeed. I'll wager he does not waste the sail to bring goods all the way from the Orient. I'll wager he smuggles them from France despite the embargoes."

"Rather too brusque a character for my liking, and yet he does have a certain flair, what? Not afraid to speak his mind, either. He and the lieutenant were having a hot go at it just before you arrived."

"Really? About what?"

The lines parted and the dancers traced through several intricate moves before stepping together again.

"What does anyone argue about these days?" Merriweather sighed. "Politics, of course. I admit to a certain penchant for stirring the odd hornet's nest meself, but our bold Mr. Montgomery came right out and whacked it with a stick. Rather took the buzz right out of my own efforts."

"He advocates war?"

Merriweather pursed his lips thoughtfully. "Dash me if I know what he advocates. Or for whom."

Catherine frowned and stole a peek over her shoulder. Neither Montgomery nor Hamilton Garner were involved in the discussion now taking place. They both stood silently contemplating their drinks or the milling guests. Noticing this, Catherine could also not help but notice that other eyes were drawn toward the small group, most of them sparked with curiosity about the tall, dark stranger.

Catherine looked back at the velvet-encased shoulders. His face was in profile, but there was no question he was a striking blend of contrasts, definitely not a dandified city dweller or a lazy, bored country scion. Further, there was an indefinable air of assurance about him, as if he knew every female eye in the room was on him and could care less.

Catherine moved instinctively through the routines, her mind racing well ahead of the music. She was being presented with the ideal opportunity, if she could play it correctly. Despite her intense loathing for the man, Raefer Montgomery had managed to capture the interest of everyone present — a fact which could not have gone unnoticed by the man who usually claimed the honour for himself — Lieutenant Garner. They had already clashed once, according to William Merriweather, and indeed were poised now like two cobras anticipating a strike. A casual flirtation with the merchant from London could be just the nudge Hamilton needed to spur him into an impassioned proposal. If he hadn't been moved before to publicly lay claim to her hand, he certainly would now, if only to score against Montgomery.

Of course she would have to manipulate the parties carefully. She did not want to overplay her part or give Montgomery undue cause for imagining a victory of his own. He had, after all, been boorish and unforgivably rude this morning and she could not allow him to receive the mistaken impression that she was succumbing to his arrogant charm. He would have to be put in his place, and know quite clearly by whom.

The minuet ended on a trickle of applause and Catherine was escorted back to the group of gentlemen. With Faversham unobtrusively melting away to join a less hostile crowd, and Damien and Harriet excusing themselves to participate in the next dance, their numbers had dwindled.

"I thank you, Mr. Merriweather," she said with a smile and released his arm. "You have managed to quite steal my breath away. Hamilton," she murmured glancing up at him from beneath the thick crescents of her lashes, "might I impose upon you for a glass of cool water?"

He bowed curtly. "Of course you may. I won't be but a moment."

"Thank you. Oh, and Father . . . I believe Mr. Petrie is looking for you."

"Petrie?" Sir Alfred perked up instantly. Hugh Petrie could always be counted upon, on any occasion, to dispense with the nonsense and frippery and get down to the more serious business of whist and backgammon. "Well, er, *harrumph!* Lawrence — what say we look Petrie up and see what he is wanting? Something that warrants our immediate attention, no doubt."

"No doubt, no doubt." The colonel nodded and was rapidly ushered away.

Merriweather lingered a moment longer, but the temptation of a rousing good game of cards was too much to endure, and he made his excuses. Montgomery and Catherine were left alone.

Her cheeks warmed faintly, but when a full minute passed without an attempt to open a conversation, she tilted her head and mused to no one in particular: "What a lovely waltz."

"Lully, I believe."

She smiled tightly. "I had no idea they taught music appreciation in poaching school."

"Dance appreciation too," he said and offered his arm. "May I?"

Catherine studied the rakish grin a moment before accepting his company onto the dance floor. Aware of the heads turning and following them as they walked past the row of whispering matrons, she was even more conscious of the pair of jade-green eyes boring into their shoulders as they joined smoothly into the midst of the dancing couples.

Montgomery's movements were fluid and assured, amazingly graceful for a man of his size. Catherine felt lost against the breadth of his chest and was scarcely conscious of her feet touching the oak floor. She did not anticipate so strong a reaction to the feel of the steely muscles against her fingertips or the memory that came flooding back of what lay beneath the starched and ruffled linen shirt. An image of them dancing together, he stripped to the waist, his black hair dripping water onto his naked flesh, caused her to miss an easy step. He took advantage of the slip to tighten his grip about her waist and draw her closer against his body.

"Do I still frighten you, Mistress Ashbrooke, even in a crowded room?"

Catherine caught her breath and tilted her head up. "I beg your pardon?"

He smiled and let his eyes linger on the tender pink blush in her cheeks. "I vaguely recall Damien mentioning he had a sister, but for some reason I thought she was much younger. You must forgive me for being so abrupt this morning, I — "

"Apologies hardly suit your character, Mr. Montgomery. And why did you not say you were a friend of my brother's? It would not have excused your abominable behaviour, but it might have helped explain it."

"You're absolutely right," he said after a speculative pause. "I should not have to apologize. It wasn't me who was doing the spying."

"Spying?" she gasped.

"What else would you call it, standing in the bushes watching a man bathe?"

Catherine's mouth dropped open. "I certainly was not *watching* you, sir. Had I known there was anyone lurking in the clearing, I should not have gone within a hundred yards of it. I was merely trying to water my horse and — " She stopped and clamped her mouth shut. The maddening, all-knowing smile was back on his lips, and there was a distinct gleam of amusement in the dark blue eyes. "Please take me back now. I see Lieutenant Garner has returned with my refreshment."

"My dear Mistress Ashbrooke, it has been many long weeks since I have held such an incredibly lovely woman in my arms and I have no intentions of forfeiting the pleasure just yet. The lieutenant will have to wait."

The softness of his voice startled Catherine and sent an unexpected flood of warmth coursing through her body. The music, the laughter, the buzz of conversation seemed to fade away as she lifted her eyes to his. She felt the hand at her waist tighten yet again, but she could do nothing to resist the pressure. She was only dimly aware of the flashes of coloured silk that passed them by, of the brilliant splashes of candlelight reflected off the cut-glass panes of the french doors. He whirled her away from the close confines of the ballroom and out onto the terrace and she could do nothing to stop him. Around and around he danced her. Around and around, until they had only the dusting of starlight overhead to light their way.

Drawing her closer, Montgomery embraced her in a way that made her feel molded to the hard contours of his body. The circles they made became smaller, their footsteps slower until they were barely moving at all, hardly swaying to the strains of the music. Catherine felt a mindless drumming in her blood. He was holding her too closely. The night was too dark, the air too fragrant with the scent of roses. She lowered her eyes a fraction and it was no longer his gaze that transfixed her, but the sensual curve of his mouth — a mouth that was descending toward hers even as his hand slid up from her waist to cradle the nape of her neck.

His lips touched hers and the shock rippled through her body. A feeble protest shivered free on a sigh, but she could not even summon the strength or wit to make it sound convincing. Her whole being centered around the feather-light pressure of his mouth, on the teasing, taunting dalliance of his tongue as it sampled, tasted, prepared her for the possessive boldness that followed.

As his lips slanted more forcefully over hers, as his arms tightened and his tongue thrust demandingly into the soft recesses of her mouth, Catherine gasped at the waves of pleasure curling both inward and outward. Her stomach turned to jelly, hot jelly, heavy as molten lead that slid downward into her limbs at each silky, probing caress of his tongue. Her fists unclenched, her fingers spread against the velvet thickness of his frock coat and inched higher . . . higher, until her hands were circling his neck, then clinging to the powerful breadth of his shoulders. She pressed eagerly into his embrace, glorying in the strength of his arms as they enfolded her.

She had thought she'd known every kind of kiss a man could offer — what mystery could still remain in the simple touching of lips? Hamilton's kisses, to be sure, warmed her and sent tiny shivers of contentment through her body, more so than those of any other man before him. Yet he had never inspired the surge of liquid heat that was setting her veins on fire. His body had never commanded hers to melt against him, to move with him, to question the cause and remedy of this incredible, burning tension. The flesh everywhere on her body had grown tauter, tighter, and her belly was fluttering with stronger and stronger urges.

She was kissing him back, she knew she was. She wanted more, she wanted all of him. She was being plundered, ravished, conquered, and she had no desire to stop it from happening.

Montgomery ended the kiss suddenly, and Catherine could not prevent the small cry of disappointment that escaped her lips. His face was in shadow — she could barely discern the rugged features — but she sensed a shared feeling of total surprise, as if he had not expected the effects she could feel thundering within his chest. He held her away from his body, as if he did not trust any further contact, and when he spoke, he tried to make his words light and casual.

"I did warn you about unscrupulous rogues who would not hesitate to take advantage."

"So you did," she murmured. "You also promised me a lesson in reality. Was that it?"

The dark eyes narrowed and studied the lines of her face as if to memorize them. "Reality?" he whispered. "I don't believe I know what that is anymore. I thought I did . . ."

Catherine shivered as she felt his fingertips brush along the curve of her throat. She turned her head slightly, the better to feel the warmth of his flesh on hers . . . and her eyes opened wide in horror.

The figure of a man was standing less than ten paces away, his silhouette framed in the glare of lights that spilled from the open french doors. His hands were held rigidly by his sides, the fingers crushed into fists.

"Hamilton!" Catherine gasped and jerked out of Montgomery's arms.

"I hope I am not intruding," the lieutenant said, his voice cracking with anger.

"Hamilton . . . it isn't what you think!" Catherine cried and took several halting steps toward him.

"Isn't it? Pray then, by all means, tell me what it is. You send me for a glass of water, then dance away with a fellow to whom you have only just been introduced. Ten minutes later and" — he finished the sentence with a sneer — "you're telling me it isn't what I think."

Catherine flushed hotly. "Hamilton, please . . ."

"I think, madam, you were kissing this gentleman. The act hardly requires more explanation than that . . . unless of course you have formed the habit of kissing perfect strangers and see nothing untoward in the deed?''

Montgomery sighed audibly. He reached into an inside pocket and extracted a thin black cigar. ''You are not giving the lady much of a chance. If you did, she might tell you we weren't perfect strangers, that we have met before. She might also tell you the kiss was my idea, not hers, and that she simply . . . endured it.''

The gratitude in Catherine's eyes was visible over the flare of a sulphur match. Garner's face remained impassive, as if carved out of stone, but the suspicions in his eyes were bright and palpable as he glanced from one culprit to the other.

''You have met before?''

''You could say this was a farewell scene,'' Montgomery said before Catherine could stammer a reply. ''I will be leaving Derby in the morning and doubt if I will be coming back this way again in the near future.''

''And so you thought to force your attentions on Mistress Ashrooke?'' Hamilton's fists clenched tighter. His pride demanded he ignore the fact that he had seen no evidence of force. ''Catherine, I think you should go back inside now and rejoin the party; the air has developed a distinct chill.''

''Will you come with me?'' she asked in a whisper.

''Not just yet. Montgomery and I have not finished our conversation.''

She reached out and touched the sleeve of his tunic. ''Hamilton, please — ''

''I said, go inside, Catherine.'' The icy green eyes turned to her. ''This is between Montgomery and myself.''

''On the contrary,'' Montgomery said, studying the glowing ash at the tip of his cigar. ''There is nothing further to discuss, and if there was, it would be between Mistress Ashrooke and myself. However, if an apology will put an end to this simple misunderstanding, then I freely offer one. I had no idea the lady's time was spoken for.''

Hamilton Garner ground his teeth together. ''Mistress

Ashbrooke's time is her own. If she chooses to throw it away in the company of an unprincipled bastard, then so be it.''

Montgomery stared at the dragoon officer for a long, taut moment. When he spoke, his voice was deceptively silky. ''I have offered my apologies. Now if you will excuse me — ''

He bowed curtly to Catherine and started toward the french doors. There was a shrill whistle of steel leaving its scabbard, and Hamilton's sword slashed down in front of Montgomery, the point of the blade touching the ruff of lace at his throat.

''An apology is no longer acceptable,'' Garner hissed. ''Unless, of course, you will admit to being a *coward* as well as an ill-mannered boor.''

''What the deuce is going on here?''

Catherine flinched as her father's voice boomed out across the terrace, and her face drained of what little colour she had remaining as she saw him stride out of the doors with Damien, Harriet, and Colonel Halfyard close on his heels.

''Well? Speak up! What is the meaning of this? Lieutenant Garner, put that damned thing away and explain yourself.''

''Indeed,'' the colonel barked. ''You are a guest in Sir Alfred's house. This is no place for swordplay, especially since the gentleman appears to be unarmed!''

''This . . . *gentleman* . . . has seen fit to tender grave insult both to myself and to Mistress Ashbrooke.''

''What? What manner of insult?''

Catherine wished she could shrink away into the shadows. Harriet was gaping at her open-mouthed, Damien was staring at her as if she'd lost her mind. Colonel Halfyard, his hand on the hilt of his sword, looked as if he were prepared to cut down the first soul who dared to move.

Sir Alfred's face darkened to the shade of a thundercloud on the verge of erupting. ''I said, put the sword away, Lieutenant. If there has indeed been an insult tendered, we shall get to the bottom of it.''

The sword wavered, slowly descending from Montgomery's breastbone to a point midbelly. With a sudden, oft-practiced flourish, the sabre was whipped about and flashed into its sheath again.

"Now," Sir Alfred said gravely. "What is all of this about an insult?"

Montgomery had not so much as blinked since Garner's sword had appeared. "I have no desire to kill this man," he said quietly. "I suggest a strong glass of brandy might cool him down."

"Kill me?" Hamilton scoffed. "It would be my pleasure to let you try."

"Hamilton, for God's sake — " Damien stepped forward quickly, placing himself directly in the lieutenant's path. "Raefer — ?"

His eyes still on the dragoon officer, Montgomery allowed a slight smile to curve one corner of his mouth. "I saw something I wanted and took it. The lieutenant seems to feel I was out of line, and yet he says he has no claim on the lady himself. To my way of thinking, that leaves the decision up to Mistress Ashbrooke as to whether there was an insult delivered or not."

"They're engaged, for God's sake," Damien hissed urgently.

Hamilton's gaze broke away from Montgomery to stare first at Damien, then at Catherine, who felt the full brunt of his anger before he glared at Montgomery once again. She was too distraught to clearly analyze why everything had started to go wrong. This morning in the clearing? Should she have ridden away before Montgomery ever noticed her? She knew full well she'd been tempting fate: alone in the forest with a stranger — dear God, no wonder he'd taken such a liberty tonight.

"Well daughter?" Sir Alfred's voice came down on her like a gavel. "We're waiting. Did this gentleman insult you or not?"

Catherine's eyes were burning.

"At least tell us the nature of the supposed insult," her father roared.

"He . . . he . . ." Her words were barely a whisper. "He kissed me."

"Kissed you? Against your will?"

"I . . ." She curled her lower lip between her teeth and bit down savagely. What could she say? If she said no, she would lose Hamilton as surely as if she slapped his face publicly. If she said yes, his damned code would require him to defend her honour. "I . . . One moment we were dancing, and the next . . ." She floundered again and lowered her head, unable to meet either man's stony gaze. "Yes. Yes . . . against my will."

Colonel Halfyard sucked in a deep breath. "Well then, it appears cut and dried. Lieutenant Hamilton was correct to issue a challenge. By God, in his place I'd do the same thing."

Hamilton's mouth drew into a sneer as he faced Montgomery. "Will you or will you not give me satisfaction?"

Raefer Montgomery exchanged a quiet look with Damien. He lowered his eyes after a moment and stared thoughtfully at his cigar.

"When and where?"

"Dawn tomorrow," Hamilton said crisply. "Kesslar's Green."

Montgomery smiled evenly. "I have pressing business in London. By dawn tomorrow I plan to be well on my way back. I'd as soon have this over with before then, if you don't mind."

Garner's expression became whiter, more pinched at the additional mockery. Even Sir Alfred stared at the tall merchant in surprise, which turned instantly to outrage.

"Then you shall meet here and now!" he declared. "The courtyard in front of the stables, in one half hour. Damien — since Mr. Montgomery is here by your invitation, you shall act as his second. Choice of weapons?"

The indigo eyes fell to Hamilton's waist. "As the lieutenant seems to be comfortable with sabres, I have no objections.''

"Hamilton, no . . . please!" Catherine implored one last time. "He's already apologized — "

"Daughter! You are a little late with your concern," Sir Alfred snarled. "I have no doubt you were more than slightly at fault here, if, indeed, not entirely to blame."

He took her roughly by the arm and dragged her unceremoniously toward the door.

"I warned Lady Ashbrooke we should have married you off years ago," he hissed in her ear. "I warned you as well, young lady, that I would tolerate no further scandals. You will take yourself to your room at once, and there you will remain until I decide what is to be done."

Catherine could no longer hold her tears in check. They welled along her lashes and brimmed over, streaming wetly down her cheeks. "Father — "

"Now! At once. Don't you dare ply me with any of your tricks. Your days of having your own way are over. Over, do you hear me!"

But Catherine could not hear anything above the frantic beating of her heart. She fled the terrace, fled past the startled, staring guests in the ballroom and did not stop until she was locked in her room, safely away from all prying eyes.

Chapter Four

Men were busy setting up a ring of brass lanterns in the courtyard, where a light fog had drifted in from the river, no more than a haze, but enough to blur the yellow posts of light and distort the ghostly shadows on the damp cobbles. Word of the impending duel had spread through the party like a bushfire, and every man worth his salt was present, forming a second, murmuring ring around the lanterns. Some of the more daring women, cloaked and hooded to prevent easy recognition, huddled in small, excited groups by the stables. Servants, liveried coachmen and grooms perched on the carriages, hung from windowledges and doors, eager anticipation upon their faces.

Two stories above, her hand clutching the sheer lace curtains as if to tear them from the track, Catherine stood at the window of her bedroom, grimly watching the scene below. Her face was still damp with tears, her eyes puffy and red from crying. Harriet stood behind her, her hands twisting a lace handkerchief.

"Someone has to stop this madness," Catherine whispered. "I never meant it to go this far. I didn't want anyone to be hurt. Oh, Harriet, you do believe me, don't you?"

"I believe you," Harriet murmured, seeing the genuine distress on her dearest friend's face. But the truth was, as she well knew, that Catherine often hurt people — herself included — simply because she rarely stopped to think through the consequences. There was goodness in Catherine, and kindness, but these were kept well hidden behind a protective shell of indifference. She was flighty and flirtatious, yes, but these qualities stemmed from a kind of desperation. She was too stubborn to admit she was vulnerable, too proud to reveal to anyone that she wasn't nearly as strong or self-sufficient as she professed to be. It was one of the reasons she and Harriet had become fast friends; each knew the other was terribly lonely and it was nice, once in a while, to simply take the masks away and have someone with whom to share the pain. Harriet had no one else, as she was an only child whose mother had died giving birth, and Catherine might as well have been an only child and an orphan for all the attention her parents gave her.

"Did Lady Caroline say anything when she came to see you?" Harriet ventured to ask.

"Mother?" There was a derisive sigh. "She was more irritated at having her tryst with Lord Winston interrupted than at anything I might have done. I don't think she listened to a word I said. Perhaps I should have told her Montgomery raped me; that might have aroused some curiosity."

"Oh Catherine . . ." Harriet bit her lip. "You shouldn't speak so of your mother. She cares for you, she just . . . doesn't know how to show it."

"She knows how to show it to her lovers," came the bleak retort. "Oh, why is this happening, Harriet? Why? Such a stupid little thing: a kiss. I've kissed dozens of men before this. Why make a fuss now? And why can't Hamilton be satisfied with first blood? Why is he insisting it be a duel to the death?''

"Because he is Lieutenant Hamilton Garner of His Majesty's Ninth Dragoons,'' Harriet snapped angrily. "What did you think he would do, Catherine? What were you playing at when you let Montgomery take you out onto the terrace?''

"I didn't *let* him take me. We were dancing, for heavens sake. I didn't even realize where we were until it was too late.''

"You didn't realize where you were? It must have been some kiss.''

Catherine looked around in annoyance, but the angry words never left her throat. How could she explain what had happened? She couldn't even explain it to herself. It was as if he'd cast a spell over her, swallowed her into his eyes so that she could not think or move without his command. And the kiss — yes, it had been some kiss. Her lips still burned with the memory . . . But that was all it had been: a kiss. A simple kiss and her life had been turned upside down. A simple kiss that would undoubtably cost her Hamilton's affection, and Montgomery his life. The lieutenant was a master swordsman, instructor for his regiment and the pupil of one of the greatest masters in Europe. Catherine had heard stories about his speed and instinct — two factors that often outweighed skill. Despite Montgomery's confidence — or perhaps because of it — Hamilton would cut him to bloody ribbons before dealing out the killing stroke.

"Oh God,'' she whispered and leaned her brow against the cool pane of the window. Hamilton had emerged from the shadows around the courtyard and was walking with his seconds — two junior lieutenants — into the centre of the lighted ring. He had removed his scarlet tunic and decorative white leather belts and wore only his buff-coloured nankeen breeches and a white linen shirt. He halted by the fountain and one of the seconds unsheathed his sword and handed it to him. He held it lovingly, running a finger down the gleaming surface of the steel before he held it in both hands and flexed the supple blade into a slight arc. He whipped it free almost at once and began warming his wrist with spirals and deadly swift slashes.

A smaller commotion on the far side of the courtyard indicated where Raefer Montgomery and Damien had approached the ring of lanterns. Montgomery had also removed his frock coat and waistcoat, his fancy lace jabot and high collar. His shirt was opened at the throat, the formal wig had been discarded, and his jet-black hair lay in thick waves against his neck and temples. The cigar clamped between his strong white teeth left a thin wake of smoke behind him as he walked.

Catherine's hand twisted deeper into the curtain. Hamilton moved like a dancer, preparing for a macabre performance. Montgomery was motionless. He stood with his hands on his hips, observing his adversary, seemingly oblivious to the crowd around him.

"Why does he just stand there?" Catherine asked in a horrified whisper. "Why is he there at all? He could have mounted his horse and been miles away by now . . ."

Harriet moved to the window and looked down into the courtyard. Damien was standing with Montgomery and she could see that he was worried. He was speaking with taut, angry little gestures, no doubt asking the same questions of his companion.

"Men are all the same," she said in a hushed voice. "They will never admit they have made a mistake, not where their pride is concerned."

Catherine was only half listening. Colonel Halfyard had apparently been chosen to act as judge, for he was walking solemnly to the centre of the lighted cobbles. He stopped and waited for the murmur of voices to fade to silence, then cleared his throat.

"Will the principles come forward."

Hamilton handed his sabre to one of the junior officers

and strode purposefully toward the colonel. Montgomery advanced, his dark hair glistening in the mist and lanternlight.

"Gentlemen, I am bound by convention to appeal to both of you to settle this *affaire d'honneur* without bloodshed. Lieutenant Garner, as challenger, will you accept an apology if tendered?"

Hamilton shook his head once, slowly.

"Mr. Montgomery," Colonel Halfyard glared at him from under beetling white brows, "do you believe there is any other way of settling this dispute?"

"I think not," he said quietly. "The lieutenant has been quite clear on that point."

"Very well." The colonel nodded brusquely to the seconds, who exchanged sides to formally inspect the weapons of both parties. "If all is in order, we shall proceed. Is there a doctor in attendance?"

A barrel-shaped, bewigged gentleman stepped forward and raised a hand. "Dr. Moore, at your service."

The colonel harrumped and looked gravely at each combatant. "At the command *en garde*, you will take up your positions. Since first blood has been waived by both parties, the duel will be to the death. God have mercy on your souls, gentlemen. Take your marks."

Montgomery inhaled a long last time on his cigar and dropped it on the cobbles. He ground it beneath his heel before stepping over to where Damien waited with his sabre. He wore a curious smile on his face, as though thinking of some private joke, but there was nothing amusing in the way the white silk of his sleeve fluttered as he slashed an invisible *Z* through the air with the slim steel-blue blade.

Catherine felt the blood drain from her face. Her heartbeat rose to a crescendo, pounding painfully against her ribcage as if it might burst free. She whirled suddenly away from the window and ran to the door.

"Catherine! Where are you going!"

She did not answer. Flinging the door wide and gathering the folds of her skirt in her hands, she flew along the hallway to the stairs, down and through the front doors as if a demon were snapping at her heels. She ran across the fine gravel and onto the manicured lawns, slipping on the dew-laden grass and twisting her ankle sharply. She did not stop. She kept running toward the stables and the rear courtyard, and before she rounded the corner of the house, she could hear the angry bite of steel on steel, shrill metallic screeches of offense and defense, swift, deadly strokes cutting, probing for blood, for life.

Fear forced her to a halt, her lungs heaving for air, her blonde hair flying wildly about her shoulders. The duelists faced each other, left arms bent and raised for balance, right arms in straight thrust; parrying, engaging, counterthrusting without a break in the stride or rhythm of their movements. It was like a ballet — a lethal, demoniacal ballet, and all present were holding their breath, knowing from the first few strokes that they were witnessing a test of supreme skill. There was no hacking or panicked slicing to ward off a blade. Each step was precise, calculated for the most efficient use of speed and strength. Each thrust and riposte was affected with a terrifying grace and beauty; less experienced swordsmen would have been dead a score of times over.

Hamilton was on the attack, his face set, his eyes pale and glittering with malevolent pleasure. A slash. A stinging whip of steel on steel and Montgomery reversed into a counterattack, his forward foot striking the cobbles with the clipped regularity of a metronome. He forced Hamilton into a temporary retreat, his sword moving like a silver blur.

They came together, their blades sliding to the hilts, and Hamilton spun away, feinting to the left while he cut an agile backhand low across Montgomery's exposed thigh. The crowd gasped collectively. First blood had been drawn, and, as was customary, the men separated, paused a moment to acknowledge the hit.

Montgomery's face and throat were covered in a sheen of sweat, as were Hamilton's. He waved away the physician with an impatient gesture, then raised his blade in a mocking salute to Garner, the fury in his eyes making them glow like embers in a fire.

At the call to "encore," Hamilton went on the full attack at once. His teeth were bared in savage delight, his arm moving with surety and confidence as he challenged the resilience in Montgomery's wrist. He did not find it lacking. They were evenly, awesomely matched, and Garner experienced the first twinge of surprise: he had misread Montgomery's nonchalance as mere bravado, a mistake that would require all of his superb instincts to correct.

Instinct found another opening and the tip of Hamilton's blade creased a ribbon of flesh from Montgomery's temple, just above his right ear. A dark red snake of blood swelled and slithered from the wound, running down the smooth-shaven jaw to drip in slow, thick drops onto the white silk shirt. He barely registered the injury or the further cries of approval from the onlookers. His teeth bared in a snarl, he launched himself at his adversary, the power of the attack driving Garner from one side of the ring to the other, then beyond, their swords alarming a wide swath through the scattering guests. Montgomery forced him all the way into the shadows of the stable, where a thundering riposte reversed the charge and carried it back almost to the stone lip of the fountain. The crowd was cheering feverishly, betting amongst themselves as both men, drenched in sweat, re-entered the lighted circle.

Hamilton now bore two cuts to his arm and neck. Montgomery's thigh was bleeding profusely, his shirt smeared and splattered with crimson from the wound on his temple.

Catherine's tears were shocked dry as she watched. The ringing clashes of steel showed no signs of relenting; all she could see was the blood and the rage of both men.

Hamilton parried each deadly stroke with unwavering determination. He knew Montgomery's last attack had cost him in stamina — such a sustained onslaught could not help but weaken the wrist, strain the reflexes. He could even feel the subtle shifting in the fluid stride as Montgomery began to draw heavily on his reserves. Hamilton was himself feeling the tension, but he willed it aside with a rush of unholy pleasure. The time would come at any moment. He could see it, feel it, taste it, even in the metallic sweetness of his own blood.

The opening came with the next double touch, when both blades struck for home and bit into hard flesh. Montgomery flinched and retreated to disengage his sabre, and Garner followed through, putting every last ounce of strength he possessed into the thrust. Montgomery appeared to fall, to stumble off balance, but at the last possible moment he shifted his weight forward in a lunge that should have been impossible to execute. It was certain Hamilton had not expected it, not this late in the contest. The two blades careened sharply together as Montgomery forced two, three inconceivably swift turns along Hamilton's sabre, causing the lieutenant's wrist to roll and break tension. Montgomery wasted no time in wrenching his own wrist so that the hilt of Garner's sword was torn out of his numbed fingers. At the same time, Montgomery twisted his body, pivoting on the balls of his feet so that his stance was recovered as his sabre slashed forward for the *coup de grace*.

The tip of the blade, aimed unerringly for a point midchest, was deflected — whether by Montgomery's intention or Hamilton's final, desperate defense against the inevitable strike, it was not possible to judge. Whatever the reason, the sword plunged instead into the soft flesh between two ribs, and slid the full length of the blade to the silver filigreed hilt. The impact of the cold steel punching through muscle and sinew took his breath away and Hamilton staggered back, his only conscious thought to keep from crying out. There was no pain, not immediately, only a curiously shrinking, sucking sensation that was made more pronouced as Montgomery leaned back and pulled the sabre free. It was thinly smeared, glinting redly in the lantern light, and Hamilton stared at it with a kind of horrified fascination, knowing it was coated with his blood, knowing it would be piercing him again as Montgomery drove for the heart. He stood his ground, steadfastly refusing to give way to the urge to sag to his knees — not to plead for mercy, but to instinctively keep his life from flowing out between his fingers.

When the blade still hovered some distance away, Hamilton raised his eyes to Montgomery's.

"What are you waiting for?" he hissed. "Finish it, you bastard."

Montgomery straightened, the unnatural glow fading slowly from his dark eyes. As if it had suddenly become repulsive to him, he threw the sabre aside, sending it skittering across the shiny cobblestones.

Hamilton's seconds rushed over and grabbed him beneath both arms to offer support. Montgomery was dimly aware of Damien pressing a wad of folded cotton into his hand, then guiding the hand up to staunch the flow of blood from his temple.

"Come on," Damien urged quietly, aware of the silent hostility of the crowd, which consisted of a goodly number of Garner's fellow dragoons. "I don't think you've made many friends here."

"Montgomery!"

Raefer stopped and turned. Hamilton was swaying against his men, adamantly refusing to be led to the side of the ring.

"Don't you walk away from me, you bastard. I said to the death, and by God, I meant it!"

Montgomery's eyes narrowed. "I have no further quarrel with you, Lieutenant. Take your life and leave it at that."

"Leave it? I'll leave nothing!" He shrugged off the hands of his men and lurched forward, the spittle tinged pink as it formed on his lips. "You think this makes you the better man, Montgomery? You think this makes you any less of a *coward?* You were lucky, that's all. Lucky!"

"I'll say goodbye to you, Lieutenant, with a sincere wish that we never meet again. I rarely make the same mistakes twice."

"Bastard," Hamilton grated, his jaws clenching through a shudder of pain. *"Bastard!* You're damned right we'll meet again, and when we do you'll regret you turned your back on me. *Do you hear me, Montgomery, you bastard? Don't you walk away from me!"*

His seconds caught him as he collapsed in a violent surge of agony. His eyes rolled back so that just the whites showed, and he slumped unconscious into their arms. Two men hurried over with a long plank, he was placed on it and carried into the house, the doctor issuing anxious orders by his side.

Damien led Montgomery to the tackroom at the rear of the stables and made him remove the blood-soaked shirt and breeches. Neither of his wounds was deep enough to require stitches, and for that Damien was thankful.

"The sooner you are away from here the better," he muttered. "God*damn!* I knew something like this would happen, I just knew it."

Raefer bit the end off a fresh cigar and lit it over the flame of the lantern. "Maybe I should have killed the bastard."

"There is no maybe about it. You should have. Garner isn't a man given to idle threats, and he certainly isn't the type to forgive or forget. By tomorrow morning he will have himself convinced you spared him deliberately, as an added insult."

"Not exactly the type of man I'd want for my brother-in-law," Montgomery said wryly and splashed water over his neck and torso.

"Yes, well, I don't think I'll have to worry about that. At least I hope I don't have to worry about that. Father is a bit prickly at the best of times, I would not want to say what his reaction to this will be."

Montgomery glanced over, but his response was delayed by the appearance of Sir Alfred Ashbrooke at the tackroom door.

Damien straightened at once. "Father!"

Sir Alfred ignored his son. "Mr. Montgomery, I felt obliged to come and compliment you on your skill. I don't believe I've seen such fine swordsmanship in all my days."

Montgomery dried himself and pulled on clean breeches. "It's not a compliment I go out in search of, but I thank you nonetheless."

"You might also be pleased to know the wound in the lieutenant's side, while definitely serious, is not fatal. The vital organs seemed to have been missed. Doctor Moore expects a full recovery, in time." He paused a moment and clasped his hands behind his back. "I see your own wounds are minimal. Your . . . wife and family should be grateful to get you home in one piece."

Montgomery's eyes flicked to the door as Colonel Halfyard stepped through and stood behind Sir Alfred. "I appreciate your concern, but I'm not married."

Sir Alfred smiled and nodded to the colonel, who in turn gave a signal to someone standing out of sight. The "someone" proved to be six armed soldiers.

Montgomery scanned them warily before arching a questioning brow. "Have you come to arrest me?"

"The duel was fairly fought," Colonel Halfyard declared. "Fairly won. No need for an arrest."

Montgomery shrugged his broad shoulders into a clean shirt. "Then may I ask why the friendly escort?"

"The escort, sir, is to ensure your co-operation in fulfilling the rest of your obligation."

After several long moments, Raefer said evenly, "I'm not sure I understand."

"Neither do I." Damien frowned. "Raefer was challenged, he met the challenge and won — honourably, as Colonel Halfyard has already noted. What else is expected of him?"

Sir Alfred pursed his lips and rocked back on his heels. "Simply this: You were challenged for taking liberties with my daughter. You accepted the challenge. You won. These men are here to see that you claim your prize."

Montgomery exhaled a slow stream of blue-white smoke. "My . . . prize?"

"Indeed. You fought for my daughter, sir; you have won her. Both she and the Reverend Mister Duvall await you in my study."

Montgomery said nothing. Damien stared at his father incredulously. "You can't be serious."

"I assure you, I am very serious. Deadly serious, in fact. As are each of these six young men who will challenge Mr. Montgomery's honour, if necessary, unto death."

Montgomery stared. Hard. Only the squared ridge of his jaw betrayed the control it was taking to keep his anger in check. "Let me get this straight: You expect me to marry your daughter . . . here? Tonight?"

"By your own admission, sir, you are free to do so. Also by your own admission, you do not find her repulsive. Your exact words, I believe were along the lines of the Roman, *veni vidi vici:* I saw something I liked and I took it. You appear to live by a strong hand, Mr. Montgomery. I have no doubt that you will be able to reform my daughter to your wishes."

"You know nothing about me."

"I pride myself in being able to judge the cut of a man on first impressions," Sir Alfred countered smoothly. "I judge you to be more than adequate for the task. Further, she will not be coming to you entirely empty handed, for she was bequeathed quite an attractive dowry by her maternal grandmother. As a merchant and a successful businessman, I am sure you can recognize sound value for a sound investment."

Damien stepped forward, his face a tight white mask. "You're talking about Catherine as if she were a piece of dry goods to be negotiated over. She's your daughter, for Christ's sake. My sister!"

"I am indeed her father," Sir Alfred said calmly. "And she has seen fit to defy me time and time again. I warned her after the last escapade, and if nothing else, I am a man of my word. You, sir, have nothing to say in the matter unless it is to produce irrefutable proof that Mr. Montgomery is a liar or a cheat, a thief or a murderer. If he is none of those, then I can see little argument. If he is any, or all of those, then these six fine officers will be more than amenable to escorting him to prison where he belongs.''

The muscles in Damien's jaw worked furiously. ''What about Catherine? Has she nothing to say in this?''

''Not a single thing,'' Sir Alfred said bluntly and looked over at Montgomery. ''Well, sir? What shall it be? Six more stout young duellists or my daughter's hand in marriage?''

''He could refuse to fight,'' Damien persisted. ''What would your recourse be then?''

Sir Alfred pursed his lips. ''That is a difficult question. One that could take weeks, perhaps months, for me to ponder a judiciary solution. Mr. Montgomery would, of course, be detained in the town jail until such time as I could render a decision. Naturally he would be provided with all the amenities . . . bread, water, rats . . .''

Raefer Montgomery's expression grew tauter, his dark eyes flaring with rage as he realized there was no immediate recourse.

''The reverend is waiting,'' Sir Alfred said mildly.

Montgomery clamped his teeth down on the end of the cigar and tucked the loose ends of his shirt into the waist of his breeches as he stormed angrily to the door.

''Let's get it over with,'' he snarled.

''They can't force you to do this,'' Damien said urgently.

''They aren't leaving me much choice,'' Raefer shot back. ''I have neither the time to waste rotting in his jail nor the inclination to fight any more of your sister's misguided champions.''

''Your waistcoat, sir. Your jacket?'' Sir Alfred snatched up both as the two men brushed past him.

The tall Londoner stopped and glared down at him. ''If you want me that badly, you'll take me as I am.''

He pushed past Colonel Halfyard and the dragoons and strode angrily into the courtyard. There were still guests and servants lingering in the mist-shrouded lantern light, talking excitedly among themselves, discussing and replaying every detail of the duel as if they could yet see it before their eyes. They fell silent as Montgomery walked into the courtyard, their huzzahs and words of congratulation fading before the ominous blackness that clouded his features. A few, picking up the scent of a new scandal, fell into step behind the colonel and Sir Alfred, neither of whom would acknowledge the ensuing buzz of questions.

Montgomery paused inside the main entrance, his appearance startling cries and gasps from the ladies milling in the great hall. Sir Alfred bustled past him, leading the way along the hall and up the staircase to the second-floor library. He flung the doors wide with a flourish and waited for Montgomery, Colonel Halfyard, and a dazed and disbelieving Damien Ashbrooke to enter. Before he closed them again, he gave crisp orders to the escort of dragoons to stand guard outside and let no one enter or leave without his express permission.

The library was dark and sombre, with its tall bookcases filled wall to wall, floor to ceiling with moroccan-bound volumes. A huge fireplace centrally located on one wall contained a cheerfully burning fire that was the only sign of animation in the room. Harriet Chalmers sat on a red damask settee and sobbed quietly into her handkerchief. The Reverend Mister Duvall, invited as a guest to the party, looked both bewildered and agitated as he waited by the enormous carved oak desk, his hands worrying the pages of a Bible as if in search of strength.

Lady Caroline Ashbrooke sat on a leather chair near the fire and fussed with imagined wrinkles in her skirt. She was a beautiful woman, straight-backed and slender, whose fine, delicate features had been luminously duplicated in Catherine. Her hair was golden yellow beneath the white rice powder, her complexion pure enough to disdain the use of paints and powders. Her eyes were a deeper shade of violet than her daughter's and at one time must have melted the hearts of any young swain they lighted upon. Now, however, they were dull and lifeless, as indifferent to her surroundings as twenty years of a lacklustre existence could render them. There were further signs of erosion in the thin, dry lips, in the tiny white creases beneath her chin and on her forehead that night vizards failed to keep in check. Her affairs were no secret to anyone in the immediate family, not even Sir Alfred, who had himself taken his first paramour three weeks after his marriage.

Lady Caroline looked up now as Raefer Montgomery entered the library, and a faint smile tugged at her lips.

"Why Alfred dear, you neglected to tell me our new son-in-law was so . . . attractive."

Sir Alfred glared at his wife, then switched his attention to the reverend.

"We have arrived at an agreement, Mr. Duvall. Mr. Montgomery willingly accepts the hand of my daughter in marriage."

"And, er, Mistress Catherine?" The reverend raised his eyebrows in a gesture of helplessness.

Catherine Ashbrooke stood at the window, her back to the room. She hadn't moved, hadn't said a word to anyone since her father had dragged her into the library.

"Catherine!" her father barked sharply. "You will oblige your mother and I by joining Mr. Montgomery in front of Reverend Duvall. We have the means here at hand to repair at least some of the damage you have brought about tonight. Catherine — *do you hear me?*"

The minister trembled visibly at the harshness of Sir Alfred's command. "R-really, Lord Ashbrooke, I don't think — "

"Precisely. Do not think. Simply read the blasted service. She can make her vows from where she stands if she so desires."

"B-but the legality — "

"I am more than willing to pay generously for any special dispensation you may require. In fact, I am willing to pay for a complete new roof for the chapel, if that is what it will take to dispense with any further delays.''

"It . . . it isn't that, Your Lordship, it's . . .''

"It's what? God's blood, speak up!''

"You cannot force your daughter into a marriage by threats and coercions. It would not be morally legal.''

"Poppycock! It's been legal, morally and otherwise for centuries gone by. That's the root of most of society's troubles these days, allowing children to decide what is best for themselves. My daughter will be married this night! If not to Mr. Montgomery, then to the first lout I can lay a hand to outside the door!''

Catherine turned from the window. Her face was pale, her lips bloodless, and when for the briefest of moments she looked into her mother's eyes, she thought she saw the faint glimmerings of pity. She, too, had been forced into her own marriage to Sir Alfred; a prudent union between two families of substance, with no thought whatsoever to affection, or even whether the two parties concerned liked each other.

"Reverend Duvall,'' Catherine said softly, "I'm ready to proceed.''

Damien hastened to her side and grasped both her ice-cold hands in his. "Catherine . . . you don't have to go through with this . . . he cannot force you . . .''

Her face softened and she raised a hand to lay it against his cheek. "My dear brother, my dearest friend,'' she whispered, "he is not forcing me. He has simply explained the advantages and disadvantages of refusing to do as he asks. It will be all right.'' Her eyes flicked to the glowering Montgomery, then back again. "I promise you, everything will be all right.''

She was calm. Too calm, Damien decided, and far too docile where she should have been screaming and tearing at her hair. What was she up to? What was she trying to tell him with that strange little smile?

The reverend cleared his throat and opened the missal to the appropriate pages. Catherine took her place before him and there was one final moment of tension as Raefer Montgomery drew deeply on his cigar and let his stare fall on every face in the room. With a brusque gesture of annoyance, he tossed the cigar butt into the fire and took his place beside Catherine.

The reverend shuddered away the last of his misgivings and began droning passages from the missal. Under any other circumstances, he might have taken pause to admire the handsome couple that stood before him: he, tall, strapping, and darkly handsome; she, slender and glowing in her blonde beauty. But the one instance he did happen to glance up and offer a smile of encouragement, he was rewarded by hot violet-blue eyes filled with contempt, rife with bitterness, flecked with sparks of pure hatred.

Chapter Five

Catherine Ashbrooke Montgomery stood in numbed silence beside her bedroom window watching a small battalion of maids swarm through her armoires, her dressers, her tables, and her sideboard to select the possessions she approved before packing them into the two enormous wooden trunks her father had placed at her disposal. A nod or a shake of her head decided the fate of dozens of gowns. Those she rejected were carefully laid aside, not to be burned, as she had initially commanded, but to be distributed among the servants. Her new husband had informed her in curt, cold tones of his intentions of leaving Rosewood Hall at dawn. He had stalked out of the library immediately after the brief ceremony and she had not seen him since.

Numb was exactly how she felt. Her mind, her body, her senses — it was as if she hung suspended somewhere in the air above the room and could watch but not participate. Someone else was saying yea or nay to the selection of gowns. Someone else was watching Harriet Chalmers burst into tears at every turn, and that same someone else was unable to cry herself. What possible good would tears do now? She was married — to a man she did not know, much less love. Mrs. Raefer Montgomery: The name sent a shiver down her spine. How could things have gone so wrong in so few hours?

Her father had not called a halt to the birthday party, as anyone else might have done; he had simply announced to the guests that there was new cause to celebrate. Her utter and complete mortification had sent Catherine to her room, from where she vowed not to emerge until Montgomery's coach was at the front door of the manor. Twice she had thought to go and see Hamilton, and twice she had stopped herself. The doctor had labored over his wound for more than an hour before declaring it might be safe to move him from the table in the kitchen to one of the guest rooms.

Catherine stepped around the clutter of garments strewn on the floor and, almost in a trance, walked to the door and put her hand to the brass latch.

"Catherine?" Harriet sniffled. "Where are you going?"

"I must see him," she said softly.

"See him? See who?"

"Hamilton. I must try to explain . . ."

"Oh Catherine, no. Why torment yourself? Why torment Hamilton? Aren't you both suffering enough?"

Catherine squared her shoulders and walked out the door. She was still dressed in the pink silk gown, and the skirt made soft whispering sounds as she made her way along the darkened hallway. There were candles alight in the wall sconces, but only as many as were necessary to prevent a guest from stumbling in the dark. It was four o'clock in the morning and, thankfully, she met with nothing more than muffled snores on the way to the west wing, where Hamilton had been taken.

The door to his room was slightly ajar, enough for a finger of light to beckon to her through the gloom. Catherine approached it warily, not knowing who or what to expect to see inside. Even in the hallway she could smell the lingering aura of the herbs and unguents Dr. Moore had used to treat the wound. She could also smell sweat and fear, pain and humiliation.

A single candle lit the room. Its flame was weak, the wick trimmed to assure the minimum disturbance for the patient. The glow it cast illuminated the sheer canopy that hung like a tent around the bed; the image it created was of a pagan altar prepared for the offering of the ultimate sacrifice.

Catherine edged closer, her hands pressed to the deep cleft between her breasts. Hamilton's eyes were closed, the lids flickering sporadically beneath a film of sweat. Droplets slid from his brow and temples, turning his tawny gold hair into a damp, clinging cap. His flesh had turned gray and his hands, resting along either thigh, were splayed upon the linens, trembling with each wave of pain. His clothes had been removed and he lay bare to the waist. The thick, wide bandage that was wrapped around his midsection was oily yellow from the doctor's poultice and tinged with blood.

Catherine moistened her lips, uncertain of whether to stay or go. He was asleep, drugged most likely with the tincture of laudanum that sat in a vial on the nightstand. Hot, fat tears swelled over her lashes and glistened down her cheeks as she leaned over and gently rearranged the covers he had thrown aside.

"No!" he hissed and a hand shot up, grabbing at her arm. The jade eyes bulged open but it took several seconds for recognition to break through the glaze of pain.

"Catherine?" he gasped.

"Hamilton," she sobbed in a whisper. "Oh, Hamilton, what have I done to you?"

He swallowed with difficulty and the grip on her forearm became less fanatical. "You've nothing to blame yourself for, Catherine. It was my contest. I lost it. He proved himself the better man."

"No, Hamilton! No! Not a better man. He's vile and brutal and cold-hearted — "

"Did you — " The hand tightened, squeezing her viciously to silence. "Dear God, Catherine, did you actually do it? Did you marry him?"

Catherine cringed from the anger in his voice as well as the sharp burning pain in her arm. "I had no choice, Hamilton! Father forced me to do it. He was in a rage, he threatened to throw me out into the night — "

"You *married* him?" he snarled, his head splitting, reeling with this further scourge on his honour.

"I had no choice," she cried weakly. "He would have done it. He would have thrown me out of the house, and where could I have gone? What could I have done? Who could I have turned to knowing that you hated me, and Damien hated me, and — "

"Hate you?" His eyes burned feverishly and fresh beads of moisture broke out across his forehead. "You're mine, dammit. *Mine!* No strutting, arrogant bastard is going to touch you, not while there's breath left in my body."

He began to struggle upright, his hand flailing angrily at Catherine's attempts to stop him.

"What are you doing? Your wound!"

"He's not going to have you, by God! I'll kill him before I'll let him take you away from me."

"Hamilton, no! You're too weak. Your wound will open again and — "

"You're mine, Catherine! Mine!" A searing bolt of pain lanced through his side, twisting his features into a mask of agony. He slumped back on the pillows, the sweat pouring from his face in rivers. His mouth moved and he tried to speak again, but there was no sound.

Catherine clamped her hands over her mouth and stared down in horror at the man who had willingly risked his life for her — had been willing to die to protect her honour — and her father's threats paled in comparison, as did her own pathetic lack of courage. She should never have doubted Hamilton's love or devotion, never worried that his ambitions would have taken precedence over his need for her. She should have listened to her heart, not her pride. He loved her, he truly loved her, and now she belonged to another.

"Catherine." He regained control with an effort and his eyes opened slowly. "Stay with me. Don't leave. Tell him . . . tell them all you've changed your mind, that you cannot go through with this travesty, that you love me . . . *me*!"

"Hamilton, I do love you, I — "

He dragged his tongue across his parched lips and stared at the shadows beyond her shoulder. "No one makes a fool of me," he hissed. "No one. If he tries to take you away from me, I'll follow. I'll track him to the ends of the earth, if need be. He can't get away with this. He *won't* get away with it!"

Catherine heard footsteps out in the hallway and quickly leaned over the bed. "You mustn't do anything until you're well. Please, Hamilton, please promise me you will not do anything until you have your strength back."

His eyes glittered and his hands clenched and unclenched spasmodically. "It was a trick, it had to be. I don't know how he did it. No one has ever bested me before; no one ever will again. Yes . . . yes, somehow a trick — "

"Hamilton . . . I want to stay with you, you know I do, but we need time! We need time for your wounds to heal, and time for Father to realize what a dreadful thing he has forced me to do. No, listen to me" — she placed her fingers gently over his mouth to prevent an interruption — "I will leave with Montgomery in the morning, as planned. I must. But at the first inn we come to, I shall tell him I'll go no farther. I will wait for you there, Hamilton, and . . . and we can run away together. I will go anywhere you want me to, my love. Anywhere."

"Montgomery is your husband," he croaked, his voice breaking with emotion. "He has a claim to you. He can force you — "

"He cannot force me to do anything," Catherine said vehemently. "He is my husband in name only — and only for as long as it takes us to find someone willing to annul this entire mockery. He will not touch me, Hamilton, that much I swear to you. As long as you love me and want me, I am yours. No other man shall have what belongs to you alone.''

His eyes held hers for a long moment. His hand snaked up, curled around the nape of her neck and pulled her roughly forward, crushing her mouth down over his. The kiss was far from gentle; his teeth were savage as they bruised her lips, his tongue thick and furred and soured as it plunged repeatedly in her mouth. But she shuddered away her revulsion, knowing it was a kiss of desperation, knowing the violence was borne of pain and anger and helplessness.

''Tell me you love me,'' he commanded harshly.

''I . . . I love you, Hamilton, you know I do.''

''Tell me you want me. Only me!''

''I want you,'' she whispered, aware that they were no longer alone in the room. She kissed him again, briefly, tenderly, then straightened away from the bed. ''Rest now, my love. We'll be together soon, I swear we will.''

The coach drew to a halt at the front of Rosewood Hall just as the dawn light was blushing pink across the horizon. The last of the brightest stars still winked overhead and the ground shimmered under a carpet of mist and dew. Catherine stood in the foyer, her gray velvet travelling suit covered beneath the wings of a light woolen cape. Her hair was protected against the morning dampness by a muslin cap trimmed in lace and ribbon and surmounted by a small gray felt hat. Her hands were gloved, her slippered feet tucked safely inside leather pattens to guard against mud and water.

She was determined not to cry. Her expression was taut, her eyes heavy and strained from sleeplessness, and it gave her some measure of satisfaction to see that Sir Alfred was not bearing up well under her accusing stare. He avoided meeting her gaze directly. His lips were held in a pucker and moved now and then as if he were holding a private conversation with himself. His multilevel presentation of chins quivered with the frequent need to clear his throat and appear unmoved.

"Kitty?"

She turned from her father's discomfort and leaned gratefully into Damien's supportive embrace.

"Kitty, I don't know what to say . . ."

"It's all right, Damien. *I'm* all right. It isn't as if I was the first woman in the world to be tossed away like so much excess baggage. Mind, if I were you, I would be quick about having the banns read for you and Harriet . . . before someone takes it upon themselves to destroy *your* life and happiness."

The sarcasm was not lost on Sir Alfred. He reddened and cleared his throat with a vengeance, but if an apology or some word of consolation was expected, Catherine was to be sadly disappointed again.

"Stay well, daughter. Behave yourself. Show this fellow Montgomery what stock we Ashbrookes are made of. Say goodbye to your mother now, and promise to send your address in London so she can communicate with you."

Catherine's eyes stung with tears despite her resolve. She felt Damien's arm tighten on her shoulder, but it still took every last ounce of her willpower to remain calm as she faced her mother. There were signs of a long sleepless night on Lady Caroline's face as well, but somehow Catherine did not think they were placed there out of concern for her daughter's welfare. Her mouth was puffed and tender-looking, her cheeks and throat chafed pink. Her eyes were heavy-lidded and held the faraway glaze of passion-drugged exhaustion; obviously she and Lord Winston had made the most of the night's commotions.

"Goodbye, Mother," Catherine said coldly. "Try not to worry about me."

"I shan't, my darling," she purred, and fussed absently with a misplaced ribbon on Catherine's cap. "There is far too much of my blood in your veins for me to doubt that you will eventually come to make the best of this situation. Your husband is rich, he is handsome, he is incredibly'' — she took a slow, deep breath while she searched for the precise word — ''*male*. Do bring him home for a visit now and then. You know you will always be welcome.''

Catherine turned away.

''Catherine! Oh, Catherine!'' Harriet Chalmers came flying out of the door, a wrapper flung hastily over her nightdress, both garments ballooning out behind her. ''You were not going to leave without saying goodbye, were you?''

''You were up with me most of the night,'' Catherine murmured, her words muffled within a frantic hug. ''I did not think I should disturb you.''

''I want you to write me every single day, do you hear? *Every day*, no matter what!'' She lowered her voice to a fervent whisper. ''And if that brute mistreats you in any way, Damien and I will fly to your rescue, I swear it. In *any* way!''

''You are a good friend, Harriet,'' Catherine said softly, a sob pressing even more urgently against her throat at the sight of Harriet's distress. ''I will write, I promise. Every single day.''

The desperate embrace ended abruptly as the tiny group gathered in front of the coach heard the pounding of horses' hooves approaching. Raefer Montgomery, his broad frame cloaked in a many-collared flowing black cape, rode into view. He was astride the gigantic black stallion Catherine had seen in the clearing, and his face, glowering out from beneath a three-cornered beaver hat, was as bleak and grim as the gray morning sky. Dressed all in black, with his black eyes and his black stare, he seemed a larger-than-life spectre out of some terrifying nightmare.

''Well, Mrs. Montgomery, have you dispensed with your farewells?''

Catherine flushed at the coarseness in his voice, at the deliberately mocking inflection placed on her new name.

''I'm ready,'' she grated.

''Very well. Time is wasting. Damien — ?'' The cold

black eyes sought Catherine's brother. "My thanks for an interesting and eventful evening. We must get together and do it again some time."

He wheeled the stallion around before Damien had a chance to respond to the cutting remark. Catherine gave her brother a last quick hug, wishing she could ease his anxiety by telling him of the plan she had devised with Hamilton, but she could not. She dared not tell anyone, not even Harriet, for fear of her father finding some way to interfere again.

She gave Harriet a final kiss on her plump, tear-stained cheek, then walked swiftly to the waiting coach without a glance spared for her father or mother. The attending coachman closed and latched the door behind her, and before Catherine could raise a hand in farewell, the driver was cracking the whip over the heads of the matched bays in response to a barked command from Montgomery. Slammed back into her seat, Catherine swore aloud and for the next few minutes enjoyed imagining various methods of torture to exact revenge upon her new husband.

Sir Alfred had spared one of the smaller carriages, a vehicle that could seat Catherine and her personal maid, Deirdre, in relative comfort, as well as carry her two massive trunks in the boot. Constructed of glossy black mahogany, the side panels were chased in brass and emblazoned with the Ashbrooke family crest. The team of bays was handled by a driver and coachman on loan from the Ashbrooke estate.

Judging by the speed at which they churned along the road, Catherine assumed Montgomery had instructed the driver to defy both gravity and safety for the sake of haste. The trunks rattled and shook so much she feared for their bindings. The thunder of the horses' hooves was so loud and incessant that a constant vibration hummed in her ears. She could not relax, could not even contemplate recouping the hours of sleep she had lost. She had no way of marking the passing hours other than to peer for the sun through the clouds of boiling dust thrown up by the roaring hooves and carriage wheels. Deirdre O'Shea, normally bright and cheerful, was pale from fear and doubtless could not have bolstered her own spirits much less attempted to lighten Catherine's.

Montgomery made no attempt to see her or speak to her during the morning, and it was not until well past noon before he deigned to spare a thought for her mental or physical comforts. By then she was in a fine temper, ready to gouge out his eyes at the first hint of insolence.

"How very thoughtful of you to inquire after my necessities," she said through clenched teeth. "How considerate of you to stop every few miles so that we might stretch our legs or ease our thirst with a sip of water. And how *very* kind of you to instruct the driver to slow down at the corners and to do his utmost to avoid driving into every rut and canyon in the road!"

Montgomery was standing by his horse, stroking the beast's gleaming neck as it pushed its snout into the cool water of a stream. He glanced up at her tirade but showed no overt reaction aside from a faint curving up of the corner of his mouth.

"Have you nothing to say?" she demanded with a frustrated stamp of her foot.

"If the accommodations were not to your liking, you should not have come."

Her eyes blazed violet fire as she planted her hands on her waist. "You know very well I had no choice in the matter."

"People always have choices."

"Really?" He was infuriating! "And what were yours, pray tell? You looked even less pleased than I did — *if that is possible* — and yet you went through with the wretched ceremony anyway!"

His eyes lifted from their indolent study of her mouth. "It seemed the most expedient way of getting through an awkward situation."

"Expedient!" she exclaimed. "You call entering into a marriage that neither of us wanted . . . *expedient*!"

"I told you, I was pressed for time. I still am, so if we

could dispense with the rest of your righteous indignation, I'd like to see if we can't reach Wakefield by nightfall. Hopefully we'll be able to find a sympathetic — and greedy — magistrate thereabouts who will legally annul your father's error in judgement.'' His smile broadened and he arched a black brow. ''Unless of course, I have misread the lovely flush in your cheeks and you are quite eager to remain Mrs. Montgomery?''

Catherine's rage drained away in a dizzying rush. She stared up at his bronzed features, totally at a loss for words. She was not even sure she had heard him correctly.

Montgomery laughed softly. ''My dear Mistress Ashbrooke, while I will admit to a certain attraction to your more earthly charms, I would not now, or ever, consider them worth relinquishing my freedom. I would not relinquish that for you, or any other woman.''

The candour heightened the blush in Catherine's cheeks. ''You have an aversion to marriage, sir?''

''Distinct and everlasting, madam. But aside from that, did I honestly strike you as the type of man who would take an unwilling wife to heart and home?''

''I suppose . . . if I'd thought about it . . .''

He laughed again. ''If women thought about a tenth of the things they should think about, I warrant the world would be a far less complicated place to live in.''

''Are you suggesting this is all my fault?'' she asked, her eyes narrowing with renewed vindictiveness.

''Are you trying to tell me you considered the consequences — *all* of the consequences of using me to rouse your lover's jealousy?''

Catherine's cheeks flamed a deep crimson. ''Lieutenant Garner is not my lover!''

''A moot point. Obviously no one ever cautioned you against tinkering with proud men or wild animals — neither is completely predictable.''

''I assume you consider yourself to fit into one of those categories?''

''I'll leave the choice solely to your discretion,'' he mused and bowed solicitously. "And I am still in a hurry, so if you don't mind — " He tilted his dark head in the direction of the lunch Deirdre was laying out on a blanket.

With a toss of her head she walked away, but Montgomery did not appear to suffer for the snub. He finished watering and feeding his stallion, then spent the better part of an hour chatting with the coachmen and sharing out his cigars. When he strolled over to where she and Deirdre were sitting beneath the shade of a huge oak tree and inquired politely if they were finished, she stood and brushed past him without a word and reboarded the coach.

The afternoon passed in as much discomfort as the morning. Her only consolation for the bumps and bruises was the promise of speedy salvation at the end of the trek. An annulment at Montgomery's suggestion was the best possible solution she could have hoped for. No arguments. No questions asked. He was actually being quite civil about the whole thing, rather good-natured . . . almost indifferent. In fact, if she thought about it, she could easily become just as angry for the totally opposite reasons. Did he think he was too good for her? An aversion to marriage . . . the scoundrel should have counted himself the luckiest man alive to have won the hand of Catherine Augustine Ashbrooke at the small sacrifice of a cut temple and a skewered thigh!

By the time the coach halted, Catherine was again bristling and determined more than ever to ignore the rogue completely. She tucked a finger beneath the blind to pry it away from the coach window and was mildly surprised to see that dusk had fallen.

"We are outside of Wakefield," Montgomery announced, his broad frame suddenly filling the doorway. "I would like you ladies to remain in the coach until I have completed arrangements with the innkeeper."

"And the magistrate?" Catherine blurted hopefully.

"Unfortunately that will have to wait until the morning."

"Well . . . just see that there are clean sheets on the bed

and a hot bath waiting in my room. And food. Lots of it, I am famished.''

He stared at her a moment. "I'll see what I can do.''

Catherine leaned back on her seat. She felt grimy and dusty, but somehow elated to have the worst behind her. Three or four days, a week at most, and Hamilton would be in Wakefield to rescue her. With her annulment in hand they would not delay in making new vows, the proper vows this time between two people who loved each other and belonged together for all time.

She heard the crunch of boots on the hard ground outside and gathered the voluminous folds of her skirt and petticoats together in anticipation of disembarking. The door swung open again and Montgomery reached a black-gloved hand inside to offer assistance. Primly she accepted it, and daintily she ventured one petite foot out onto the coach step, but she had barely cleared her head through the portal when she stopped dead and gaped in horror at the "inn.''

The building was no more than a run-down country cottage. The walls were mud and mortar, the roof was thatch, rippled like the surface of a pond. Wooden shutters leaned drunkenly from the oilcloth windows, and there was more smoke escaping through cracks in the roof and walls than from the half-rotted chimney.

"Is this some kind of a joke?'' she demanded with quiet fury.

"On the contrary. The landlady takes her hospitality very seriously. It may not be much to look at from the outside, but I am assured of the tastiest meat pastries in two counties and the best black ale in all of England.''

"Surely you do not expect me to sleep in this . . . this pigsty!''

"You shall have a clean room. It will not be as fancy as what you are accustomed to, but — ''

"The room could be painted in silver and the floors dusted with gold,'' she hissed. "The king himself could be lodged in the next room, for all I care. I will not spend so much as a single *hour* in this hovel, much less challenge providence by sleeping under that roof.''

''My dear Mistress Ashbrooke — '' He slipped his hand under the crook of her arm but she jerked back angrily. ''All right then — '' His arm curled around her waist and he lifted her clear off her feet, crushing her to a breathless silence against his chest. ''My dear Mrs. Montgomery, you can either walk in that door and up to your room under your own power, or you can be carried up the stairs like a sack of grain.''

''You're hurting me,'' she gasped.

''Madam, you do not know the meaning of the word. But if you would care to learn . . . ?''

His voice was as ominous as the gleam deep in his eyes and Catherine felt a flash of real fear drain away her courage.

''You are even more despicable than I had imagined. Morning cannot come too soon to please me.''

''I share your sentiments, madam, but until then you will behave yourself. You will walk inside the inn and you will smile pleasantly at Mistress Grundy, for she is quite beside herself at the thought of providing for a lady of *quality*.''

Catherine prickled at the sarcasm and wrenched out of his grasp. She might have said more but for Deirdre's presence beside her on the coach step.

''Faith, Mistress Catherine,'' the maid breathed, gaping at what supposedly passed for a posting house, ''is it here we're expected to sleep?''

''So I have been informed,'' Catherine said pertly, her gaze clashing with Montgomery's. ''But only for the one night. Tomorrow we shall find a *respectable* lodging where we needn't tolerate *any* manner of vermin.''

She clutched Deirdre's arm for support as she walked toward the lighted doorway. An effort had been made some century past to plant a garden along the pathway, but the weeds had long since taken over, mostly yellow goldenrod, the pollen of which tickled the inside of Catherine's nose and throat the instant she set foot on the chipped cobbles. Inside the rickety door, the prospects were no less discouraging. The lower floor was all one room, dark and airless, the floor covered with stale rushes. A fireplace occupied one wall, overhung with pots and utensils and vile-looking tubes of curing meat. A dismal fire was licking at the metal grate, but the effort produced more smoke than light or heat. The ceiling sagged threateningly between thick-hewn beams, a malady it had apparently caught from the roof. A narrow flight of steps, more like a ladder than a stairwell, rose from the centre of the room, dividing the living quarters from . . . and here Catherine experienced a flutter of true nausea . . . a large wooden pen containing goats and filthy bovine creatures too covered in mud to properly identify.

She took a reflective step backward, only to come up hard against Montgomery's body. She flinched from the contact and spun around to glare up at him, the anger and degradation pulsing through her veins in slow waves. He was doing this deliberately, she had no doubt. Was it out of spite? Did he want to see her break down in tears or beg and grovel because *he* happened to have been fool enough to enter into a duel with Hamilton Garner?

"I wish Hamilton had run you through," she said tersely. "I wish it with all my heart."

"Perhaps next time," he said wanly.

"You doubt there will be a next time, sir? Lieutenant Garner is not so easily brushed aside. If he says he intends to finish what he started, you had better believe he will."

"In that case, perhaps I should give him a good reason," he murmured. "Perhaps we should finish what we started out in the garden last night."

Catherine gasped and stumbled back out of his reach. A very short, very stout, very red-faced woman scurried out of the shadows beneath the stairs and executed a clumsy curtsy.

"Milady," she wheezed. "I'm ever so sorry for the mess 'ere about. We wasn't expectin' 'is lordship ter bring a lady with 'im. I'll 'ave the linens in yer room changed in a lick.''

"Her ladyship would also like a bath, Mrs. Grundy."
Montgomery's smile oozed charm like snake oil. "Is that
possible?"

"W-a-all, I surpose I could send up a warshtub."

"That would be fine." On a gentle nudge from the black-
gloved hand, Catherine moved toward the stairs. The ban-
nister, as such, was a frayed length of ship's rigging, which
she held gingerly as she placed her feet carefully on each
cracked and sagging tread. Deirdre, who had observed the
exchange between her mistress and supposed new master,
followed at a discreet distance, her hands clutching the small
portmanteau that contained Catherine's personal articles
and jewelry.

The upper floor was partitioned into four rooms, one at
each corner of the cottage. Catherine paused at the top of the
stairs and allowed the innkeeper to lumber past, leading the
way to the door in the far corner. Having braced herself to
expect the worst, she was somewhat relieved to find the room
small but surprisingly clean. The walls were whitewashed,
the bed draped in a canopy that was no more than a decade
old. The only other furniture was a small spindle-legged
nightstand, chair, and stool. There was no curtain on the
high, square window, only shutters that could be closed from
the outside. There was no rug to cover the warped and
splintered floorboards, and not even a brazier to provide
warmth in the winter.

"I'll 'ave that warshtub sent up roight away," Mrs.
Grundy said.

"Please . . . don't trouble yourself," Catherine demurred
wryly and, catching a warning glance from Montgomery,
added, "I'm much too tired to bother with a bath tonight."

"Ayrr, I know what ye mean, milady. Never ye mind. I'll
send yer up some nice 'ot broth and mutton pies ter fill yer
belly."

"That would be lovely," Catherine murmured and crossed
over to the bed. She peeled off her gloves and tossed them on

the faded coverlet, dimly aware of Montgomery's voice droning with Mrs. Grundy's. What they were saying somehow didn't matter anymore. She leaned her brow on the bedpost and sighed, suddenly weary beyond all recollection.

"Now that wasn't so difficult, was it?" Montgomery asked. "And you must admit, the room is reasonably clean."

Catherine straightened and turned to face him.

"Get out," she said quietly. "I would prefer not to have to look at your face again until the morning."

After a brief hesitation, his husky laugh prickled the fine hairs at the nape of her neck. "It would be my pleasure, madam."

He bowed with a flamboyant swirl of the black cape and was gone, leaving Catherine with the burning memory of his amusement. She heard his boots echo on the floorboards and she mentally cursed every step he took along the narrow hall, hoping against hope that a stair would give way and he would plummet to his death in the pigpen.

But he did not go down the stairs. The footsteps halted at the end of the hall and he turned to enter the room next to Catherine's. She heard a muffled exchange of voices — men's voices — but since she could care less what Montgomery did or who he saw from this point on, she ignored the sounds and sat on the edge of the bed.

Deirdre, seeing her mistress's exhaustion, hurried over to the bed. "Oh, Mistress Catherine I wish there was something — "

"What the bloody hell did you bring her here for?"

Both Catherine and Deirdre started at the outburst of profanity. It had exploded from the other side of the wall and just as swiftly had been ordered to silence by a sharp reprimand. Catherine tensed and waited, but there was nothing more than the beating of her own heart to listen to.

She was about to shrug away the incident when she noticed a bright slice of light halfway up the wall partition. The boards had holes in them, probably knots in the wood or splits. Curious, still angered by Montgomery's brusqueness, she carried the wooden stool over to the wall and stood on it, bringing her eye to the level of the knothole.

"Mistress Catherine!" Deirdre whispered, shocked.

"Oh hush. I just want to see who he is talking to, I'm not going to eavesdrop or anything. I'm sure he couldn't say anything I would be the least interested in, anyway."

There were two other men in the room with Montgomery. One of them stood beside a rusting tin stove in the corner; he was of medium height, rangy-looking and thin, as if he had not had a good meal in some time. He did not appear to be much older than Catherine, as his cheeks had only the sparsest of dirty brown stubble covering them. He also looked extremely flushed and agitated, and Catherine surmised his voice had been the one they had overheard.

The second man, who'd had his back to the wall, now began pacing thoughtfully across the width of the room. He was almost as tall as Montgomery, but lean and graceful, with the quiet, contemplative features of a man who could have been a poet or a philosopher. Both men were dressed casually in loose-fitting homespun shirts, leather jerkins, and plain breeches.

"She won't be a problem after tomorrow," Montgomery said, moving away from the door and more directly into Catherine's line of vision.

The other two men exchanged a glance and the older man stopped pacing long enough to inspect the fresh cut on Montgomery's temple.

"Her husband give you that?"

Montgomery touched the edge of the angry red slash and grimaced. "A slight miscalculation on my part. Nothing to worry about. We should be more concerned about the rumours we heard in London. They were true. Several regiments are making preparations to move north; they expect to have their orders by the end of the month."

"Then they suspect something is going on?"

"They know our friend isn't in Normandy any longer,

and they don't believe he has gone to Rouen as they were led to understand.''

''Where do they think he is?''

''It depends on what story you are prepared to listen to: There are confirmed reports that he is in any of a dozen cities between Paris and Rome.'' Montgomery removed his tricorn and threw it onto the bed. ''Some are even convinced he has already crossed the Channel with an army.''

''What about the colonel? What did he have to say?''

Montgomery shrugged out of his heavy cloak. ''He's worried that the English know too damned much about our business. Too much for it to be coming from their people alone.''

''It goes both ways,'' the man said quietly.

''Aye, he's nae ane tae talk, bein' *Sassenach* himsel',''the younger man noted.

Catherine lifted her eye from the knothole, momentarily taken aback at the sound of the broad Scots accent. A further prick of anger was stirred by the use of the word '*Sassenach*' — a vulgar idiom denoting anyone of English birth.

''Is something wrong, mistress?'' Deirdre asked.

''I . . . I don't know,'' she murmured and leaned forward again.

''. . . much longer can you expect to use the name Montgomery?''

''As long as it is still useful. I was beginning to grow rather fond of it,'' Montgomery said wryly. ''For that matter, I must confess, I was beginning to grow fond of everything to do with Raefer Montgomery's lifestyle.''

''Then it's lang past time ye came hame, cousin,'' the young man declared with a frown. ''Yer brithers need ye, yer clan needs ye, an' if that's nae reason enough, happens we should hae brung yer faither, Old Lochiel, back into England, na you.''

''Maybe you should have, Iain,'' Montgomery agreed.

"And for your troubles, he would have been the first man the English would have arrested and hanged without the benefit of a trial.''

"Why dae ye think ye'll fare any better? There's still a price ridin' on yer heid — ten thousan' crowns — an' that were just tae tempt the foxes tae track ye doon in France. When the Duke o' Argyle hears ye're back at Achnacarry, he'll double it.''

"I'd like to be there when he does hear,'' Montgomery murmured, his eyes flickering briefly with some distant memory. "The look on his face alone would be well worth the trip.''

"I, for one, would prefer to look inside his head,'' the more practical of the newcomers remarked. "I'd like to know what he plans to do about it.''

"Aluinn's right,'' the boy said. "He'll dae somethin'. The Duke has a lang memory, aye, an' so dae his clansmen.''

"It's been fifteen years.''

"Aye. Fifteen years o' rememberin' how ye cut doon the sons o' a powerful laird an' lived tae tell aboot it. It's the third whoreson bastard, the ane ye let live, who'll stair the whole bluidy lot up again. He'll hae every Campbell wi'in a hundred mile screamin' murder an' sharpenin' their broadswords.''

"Assuming they aren't already,'' Aluinn pointed out.

"There is no reason to think there has been any word of our arrival preceeding us,'' Montgomery said. "If Donald did not think we could make it through, he would not hav sent Iain to find us, and he certainly would not have suggested we travel overland.''

"What if someone recognizes ye?''

Montgomery regarded the lad calmly. "We will just have to be extra careful when we cross the border. Not that I think the Duke of Argyle would declare all-out war in any case. He'll control his clansmen and his nephew. A raid on

Cameron land now, after all these years, would unite the Highlands faster than if Prince Charles landed with a hundred thousand Frenchmen. The English government would not be too pleased with the Campbells either, since my brother is the last nail holding the lid on the powderkeg. Donald is a man of peace — a diplomat, not a fighter. Men listen to him. They respect him.''

''Aye, but they'll fight f'ae ye.''

The black eyes glanced over sharply. ''What is that supposed to mean?''

The lad shrugged, undaunted by the look on Montgomery's face. ''Mayhap it means Lochiel kens there's a fight comin'. Mayhap he kens the time f'ae talk is lang past, an' he needs someone beside him who could lead the whole clan tae bluidy victory.''

''Bloody slaughter, you mean,'' Montgomery said tautly. ''I can't believe that is Donald's intention.''

''Dae ye doubt his loyalty tae the Stuart cause?''

''Loyalty and stupidity are two different things.''

The young man drew himself up indignantly. ''Ye believe our fight tae see King Jamie back on the throne o' Scotland . . . a stupid thing?''

''At this particular point in time, I believe the world is full of righteous fools who think it their divine right to chase each other around in circles. A prudent man might want to consider which fool has the larger, stronger army.''

''King Louis has promised tae send troops,'' Iain objected.

''If and when the Highlands raise an army of their own.''

''He wouldna betray his ain cousin!''

Montgomery smiled tightly. ''King Louis would betray his own mother if he thought there was a profit in doing so.''

The boy clamped his lips into a thin line. ''If ye believe so strongly that we're after wastin' our time, why did ye come back?''

''Damned if I know,'' was the dry response.

Iain's face flushed hotly. "An' ye, Aluinn MacKail?"

The smoky gray eyes of the poet returned the stare indolently. "I go where Alex goes."

The boy glared furiously from one blank face to the other. "By all tha's holy, I never would hae believed it if I didna hear it wi' ma ain ears. The *Camshroinaich Dubh*, tremblin' at the thought o' a few Campbells takin' wind o' him; fearin' he'll na be able tae go back tae his soddin' life as king o' the roost. By Christ, ye've forgotten who ye are!"

"I haven't forgotten," Montgomery said in a voice as cold as steel.

"Then ye've misplaced yersel' somewhere alang the way, for ye're no' a Cameron," Iain spat disdainfully. "Ye're no' the same Alexander Cameron what slew the dragons frae Inverary Castle."

"Those dragons were made of flesh and blood. They died as easily as you or I could die tomorrow. For God's sake, don't make the mistake of canonizing me over an act that was cold and brutal and ugly."

"Ugly? Aye, it were that," Iain grated harshly. "But no' as ugly as what I'm seein' now. They've made a coward out o' ye, cousin. A rare English coward."

He turned and strode out the door, slamming it with such force the rusted hinges were in peril of separating from the wall. For a full minute after the echo of the departure had faded from the tiny room, neither Montgomery nor Aluinn MacKail as much as blinked.

"A little rough on each other, weren't you?" MacKail murmured.

"He's exactly the kind of hothead who's going to push Scotland into a war she's not ready for."

"He's what . . . nineteen? Twenty? Not much older than you were when you thought you could take on the world single-handedly."

"My fight was personal: a life for a life. And if we're speaking of windmills, I recall you jousting a few of your own, my temperate friend."

"Only because I had to watch out for your back."

"No one asked you to," Montgomery snapped.

"No," MacKail agreed. "No one asked me to. I ascribe it to a kind heart and an addled brain, myself. Also to the fact that there isn't a day I don't wake up wondering what the devil you're going to throw us into next. It has made for a pretty interesting life so far."

"I'm glad I've amused you," Montgomery said dryly and paced to the window.

"Alex . . . why *did* you agree to come back?"

"I've been away fifteen years. Isn't that long enough?"

"Iain made a good point about the Duke; you're still wanted for murder."

Montgomery smiled crookedly. "And he still has to catch me first."

"Don't you ever worry that your luck is going to run out?"

"Never. The minute I do start to worry, I'll know it's gone."

Aluinn sighed and shook his head. "So why do I have the distinct feeling I should have stayed tucked comfortably in Countess Marie de Mornay's bed and kept the covers pulled tightly over my head?"

"Because it was only a matter of time before her husband noticed the horns growing out of his head . . . and because you were just as anxious to go home again as I was."

Aluinn's gray eyes softened and a smile tugged at his mouth. "Just a couple of sentimental bastards at heart, I suppose, too stupid to know when to keep their noses to themselves. Ah well, this should prove interesting, anyway. The borders are being patrolled day and night; the Black Watch is out in all its bloodthirsty glory searching for rebels, inventing them when none can be found to fill their quota. All that and a few thousand Argyleshire men sniffing at our tracks . . ." he smacked his lips sardonically. "Any other little details I've missed? You have neatly avoided talking about that charming young bundle you arrived with here tonight. She has the word 'complication' stamped all over her.''

''It's a long story,'' Montgomery admitted and glanced toward the door. ''I don't suppose we could discuss it over a few pints of ale and some of those meat pies I'm smelling? I haven't eaten anything since I left here Thursday.''

They moved toward the door and Catherine, on the other side of the partition, stepped quickly off the stool and pushed it back to its former post at the foot of the bed. Her hands were trembling and clammy — and no wonder! The man she was married to, however temporarily, was not at all what he had presented himself to be. He was *not* a merchant, he was *not* a London businessman, he was *not even an Englishman*! He was one of those bare-legged, skirted savages who belonged to a race of people as barbaric and primitive as the barren land they inhabited! He was a Scot. And a Jacobite! Sir Alfred Ashbrooke would have taken a pistol and shot the rogue out of hand had he known a papist traitor was masquerading as a gentleman — under his own roof, yet!

A Scot! Alexander Cameron . . . not Raefer Montgomery. She had known, had *sensed* there was something unnatural, something sneaky and underhanded about him from the very beginning. How could Damien have been duped so easily into a friendship! Good heavens, his career would be in ruins if word leaked out that he had kept company with a Jacobite, even for business reasons. *Especially* for business reasons, since everyone knew the Jacobites were in the business of smuggling, kidnapping, extortion, theft, treason, murder. . . .

Murder! Cameron was wanted for murder — there was a price on his head of ten thousand crowns!

Catherine sat down heavily on the edge of the bed. She was married to a spy and a murderer. He had brought her to this filthy inn under false pretenses, undoubtedly with no intentions of letting her go or of taking her into Wakefield to have the marriage annulled. He would annul it himself with a pistol or a knife! No wonder he had chosen this hovel with its acres of dark and gloomy woodlands surrounding it. He would kill her and dispose of the body and no one would ever be the wiser.

Catherine gasped as a pale hand touched her on the shoulder.

"Deirdre!" Catherine swallowed hard and laid a hand on her throbbing breast. "I'd forgotten you were here."

"Mistress?" The girl looked perplexed.

"Deirdre, did you . . . did you hear any of that?"

"Some of it was muffled, mistress, but I heard most."

"Then you agree we are in terrible danger. We must find a way to get out of here, away from those men . . . to alert the authorities and have them arrested!"

"But . . ." the maid cast her eyes around the bare room. "How, mistress? There's only two of us, in the middle of nowhere for all I could see."

"He said we were outside of Wakefield. If we . . . if even one of us can reach the town and bring back the militia . . .''

Catherine stood up and tiptoed to the door. She tried the latch, which moved freely enough, but in her mind's eye she recalled the lower room and knew there was no possibility of slipping unseen out into the yard. She turned and pressed her back against the door. There was nothing in the room they could use as weapons, either to attack or to defend themselves. There was a musket in the coach, and a pistol — all of Sir Alfred's coachmen were armed when they travelled abroad. She had shot her fair share of grouse and pheasant and had no doubt she could shoot a man if he stood in the path of her freedom, but first they had to find some way to reach the coach.

"The window, mistress?" Deirdre whispered, her thoughts obviously following along the same lines.

"Window?" Catherine said and glanced at the small, paneless aperture. She ran to it and pushed the two hanging shutters fully back on their hinges. A foot or two beyond her grasp was the thick, gnarled branch of an oak tree. As ancient as the cottage it stood beside, the tree was partially dead. It had been at least ten years since Catherine had dared to shinny up or down a tree, and then never more than a few token feet off the ground to impress her brother. The drop from the second-story window was better than twenty feet.

"What do you think?" she whispered. "Could we do it?"

Deirdre, born and raised on a farm, one of thirteen children sired by an estate gameskeeper, had spent half her years clambering through the forests behind her eight older brothers.

"Oh, easily!" she assured her mistress with a smile. "See . . . the branches lie like steps all the way down, and they look to me a good deal sturdier than those we had to use to climb to our room. I can take a quick look first, if you like, but I'm sure it's safe."

Catherine chewed savagely on her lip and glanced at the door. "All right. You'll have to go first, to show me what to do, but if anything happens, you mustn't stop. You must keep going; try to reach Wakefield and bring back help."

Deirdre's soft brown eyes rounded. She had been Catherine's abigail for the past seven years and was fiercely loyal. "I couldn't leave you, mistress, not to the likes of *them*."

Catherine gripped the girl's arms. "Deirdre, it might be our only chance. If I can't make it, you have to. Someone has to stop these men! They're murderers, they're traitors and spies! You don't actually think they will let us live beyond tonight, do you? This is life or death, it's no time to argue who will go and who will stay."

Deirdre studied her mistress's face a moment then bent over and hoisted her plain black skirt and single layer of petticoat up over her knee. Strapped to her upper thigh just above her stocking garter, was a thin, deadly-looking dagger. She slid it out of its sheath and held it out so that the lamplight glittered off the polished steel blade.

"It's come in useful many a time, with many a frisky houseman," she explained. "You take it, Mistress

Catherine. Tuck it here, like so — '' She carefully fitted the knife beneath the bodice of the gray velvet travelling suit. ''Should we become separated for any reason, and should one of them try to do you harm, take no chances and aim between the legs. You needn't strike hard to have them rolling helpless on the floor.''

It was Catherine's turn to study Deirdre's solemn features, this time with a new respect. It was a shameful admission to have to make, and one that came at an awkward time, but she had never really paid much attention to the girl before. Servants had been taken for granted all her life, and Deirdre had behaved no differently from any of the other shadowy figures who moved silently and unobtrusively through the rooms and corridors of Rosewood Hall.

Yet they were the same age, nearly the same height, and the figure trapped beneath the homely starched black cotton frock was slender and fine-boned.

''Bless you, Deirdre,'' Catherine murmured, taking the girl's hands in hers. ''And I'm thankful for your company at this time. I don't know if I could have found the courage to do anything without you.''

Deirdre flushed under the praise and gave Catherine's ice-cold hands a return squeeze for encouragement. ''Shall I go first, then? They talked of sending food up to us; perhaps we should wait — ''

''No! No, I don't want to spend a single moment longer in this house than I have to. Besides, if we wait,'' she added on a more honest note, ''I may think too long on the obstacles against us. Hurry now, before they — ''

Just as Deirdre gathered her skirt and petticoat together and put a hand to the window ledge, a sound from the hallway startled them. They spun around as the door opened and an equally startled face greeted them.

''What the devil are you two up to?''

Chapter Six

"Damien!" Catherine was so surprised to see her brother standing in the doorway that she could do little more than stare at him in shocked disbelief. "Damien! What are you doing here?"

"Well, I — " He was prevented from giving a coherent answer by the armload of sobbing female that flung herself across the room. "Hello? What's this? What is going on here?"

"Oh Damien . . . Damien!" She could manage nothing more, so, arching his brows in bewilderment, he soothed her as best he could until the wrenching sobs had run their course. Only then was he able to guide her gently to the bed and sit her down while he rummaged in a pocket for a handkerchief.

"There now, blow like a good girl then tell me what this is all about. You act as if you've been frightened half to death."

"Oh Damien — " She looked up at him, her eyes drowning in a pool of tears. "Damien, thank God you're here."

"Didn't Raefer tell you I was coming?"

"H-he *knew*?"

"We made arrangements last night; well, this morning actually. I was to follow as soon as the ruckus died down, meet you here at the inn, witness the annulment in the morning, then take you back home again."

Catherine was astonished. "He . . . he told you to meet us here?"

"Of course. He may be a rogue and a bit temperamental, but he isn't without common sense. He couldn't very well send you home alone, without an escort, and he certainly couldn't take you back himself. He'd be fighting duels until next spring, providing Father didn't shoot him outright."

"He really was going to send me home?" she asked in a whisper.

"Of course he was. He isn't in the habit of collecting wives, that I know about." He frowned at the stricken look on his sister's face. "Did you think . . . ? Good God, is that why you were about to scupper out the window, to avoid your wifely obligations? Now really, Kitty — "

"Damien! What exactly do you know about him?"

"Know about him? About who? Raefer? Why?"

"What do you know about him!"

He was taken aback by her vehemence. "About as much as I need to know, I suppose. I met him three or four years ago in Brussels, and since then he has sent a great deal of business my way."

"What kind of business? What has he told you his business is?"

Damien's frown deepened. "Import, export. He's a merchant . . . Catherine, what is the matter? Why are you asking me all these questions."

Catherine swallowed hard and clutched his forearms with enough fervour to erase the beginnings of a smile from his face. "Damien . . . he isn't who he says he is," she hissed. "He is *not* Raefer Montgomery, he is *not* from London, he is *not* a merchant and he most certainly isn't even an *Englishman!*"

"Isn't . . . ? Catherine what are you talking about?"

"I'm talking about *him*. About who he says he is . . . only he isn't. He's a spy," she said fiercely, "a *murderer!* I heard him admit it. I also heard him say he was only at the party last night to speak to some colonel and that they had to reach the border before someone found out they were here."

"They? Who is 'they'?"

"Didn't you see those two men when you came in? Well, they're his partners or his cohorts or something, I don't know exactly what — but they were here when we arrived. They were waiting here for him."

"Catherine" — Damien's handsome face took on the dubious look of a man who believes a loved one has gone completely mad — "I can understand why you wouldn't like the man, but really, Raefer is neither a — "

"I heard it too, Master Damien," Deirdre blurted, stepping forward. "Mistress Catherine is telling the truth. I heard him say himself he was going home to Scotland and how it would be a shame to give up the name Montgomery because he'd grown rather fond of it."

Catherine's eyes gleamed triumphantly. "His real name is Cameron. Alexander Cameron, and he's wanted for the murder of two men near some place called Archberry. If we had time, I'm sure you could check it out yourself!"

"And if I did, I'm sure we would find out there were circumstances. Men change their names for all sorts of reasons, but it doesn't make them spies and murderers."

"There is a bounty on his head," Catherine declared adamantly. "Ten thousand crowns. And he was definitely at Rosewood Hall yesterday to spy. He said he met with this colonel person, who passed information to him about government troop movements and something about the Stuart prince. I did not hear too clearly. Oh Damien, can you not see that he's only been using you, using your friendship and your position to disguise his real activities?''

Damien's face had paled and although there was still the shadow of doubt in his eyes, there were also the glimmerings of belief.

''When did you say you heard all of this? How?''

Catherine pointed to the crack in the wall. ''I could see and hear everything perfectly. They obviously do not realize how thin the walls are.''

He continued to stare at the knothole . . . so long that Catherine grew impatient.

''What are we going to do?'' she demanded.

''Do?''

''They're spies. They're traitors to our king and country. We cannot simply let them mount their horses and ride away unscathed.''

Her words startled some colour into his cheeks. ''What other choice do we have? Look around you. We're virtual prisoners in this house.''

''In this house, yes,'' she whispered meaningfully. ''But if what you say is true, if he really does plan to go into Wakefield tomorrow, and if he is given no cause to suspect that we know who and what he is . . . ?''

''Yes?''

''Well, don't you see? All I would have to do is wait until there is a crowd around us, scream, and faint dead away. It would arouse all the attention we would need, all the help we would need, as well, to see the criminals caught and thrown into jail where they belong.''

She leaned back, proud of her plan, pleased at her own in-genuity. Her earlier fears had now given way to confidence and, admittedly, some excitement at the prospect of captur-ing a dangerous criminal. Her conduct the night of the party would now be exonerated and she would be given a hero's welcome. Hamilton would be bursting with pride, eager to claim her as his wife. Her plan was perfect, flawless, far less risky to their necks than if they had to scrabble down a tree in the middle of the night.

"Well? Is there or is there not a detatchment of militia in Wakefield?"

"An entire regiment, if I'm not mistaken," Damien murmured speculatively.

"Well then?"

His expression cleared. "It could work. We would have to be damnably careful. If these men are who you say they are, they haven't survived this long by taking anything for granted. They're bound to know there is a troop of militia in Wakefield, and they'll be on their guard for anything suspicious we might do. The risks will be incredible . . . for all of us. Are you sure you want to go through with it?"

Catherine smiled vindictively. "He kept us cramped in that horrid coach all day and hardly stopped long enough for food and water. He did not deign to tell me his intentions of annulling the marriage until well after noon — and you can imagine the state I had worked myself into by then. Worst of all, he did not even have the common decency to ease my mind by mentioning that you were following behind us. I'm so angry I could scream right now, and hang the risk!"

"You don't want to do that," Damien cautioned hastily. "In fact, for this to have any chance of success, you are both going to have to act as if nothing has changed. As if you haven't noticed or heard anything out of the ordinary."

"I would rather scream."

Damien rubbed an agitated hand across his temple. "You keep saying he met with someone at the party last night?"

"He didn't mention a name, he only referred to him as the colonel. I absolutely refuse to believe he could have meant Uncle Lawrence. He is no more a Jacobite sympathizer than you or I."

Damien continued to rub his forehead distractedly. "No. No, of course he isn't. All the same, Father will be livid when he hears. He prides himself at being able to smell out a rebel within a hundred yards."

"Oh, Damien, I'm so glad you're here." She hugged him impulsively. "We were beginning to imagine all sorts of horrible things. I mean, he admitted to committing murder and as much as boasted that he plans to return to this Archberry place and commit more."

Damien patted her hand and glanced at the door. "I should go back downstairs. They might become suspicious if I stay up here too long."

Catherine clutched his arm. "You're not going to leave us alone!"

He raised a hand and gently stroked a tendril of golden hair off her cheek. "I am going to go downstairs — exactly what I would have done if you hadn't accosted me at the door — I'm going to sit with them and drink with them, and now that I know who they are, I am going to listen very carefully to everything they say and perhaps learn something that will be of use to *our* side. You, on the other hand, are going to try to relax and get some sleep. You will need all of your strength and courage tomorrow, and remember: You are perfectly safe as long as you do everything they expect you to do."

Catherine's lips were bloodless. Her eyes were wide and suddenly shiny with fear again.

"Deirdre is here with you," he assured her. "Good God, they can't kill all three of us without someone taking notice. For insurance, I will be sure to mention to them that I told at least a dozen people where I was bound and why."

"You'll be careful?" she pleaded.

"I shall be the soul of discretion. It will be difficult, since I rather liked the fellow up until now. But I admit I like my own skin more." He planted a tender, brotherly kiss on Catherine's forehead. "Remember now: Eat and sleep. No more vaulting through windows and no more hysterics. I don't want you truly fainting on me tomorrow."

Catherine managed a weak smile. "I won't faint, I promise. As long as *you* promise that when this is over, you will exaggerate shamelessly to Father and all our friends about how brave I was."

Damien grinned. "You won't recognize it as the same story."

He still wore the faint traces of a smile as he walked out of the room and along the short hallway, but by the time he had arrived at the bottom of the rickety stairs, a frown was firmly entrenched upon his brow.

The three men were seated at the table in front of the fire. Raefer Montgomery, his back to the wall, his long legs stretched out and crossed at the ankles, held a pewter tankard cradled in his hands, half filled with mulled wine.

"Well?" he asked without looking up. "What did I tell you? Alive and well, although if this fiasco had been for real, she might have found herself with a well-tanned backside. Pull up a chair and help yourself to some wine or ale. You must be cold from the long ride."

Damien's gaze shifted to the two men seated opposite him. The younger one, his expression gloweringly distrustful, was staring back balefully. The third man seemed preoccupied with tracing the pattern of moisture his mug was leaving on the scored surface of the wooden table.

"My sister has just finished telling me a very interesting tale," Damien said quietly, the anger causing a tic to shiver in his cheek. "It seems the walls between the upstairs rooms are very thin. So thin, in fact, that both she and her abigail heard every word the three of you said. They know who you are and what you are."

Alexander Cameron's expression did not change as he lifted his eyes from the fire, not even when Damien's fist came smashing down on the tabletop.

"Goddammit! Why weren't you more careful? I pleaded with you . . . I *begged* you to watch what you said and did in front of her. Good Christ, it was insane enough that you showed yourself bold as brass at the house last night, never mind playing centre stage in the duel, then the marriage . . . and now this!"

Aluinn raised his head. "Marriage? What marriage?"

"You mean he didn't tell you?" With a sardonic wave of his hand, Damien said, "I'm not surprised. What's to tell?

Only that he showed up at my home and single-handedly managed to earn challenges from half the company of dragoons attending the party. Only that he settled on one gentleman in particular, whom he fought and left more dead than alive, and in doing so, won the hand of my sister in holy matrimony! Not an entirely wasted evening by any standards. Nearly fatal, however, or were neither of you intrigued enough to ask how he came by the wounds on his temple and thigh?''

Cameron patted his pocket and produced a cigar. ''You're becoming a little overexcited, aren't you?''

''Overexcited? Haven't I every right to be? You appear out of nowhere, possibly jeopardizing my position, certainly running a risk that could have seriously compromised both of us. You manage to antagonize a colonel in the local militia and an officer of the royal dragoons, then compound the situation by whisking my sister — who just happens to be that same lieutenant's fiancée — into the garden where you make damn sure Hamilton Garner sees what you are about and has no recourse but to challenge you to a duel. My father, who has been about as stable as gunpowder himself these days, forces you at gunpoint to marry Catherine, and you have the audacity to bring her here! Now we're all together, reminiscing over a tankard of wine while she's upstairs set to scream her fool head off about spies and murderers — and you accuse me of being *overexcited*!''

Aluinn and Iain both gaped at Alexander Cameron, waiting for his response.

''In the first place,'' he said slowly, ''there was no way to forewarn you that I would personally be coming to Derby to meet with you — I only made the final decision a week or so ago. Secondly, I did not deliberately set out to antagonize either the colonel or the lieutenant. I merely answered their questions to the best of my knowledge . . . and patience. Thirdly, your sister was asking for trouble. I may have taken advantage of that particular situation, but believe me, if it hadn't been me, it would have been someone else. Furthermore, you know damn well I tried my utmost to avoid fighting that pompous fool; he just wouldn't let it lie.'' He shrugged his broad shoulders and moistened the end of his cigar. ''There you have it. While I can fully appreciate your father's desire to bundle your sister out of his house, I was in no position to argue his methods.''

''Ye mean it's true?'' Iain blurted with a grin. ''Ye really are married tae the wench?''

Damien glared at the younger man. ''I'll thank you to remember that the 'wench' is my sister. My *only* sister. And in case you've forgotten, she also knows who you are.''

Alexander clamped his strong teeth around the butt of the cigar. ''Now that truly is an unfortunate turn of events.''

''Is that all you can say?'' Damien snorted and reached for an empty tankard. ''Having the pox would be an unfortunate turn of events right now. Having Catherine, however . . . .'' He shook his head and splashed ale into the mug.

''We can't afford to let her spread the news about us just yet,'' Aluinn said quietly. ''She'll have to be kept away from the authorities — at least long enough for us to get across the border into Scotland. The last thing we need at the moment is more patrols searching for us.''

''Yes, yes. Agreed,'' Damien grunted. ''I just don't know how you're going to do it. When she has her temper up — and believe me, it's at full cock now — you'd as soon try to plug a hole in the wind as keep her silent.''

''Ye could always tell her ye're ane o' us, *Colonel*,'' Iain said with a smirk. ''Mayhap she'd take up the Prince's standard as well.''

Damien stiffened and his blue eyes turned into chips of ice. ''I doubt that very much. She would probably scream twice as loud, twice as long.''

''Are you saying you don't think you can control what she says or does over the next few days?'' Alex asked.

''In all honesty? I think as soon as she is set free, all hell will break loose. She'll have Colonel Halfyard calling out every hound in England to hunt you down, and if she knew

I'd been helping you, she would send them out after my skin as well." He lifted his tankard in a mock salute. "Your health, gentlemen."

"Is there nothing you can do to win a promise of silence from her?"

"As much as I am loathe to say it, there is *nothing* — no bribe, no threat strong enough to win any guarantees. She has . . . confused priorities at the present time, and unfortunately I don't think I carry as much weight with her as I used to."

Cameron took a deep breath, uncrossed his ankles and stood up. "What if the threat came from someone else?"

Damien studied the swirling contents of his tankard. "I don't want her hurt . . . or frightened any more than she already is."

"Threats don't usually come sugar-coated."

When there was no further rejoinder, Alexander threw his unlit cigar on the table and strode across the room and up the stairs. Damien started to follow, but Aluinn's hand on his arm stopped him.

At the top of the stairs, Cameron turned and headed directly to Catherine's room, not bothering to slow down or knock before he kicked the door open. The force tore the iron bolt out of the wall and sent it cracking against the wood with the report of a gunshot. Deirdre, in the midst of undressing Catherine's hair, jumped and scattered a handful of steel pins across the floor. Catherine gave off a little cry, one which turned instantly into a gasp of indignation.

"What is the meaning of this?" she demanded. "How dare you burst into my room uninvited!"

The dark eyes held hers for the span of several throbbing heartbeats, then flicked to the maid. "Leave us alone for a few minutes."

"Stay where you are!" Catherine cried and reached up to grasp Deirdre's hand. "Whatever you might have to say, sir, can be said to both of us."

"I suppose that is only fair, since you will both undoubtably share the same fate."

"Just what is *that* supposed to mean?" she asked coldly.

"In plainer language? You were eavesdropping on my business. Eavesdroppers sometimes hear things they shouldn't. Sometimes too much to allow them to remain healthy for too long."

Catherine's eyes widened and her cheeks blanched as she glanced past his shoulder at the open door. "Damien. What have you done to him?"

"Nothing . . . *yet*."

She stood up slowly. "I want to see him. I want to see my brother."

Cameron crossed his powerful arms over his chest. "You are hardly in a position to make demands, mistress."

Catherine recognized the same icy calm in his voice that had been present in his confrontation with Hamilton Garner. And yet it was not quite the same. It was more . . . rehearsed.

"You cannot kill us, *Mister Cameron*. You cannot kill Damien either. He has told Father he was coming after me, and if anything happens to either one of us, they will send every soldier in England after you. They will have you dragged back and put in a cage and they will see that you die slowly and horribly before they hack you to pieces and feed you to the dogs."

"My, what a picturesque imagination you have. Just how do you propose your father will find me?"

"Find you?"

"Indeed. He will be looking for Raefer Montgomery — who no longer exists, thanks to your interference. I warrant he and his able-bodied soldiers will make a fine mess of London before he thinks to send his horde of avenging devils north."

Catherine stared in horror at the darkly handsome face. The truth of what he said struck her like a cold, cruel slap.

Even Hamilton, who had sworn to come after her, would instinctively scour the roads south toward London in search of her. By the time the deception was discovered, their slain bodies would be long overgrown with weeds.

"What do you plan to do with us?"

"That, madam, depends entirely upon you."

He was watching her intently, and if she had learned anything at all in the past twenty-four hours, it was that he seemed to have an uncanny ability to know exactly what she was thinking. If he saw her fear, he would know he had won.

"Traitor," she said evenly. "Murderer. I told you once before you did not frighten me. You do not frighten me now."

The black eyes narrowed. She had more fire in her than he would have guessed, definitely more than was wise to show him at the moment. He should have known last night . . . even earlier, in the clearing . . . that she was trouble. Yellow-haired, violet-eyed trouble.

"I will tell you what I need from you," he said slowly. "And then we can decide what method of persuasion to use to win your co-operation."

"Never," she said promptly. "I will never co-operate."

"I need a week," he continued as if he had not heard the interruption. "I need time to reach the border, cross into Scotland, and ride up into the Highlands without imagining a shot in my back every step of the way."

"A musket would be too merciful. They hang spies. They draw and quarter them and stick their severed heads on fence pikes until they shrivel and blacken like figs."

Cameron grimaced wryly but refrained from asking where she came by her colourful information. "During that week, I would expect you to speak to no one, tell no one what you have seen or heard."

"Oh, I have no intentions of speaking to anyone," she said sweetly. "I intend to scream the news at the top of my lungs, and there is nothing you can say or do to stop me."

"Nothing?"

"Nothing," she declared.

His eyes descended from the blaze of defiant violet, down the slender curve of her throat to come to rest where the soft white flesh of her breasts temptingly swelled against the *V* of her fitted bodice.

"Have you forgotten, madam, our participation in a certain poignant ceremony last evening? I believe it gave me . . . shall we say, some rather specific rights and privileges?"

Catherine gave no outward sign of the sudden wave of panic that rippled through her. "If you are referring to conjugal rights, sir, you could indeed claim them, and in doing so, add the charge of *rape* to your already illustrious array of crimes. However, I fail to see how rape would guarantee my silence. If anything, it would only add fuel to my desire to see you crushed beneath the heels of justice."

Cameron felt his temper rising, felt his own desire to crush something itching in the palms of his hands. It was time to put the minx in her place.

"What if I said to refuse your co-operation would mean you would never see your brother alive again?"

Although Catherine managed to control the involuntary flutter of her hand to her breasts, she could do nothing to prevent the hot surge of blood into her cheeks.

"I do not believe you would do that," she said quietly. "Damien befriended you."

"I befriend a lot of people in my line of work."

Catherine laced her fingers together so tightly the knuckles turned white.

"He . . . invited you into our home. How could any man kill another after accepting his friendship and hospitality?"

Cameron reacted visibly to her words in a way that was more shocking and terrifying than any threat he could have put forth. His eyes flared with open rage, his hands curled into fists and curved forward as if he were attempting to staunch the flow of blood that was draining from his face.

Catherine recoiled instinctively from the sight. She had somehow, unknowingly, touched upon an open wound — touched it and apparently scoured it with salt.

Without warning he lunged forward, and Catherine — convinced she had seen her fate clearly proclaimed in the bottomless black eyes, lifted her hand to her bodice. The knife gleamed in the candlelight as she brought it slashing in an arc downward, but with almost insolent ease he sidestepped the attack. Catherine had a glimpse of his surprise, then of his heightened fury before he caught her wrist and twisted it cruelly into the small of her back. An expert squeeze on the appropriate nerves produced such a brilliant flash of agony that her fingers sprang apart and her knees buckled beneath her. The knife fell to the floor and was instantly swept into a swirl of petticoats.

Deirdre was already in motion. She was pushing the crush of velvet and lace aside, scrabbling to take hold of the knife when a second strong pair of arms went around her waist and she was lifted bodily away from where Catherine still struggled and thrashed within Alexander Cameron's grasp. Aluinn MacKail cursed aloud as Deirdre's hard-heeled shoes barked his shins, causing several deep gouges and bruises on his flesh. He flung the writhing Irish virago aside, into the corner, and was starting to reach for the knife when the maid launched herself at him again. This time his arm swung up reflexively to protect his face and throat from clawing nails. Instead of deflecting the anticipated hail of scratches, however, his fist slammed solidly into Deirdre's temple. The blow snapped her head to one side with such force that she sprawled to the floor and did not move again.

Catherine ceased her struggles instantly.

"You've killed her!" she gasped. "Oh my God, *you've killed her!*"

Aluinn pressed a hand against the girl's throat. He found the erratic pulse and looked up quickly. "She's all right, she's just out cold. I'm sorry, I didn't mean to — "

"*Murderers!*" Catherine screamed. "Traitors! Spies! I'll

see you both hanged for this! I will, I swear I will, if it's the last thing — ''

"Oh, for the love of Christ," Cameron muttered and leaned forward, scooping Catherine up and over his broad shoulder. He carried the shrieking, flailing bundle out into the hall and down the stairs, dumping her unceremoniously by the hearth.

"Catherine!" Damien rushed to her side, a wild eye on Cameron as he helped his sister to her feet. Instead of cringing into his arms, Catherine flung herself at Alexander again, vilifying him with every curse and expletive she could ever recall hearing. Grabbing her around the waist, Damien had to brace his feet to hold her away from Cameron.

"Let me go!"

"Catherine! Please — ''

"Let me go! What difference does it make what we say or do, they're going to kill us anyway! Oh! *Ohh — !*'' She whirled and sagged against her brother's chest, wracked by sobs which finally burst free.

Damien glared at Alexander Cameron over the top of her head. "What have you done to her? What have you said?"

"Nothing — on both counts. It was your charming little sister who tried to settle the matter with a knife."

Damien looked shocked and tightened his arms around Catherine as Aluinn MacKail came back down the stairs.

"The other one will probably be out for a couple of hours," he murmured uncomfortably. "I don't think anything is broken or cracked."

"What happened?" Damien demanded.

Cameron ignored the question and snatched up the cigar he had tossed onto the table. "More to the point, what happens now? With or without a sugar coating, your sister is adamantly refusing to listen to reason."

"Murderer!" came the muffled retort. "Traitor! Spy!"

Cameron arched his eyebrows pointedly, as he selected a burning taper from the fire and held the glowing end to his cigar.

"We need time," Aluinn said quietly. "A couple of days at the very least."

"Never!" Catherine sobbed and lifted her head from Damien's coat front. "I'll see you hang. I'll see you caught and — "

"Shut up!" Cameron's eyes glowered with a promise. "I've taken about all I care to from you, Mistress Ashbrooke. One more word and I won't guarantee what condition your hide will be in when and *if* you live to see daylight!"

Catherine returned his stare for a sullen moment. It appeared as though she was bracing herself for a further battle of wills, but then she clamped her mouth firmly shut and buried her face in Damien's shoulder again.

"Any suggestions?" Cameron's gaze shifted to Damien. "I'm willing to listen to anything you have to offer."

"Let Catherine and Deirdre leave," Damien said at once. "Keep me with you, take me along as a hostage and I can fairly well guarantee their silence."

"Damien!" Catherine raised her tear-streaked face. "No!"

"It is the only way they will trust either one of us," Damien said urgently.

"He's a murderer!" Catherine persisted, aghast. "He won't let you go. Once he is safe, what will stop him from simply killing you and disposing of the body beneath a hedgerow somewhere!"

"What stopped him from killing *you* and leaving *you* beneath a hedgerow as soon as he was away from Rosewood Hall? Why did he trouble himself with bringing you all this way when he could easily have rid himself of the bother in a dozen different ways?"

"Perhaps he thought he needed me as a camouflage to get away from Derby. Perhaps he thought to use *me* as a hostage — *I don't know*! And I don't know why you are defending him! He certainly is neither the friend nor the gentleman you thought him to be. He's a *criminal*! A hunted killer!''

Damien set his jaw in a taut ridge. ''I don't know anything about any murders he may or may not have committed. I *do* know he could commit three right now if the mood was upon him and no one would be any the wiser for weeks . . . months, even. As for him being a gentleman, his name may not be recognizable to me, but the man himself cannot change that drastically. If he says he will let you go free now, I have to damn well believe he will let you go free. And if he asks you for a promise of silence, you will damn well give it to him and you will damn well keep it!''

Catherine stared up into her brother's face, stunned by the unexpected display of anger — *directed at her*! Something was different about him. Drastically different. He was not behaving at all like the easygoing, good-natured squire's son whose most important concerns in life were gaming, the pursuit of Harriet Chalmers, and a halfhearted dedication to a barrister's office in London. There was something hard in his eyes. Something cold and distant, as indefinable as the brooding intensity in Cameron, and she did not like it. It alienated her far more than if he'd crumbled into a snivelling, grovelling coward and begged for their release.

''I will not do it,'' she seethed. ''He may have charmed you into thinking him a prince, but I do not believe for a single moment that he would honour a pledge to let you go free.''

She turned hot violet eyes on Alexander Cameron, who studied the stubborn set to her jaw with a thoughtful look that combined anger, impatience, and just a hint of grudging admiration. He suspected that even if they could frighten a promise of silence out of her, it would last only as long as it took her to find the nearest outpost of militia.

''Iain? How long do you estimate it will take us to reach Achnacarry?''

The younger man shrugged. ''Four days. Happens less,

happens mair, dependin' on how thick the patrols are.''

"How thick were they when you came south?"

"Thick as a sheep's coat against the sheers."

"What of the roads? Are they any better than they were when we left? Are they passable?"

"Roads? Aye, the militia keep them well tromped." Iain looked puzzled by the sudden interest in a route they would never dare unless they had a sudden wish to inspect a hangman's gibbet up close. He glanced at Aluinn, but the smoky gray eyes were intent on Alex's face, as if he knew what the other man was leading up to — and didn't like it. Iain turned back to Alex. "Wade's roads are passable, aye, if ye want tae visit the *Sassenachs* at Fort William.''

"Or if we wanted to travel by coach," Alex said quietly.

"By coach? Are ye daft? Why would we be dain' such a fool thing?''

Aluinn sighed expressively. "Because three men — or four — on horseback, riding north, staying well off the main tracks, travelling by night, will draw far more attention if they are stopped by a patrol of lobsterbacks than will a fine English coach carrying an English peer of the realm, his wife, her maid, and a couple of liveried coachmen . . . travelling in broad daylight, of course, strictly on the main roads in plain view of any or all who question their presence. Have I interpreted the gleam in your eye accurately enough, Alex?''

"You usually do," Cameron acknowledged with a grin.

"But will it work? A coach will add anywhere from a week to ten days in bad weather.''

"I'm still open to alternatives. But while you are thinking, keep something else in mind: Damien's unscheduled absence from Derby might cause a question or two to arise, whereas the newly wed Mrs. Montgomery has a very good reason to disappear for several weeks during her . . . impassioned honeymoon trip.''

Damien stiffened. "You cannot seriously be suggesting that Catherine accompany you?''

"Accompany him?" she asked. "Accompany him where?"

"Consider it a vacation," Cameron said dryly, the cigar jutting from between his strong white teeth. "Scotland is beautiful in July."

"Scotland! You *are* out of your mind! I'm not going to Scotland. I'm not going anywhere — especially with you!" She clutched her brother's arm. "Tell him, Damien. Tell this madman he's insane."

Damien was at a loss for words. He was also fighting very hard to control the overwhelming desire to shake his sister until her bones rattled. If she'd only kept silent and agreed to their terms. Things were happening too quickly. The duel . . . the marriage . . . events had blown out of control before either wit or prudence could arrive at a logical, rational solution. Was there one? Should he just blurt out the truth? What would she do if she knew he had been working for and with the Jacobites for several years? He had come close to telling her — telling them all — so many times over the past few months. Perhaps he should have. He was certainly not alone in his disaffection for the Hanover government, for many Englishmen were working both secretly and openly to hasten a change in the reigning power. But to reveal his true leanings would have meant forsaking family and friends at Rosewood Hall, abandoning his contacts in London — vital sources of information that had taken months, years to establish. No, he could not have done it then, he could not do it now, even though his own sister had become an unwitting pawn in a very dangerous game.

"Damien?" She was again staring up at him with growing unease. "*Tell* him."

"I cannot allow it," he said lamely. "You have to think of another way."

"There is no other way," Cameron replied bluntly.

"But . . . she's my *sister*."

"And I promise you, she'll be treated exactly as if she were mine. Two weeks, three at the most, and she'll be on her way home again, safe and sound — '' He paused and smiled tightly. ''No doubt with enough stories of the 'wild savages' to keep her peers agog for months.''

Three weeks! Catherine stared at her brother, waiting for his outraged protest. When it became horrifyingly apparent there was not going to be one, she felt a wave of faintness wash through her, one that nearly threatened to undermine what little composure she had left.

''Damien,'' she whispered, ''you cannot let him do it. You cannot let him take me away!''

''You haven't given him any choice,'' Damien replied harshly.

''There are always choices . . .'' she began, whirling to face Alexander Cameron, but neither the bronzed features nor the cold black eyes revealed any emotion that she could appeal to. In that instant she came to know the true meaning of the word hatred — icy, steepening hatred that infused every nerve and fibre of her being. If Cameron read it in her eyes, or felt it in the silence that stretched on a razor's edge between them, there was no reaction on his face or in his next words to Damien.

''You have my word, Damien. No one will touch a hair on your sister's head as long as she behaves herself and is willing to co-operate.''

''On your life, Alex,'' Damien said, so softly Catherine could hardly hear him over the throbbing of her heartbeat. ''Swear it on your life.''

''You have my word,'' was the quiet response.

''And if I refuse?'' Catherine cried, shattering the brittle tension.

''If ye refuse,'' Iain snapped coarsely, ''it'll be a quick skelp on the heid an' a shallow grave. Frankly, I dinna see why we shouldna dae it now an' get it over wi'. Three graves, nae witnesses tae worry aboot now or then!''

Damien's patience exploded on a curse. He thrust Catherine to one side and his hands clawed into Iain's shirt front with such force the seams parted at the shoulders. The sound of the cloth tearing was followed instantly by the sound of a fist crunching into flesh and jawbone. Aluinn was jarred into motion, but not before Damien managed to connect two more solid punches, which started a gout of blood sheeting down young Cameron's chin and throat from a broken nose.

"Let me go," Damien snarled, wrenching his arms out of Aluinn's grasp. "He went too far, goddammit! Too far."

Iain, having staggered back against the wall, dragged his hand across his upper lip and stared at the slick red smear like an enraged bull. With a roar, he launched himself across the room, a dirk clutched purposefully in his outstretched fist. It was all Aluinn could do to shove Damien roughly out of the way and pivot clear himself.

"Iain!" Alex shouted the name, halting the boy as he spun around to redirect his fury at this new threat. "Put that thing away!"

"I dinna trust him, cousin," Iain spat, the blood gushing out at each word. "I told ye afore na tae trust him!"

"And I said, *put the knife away*!"

"Aye, I'll put it awa . . . in his guts, I'll put it awa!"

Iain hurled himself across the floor again, but Alex had anticipated the move and with an almost effortless grace caught the outthrust wrist and snapped the knife free. The boy screamed with the pain and hooked his left fist toward the aquiline features, and again Cameron sidestepped the punch, pulling the already bloodied jaw into a meeting with his own clenched fist. The blow sent Iain scraping across the floor, where he remained for several dazed minutes, an astounding array of lights and colours cartwheeling before his eyes.

Cameron, satisfied the boy would not attack again, directed his attention to Damien. Catherine, fearing her brother would earn the same treatment in this madman's hands, dashed to Damien's side and placed herself between the two men.

"No! No, don't touch him! I'll do it. I'll do whatever you

want me to do. I'll go to Scotland with you and I'll behave however you want me to . . . only let Damien go. Right now. While we're all together in this room, let him walk out the door and ride away. I want to *see* him ride away, and if you refuse, or if anyone tries to follow, then . . . then you will have a great deal more blood on your hands, Mr. Cameron, because you will have to kill both Damien and me to keep us quiet."

"Catherine — " Damien gripped her by the shoulders and spun her around to face him. "Do you realize what you're saying? What you are agreeing to?"

"I'm agreeing to be their hostage." Her eyes grew bright with the shine of tears. "And I'm agreeing to believe their promise that we will all live through this one way or another."

"Catherine — "

"Damien, *please*. I won't be able to do it if I have to think about it. I . . . I *won't* think about it. I . . . I'll treat it like a holiday, like the one we took in Plymouth that summer when neither one of us wanted to go but Father insisted. *Do you remember?*"

His hands grasping her slender arms, Damien's fury mingled with exasperation. What the devil was she on about? Holidays? Plymouth? That had to be ten, twelve years ago.

"Catherine, this isn't a game — "

Her eyes widened and the gleam in them became almost piercing.

Game, Damien thought. They had played a game on the crumbling walls of a castle, something about knights rescuing damsels in distress. Catherine had played the part of a captured princess, he had . . . he had pretended to ride away to collect the ransom to pay off the Black Prince, but instead had circled around the castle walls and stormed her imaginary captors by surprise. Was that what she was asking him to do now? Was that what she was suggesting: that he ride away in seeming agreement to their terms and instead ride for help? Yes, of course, that was it. That was what she was asking, and what she was expecting him to do . . . and indeed, it was undoubtably what he *would* have done if circumstances had been any different . . . and the hope shining in her eyes almost made him groan out loud.

"Catherine, I don't know . . ."

"I will be all right," she said firmly. "Deirdre and I will both be all right. Please, just go while you have the chance . . . and before this *gentleman*" — she cast a scorching eye in Alexander Cameron's direction — "changes his mind."

"But — "

"Damien, you only make it worse by delaying. Please!"

He drew her into his arms and held her tightly, knowing she might well never forgive him for what he was about to do. And that was to ride away and do absolutely nothing.

His eyes locked with Cameron's over the top of her head.

"On your life," he reminded the Scotsman tersely.

The dark eyes acknowledged the unspoken threat, then glanced at Aluinn. "There are two coachmen out in the stable. Tell them you've been hired to relieve them of their duties and they can return with Mr. Ashbrooke to Derby."

He saw Catherine's head turn toward him and he smiled wryly. "Will that satisfy your concerns, Mistress Ashbrooke, for the safety of your brother?"

"My only satisfaction, sir, will come upon seeing you walk up the steps to the gibbet."

There was another lengthy silence, marked only by the sudden scuffling of pigs' hoofs in the pen across the room. Somewhat abruptly, Damien gave Catherine a final kiss and hug of reassurance, then followed Aluinn MacKail out into the moonlit yard. Catherine stood in the doorway, her face, bathed in the soft luminescence was scored by the bright sparkle of tears that trickled slowly down her cheeks. She watched as the two men walked across the yard to the dilapidated stable to emerge several minutes later, Damien leading his horse, the two coachmen following close behind, their postures reflecting their confusion.

Damien paused to exchange a few muffled sentences with MacKail and then glanced intently at the pale figure outlined in the cottage doorway. Catherine watched him mount, heard him shout a brief order to the lagging coachmen . . . then the three of them were riding down the dirt road, away from the cottage, away from Catherine.

When their figures had been swallowed into the shadows of the forest, Catherine released a burning breath she had not even been aware she had been holding. She turned abruptly to go back inside, only to find that *he* was standing directly behind her, so close she very nearly bumped into him. His features were partially blotted by the darkness, his frame backlit by the weak glow of the fire. She stared up into the ebony eyes.

"Is this how you brave Scots fight your battles, Mr. Cameron? By shielding yourselves behind frightened women?"

Without waiting for an answer — for indeed, how could there be one, she surmised haughtily — she brushed past him and climbed the rickety steps to the upper floor, her head held high, her shoulders squared with as much dignity as she could muster.

Chapter Seven

Deirdre was stretched out on the bed, her eyes closed, her head lolled to one side, and for a terrible, heart-stopping moment, Catherine thought she was dead.

"Deirdre?" She leaned over the prone figure and touched a hand gingerly to the girl's cheek. There was a flutter of movement behind the closed eyelids and a soft groan escaped the pale lips.

"Thank God," Catherine murmured and focussed her concern on the swollen, purpling bruise high on Deirdre's cheekbone. The skin was cut and Catherine suddenly remembered seeing a flash of gold on Aluinn MacKail's finger.

"The beast," she hissed. "All three of them deserve whatever fate awaits them. Oh, Deirdre, wake up. Wake up! I can't bear this alone!"

She straightened at the sound of a heavy footstep in the outer hall. The door, with its shattered latch, swung open easily at a nudge from Aluinn MacKail's elbow. He was carrying a wooden trencher crowded with small meat pastries, bread, and cheese. Casting his gray eyes to the unconscious form of the maid, he then surveyed the room for a suitable place to unload his burden. The contents of the platter, when he set it down on a small table, filled the room with a warm, tantalizing odour.

"You can take that right back where it came from," Catherine announced with a righteous toss of her blonde curls. "We want no more samples of your hospitality this night."

Aluinn ignored her and walked to the side of the bed. "I did not mean to hit her. It *was* an accident."

"Tell that to Mistress O'Shea when she wakens. *If* she ever wakens."

The steely gray eyes lifted and held Catherine for a brief moment, before he turned away wordlessly and left the room. Catherine followed, slamming the broken door shut behind him, and after a few seconds of thought, she dragged the chair over and propped it firmly against the broken latch. Satisfied the makeshift lock would hold, she backed away and glared bravely at the empty space.

"An accident," she muttered disdainfully. "If I were but a man . . ."

Her fear had now given way almost completely to indignation over the way she was being mistreated, manhandled, and humiliated. She would not let them get away with this. She would not, *could* not, go docilely along with three spying, murdering thieves regardless of whatever foolish promises they thought to hold her to. She would have agreed to anything in the heat of the moment, so long as it meant they would release Damien. Fools! Dolts! Did they honestly think he would ride away and leave her alone in their clutches? She knew he had understood perfectly her oblique reference to the summer spent in Plymouth. He was probably even now circling behind the cottage, planning how to rescue her, stalling long enough for one of the coachmen to ride into Wakefield to summon the militia. An hour, no more, and the cottage and woods would be swarming with soldiers. They would . . .

They would what?

Catherine's heart thudded dully in her ears as she stared at the door. Cameron and his cutthroats would undoubtedly try to use her and Deirdre as hostages, that is what they would do. They would hold a gun or a knife to her head and use the threat of instant death to buy a safe passage out of the trap. Unless . . . Her gaze flew to the window. . . . unless she and Deirdre could somehow get clear of the cottage without their gaolers knowing it. They had been on the verge of escaping that very way when Damien had arrived — they could still do it!

"Deirdre! Oh, Deirdre, wake up. Wake *up*!" She patted the girl's face — slapped it rather hard, if truth be known — and rubbed her wrists. She ran to the washstand and soaked a towel in cool water, then draped it across the maid's brow. A groan was the only result achieved from all her ministrations, and a slight shifting of head and shoulders to try to avoid the cold, dripping wetness of the compress.

. . . *If something happens to me, mistress, look to yourself. Run and save yourself* . . .

It was unthinkable to abandon Deirdre to the mercy of brigands and criminals, and Catherine recoiled from the idea as soon as it entered her brain. And yet, if she did manage to get away . . . if help could be brought back . . .

"Deirdre!" Catherine cried urgently. "Wake up. Please wake up."

The soft, fawn-brown eyes opened briefly, but the effort and the crushing pain were too much and the girl slid into unconsciousness once again. There was nothing more Catherine could do. Even if she could have roused the maid to a state of semi-awareness, she doubted if Deirdre would have the strength to make the descent from the window.

Her heart throbbed anew as she crossed over to the window.

. . . *simple as climbing down a ladder, Mistress* . . .

Chewing her lower lip — a habit dear Miss Phoebe had

tried unsuccessfully to break her of since childhood — she contemplated the darkness outside. The moon hung swollen and glistening above the trees, its rays bathing the open ground nearly as brightly as sunlight. The branches of the tree outside the window were etched against the light like the bones of a skeleton; a gnarled aged specimen, there were few leaves or shoots of new growth to hamper the way down.

Catherine gathered together the folds of her skirt and tucked the excess into her waistband. Removing two of the bulkiest layers of petticoats, she reduced the volume of material she would have to control, not, for a moment, stopping to contemplate what she was about to do. Nor did she want to entertain any thoughts of what might happen if she was caught in the act of trying to escape.

A last glance over her shoulder was divided equally between the still form on the bed and the chair propped against the door. With a quick, silent word of prayer, she lifted herself onto the sill and managed, with much wriggling and cursing, to place herself on the outer ledge, balanced precariously between the window and closest tree branch.

All or nothing, now or never — every trite cliché she could think of ran through her mind as she summoned the courage to lean forward, to grasp the scabbed branch and swing herself free of the windowledge.

Immediately she felt the uncomfortable chill of a cold sweat break out across her brow. The branch was thick and she felt reasonably secure, but for the life of her, she did not want to move. She did not want to release or relax her hold, nor did she want to open her eyes and look at the ground so many dizzying feet below.

In the end, it was the image of what she must look like, clinging like a terrified monkey to a vine, that stirred her hands and feet into motion. She began a slow and careful slide along the thick branch, lowering herself footstep by scraping footstep until she arrived, panting and considerably damper under the armpits, at the junction of the tree trunk. Her clothing was cumbersome and totally impractical for what she was doing, and she upbraided herself scathingly for not thinking to remove, or at least loosen, the laces of her stiff pasteboard stomacher before venturing out on the limb. She was sweating profusely, a condition she abhorred at the best of times and one no lady would ever admit to enduring. Even her undergarments — her pantaloons and stockings — tangled on every twig and protruding knot she encountered.

At last, the slippered toe of a searching foot found solid ground, and with an enormous sigh of relief, she rested her drenched brow against the rough bark. Flushed and fighting for every breath, she did not linger to celebrate her victory but picked her way cautiously around the side of the cottage. The stable was dark, a striking contrast with the moonlit stretch of yard that lay between. She experienced another twinge of panic as she envisioned Alexander Cameron passing by a window, happening to glance out, and seeing a fleet-footed shadow streaking across the open space. But there was no way to avoid the risk, unless she wanted to walk all the way into Wakefield, and since she had no idea how long a walk that might involve, or even what direction to set out in, she had no alternative but to try to steal a horse.

Fear and panic snapping at her heels, she dashed across the yard and flattened herself into the shadows of the crooked, mouldering building. Thankful, she saw that the door was not in the direct wash of moonlight; she would be able to open it and get inside without being seen from the cottage, but at the same time she would not be permitted the luxury of leading a horse very far in case it balked or shied out of control.

With infinite care, she pushed the door open. The hinges, crudely worked in rope and wood, made no noise, but Catherine herself gave off a sharp little cry as she stumbled forward over an unseen length of pole. She bent over to move it and clutching it to her, took a few precious seconds to let her eyes adjust to the heavy gloom. Again, luck was on her side, for the roof was so rotted in places that the moon shone through as bright as lantern light. She could see there were six rudimentary stalls in all, built of fieldstone and wood. The ceiling overhead was a hanging garden of leather reins and harnesses. The odour of horses, past and present, was as strong as acid at the back of her throat, and, holding a hand over her mouth and nose, Catherine hurried to the nearest stall.

She pulled up with a gasp as the velvet black snout of Cameron's stallion loomed out of the darkness and shrilled an angry challenge. Backing away, she made a wide berth around the front of the stall as she sidled to the next one, where a sleepy-eyed bay was tethered. She slipped loose the halter knot, then, on a further thought, ran quickly into each of the other stalls — except that of the black demon's — and loosened their bindings.

She was heading back to the bay when a shadow detached itself from the wall and stepped into her path.

"An' just what the hell d'ye think ye're dain?" Iain Cameron asked belligerently. "Surely ye werena thinkin' o' ridin' out in the middle o' the night wi'out so much as a fare-thee-well."

Edging back, Catherine heard his low, coarse chuckle.

"Caught ye, did I na? Red-faced, red-handed — " The glittering blue eyes raked down her slender body, the grin widening when he saw the shapely outline of her legs.

Catherine suddenly realized that her skirts were still tucked into her waist, affording him more than a reasonable glimpse of stockinged calves and frilled pantaloons. She rectified the situation hastily, and in so doing, became aware that she still held the wooden stave she had picked up off the floor.

"Here now, mayhap ye an' I can make an arrangement o' our ain," Iain suggested lewdly. "Ye're supposed tae be on yer honeymoon trip anyways . . ."

"Stay back," she warned hoarsely as she saw his figure loom closer.

"Or ye'll dae what? Nae doubt ye could scream an' bring

ma cousin out here on the run, but could ye explain how ye came tae be out here in the fairst place . . . or why?''

''Don't come any closer,'' she cried, and her fingers tightened around the hard wooden stave.

''Come closer? Aye, I plan tae come a mout closer, Miss High an' Mighty. I plan tae come so close — ''

Reacting instinctively as his hand reached out to grasp her, Catherine swung the stave out of its hiding place within the folds of her skirt and cut it in an arc across Iain's neck and shoulder. Not as quick-witted as he might have been before the scuffle inside the cottage, Iain saw the pole coming at his face, but too late to duck. The blow knocked him sideways and he staggered against the wall, where, as luck would have it, his temple met with a protruding edge of stone, which stunned him long enough for Catherine to run to the bay, pull herself up on the horse's back, wheel it around and out the open stable door. Iain shouted and lunged after her, but the noise only startled the other animals into bolting out of their stalls and thundering past him into the darkness.

Catherine did not pause to look back or to gloat over the success of her escape. Her last clear image was of the cottage door bursting wide, spilling harsh yellow light and two running figures into the courtyard.

Urging her horse to greater speed, Catherine held on for dear life, her hands twined around fistfuls of brown, wiry mane that whipped and stung her face with each racing stride. Her knees and thighs were pressed so tightly to the straining muscles that hurtled her along the moonlit road, she almost felt a part of the animal.

Tears scalded the back of her throat and the cold wind lashed her face. Her hair streamed out behind her in the tearing wind, her skirt was peeled back above her knees and snapped out behind her. She knew the moon was her worst enemy, and had to decide whether to remain on the open road or try to weave her way through the bordering black forest.

Some instinct made her fight the wind and motion to glance back over her shoulder. The horse and rider chasing her were plainly visible — as visible as she was no doubt to him — and she wailed a stricken plea for salvation as she realized her mistake in not freeing the stallion. She could not have know that it would have made little difference, as Shadow, trained to respond to the orders of one master, would not have wandered more than a dozen paces in any direction even if she had whipped him to a bloody frenzy.

Catherine gouged her heels cruelly into the bay's flanks, ignoring the dangers of hidden footfalls and overgrown roots, and steered the terrified animal off the road. Even though the trees were widely spaced and enough moonlight filtered through the branches to define the path they were taking, she now had to sacrifice speed. Low-hung branches slapped at her and tore at her streaming hair. For long stretches at a time the light was so dim that only the horse's instincts kept them from smashing into the razor-edged bark of the trees. The land dipped and twisted, disappeared into a narrow gorge, and for many strides both horse and rider were badly off balance. They skidded through a shallow stream, sending gouts of glistening water off each panicked hoofbeat, then tore through dense patches of gorse and weed, scattering quail and ptarmigan into the darkness.

The angry hoofbeats behind them were gaining, and Catherine pleaded for more speed from the bay. She lost her sense of direction and could no longer distinguish trees from shadows. Her horse plunged downward again, whinnying as the embankment crumbled beneath its flailing hoofs and Catherine lurched back to compensate. She heard a loud *crack* and the world slid sideways. Her hands lost their grip on the reins and she was flung into space, spinning through the blackness as the ground rushed up to meet her. Her scream was cut short as she slammed into a bed of moss, the angle so steep she slid again, tumbling with the momentum of her fall until a final spin sent her over a bank and into the icy, rushing water of a stream. The water was only waist-deep, but the current was strong and dragged her beneath the surface before she was able to find her footing.

She grabbed for a handhold, but the bottom was covered with inches of slime and decaying organisms. She managed to halt her forward motion long enough to thrust her head above the water but she drew no more than a gulp of air before she was dragged under again and swept painfully along the slippery, boulder-strewn bottom. Her skirt was soaked, twined around her ankles like an anchor, and the panic burst from her chest in an agonized, water-burned scream of despair. She was drowning. Her body was on fire from the cuts, scrapes and bruises she earned at every twist and turn of the current, and she was struggling not to give way to the agony of hopelessness when a rough pair of hands caught her under the arms and hauled her clear of the water.

Coughing and choking for a clear breath of air, she swung her arms in a desperate attempt to free herself. Her hair was plastered to her face like a blanket of seaweed, cold and clinging, blinding her to everything but her own inner pains. Numb with terror, she imagined the cruel smile on Cameron's face and the dripping blade that was surely clutched in his hand. He was going to kill her! Coldly, brutally, he was going to kill her!

Catherine screamed and, lashing out with her fists, managed to land a solid blow to his jaw. Without hesitation, he struck back, the flat of his hand stinging smartly across her cheek. The shock stunned her long enough for Cameron to lift her the rest of the way onto the embankment, where he left her crying and retching muddy water onto the moss.

He walked swiftly back to where her horse lay writhing and screaming in agony. Both slender forelegs were broken, snapped like twigs. The bones were gleaming through the shattered skin and tendons, and each thrashing movement produced a scream and a spray of warm blood. Cursing loudly and steadily, Cameron knelt beside the suffering animal and unsheathed a knife from the top of his boot. He made two swift, deep slashes in the straining throat, then remained on his knees, stroking the horse's sweat-flecked coat until the legs had shivered to a lifeless halt.

Angry enough at that moment to have willingly used the same knife on Catherine, he did not trust himself to speak or to look her directly in the eye. Instead, he jerked her up onto her feet and half carried, half dragged her to where Shadow stood nervously prancing from one foot to another. He had heard the dying screams of the other horse and smelled the blood, and his fine, chiselled head was held high in revolt.

"Stand!" Cameron commanded harshly and the stallion quiveringly obeyed while he slung Catherine's soaked and shivering body across the bare back. Cameron swung himself up behind her and guided the horse slowly and carefully back through the forest toward the road. Catherine, faint from nausea, sick at heart, and aching from the near-fatal fall, was too weak to do more than cringe against the warmth of Cameron's broad chest.

Back at the cottage, Aluinn was waiting anxiously in the yard.

"Is she all right? Where is the horse?"

"She's fine, the horse is dead," Cameron said bluntly. "It's unfortunate it did not end up the other way around."

"What the hell did she think she was doing?"

"I have no idea," he snarled and jumped to the ground, hauling Catherine down after him, "but I'm damn well going to find out. Where is Iain?"

"Running down the other horses. His pride has certainly taken a beating tonight."

"It may not be all that takes a beating when I'm through with him."

He scooped Catherine into his arms and carried the sodden, dripping bundle into the cottage. He did not take her to the room where Deirdre still lay unconscious on the bed, but to the room where she had seen him meeting his two companions. He kicked open the door and flung her down on the bed, glaring at her for a moment as if daring her to move. He turned and slammed the door shut with such force she felt the concussion in her ears.

"Well, madam?" He planted his feet wide apart and crossed his arms over his chest. "I presume you have some explanation that will convince me not to wrap my hands around your throat and throttle the life out of you?"

Catherine pushed herself upright, her lips blue and trembling from the cold.

"G-go to h-hell," she whispered and attempted to brush back the tangled mass of hair from her face and shoulders. There was too much of it, however, and it lay thick and wet, clinging to her white skin.

Cameron's eyes flicked briefly to the torn gap in the front of her bodice.

"Madam, I shall only warn you the once — "

"*You* shall warn *me*?" she cried indignantly. "A spy, a m-murderer . . . a . . . traitor to king and country . . . and *you* intend to warn *me*!"

"You could have killed yourself out there," he exploded.

"Then I would have saved you the trouble, wouldn't I?"

His eyes narrowed. "As much as I feel the inclination could change drastically over the next few minutes, I am not in the habit of killing women . . . or *children*, as the case may be."

"N-no, you only kidnap them against their will and then amuse yourself by frightening them half to death."

Cameron's lips compressed ominously. "You, madam, are an insecure, pampered piece of irresponsible foolishness who suffers under the delusion that all mankind was placed on this earth for the sole purpose of catering to your every whim. You use people as it pleases you, for as long as it pleases you, then discard them like so much rubbish. I doubt very much whether you have ever gone hungry a day in your life, or known the meaning of the word fear — *real* fear, Mistress Ashbrooke. The kind that gnaws at your belly and leaves you too empty and shaken to even cry.''

His tone infuriated her, but something in his eyes made her wary of the fine edge he trod between savagery and civility. She had prodded an open nerve once already, with unexpected and unnerving results, and had no desire to do so again. By way of compromise, she tossed her head in a gesture of disdain, but was shivering so badly the rebuke was ineffectual. Her hands were clasped around her upper arms and she was hugging herself so fiercely she would leave bruises of her own making on her flesh.

''You had best get out of those wet clothes.'' He scowled and turned abruptly toward the door. ''The last thing I need is a child with pneumonia on my hands.''

''I'm quite through taking orders from you, sir,'' she gritted through her teeth.

He stopped and glared back. ''Either you take those wet things off now, or I'll rip them off for you.''

''No doubt you would enjoy it to the utmost, you perverted, pretentious . . . *noooo!*'' She lunged sideways on the bed to avoid the hands that were reaching down for her, then balled her fists and batted them against his chest as he pulled her to her feet. He was not deterred in the least. He spun her around and held her bent over one arm while he plucked and tore at the fastenings of her bodice. When it was loose, the sleeves were peeled roughly from her arms and the ruined velvet discarded. She was shockingly aware of the hardness of his thighs pressed against her buttocks, but that shock paled in comparison to the one she experienced when she saw her clothing tossed into a growing heap on the floor. The lacing of her corset succumbed to an irritated series of tugs, and despite the indignity of her position and of what he was doing to her, her ribs expanded gratefully as the last loop was freed and the buckram cast aside.

The sodden velvet folds of her skirt joined the sorry heap of garments, as did the solitary petticoat she wore. Her knees buckled as she felt his hands skim the stockings from her calves. Jerking herself upright, sobbing, she renewed the struggle with him, but her quaking shivers rendered her efforts all but useless. He was going to rape her. He was going to strip her, rape her, then kill her as coldly and remorselessly as he would kill a troublesome flea! He would have his way with her, and when he was sated no doubt she would be passed to the others to ease their carnal lusts.

She gasped as she was turned again within Cameron's arms. It was worse — much worse having to face him while the ravishment proceeded. She could see the animal hunger in his eyes, she could feel the rasping heat of his breath against her bared flesh, and she could feel the effects of both curling hotly within her loins. The ache of outrage that had closed her throat at his first touch blossomed into true terror as she stared up into the deep, dark glitter of his eyes.

"Stop! Please!" she cried, but he was beyond hearing. His hands were on the drawstring that shaped the sheer silk wisp of her shimmy to her waist and with a seemingly indifferent twist of his fingers, the string was released, the silk brushed from her body like an annoying film of dust.

In the next instant he was tearing the quilted coverlet off the bed. He flung it about her shoulders and started rubbing, so vigorously that she almost forgot her nakedness. When he had chafed some warmth into her chilled body, he bundled the quilt tightly around her, then plunked her into the chair he shoved near the small rusted brazier. He knelt down beside her and fanned the glowing embers to life, feeding them with small scraps of dry kindling. Catherine, confused by his sudden changes of mood, could do little more than stare at the glossy black waves of his hair.

Did this mean he was *not* going to rape her? Or did it simply mean he preferred to commit his crimes in comfort?

"Wh-what are you going to do with me?" she asked in a whisper.

"What do you suggest I do?" he snapped angrily. He kept his back to her as he spoke, and his voice was so low she was tempted to lean forward to hear. "What would *you* do with a tiresome, officious nuisance of a woman who is the first to question a man's word of honour, yet the last to keep her own?"

Catherine was taken aback by the accusation. "I hardly consider myself bound by honour to a murderer and a spy!"

He sighed and regarded her steadily. "Then may I ask by what logic you suppose a murderer and a spy would be expected to honour *his* guarantees?"

Catherine's hands tightened on the edges of the quilt. "Damien knows where you are taking me. If you kill me . . . or abuse me in any way . . . he will follow you. He will hunt you down and see that you die a truly horrible death."

"So you have already said," Cameron mused and straightened to his full height, forcing Catherine's gaze to climb to alarming heights with him. "You obviously have never been to the Highlands, have you? A man can lose himself in the mountains and glens and never be seen by another living soul if it so pleases him."

"Is that why you ran away to France to hide?" she asked tartly, sounding much more composed than she felt . . . especially when he leaned over to respond, his hands placed on either armrest so that she was trapped in between.

"I did not *run*, Mistress Ashbrooke," he said evenly. "I was *sent* to France by my brother. But if I had had my choice all those years ago, I most certainly would have gone up into the mountains, and then I might not have become so civilized. For that you have my brother Donald to thank . . . if and when you ever meet him."

Catherine blinked back the rush of tears that threatened to betray her fear. "I have no intention of going anywhere with you, Mr. Cameron, despite whatever foolish promises I may have made. If you are desirous of my meeting any members of your family, I dare say the only way you will have me do so is to bind and gag me and drag me behind the coach — which would win rather more attention to your plight than you would want."

Cameron's eyes narrowed further. Oddly enough, he felt the urge to throttle slowly giving way to the urge to smile. Even more discomforting was his growing awareness of the bright shine in the violet eyes, of the slender curve of her throat and the soft texture of the flawless skin. A wet, clinging tendril of golden hair seemed bent on drawing his attention to the slipping folds of the quilt, but he knew that if his glance strayed there he might not be able to look away again.

"I am not a man given to playing at games," he warned softly.

"So you keep saying," she countered, startled by her own audacity. The courage, she suspected, was being falsely raised in defense against the probing stare only inches away. It was also a defense against the lightheadedness, the faint breathlessness that came with being so close to his raw animal presence. "Your threats sound very much like the bluff of a desperate man, Mr. Cameron. I do not believe you will kill me, and since you obviously have few other alternatives, I suggest you mount your horses and ride as fast and as far away as they will carry you."

The smile that had been battling with his better judgement won and spread meaningfully across the handsome face.

"Oh, I think I have at least one other alternative," he mused. His hand moved from the armrest and brushed aside the curl of yellow hair that had been taunting him from the deep *V* of white flesh. Catherine started when she realized how low the quilt had fallen, but before she could rearrange the folds his long tapered fingers were closing firmly around her wrist.

"A wife, madam, is far more obliging to her husband's wishes if she knows the price of her disobedience."

"Wife!" she gasped.

His gaze roved down to the plump swell of flesh rising against the worn quilt. "It would not be such a great hardship for me to validate those vows we took last night, and it would be one sure way to guarantee your silence."

Catherine's eyes widened. Her hand, released from the

captivity of the iron grip, remained hovering in front of the quilt, frozen to inaction by the sight of his hands beginning to slowly unfasten and unwind the linen stock he wore about his neck. His jacket was stripped off and shrugged to the floor, as was the embroidered satin waistcoat. His shirt was loosened at the throat and the tails pulled from the skintight black leather breeches.

With a cry, Catherine lunged out of the chair, knocking it over in her haste to scramble to safety. Unfortunately, there was only the bed to place between herself and Cameron, for a single step of his long legs effectively blocked any hope of escape to the outer hall.

"Don't you come near me," she hissed fiercely, dragging the quilt with her as she pressed into the farthest corner of the room. "Don't you dare come near me or I'll scream!"

"Scream, dear wife," he said mildly, "and I'll blacken both your eyes."

Catherine's mouth gaped open. "You . . . you wouldn't dare."

"Wouldn't I?" He lifted his shirt over his head and tossed it onto the bed.

"Y-you promised . . . you gave y-your word . . ."

"I gave my word not to lay a hand on you . . . *if* you behaved."

Catherine was too stunned by the quiet vehemence in his voice to make any attempt to elude him as the great wall of naked, bronzed muscle came toward her. She felt her skin shrink and tingle with a thousand pinpricks of tension. Her mouth went dry and her legs trembled; her belly flooded with a heat unlike anything she had ever felt before. His hands, cradling each side of her neck, angled her head up so her mouth would meet the hard, bruising lips that moved determinedly down to cover hers. Her breath escaped on a harsh groan and she tried to twist her head away, but his fingers only ran deeper into her hair, twining around the tangled thickness to hold her fast. His lips forced hers apart. His tongue met each muffled gasp, thrusting, ravishing the inner sweetness with a surety that left her weak and helpless. It was happening again, just like the kiss in the garden. She was being plundered, robbed of all control; her mind was fighting the conquest, but her body was revelling in the possession. That same, slow wave of pleasure was unfurling within her, building, growing, pulsating into every nerve and fibre until her hands ached with the need to reach up and cling to him.

Somehow she resisted. She was pressed against the wall, crowded there by the heat of his body, and yet she resisted the need, the *desire* to run her hands across his chest and explore the forbidden pleasure.

His mouth lifted from hers and she instantly felt the loss ripple throughout her body. She could not raise her eyes to meet his even though she was acutely aware of his silent command to do so. She could only stare at his chest, at the cloud of crisp black hairs that lay crushed against her fingertips.

"Please," she whispered, "don't do this."

"Then stop me," he murmured, and his mouth descended lazily to the smooth arch of her neck. Her hands, occupied with holding the quilt in place, trembled under this new onslaught and moved ever so slightly higher on his chest.

"I'll do anything you want. I'll say anything you want." She shivered as his tongue flicked expertly around the dainty curl of her ear. "I'll . . . I'll go anywhere you want, I swear I will, and . . . and I won't make any more trouble."

"More promises?" he mused, and the huskiness in his voice reverberated the length of her spine. "Worth as much as the last one?"

Catherine's stammered assurances were stifled as his lips molded to hers again. His hands slipped to her shoulders, then to her waist, carrying the folds of the quilt with them. Her naked breasts were crushed against his, her thighs were no longer guarded against the determined roving of his hands. Just as his mouth was bent on imposing sensations she had never experienced before, his hands scorched a blazing trail of shocking caresses over flesh that had never known, never dreamed of such incursions. Her thighs, her hips, her waist, her breasts — her flesh was set on fire, the flames leaping and flickering behind her tightly clenched eyelids.

She heard a soft, startled moan of disappointment and realized her mouth was no longer prisoner beneath his. Her eyes fluttered open only to find his darker ones staring down at her, studying her features with an intense stillness she dared not challenge. She could sense how every muscle and sinew in his body was strained to its limit. She could see in his eyes that he wanted her, that he was fighting the hunger even as he fought to deny its existence. At that moment, Catherine felt more like a woman than she ever had in her life. A single stroke of his hand had rendered her past girlish flirtations infantile, her proclamations of superiority as lacking in substance as the breath wasted in expending them. And possibly, for the first time, she understood the gravity of her situation. Cameron was right: He was no fop or dandy to be toyed with and dismissed as easily as a bandy-legged schoolboy. He and his companions were desperate men on a desperate flight to the border, and they would let nothing, no one stand in their way.

The tears that had been swelling along her lashes dropped onto her cheeks and ran in two glistening streaks to her chin. Her lips, still puffed and moist from his assault, quivered as she found her voice and gave life to a final, heartfelt plea.

"I . . . I won't cause you any more trouble. I won't try to run away again, or betray you in any way. I give you my most solemn word against God, I won't, only" — she turned her face and averted her eyes — "please don't hurt me."

Alexander Cameron, already fighting against an urge so strong it had paralyzed every thought and emotion, saw the tears, watched them collect on her chin and splash onto the milky white rise of her breast. Her breath was laboured, and each gasp brought the buds of her nipples into contact with the dark fur of his chest. It had been so long — too long, he rationalized with the logic of a drowning man — since he had lost himself within the softness of a woman's body. The need was overwhelming and he had to force himself to ease away from her, to drag away the hand that longed to gently smooth back the tousled yellow hair from her cheek.

Catherine sensed the movement and looked up at him through the blur of her tears. His face was too close to distinguish more than the slash of his brows and the straight prominence of his nose, but it was his eyes that she sought, and the odd gleam in their depths drew her and held her.

It faded in the next instant, as if he had felt an unwanted intrusion and retreated instinctively behind a protective barrier of ice. He stepped back even farther, deliberately glancing away as Catherine crossed her arms over her nakedness.

"I'll have your trunk sent up," he said in a low, hoarse voice. "You will need clean, dry clothes for the morning. We will be leaving at dawn . . . do not make me come up and get you."

With that, he retrieved his shirt, waistcoat, and jacket, and without another word or glance in her direction, strode out of the room.

LOCHABER: August 1745

Chapter Eight

Alexander Cameron reined Shadow to a halt on the rim of a vast amphitheatre, the mouth of a chasm that stretched thirty miles to the north to form the Great Glen. The rivers, streams, and cataracts that tumbled down from the formidable reaches filled the basin of the chasm and formed a canal of lochs from Inverness in the north to Fort William in the south. The largest by far was Loch Ness, with waters deep and black and mysterious.

By Alex's reckoning they were a six-hour journey from Achnacarry — six hours filled with the most savage, yet unquestionably the most spectacular terrain they would encounter. From where he stood he could see the proud splendor of Aonach Mor rising like a shark's tooth against the clear blue sky. To the south and west were the Gray Corries, gnarled and ominous with shadow; to the north the jutting majesty of Ben Nevis, the tallest peak in Britain. Directly below was a gorge, sparkling with the swift-flowing waters of the River Spean, and beyond, the jagged crests and fertile glens that were the ancient landholdings of Lochaber. These tall, mystic tracts of mountain were the heart of the Highlands. To Alex, they were home.

Their progress so far, as Iain had predicted, had been slow and dusty over the red sandstone military roads. Travelling by coach with the two sullen women had definitely hampered them; on horseback the trio could have covered the distance in a fraction of the time. Weighing heavily on the other end of the scale, however, was the fact that they had been seen and stopped by half a dozen patrols of soldiers who, after a cursory inspection of the Ashbrooke coat of arms and a courteous introduction to Lord and Lady Grayston (Alex Cameron had assumed a new identity as easily as a chameleon changed its colours), were more concerned with warning the travellers of the dissident Jacobites in the area than verifying their identities.

"We could bring half the French army into Scotland under the petticoats of a well-turned ankle," Aluinn had remarked after one such delay. "Although I must confess, I am glad we have those ankles along. These troops are so jittery they're ready to shoot at anything that moves."

The tension and suspicion they had encountered while crossing through the Lowlands was disturbing. Hospitality — an inbred tradition to Caledonians — was given grudgingly and guardedly. The Lowlanders were content with the Hanover government. Their pastures were lush and green, stretching for miles, filled with herds of fat, waddling cattle. The cities were prosperous, the towns crowded with English merchants, and to say a word against King George was to spit in the hand of growing affluence. Clan ties had long since become lax, loyalties strained and scattered. A man could better himself on wits and ambition without the support or protection of the chiefs and lairds. Being less dependant on hereditary laws, they were less willing to commit themselves to a cause that would see that independence taken away — or worse, bring back a dependence of another, more frightening kind.

Looming above the Lowland pastures, beckoning on the

horizon like ancient, twisted hands, were the mist-ridden peaks of the Grampian Mountains. They formed a wall of hostile, glowering rock and stone that set a clear division between Highlands and Lowlands. Within their forbidding hills and valleys, their inhabitants depended upon strict codes of subservience to the clan laws for survival. Territories were divided and claimed by power of sword, disputed by centuries-old blood feuds, guarded and protected in some cases by whole private armies. There were laws — of survival and of retribution. The chief's word was absolute; the Highlander's pride in himself, his clan, was his mainstay. An insult to the humblest of tenants was answered by an armed raiding party. A man from one clan found straying on land belonging to another could be hung without benefit of trial or defense. The Highlands were steeped in bloodshed and violence; it was a land of dark gods and druids, of legends and superstition, where a man was either born to wealth and prominence or born to serve. It was home to Alexander Cameron, and as he stood on the crest of the sweeping vista that stretched out before him, his blood sang and his body throbbed with pride.

"Incredible, isn't it?" Aluinn asked softly from his side. He, too, was gazing out at the graduating shades of purple and blue and darkest-black chasms that marked the fastness of Lochaber. "All the memories come back on a single whiff of mountain heather."

Cameron smiled and patted Shadow on the rump to indicate he was free to graze on the sweet deer grass. "I've been seeing faces in my mind's eye that I haven't been able to conjure for years. Do you remember old MacIan, of Corriarrick?"

"Ruadh MacIan? Who could forget? Seven feet of muscle-packed belligerence, arms as thick as tree trunks and hair so red it hurt your eyes." He grinned suddenly. "I wonder if he ever got around to marrying Elspeth Mac-Donald? He used to turn as red as his hair when he was anywhere near her."

Cameron's eyes crinkled with a fond remembrance as they

studied the towering cliffs on either side of the glen. There were curls of hazy mist shrouding the summits, and in the foreground a solitary eagel hovered, the sunlight dancing off its wings like liquid silver as it carved a slow, watchful circle on the wind currents.

"What do you suppose we'll find when we reach Achnacarry?"

Aluinn glanced over. "According to Iain, nothing much has changed. The war tower still stands, the fruit gardens still bloom, the roses and yews are thriving. Lochiel has planted a new avenue of elms — probably at Maura's suggestion."

Alex sighed. "That wasn't exactly what I meant."

"I know what you meant. What do you want me to say? That nothing has changed? The curse of all exiles is to dream of a homecoming where everything has remained frozen in time, exactly as they remembered it. But it's been fifteen years. The house is older, the people are older. The children are grown with wives and families of their own; the burial grounds undoubtedly have a few more cairns than we'd like to see." He hesitated and crooked his head in the direction of the coach. "Ah, speaking of wives, how are you proposing to explain the presence of Lady Grayston?"

Alex followed his glance. The coach had drawn to a halt several yards away, the door was open, and the head and shoulders of Catherine Ashbrooke were emerging into the sunlight. She had avoided Alexander Cameron for the six days since their departure from Wakefield, and thus far he had been content with the arrangement. It was easier to deal with her cool hostility than it was to try his patience with forced conversation. It was easier, in fact, just to watch her, something he found himself doing far more frequently than was advisable — or so his conscience warned him. But she was a beauty, no denying. Her hair shone in the sunlight like pure gold, her skin glowed radiantly, her eyes were bright and keen and noticed every little detail of her surroundings despite her feigned indifference. It would have taken a heart exceedingly colder than his to be able to ignore her completely.

He had been pondering the question of what to do with Catherine Ashbrooke ever since they had ridden away from the inn at Wakefield.

"I suppose I could always tell them a version of the truth — that she is the sister of a friend who was willing to pose as my wife in order to ensure us a safe passage home."

Aluinn looked skeptical. "Lochiel has been anxious to see you married off for years now. Even a hint that the vows were legally exchanged, regardless of the circumstances, and he will be converting half the castle into a nursery."

"You have a better idea?"

Aluinn pursed his lips thoughtfully. "You could always live up to the image she has of you — already well deserved — and tell Donald you have brought him a fine English prize to hold for ransom."

"You're enjoying this, aren't you?" Alex said dryly.

"It has its moments."

"Then I hope you won't be too disappointed when I tell you I plan to make a brief detour south once we have crossed over the river."

Aluinn sobered instantly. "You're taking her to Fort William?"

"It should not be too difficult to arrange passage for her on a military supply ship, especially since her uncle is a high-ranking officer in the English army."

"And I suppose you think you will be able to just walk through the gates, brandish an effete accent, and walk out again?"

Alexander turned away, squinting his eyes against the sunlight.

"I thought we agreed not to take any unnecessary risks," Aluinn reminded him quietly.

"You would rather I risk my freedom by taking her all the way to Achnacarry?" The attempted levity fell short of its mark as the soft gray eyes darkened with concern.

"I would rather you had never thought of his harebrained

scheme in the first place, much less let it progress this far.''

"If it was so harebrained, why didn't you object more strenuously at the outset?''

Aluinn sighed. "Because at the time, Iain seemed just a little too eager to dig three graves. Have you told her yet?''

"No. I thought it best to keep her temper primed. God forbid she should be given any reason to start behaving civilly.''

Aluinn looked down and stubbed at a mound of dirt with his toe. "Is that the only reason? I mean, you wouldn't want to have to start behaving civilly yourself, now would you?''

"Meaning?'' Alex demanded.

Aluinn shrugged. "Just a thought, that's all. You could do a lot worse for yourself — '' He grinned slyly. "And the castle does have a lot of spare room.''

Alex glowered, but before he could voice a rejoinder, Aluinn touched a sand-coloured forelock and walked back to the coach to help Iain feed and water the horses.

On the way, he passed Catherine and Deirdre, both of whom treated him to a cold stare that made him want to glance down to see if he had trod in something unpleasant.

Catherine looked away disdainfully and carried on toward the shade of a tree. She had found the past six days to be an excruciating test of endurance. While it was true that the three fugitives had been remarkably well mannered, she could not help but feel it was only a matter of time before they exploded into snarling wild beasts. Despite her outwardly good behaviour, the promise extracted by the Scottish renegade rankled and abraded her senses at every turn. At each stop they made, each inn, each village, each lowly cowshed they passed, she yearned to scream for help at the top of her lungs. Each time they were stopped and questioned by the militia she grew faint with desperation, hoping against hope they could interpret the silent plea in her eyes. Each time she caught a glimpse of scarlet her heart raced and her blood pounded, for she knew it had to be Hamilton Garner come to rescue her.

She was thinking of Hamilton, of the pleasure she would have watching him slash Cameron's face to bloody ribbons, when she was distracted by the crunch of boots on sandstone. The Scotsman was walking toward the coach, his fluid and purposeful stride exuding power at every step. He was hatless, and the metallic black hair was gathered loosely at the nape of his neck leaving only a few errant curls to brush forward over his brow and temples. He wore a chocolate-brown jacket and buff breeches; his waistcoat was cream-coloured satin embroidered with bright sprigs of green-and-gold leaves. His shirt was snowy white linen, the lace at his throat and cuffs of a quality costing easily as much as two of her own gowns.

It was no wonder men and women alike were duped into believing he was someone he was not, she remarked inwardly. He looked as if he would be at ease in Parliament or at court. He gave the appearance of refinement and elegance, and he certainly spoke with more confidence than one would credit a Highland sheep farmer. The faint lilt in his voice was easily taken for a Continental accent, and his easy mannerisms supported the fact that he had been educated in Europe. He was obviously accustomed to expensive clothes and a luxurious life. What could possibly inspire him to trade a comfortable life as Raefer Montgomery for a damp stone cottage and sheepskin cloaks?

He certainly had not sounded like a fanatical Jacobite in the conversation she had overheard; she doubted it was politics bringing him home. Money? Were spies well paid? She did not know, but it was an easy wager that he was good at whatever he did, be it espionage or murder. Still, there was a reward on his head. Ten thousand gold crowns was the fortune of ten lifetimes to most of the Highland rabble they had encountered. Was he not afraid someone might recognize him without her assistance and alert the local constabulary?

With a start she realized the dark eyes were upon her. He was frowning slightly, as if curious to know why he was earning such a prolonged study. Catherine lowered her lashes quickly, but not soon enough to discourage him from leaving the company of his cousin and henchman to join her where she sat.

"A lovely afternoon," he commented casually, noting the instant kiss of pink that shaded her cheeks. "Perfect for a short stroll. The hill we are coming to is rather steep and the road does not appear to be in the best condition to accept a coach. Iain will take it on down ahead and we'll join him at the bottom."

"As you like," Catherine said primly and picked at the lace ruff on her handkerchief. When he did not move away immediately, she felt annoyingly obliged to look up, and her blush deepened accordingly.

While there was never anything untoward or vulgar in his behaviour to suggest he knew what she was thinking — what she was remembering — each and every time he looked at her or spoke to her or had occasion to hand her in or out of the carriage, she could tell that he remembered by the look in his eyes. She could feel them piercing straight through the silvered-blue brocade of her bodice, cleanly through her chemise and shimmy, as if he could yet see her standing naked and trembling in his arms. And try as she might, she could not forget the searing impression his hands had left on her flesh — flesh that had never known such sinfully bold caresses.

She swallowed hard and stared determinedly past him toward the road. "May I ask how far we've come this morning?"

"We have been in MacDonald territory for the past day or so."

"That does not tell me a great deal."

"I had no idea you were interested in geography."

She mimicked his gently mocking smile. "I am interested in knowing where we are. Other than being vaguely aware of crossing the border from England four days ago, I have not seen anything that could possibly be construed as a landmark since."

"Marking our trail, are you?" His grin broadened rakishly and he spread his hands. "You aren't impressed by our mountains?"

She squared her shoulders. "I have seen mountains before."

"No doubt you have seen hills," he agreed and startled her by leaning down and extending his hand. She stared at him, at his outstretched hand, and clenched her own into tight fists on her lap.

"You wanted to see a landmark, didn't you?" he inquired politely. "I am merely offering to present you a better view."

Catherine glanced over to where he and Aluinn MacKail had been standing minutes ago. It looked harmless enough — a narrow stream cutting through some trees, a knoll like a domed head rising on the one side. She stood up with a sigh and walked past him, ignoring the proffered hand.

The slope was gradual, and as she climbed it, the crust of bluish mountains that dominated the skyline seemed to move farther away, as if sliding independently from the ground she walked on. Cameron was behind her, and she could feel his eyes burning into her shoulders as she slowly mounted the top of the knoll. When she halted, he moved alongside her and this time she offered no objections to the hand he slipped under her elbow.

Loathe as she was to admit it, there had been some vistas and landscapes over the past few days that had quite taken her breath away: sweeping russet meadows, winding silver slashes of rivers and streams, the steep and craggy peaks that thrust up into the blue sky before falling black and sheer into the deep, inky waters of a loch. There was beauty even in the irridescent green of the thunderclouds that collected at night and pounded the heavens with their fury. Only yesterday they had travelled through a glen so still and peaceful it seemed to be painted on canvas. It was called Glencoe, MacKail had told her, home of the MacDonalds and the scene of one of the most treacherous massacres in Scotland's history. Beauty and ugliness, tranquility and awesome desolation; the mood of the land was as changing and enigmatic as that of the man who stood by her side.

Less than three steps in front of her the land dropped steeply away down the face of a cliff several thousand feet in height. At its base sprawled a valley, so far below them the road was reduced to nothing more than a thin ribbon rippling across the green-carpeted floor. On either side of the valley the walls of the two closest mountains were split and broken by fissures so that it looked as if a giant had piled rocks there at random. It was a bright, crisp day, yet the battlements of the glen were hazed over and gloomy, as if there were places where even the sun was denied entry.

Catherine turned her head slightly, the better to identify the muted rushing sound to the right of the knoll. A thin, whisper-sheer cascade of water tumbled over the broken verge of the cliff, spraying a transparent, rainbow-hued mist on the rocks below.

Catherine was unaware that she had moved closer to Cameron's side or that she had insinuated herself into the protective circle of his arm, but Alex was very much aware of both indiscretions. His hand rested on the curve of her waist, temptingly close to the round swell of her breast. The sunlight was playing with the breeze-blown wisps of her hair, scattering them like threads of spun silk against the dark brown of his jacket. Her violet eyes, absorbing the colour of the sky, shimmered with sparks of vibrant blue; she smelled of wildflowers, cool and clean, and the effect was intoxicating. It acted on his senses like a deep drink of sweet wine.

"It's beautiful," she whispered.

"Beautiful indeed," he agreed softly.

Something in his voice sent a shiver racing over the surface of her skin and she turned slowly to look up at him. His eyes were measuring each rounded curve of her face, each golden thread of hair, each soft rise and fall of her breasts. She felt the slide of long, tanned fingers on her cheek, and she felt herself turning into his embrace, felt her lips parting as she imagined the bold warmth of his mouth moving possessively over hers.

She blinked and took a hasty step away from him, her mind racing as swiftly as her pulse as she tried to find something to say to break the awkward silence.

"Are we anywhere near this Archberry you keep talking about?"

"Achnacarry. We should be there in a couple of hours, with any luck."

"And then will you be sending me home?"

The question irritated him and he turned away from her to gaze out over the valley. "As soon as I think it is safe, yes."

"Safe? I fail to see where I could be any further threat to you or your furtive little mission. The farmers we have seen haven't spoken enough intelligible English for me to betray you even if I tried — which I haven't."

"You have been quite well behaved," he agreed.

"I have done exactly what you have asked me to do. I have co-operated and been pleasant to the point of nausea each time we are stopped by strangers. We have come safely across the border — " She threw up her hand in exasperation. "I don't know what else you want from me, and I really do think it is vile of you to keep tormenting me this way."

"What way is that, Mistress Ashbrooke?" he asked guilelessly, although the faint, distant grin he wore shaded her cheeks darker.

"Your cousin, for one thing," she retorted. "He stares at me constantly. Glowers at me, actually, as if he would like to do me harm."

"You did cause him a few moments of anxiety back at

Wakefield, not to mention a bruise or two in the bargain. As for him staring, you are a very lovely woman. I would be more concerned if he didn't stare.''

Catherine frowned, disconcerted by the compliment. ''He talks about me. I've heard him.''

''You understand the Gaelic?'' Alex arched an eyebrow and searched out a cigar from his pocket.

''I know when a man is talking about me,'' she said sharply. ''And I can guess what he is saying. Did you know he accosted me in the stables and if not for the good stout pike Providence saw fit to provide, I might well have been . . .''

He glanced at her over the action of his hands as he lit the cigar. ''Yes?''

''. . . raped,'' she concluded lamely, remembering how close she had come to suffering the same fate at the hands of Alexander Cameron. For a longer, even more unsettling moment, she recalled that she'd had no means at hand for stopping Cameron had he wanted to proceed, and that the question of why he had stopped had been plaguing her ever since he had stormed out of the room.

''Mistress Ashbrooke?''

''Wh-what?'' She looked up into his face. His eyes had darkened with memories of his own, his grin the same as a cat's grin after it has cornered an elusive quarry.

''Your maid appears to have set out the picnic blanket. You should have something to eat before we make the walk down into the valley.''

''I'm not very hungry.''

''You hardly ate anything for breakfast.'' He hooked his hand beneath her elbow again and steered her in the direction of the large woolen blanket Deirdre had spread under the shade of an oak. ''I would as soon not have to deal with a woman fainting from hunger, thank you very much.''

''I have no intentions of fainting,'' she said firmly. ''I have never fainted before in my life, for that matter. Let me go. I am not a child to be led about by a string.''

"Believe me, I discovered the other night you were not a child, but I do wish you would stop acting like one. Now . . . sit down."

Catherine was so shocked by the blatant reference to what had happened at the inn that she sat. Deirdre came hurrying over with the last of the provisions — a wicker basket and cutlery — but at a glance from Cameron, she deposited them on the blanket and returned to the coach.

Under Catherine's sullen glare, Alex stripped off his jacket, folded it carefully, and laid it on the grass. He adjusted the wide ruff of lace at his wrists and sat down beside her.

"What do you think you are doing?" she demanded.

"Eating lunch. I suddenly find myself with quite an appetite. Will you serve, or shall I?"

Catherine debated about elaborating on precisely where he could put the greasy leg of mutton that peeped out from its brown wrapper, but instead she snapped open a linen napkin, selected the cleanest knife from the small tray, and transferred a thin slice of meat and a hard biscuit to her plate. Without a thought to Cameron or his empty plate, she broke the biscuit and began to eat.

He grinned hugely, the cigar clamped between his strong white teeth. "Why, Mistress Ashbrooke, how uncivil of you. Here I thought you were bent on condemning me for *my* bad manners."

Catherine set the biscuit aside and glared directly into the laughing black eyes. She reached into the basket, stabbed grimly at two slabs of meat, dropped a biscuit on top and slammed the plate in front of him.

"Thank you," he murmured.

Seething, she watched as he propped his cigar on the grass and tasted the mutton.

"Delicious. You should try it."

"I find it difficult to breathe, let alone enjoy the taste of food. Dare I ask what is rolled into those miserably foul things you smoke?"

"Foul? Don't ever let a Virginia colonist hear you say that." He took a long last draw on the cigar and flicked it in an arc toward the stream.

"Better?"

"It would suit me better if we could drop this ridiculous charade once and for all. You have kidnapped me, compromised me, undoubtably ruined my reputation beyond salvaging, yet you expect me to sit and join you in a civil meal. You expect me to answer all of your wretched questions the instant you ask them, yet you haven't the decency to give an honest answer to anything I have asked so far."

He lounged back on one elbow and regarded her thoughtfully. The sunlight, he noted absently, was exploding in tiny stars in her eyes.

"Very well, ask away. I will answer anything you like — providing I am accorded equal time and liberty."

Catherine tapped her fingertips on the stem of her fork, wary of a verbal trap. Who was this impudent beast? He was brash and arrogant, with no redeeming characteristics that she could see. He was a fugitive, a hunted criminal . . .

"Did you really murder someone?" she blurted. "Is there really a reward posted for your capture?"

If he was surprised or taken aback by the bluntness of the question, it did not show. "Why? Were you hoping to turn me over to the authorities and collect it?"

"There, you see?" She threw down the fork in a gesture of disgust. "You always answer a question with another question."

"Do I?" He made an effort to contain a smile. "I suppose I do. Sorry, force of habit, I guess." His eyes wandered from hers for a moment, distracted by a movement from the coach. "What was it you asked? Ah yes: Did I really murder a man? The direct answer would be yes. I killed two men, in fact, but I do not believe I *murdered* either one of them. And to be perfectly honest, there have been a great many more over the years that haven't earned half so much attention, though they could be considered a more criminal waste."

Catherine stiffened. "You make a habit of killing people? So many that you have lost count?"

Cameron frowned. "It is difficult to judge in the heat of a battle just how many of your cartridges strike home."

"Battles? You were a soldier?"

"For a while. I have been a little bit of everything for a while. My turn: How long were you engaged to your hotheaded Lieutenant Garner? I only ask because he seemed almost as surprised at the news as your father was."

Two bright splotches of crimson rose on Catherine's cheeks. "If either one of them looked surprised, it was because we had not intended to blurt the news out quite so . . ."

"Unexpectedly?"

"*Melodramatically*," she countered tartly. "And certainly not over a spectacle such as a duel."

"Are you in love with him?"

"What possible business is that of yours?"

"A question with a question, Mistress Ashbrooke?"

She grated her teeth together. "Am I in love with Lieutenant Garner? If you must know . . . yes. Desperately. And if you think he will let this incident go unavenged — "

"Desperately, you say? How does one love someone *desperately*?"

"With one's whole heart and soul," she said pointedly. "Although it does not surprise me in the least that you should not know of such things. *My* turn: If you have stayed away from your precious Archberry for the past fifteen years, why come back now?"

"It is my home. Why shouldn't I come back?"

"But why now? Why come back to Scotland in the midst of so much dissention? You don't believe the Stuart Pretender has a chance of winning back the throne; I heard you say as much."

"You seemed to have heard a great deal."

"You are not answering me. Do you or do you not believe in the Stuart cause?"

Cameron pursed his lips and started to reach for a cigar.

When he saw the look she gave him, he shrugged away the urge with a sigh. "I believe the Scots do not know the meaning of the word compromise, whereas it has become the second nature of the English. Simply put, King James is a Scot, the man to whom all of Scotland had pledged allegiance before the English decided they did not like his religion or his manners. A rather shoddy way to treat a king, wouldn't you agree? To banish him and invite his cousin and her foreign-born husband to fill the vacancy on the throne?"

"It was perfectly legal."

"After Parliament passed the Act of Succession, certainly it was legal. But suppose they put into effect a law saying that all blonde, blue-eyed vixens must remain in a convent until the age of thirty-five? It would then be legal to lock you away, but would it be morally right?"

"That is a foolish example," she retorted.

"No more foolish than dictating to a man how he must pray to his God."

"We are speaking of kings, not gods."

"Granted, but whatever happened to the divine right of kings? I'm not saying they have all been holy, but do we chop off their heads or banish them whenever one comes along who does not meet our fancy? I'm afraid I have to agree somewhat with the Jacobite standpoint insofar as an oath made to one king cannot arbitrarily be rerouted to another. The Scots have pledged allegiance to King James and it is a matter of honour that they uphold it."

"As simple as that?"

"War is never simple, nor are the reasons for it."

"Then you believe there *will* be a war?"

"If certain factions have their way, I can see trouble ahead, yes."

"Not all of Scotland is united behind the Stuarts."

"Not all of England is especially pleased with the Hanovers."

She scowled at his quick tongue. "They dislike and mistrust papists, however. You will never see England accept a Catholic king, divine right or no."

"My, what religious tolerance you have. Do Catholics have horns and forked tails?"

"If you are anything by which to judge, I should say yes."

"But I am not Catholic, nor is my family or clan."

"So you are saying you *won't* fight for a Stuart restoration?"

He sighed good-naturedly. "Religion is not the only issue here, albeit it seems to be gaining the most focus. There is the little matter of summarily declaring Scotland to be a part of a union with England, of stripping her Parliament of any real powers, of placing English mayors in her cities, and building English forts garrisoned with English soldiers to police us. They steal our land, take over our merchant trade and dictate what we may grow and sell and buy. They lure settlers away to work their colonies, only to have them slapped in irons or indentured to blue-blooded, upstanding English colonists. We're a stubborn lot, we Scots. We believe in having something to say about governing our own destinies."

"But . . . the Highlands attempted an uprising thirty years ago and it failed miserably. What makes anyone think another one can succeed now? You don't believe another uprising can succeed, and don't tell me you didn't say that, because you did. I heard you. The night at the goat cottage you said something about a world full of romantic fools chasing each other around and you wanted no part of it!"

Alex laughed outright, a deeply resonant sound that echoed in the still air and tickled the nape of Catherine's neck in a most unnerving manner. Under different circumstances, she might have enjoyed the sound and the attention it drew, but as it was she could only fidget uncomfortably as both Aluinn MacKail and Deirdre turned to stare.

"By God, you actually do have a mind behind all that powder and rouge, don't you?" he asked when his mirth had been brought under control.

"Just because I loathe and detest talking about politics does not mean I am deaf or blind to what is going on around me. And I do not use either rouge or powder."

"A refreshing change, I assure you," Alex murmured appreciatively.

"Will your family fight in a war if it comes to that?" she asked, not dissuaded by his attempt at humour.

"In all honesty, I do not know. One of my brothers, Archibald, is a physician, dedicated to saving lives, not taking them. Another, John of Fassefern, has openly declared all along that he will not declare either way. The eldest, Donald, is the clan chief, The Cameron of Lochiel. It is his decision that will affect the way a thousand clansmen behave over the next few months. So far he has advocated peace, and so long as he keeps advocating peace, the Highlands will remain quiet."

"He must carry a great deal of influence."

"Influence, good judgement, common sense," Alex nodded soberly. "A third of the Highland clans look to Lochiel for guidance. An equal number of cooler heads in England look to him for sanity. He knows a rebellion now would be ill-fated and probably disastrous to Scotland in the long run. But he's also a man of intense honour and pride. I think if his loyalties were challenged point-blank, all of the good, sane intentions in the world would not save him . . . or his enemies."

For a brief moment, Catherine was allowed to see yet another side of Alexander Cameron. This one did indeed appear to have a conscience, as well as affection, love, and concern for a family he had left behind fifteen years ago. Was that why he was returning now despite the dreadful risks? Having never experienced family ties that could be so strong and binding, Catherine could not understand how they could reach out and beckon to a man years and continents apart. Moreover, she did not want to believe that something so basic and lacking in ulterior motives could be responsible for Alexander Cameron's journey. It would make him more human and less the monster she had willed him to be, and that was a notion she was not especially comfortable with.

The sun was warm and the black hair at Alex's temples glistened with tiny beads of moisture. The sabre slash was all but healed. In a week or two there would be nothing to mark the wound but a thin white line through the tan. The linen of his shirt was almost transparent, affording a breathtaking reminder of the hard, sinuous muscles in his arms and across his chest. He possessed the deadly grace and power of a panther, and Catherine was just as wary of the danger as if she were sitting in the open wilds. He would fight. Despite his reservations and his cautions and his logical arguments, he was not a man to stand by and watch others throw themselves onto the swords of their enemies.

An image of a violent, bloody battlefield flashed before her without warning: acres of green piled with bloody corpses, the sounds of screaming and dying men, and in the midst of it all, a tall black-haired warrior laughing out a curse as a dozen scarlet-clad soldiers lashed at him with bright, gleaming swords.

The image was so real that Catherine gasped aloud and dropped the knife and fork she was holding. Cameron turned at the sound and his eyes dropped to her hand, where a dark red bead of blood was swelling on her fingertip.

"I . . . I cut myself on the blade," she stammered, reaching hastily for her napkin. The image of the battlefield faded away against the backdrop of the azure blue sky, but a haunting chill persisted, and she could not help but wonder if she had somehow glanced through a curtain and seen the past — or if it was something the future held in store.

Chapter Nine

"I'll carry those for you, if you like."

Deirdre looked up at the sound of the voice. Aluinn MacKail had come unnoticed upon her and stopped a few feet away. During the past six days she had scarcely glanced in his direction, much less acknowledged his embarrassed, apologetic smiles. Several times he had attempted to engage her in conversation, but she had always presented a cold shoulder and walked away without uttering a single word. When the coach stopped and the passengers alighted, she simply glared a warning that he should not even dream of offering her assistance, and when it was necessary for her, as a servant, to remain with the other "servants" in the "Earl of Grayston's" entourage, she gave both Iain Cameron and Aluinn MacKail the benefit of her seven years of watching and learning from Catherine Ashbrooke: She affected a demeanor as cold and remote as a mountain glacier.

For Aluinn, it was a distinctly new sensation. He possessed a certain careless charm that women found irresistible, and in the past he had never been reluctant to capitalize upon it. Catherine's first impression of MacKail as a scholar and philosopher was not entirely off the mark. He could speak four languages fluently and was not adverse to composing lines of poetry when a beautiful day or a ravishing woman inspired him. He was hardly less dangerous than Alexander Cameron — possibly more so, because of his deceptively genteel appearance. Where Alex was seen instantly as a powerful adversary and a dangerous man to toy with, Aluinn was apt to disarm an opponent with a rueful smile seconds before slashing him to pieces with his sabre. To that end, he was Alex's sparring partner, and there had been many a mock duel where the outcome had been declared a draw or an outright victory for MacKail.

Raised as foster brothers since infancy, he and Alex were not equals in the finest sense of the word: Alex was the son of the clan chief, Aluinn was the son of a tenant crofter. They had been weaned on the same breast milk, raised as playmates until it was time to share the same tutors, attend the same schools, vie for the same pretty wenches as they vaulted through adolescence. When Alex had been sent into exile, Aluinn had neither balked at nor questioned the necessity of accompanying him throughout the fifteen long years. They were bound by obligation, loyalty, and friendship. Either would have given their life for the other without hesitation.

Deirdre knew none of this, of course. She viewed them as Catherine did: a pair of criminals. Worse for Aluinn, she regarded him as a lowlife who had raised his fist and struck a woman to unconsciousness. The bruise on her cheek had faded, but the anger of the Irish gameskeeper's daughter had not.

"It is over a mile to the bottom of the hill," he explained, his lean, handsome face reddening slightly under her steady glare. "You might find your case a little heavy by the time you get down to the valley."

Deirdre clutched the portmanteau tighter in her hands. It

was never very far from her side, certainly never out of sight when any of the three brigands were nearby, since it contained everything of value that Catherine owned.

"I am quite capable of walking the distance unassisted," she replied frostily. "Now, if you will excuse me — "

She started to brush past, but his hands shot out unexpectedly and grasped her by the shoulders.

"Look, I can understand why you are angry. Believe me, I have been angry with myself ever since . . . well, ever since it happened. I didn't mean to hit you. I have never hit a woman before in my life." He smiled haltingly and added, "Not even when they've deserved it."

His attempt at levity fell flat.

"Look mistress ——" She did not help him with a name. "It's Mistress O'Shea, is it not? Deirdre? A lovely name, by the way — " Her fawn-brown eyes sparkled with flecks of ice-green contempt and he took a deep breath. "All right, you win. I'm a cad, a blackguard, a bounder, and you are absolutely right: I beat women every morning before my tea and toast. If it will make you feel any better, you can take a swing at me. Right here — " He turned his head and angled his cheek toward her. "Go ahead. Your best shot."

There was less than a moment's hesitation on Deirdre's part before she swung hard and sharp, catching his smooth-shaven cheek and jaw with the flat of her hand. The blow startled him — stunned him more likely, since he had not expected her to take him up on the invitation. Throwing charm in the face of a woman's temper had never failed him before and he found himself gaping after the slender figure as she stormed away, his vanity stinging almost as badly as his cheek.

"Makin' friends, are ye?" Iain chuckled, having witnessed the entire exchange. "Waste o' time tae sweet-talk a lass like tha'. She'd like it better ye just throw her on the ground an' jump atween her thighs. I warrant they've spread plenty o' times afore now."

Aluinn's frown darkened with anger at the young man's crudeness, but his retort was delayed abruptly by the sight of a group of riders approaching along the road.

"Alex! Company!"

Cameron was beside the coach in an instant, his eyes narrowed against the shimmer of heat on the sun-baked road.

"They have the look o' the Watch aboot them," Iain murmured, already swinging his lanky frame up into the driver's box. He passed down a long-barrelled musket, which Aluinn took, checking the charge of powder before sliding it beneath the canopy on the boot of the coach. Alex whistled shrilly for Shadow and retrieved his own brace of steel-handled pistols out of the leather saddle pouch.

"We'll have to try to talk our way through it," he said grimly, cocking each weapon and checking the priming pans. "Stay near the coach and don't make any unnecessary moves unless you see a signal from me."

Catherine had stood up when Alex had, but she was still rooted to the picnic blanket, her eyes wide with alarm as she saw him approach with the guns.

"Who are they? You haven't needed pistols before."

"We haven't come across the Argyle militia before."

"But — "

"They're part of the local Highland militia, the Black Watch, aptly named since they are comprised mostly of thieves and cutthroats, castoffs who enjoy terrorizing local farmers for a few coins here and there." He directed Deirdre toward the coach. "I want you out of sight. Keep your eyes on Aluinn, and if anything happens get on the floor of the coach and cover your head. Catherine, I'm sorry, but you will have to stay where you are. Chances are they have already spotted you — " He nodded grimly at her cheerfully emblazoned and beribboned frock. "Any sudden dash for the coach will only put them on their guard. You keep your eyes on me. When I tell you, run for those trees and for Christ's sake, keep your head down."

She was staring at him. "Argyle. Isn't that the name of the man who has offered a reward for your capture?"

"Indeed it is, and yes, our impending visitors would undoubtedly sell their first-born sons into perdition for the honour of presenting my head to the Duke. Fortunately for their misguided souls, I have no intentions of letting that happen. Not just yet, anyway. It's much too nice a day to die."

Alex put a hand on her wrist and pulled her gently down beside him on the blanket.

"Just relax. We're having a picnic, remember?"

"How do you know who they are? How do you know they are from Argyle?"

"The tartan."

Catherine peered along the sandstone road. She could barely distinguish the drab red colouring of their jackets, much less determine the *sett* of the short woolen skirts they wore, but they were soldiers and they represented the law. There were eight of them against the three renegades, odds that sent a blush of excitement into her cheeks. Cameron was so close to his destination, something had to be done and done quickly before the last of her chances rode away none the wiser about the men they had allowed to pass unmolested.

Her breath quickened and her tongue flicked across her lips to moisten them.

"I wouldn't even think about it if I were you," Cameron advised quietly, not bothering to look up as he concealed his pistols beneath the folds of his jacket. "Whatever else they might be, Watchmen are not known for their kindness or their compassion. I'm sure they would rescue you and escort you to the nearest government outpost, but not until they'd worked your flesh raw and had their fill of amusing themselves with a *Sassenach*. Furthermore, if they thought you were worth any money to them, they would keep right on amusing themselves with you until someone showed up with a ransom. But there again, the choice is yours. You can trust them, or you can trust me."

Hoofbeats, distant but steadily advancing, came toward the knoll and Catherine's gaze reverted to the road. She could see the riders much more clearly now. Their bonnets were blue, their waistcoats and jackets red with buff facings, elongated white buttonholes and buttons. Dark green-and-blue lengths of plaid were draped over burly, stooped shoulders, the colours and patterns not necessarily matched with the pleated tartan they wore belted in a kilt about their waists. Across each barrel chest was slung a crossbelt which held a basket-hilted sword. A brace of claw-butted pistols were sheathed in each man's belt and a long-snouted musket was slung across each saddle.

"Catherine — " The warmth in Cameron's voice dragged her attention away from the advancing soldiers. "If you looked any more relaxed, you would frighten away the devil himself."

"Why should I believe you?" she hissed.

He shrugged lazily. "Maybe you shouldn't. Maybe those eight men are your salvation. Heaven only knows, we have beaten you every day, tied you hand and foot every night, starved you, mistreated you in every way imaginable. Why should you trust us now?"

His sarcasm stung and she felt the tears burning behind her eyes. "How can you joke about such a thing? Aren't you worried they might recognize you?"

"It has been fifteen years," he reminded her softly.

How could anyone forget him, having once felt the power of those accursed eyes? She said nothing, however, and looked over at the coach where Deirdre stood partially shielded behind Aluinn MacKail. He had donned his coachman's frock coat, as had Iain Cameron, and both had drawn the wide-brimmed hats low over their foreheads to shadow their features.

"They look about as much like servants as I do," she remarked through her teeth.

Cameron was pensive for a moment, then a faint smile curved his lips. "I shall trust your judgement in that, but since we are a little pressed for alternatives, I guess we will just have to make sure they have something else to look at. Put your arms around my neck.''

''*What?*''

''I said'' — he repeated, curling a muscular arm around her waist and forcing her to lie beside him on the blanket — ''put your arms around my neck. I am going to kiss you, Mistress Ashbrooke, and it would be far more convincing if you appeared to be enjoying it.''

''*You'll do no such th* —— *!*'' His mouth moved swiftly down to cover hers and she felt his weight shift so that she was effectively pinned beneath him. Her skirts flew up in a splash of lace petticoats as she thrashed her legs to dislodge him, but the absolute authority of the hand that was suddenly clamped over her windpipe quickly stilled them. His lips slanted boldly over hers, his tongue thrust insolently past the barrier of her teeth and began a slow, deliberate exploration of the silky recesses of her mouth. She was forced to submit, she had no choice, yet the temper she had held so painstakingly in check over the past few days snapped like an overdrawn bowstring. He was *not* going to amuse himself again at her expense. He was *not* going to escape completely unscathed this time!

With a malicious little gasp, she parted her lips and challenged the teasing probe of his tongue. She ran her hands up and around his shoulders, deliberately raking her fingers into the thick, glossy waves of his hair. She began kissing him back, her tongue matching his thrust for thrust, her lips as bold and energetically demanding as his.

She expected him to flinch back in surprise and was not disappointed, but his retreat was effectively — and painfully — discouraged by the sharp points of her fingernails digging into his scalp. Her teeth bit down savagely, trapping the meat of his tongue between them and she could have laughed aloud at the sound of the strangled groan that came from his throat.

Her smugness was short-lived, however, for in the next instant, his hand slid down from the arch of her neck and brazenly cupped itself around the swell of her breast. While she squirmed and tried to break away, he took advantage of her struggles to snatch at and remove the sheer blue wisp of a scarf she wore tucked into her bodice. He tugged at the upper lacing of the fitted brocade busque, loosening it by several inches before Catherine's deep-throated protests sent both of his hands up to cradle either side of her neck, holding her steady so that he could concentrate his full attentions on her mouth.

A warning cough from the vicinity of the coach forced an abrupt end to the contest as Alexander turned and raised a hand to shield his eyes against the noon sun. The eight horsemen had reined to a halt nearby; two had dismounted and were walking slowly toward the blanket, their eyes fastened on the slim length of calf bared by the mussed petticoats.

"Good God!" Cameron exclaimed, feigning surprise in his best upper-crust London accent. "Where the deuce did you fellows come from?"

"We was aboot tae ask ye the same thing," the tallest and burliest of the pair said, his eyes following the line of Catherine's exposed calf up to the brocade bodice. "Isna aften we see such a fine coach on these roads."

Cameron stood and extended a hand down to assist Catherine. She was a beat slower in her recovery. Her lips were still moist and pink, her mouth tingling with shock. She could feel the eyes of the Highlanders on her and a hand fluttered to her throat, only to discover what further mischief Alexander Cameron had wrought. Without the modest protection of the blue tucking piece, the low-cut bodice of her gown demanded immediate and prolonged attention. With the satin laces loosened, the soft plump globes of flesh swelled against the brocade prison as if they might burst free on her next breath. Indeed, she feared the tightness of her stomacher could not help but force just such a disaster. The

Highlanders stared. Even the men on horseback craned forward, their mouths agape.

"I'm sorry, Sergeant," Alex said calmly, capturing Catherine's other hand and holding it pinned against the small of her back. "What were you saying about these roads? They certainly are dreadful, I must agree. Oh, excuse me, permit me to offer introductions. The name is Grayston. This fetchingly dishabille creature is my wife, Lady Grayston. We were trying to snatch a bit of a rest before we tackled this nuisance of a hillock. I say, you wouldn't happen to know of an easier way down, er . . . Sergeant — ?"

"Campbell," the man said through dry lips. "Sergeant Robert Campbell, an' this mon is Corporal Denune. I mout be askin' where ye're bound."

"Fort William," Alex supplied promptly. "M'wife's uncle is posted there and we thought we should visit with him for a week or so. We were in Glasgow, y'know, on business. Would've gone by sea, but dear Lesley gets so noxiously ill on ships of any kind, don't you, my dearest?"

The unsubtle pressure on her wrists forced a bland smile to Catherine's lips.

"Been safer, none the less," the sergeant grunted. "These glens are crawlin' wi' rebels."

"Rebels? Here? But we're less than ten miles from the Fort."

"Aye, an' scarce ten minutes' ride f'ae the borther o' bastard Cameron land. Be north o' here — " He thrust a filthy finger over his shoulder and spat messily onto the grass. "Lochaber. Warse o' the lot, them. Never ken as when they mout fall doon f'ae the trees an' thrump yer heid f'ae yer shoulders."

"Good heavens, they wouldn't provoke an attack on us, would they?"

"Might. Dung farmers, they be. Murtherin' sods wha'd steal ye blind an' take yer lives f'ae the pleasure o' it."

The sergeant's eyes were small and ferret-like, and when

they flickered over Catherine's face, she was hard-pressed to restrain a shudder of revulsion. She did not like the looks of any of the Watchmen. They were unshaven and unwashed. Their tunics were crusted with filth, their hair shiny with grease, their hands as black and calloused as the bark on a tree. She thought of Cameron's warning and a wave of gratitude coursed through her. She did not even care to contemplate the horror of feeling their hands, their coarse, pest-ridden bodies pulling and tearing at her.

"Thieves and rebels," Alex was saying, dabbing a finely worked lace handkerchief across his brow. "I dare say the conditions in this country worsen by the hour. London, my sweet, definitely beckons us home."

"Wisest thing," the sergeant agreed with a slow nod of his unkempt auburn hair. "I'm surprised they didna send ye out o' Glasgy wi' an escort. Sure they've haird the rumours an' all?"

"Rumours?"

"That there were a battle at sea, aff the coast. The Stuart pup were on board ane o' the ships an' managed tae slip awa in a storm. Rumour says he's gaun land somewheres in the Hebrides. Rumour says he's expectin' tae be met by a grand Heeland army. Faugh! Only army he'll find is o' ants. Ants an' dung farmers wha'd attack their ain mithers f'ae a handful o' coppers."

"A battle at sea, you say?" Alex had become very still. "When was this supposed to have taken place?"

"*Did* take place. Two weeks gone. Only supposin' tae be done is whither or na the daft pup survived." He guffawed loudly and poked his companion in the ribs. The corporal offered a scant smile; he was dividing his attention between the deep *V* of Catherine's bodice and the expensive-looking coach with its boot full of luggage.

"Aye, well then, we'd best be biddin' ye guid day. Mind what I said an' watch yer back. Have ye a few stout weepons tae protect yersel's wi'?"

"Weapons? Goodness . . . I think the driver might have a

fowling piece of some sort. Yes, I'm sure he does. It seems to me he tried to shoot a grouse with it the other day, but missed. I prefer the bow and arrow for hunting. Gentleman's weapon, what? Builds the upper torso.''

The sergeant smiled wanly as Cameron flexed a bicep by way of illustration. Even Catherine stared in amazement; he had transformed himself into a buffoon with such convincing ease it took a real effort to recall his redoubtable skill with a sword. A further effort was needed to keep her features composed as he uttered a squawk of dismay and began brushing furiously at a speck of dirt he had seemingly just noticed on his shirtsleeve. The sergeant and corporal exchanged a sly glance and muttered between themselves in Gaelic.

''Is there a problem, Sergeant?'' Alex inquired, his apparent fastidiousness satisfied.

''Problem?'' The Scot turned and grinned, revealing teeth that were chipped and coated in green rot. It was obvious the Englishman was a fop and a fool, and despite his impressive size, the sergeant was certain he could be disposed of easily and a far more pleasurable way found to spend the afternoon.

The Watchmen were several miles away from their main encampment. They had been on patrol for three days and three nights with nothing to show for their efforts but a few coins extorted from a local farmer. Even that pittance would have to be shared with their commanding officer — as if the bastard wasn't wealthy enough, the sergeant thought bitterly. But the Englishmans' coach was big and fancy, sure to contain loot worth burying now and returning to claim at a later date. The women were healthy enough to afford all of them several good romps, especially the yellow-haired one. Just looking at her set a fire in his groin and an itch in the palms of his hands. Furthermore, they could arrange the scene to appear as if the rebels had fallen upon the unwary travellers and left their bodies to rot on the moor.

''Nae problem, yer lairdship. We was just thinkin' the lady mout feel better if we was tae keep ye company tae the fort. Rough country frae here tae there. We wouldna want tae fret aboot ye out here on yer ain.''

Catherine was conscious of the increasingly lurid whispers being shared among the men on horseback. They were alternating their stares between herself and Deirdre, gesturing among themselves as if they were already casting lots to see who would be first in line. Moreover, some were making ready to dismount while others were sidling their animals closer to the coach and reaching down to unhamper their muskets and swords. Cameron seemed blithely unaware of the impending danger.

''That's very thoughtful of you, old sport, but we shouldn't sleep well at all tonight if we thought we were taking you away from your sworn duties.''

The sergeant smirked and his fat, stubby hand clamped around the butt of the pistol tucked in his belt. ''Still an' all, we'll stay. The men could dae wi' a wee rest . . . an' mayhap a share o' what the lassies have tae offer.''

''The lunch?'' Alex half turned to frown down at the picnic basket. ''I'm afraid there isn't much left, old man, but of course you are more than welcome to — ''

''We werena speakin' o' the victuals, ye daft bastard,'' said the sergeant with a harsh laugh as he drew his gun out of his belt. It flew out of his hand in the next instant, blown into a cartwheeling spiral by the impact of a lead ball plowing through the hairy wrist.

Catherine heard a second explosive retort as Aluinn fired his other pistol at the mounted Highlander nearest him. With both guns empty, he flung them aside and took up his sword, whirling on another Highlander before the man had even grasped the situation.

In a blur of motion Alex spun Catherine around and away from the soldiers, pushing her to the ground with such force she slid on the grass. Diving for the guns concealed beneath his frockcoat on the grass, he sprang to his feet again in the same smooth motion, his shots tearing out the side of the corporal's throat just as he was screaming the order for his men to attack.

Iain Cameron dropped to one knee and shrugged his guns free of the feed bag. Of the two shots he fired, one caught an Argyleman high in the shoulder, jerking him back in his saddle and causing him to lose his grip on his musket; the second went wild, the lead ball ricochetting off a boulder before it spat into the dry earth only inches from where Alex had snatched up the fallen corporal's musket and was taking aim at a charging Highlander.

A piercing shriek from Deirdre warned Aluinn as a broadsword came slashing in an arc toward his head. The steel missed his neck and shoulder, slicing harmlessly through a layer of braided collar, but Aluinn was hit solidly by the horse's swinging rump and was sent crashing painfully into the spoked wheel of the coach. Deirdre flung herself out of the coach as the soldier turned his horse for another attack, but before she could reach the musket MacKail had hidden in the boot of the carriage, the Highlander was arching back off the saddle, his face twisted with the agony of a fatal belly shot.

Alex lowered the smoking musket and started to reload, his hands moving swiftly and expertly through the precise motions. Before he could finish, a horseman was upon him and he swung the musket by its metal barrel, managing to sideswipe the broadsword out of the man's hand and send him swerving toward the coach. Still off balance and slightly dazed, MacKail saw the horse and rider at the same time as he saw Deirdre step clear of the boot and raise the heavy musket to fire. The recoil sent her staggering back in a choking fog of smoke. Aluinn shouted a warning, but the unharmed soldier was already leaning out over his saddle, his arm hooked, his hand clawing for the blinded girl. Aluinn launched himself after the horse and grabbed at the folds of the soldier's kilt. His weight threw the man out of the saddle and they went down hard together, a cocked pistol sandwiched between them.

Alex despatched the last of the attacking soldiers with a mercifully swift and clean stroke of his sword. He was pulling his blade free from the man's chest when the Argyle sergeant, his bloodied and broken hand cradled protectively against his chest, lunged for Cameron's unprotected back. The tip of his sword arced past the broad shoulder, nicking the tip of an earlobe and spotting the elegant satin waistcoat with blood. Alex spun and reached into the top of his leather boot, and with the flick of a wrist, sent his dirk flashing through the air to embed itself in the soft tissue above the sergeant's breastbone.

The ferret eyes widened and the hairy fingers scratched at the white-boned handle of the knife where it protruded from his severed windpipe. He stumbled back several paces before his foot tangled in the corner of the picnic blanket and he toppled sidelong onto the ground. Catherine screamed as he landed squarely on her feet and ankles, his wound spraying crimson droplets the length of her skirt. She tried to free herself, but he was too heavy. She covered her ears with her hands and screamed all the louder, but she could still hear the sickening hiss and gurgle of air escaping the hole in his throat. She squeezed her eyes tightly shut, but the sight of his bulging eyes remained as vividly imprinted as the shredded mass of bones and tissue that hung from his wrist.

In the next moment, Alex was by her side, his hands around her waist, lifting her away from the twitching body. She buried her face against his shoulder and clung to him, sobbing as he swept her up into his arms and carried her to the bank of the stream.

"You're all right," he said gently, his hand skimming her calves, her ankles, in search of any broken bones. "Catherine . . . you're all right. You're not hurt."

She gazed blankly up into Alexander Cameron's face, her eyes wet and frightened. They grew even rounder as she saw his cut ear, saw the blood smearing his shoulder. When she saw the blood spattered down the front of her own gown she emitted a tiny, airless gasp; her lashes fluttered closed and she collapsed limply in his arms.

Alex raised a hand to her cheek and smoothed back the tangled wisps of hair as he laid her gently down on the soft carpet of grass. It was all he could do. A shout and the sound of running footsteps had him pivoting around, only to see Iain rushing up behind him.

"I couldna stop him! He was out o' range afore I could reload an' fire."

Alex straightened and stared hard after the rider galloping away in the distance. He glanced at Shadow and knew the stallion could catch the escaping militiaman, but the pursuit would take time — time better spent on removing themselves from the scene. For all he knew there could be another patrol in the neighbourhood, and if they had heard the shots . . .

He looked down at Catherine's ashen complexion and the decision was made.

"He will be long gone into the trees before anyone could get to him. Aluinn — Where the hell is Aluinn?"

There were two bodies tangled together in the red dust of the road, both of them liberally smeared with blood, only one of them showing any signs of life. MacKail was struggling to push himself to his knees as Alexander and Iain ran over. His hand was clamped fiercely to a wound low on his shoulder, his face streaming sweat, his teeth clenched against the agony. Alex supported him to the coach, where he sat down heavily on the wooden step. Blood was weeping sluggishly from the torn flesh as Alex quickly ascertained that the shot had entered and exited and that both sites were relatively clean. It was Deirdre, standing silently behind them, who stepped forward and began tearing long lengths of cotton from her petticoat to fold and wad in place over the wounds.

"There's so much blood," she whispered, conscious of the smoky gray eyes that were fixed intently on her face. "He will need a doctor if it's to be stopped proper."

Alex nodded grimly. "Iain — collect up the guns and all the spare ammunition you can find; we may have need of it. Unsaddle the horses and set them free, then unload those trunks from the boot. In fact, dump everything we haven't a use for except the blankets and water."

"The coach will slow you down," Aluinn gasped. "Take

the women and the horses and get the hell out of here."

"And leave you here to play the hero? Not bloody likely, my friend. Besides, you're not the only casualty."

Deirdre looked up and her face drained rapidly to a sickly gray. "Mistress Catherine?" she breathed.

"For someone who has never fainted before in her life, she's giving a good imitation of it over by the river. She won't be able to lift her head for a few hours, much less sit on a horse."

"I must see to her," Deirdre cried and jumped to her feet.

"No," Alex ordered. "I'll see to her, you stay here with Aluinn and keep pressure on those bandages."

"Alex — " Aluinn reached up and closed his fist around Alex's arm. "Alex, wait . . . something's not right."

"What do you mean not right? With what?"

Aluinn shook his head and blinked hard to hold back the nausea. "I don't know. I don't even like to think it, much less say it, but — "

Alex's attention was absolute. "What is it?"

MacKail looked up. "For a man we have both seen shoot the eyes out of a squirrel at twenty paces . . . Iain missed two clear shots at almost point-blank range."

It took a minute for Alex to grasp Aluinn's meaning. "Everything happened so fast, maybe he wasn't — "

"It happened fast," Aluinn agreed savagely. "Too damned fast to calmly hang back and reload."

"What are you saying?" Cameron asked bluntly.

"I'm saying he squeezed off at least one more shot, and I would almost be willing to swear its the one that passed through my chest."

"He might have been trying to pick off the man you were fighting with."

"Then his timing is as rotten as his aim. I was hit a few seconds after I had already started shaking the blood off my hands."

Alex's jaw tautened. Aluinn hadn't liked the boy from the moment he had laid eyes upon him. He'd been too outspoken and cocky, but Alex had just credited it to his youth. This was a far more serious charge, one that Aluinn would not make lightly.

A rustle of black gabardine reminded both men that there was another possible witness to what had happened.

Deirdre glanced from one questioning stare to the other. "I . . . I don't know . . . it all happened so fast."

"You were standing by the boot of the coach," Aluinn insisted gently. "You must remember if the shot came from behind you or from the direction of the river."

Deirdre frowned, but a careful search of her memory through those panic-stricken moments progressed no further than a small gasp as she caught a movement past Alexander's shoulder.

The Highlander who had escaped the scene of carnage rode like the wind until he had placed the safety of the tree line between himself and the chance accuracy of a well-placed lead ball. When he was comfortably out of range and obscured by the hedge and brambles, he wheeled his horse to a stop and slid from the saddle, knowing he had a few seconds' advantage even if someone had decided to pursue him. He had been shot in the arm by the younger of the two coachmen, and as he scrabbled atop a boulder to gain a point of vantage, he tore a dirty strip of homespun from his shirt and bound the annoying flesh wound.

Less than half a mile away, the movements of the "Englishman" and his servants were plainly visible. There was no one preparing to chase him down; they seemed to be more concerned with helping one of their own wounded.

The Argyleman counted seven motionless bodies splayed on the ground. The fact that he had been the only one to survive an assault that had lasted all of two minutes raised a beaded line of sweat across his upper lip. Who were they? The big, tall bastard had given a fine performance, so had the half-naked slut with the yellow hair. They had obviously rehearsed the ambush well in advance. The sergeant had been a stupid, cruel oaf and the Argyleman felt no remorse over his demise, but he had been a good soldier and the loss of the whole patrol would take a deal of explaining to the captain back at camp. Mind, there were no witnesses. If he was clever enough and convincing enough he might find some way to report the incident in such a way as to glorify the action and possibly even earn himself a tidy promotion.

The thought dried the moisture that had begun to collect between his shoulderblades, and he was about to leave his perch on the boulder when he noticed something odd. The young coachman had stopped with his back to the others and was reloading his musket. The job accomplished, he stood quite still, his head tilted slightly to the side as if he was listening intently to the conversation taking place behind him. All of a sudden he stiffened, turned, and aimed the gun into the centre of the group.

The Argyleman hunkered back down, his expression a blend of curiosity and amazement as he watched the young man deliberately thumb the hammer into full cock.

"Ye're a wee bit too obsairvant f'ae ma likin', MacKail," Iain said matter-of-factly. "Ye've been a fly on ma neck since we fairst met."

"Would you care to explain just what the hell you think you are doing." Alex's voice was a sheet of ice. "And it better be damned good, mister."

"Fairst things fairst," Iain remarked calmly. "The dirk in yer boot top, MacKail . . . kick it over here alang wi' the ane in yer belt. Nae sudden moves, now, or ye'll have the lassie's heid in yer lap quicker than ye hoped."

As he aimed the musket at Deirdre, Alex stepped to one side, placing himself before the terrified maid.

"I take it your quarrel is with us, boy. Let the women go and we'll discuss it."

Iain grinned coldly. "I'm nae *boy*, Cameron of Loch Eil. An' if ye're thinkin' it was ma aim gone wrang earlier, I'd best tell ye the lead went exactly where I wanted it tae go . . . an inch or two shy in MacKail's case, but easily fixed."

"Why?" Alex demanded. "What do you hope to gain by killing us?"

"Oh, I dinna plan tae kill *ye*, Alexander Cameron. Deid, ye're only warth half as much tae me."

"The reward?" Aluinn hissed. "You're doing this for the money? You're turning in your own kinsman for a few miserable gold coins?"

"Ten thousan' sovereigns are no' miserable," the lad chided. "Twenty if Malcolm Campbell has the pleasure o' drawin' the blade across yer throat himsel'. As f'ae the *Camshroinaich Dubh* bein' a kinsman o' mine . . ." His grin broadened. "Unless he's the bastard scion o' a Campbell, like as I am, then we're no' kin."

"Campbell!"

"Aye. Gordon Ross Campbell o' Dundoon, at yer sair-vice. Enough like the real Iain Cameron o' Glengarron tae be mistook f'ae brithers, or so I were tald."

Alex's face remained impassive except for the tiny vein that throbbed to life in his temple. Good Christ, he must be getting old — or sloppy. He had accepted the boy at his word because he had been expecting him and because he'd carried personal letters from Donald. He had never questioned that the letters might have been intercepted; he had never considered the possibility of a double. He had just been so damned anxious to go home . . . .

"How did you know where to find me, or that I was expecting someone from my brother?"

"We knew it were only a matter o' time afore Lochiel sent f'ae the grand *Camshroinaich Dubh*. We're na wi'out our ain spies at Achnacarry, an' when young Iain left the castle, he an' his men were followed, stopped, an' taken tae Inverary. He were stubborn, o' course. He didna want tae tell his plans, nor part wi' the letters frae yer brither, but — " Gordon Ross Campbell shrugged his shoulders diffidently. "He did, by the by."

With an effort, Alex controlled a flood of rage. "You played your part well. But if your plan was to take us to Inverary why haven't you made your move before now? You've had plenty of opportunities."

"True enough. Yet I'm nae fool tae try tae take the *Camshroinaich Dubh* by masel'. I've twenty men waitin' across the Spean f'ae that very reason."

"Your kinsmen won't be too pleased with what has happened here today. Some of these men were from your own clan."

"Aye, an' greedy sods they were too. I didna fancy sharin' ought wi' the likes o' them. Besides, ye were the anes did all the killin', na me. Now — " The barrel of the musket moved fractionally. "Enough talk. Ye've as glib a tongue as an adder when it suits ye an' I've nae mind tae be caught by its sting."

"Let the women go," Alex said evenly, tensing imperceptibly. He kept his gaze levelled on Campbell, willing himself not to look past the man's shoulder. "They have no part in this; they couldn't care less what happens to me, or to you for that matter."

"Let them go? Aye, this ane, mayhap, she seems mair trouble than she's warth. But the ither? Ho ho . . . she'll gie me a *deal* o' pleasure, that ane, what wi' her bein' the *wife* o' Alexander Cameron o' Loch Eil." He paused and smacked his lips in anticipated delight. "Mayhap she'll bring anither pretty bit o' coin frae the Duke. Mayhap he'll gie her tae Malcolm Campbell lang enough tae fill her belly afore he sells her back tae Lochiel. Now, there would be a rare irony. The wife o' Alexander Cameron gi'in birth tae a bastard o' Malcolm Campbell. Christ, but I'd like tae see The Cameron's face when — "

Releasing her pent-up breath Catherine swung the stock of the musket with every last scrap of strength she could draw upon. She had recovered from her fainting spell and walked back from the river, too dazed at first to see the weapon in Campbell's hands or to realize what was taking place. She had even started to call out, thinking no one had noticed her or cared that she had been abandoned on the banks of the icy stream. The cry had frozen on her lips when she had seen the musket move and Alexander Cameron move with it to keep himself the target instead of Deirdre. She might have swooned again there and then if not for Deirdre's discreet gesture warning her to stay away, to run into the woods and save herself.

Catherine Ashbrooke had wanted to do just that. She had wanted to turn and run as far and as fast as her legs would carry her, but instead she bent over and gingerly pried a musket from the still-warm fingers of a dead Highlander. She had nearly groaned aloud when she saw that the gun had been discharged. There was no time to reload it even if she could have located powder and shot to do so. With no other option at hand, she had grasped the steel barrel in both hands and steadfastly ignored the look of horror on Deirdre's pale face as she advanced stealthily toward the coach. Of the three, only Alexander Cameron had remained cool enough to keep the young Scot distracted with talk.

Even so, Gordon Ross Campbell flinched at the last possible moment, some instinct warning him of an unseen danger. His finger jerked the trigger of the musket just as the flat of the wooden stock caught him high on the cheek and tore a strip of flesh from the corner of his eye to his ear. It was all the distraction Alex needed. He grabbed for the gun, wrenched it from Campbell's hand, and pulled the younger man into a bone-crunching reunion with his clenched fist. A second explosive punch lifted Campbell off his feet and propelled him into the side of the coach, the impact dazing him long enough for a third blow to crack off his teeth at the gumline.

In no time Campbell's face was bloodied beyond recognition, his nose flattened to a crush of cartilage and tissue. Two of his ribs were broken and caved inward; he barely had the strength or sensibility to saw his fists back and forth in a futile attempt to defend against the hammer-like assault that came from the left, the right, the left . . .

He staggered several times and fell, gagging on the tearing waves of agony, scrabbling for a few seconds' relief before he felt Cameron's hands bunch around the fabric of his coat and haul him back onto his feet. Again and again he fell, only to be scraped off the ground and used as fodder for Cameron's rage.

Catherine had thought the horror could not escalate beyond the slaughter she had witnessed only minutes ago, but seeing the cold killing fury in Alex's eyes, watching him slowly, methodically beat the life out of another human being became too much to bear. She ran forward and threw herself at his uplifted arm, placing herself between his fist and the semiconscious Campbell before he could strike.

"Stop it!" she screamed. "Stop! You're killing him!"

"Get out of my way!" Alex hissed. His breath was laboured, his face streamed sweat and spattered blood.

"I won't get out of the way, I won't let you do this! He cannot defend himself anymore! It's murder! You are murdering him! Look! Look at what you have done! Oh, please . . . isn't it enough?"

Alex curled his lips back in a snarl and would have flung her aside without another thought if not for the sudden flaring of pity he saw wash over her expression. It was not directed at Gordon Ross Campbell, for he had a suspicion she would not have batted an eye had he taken his gun and shot the bastard out of hand. The pity was for him, for what she doubtless saw as his loss of humanity, his reversion from man to animal.

"Please," Catherine begged, her fingers digging into the taut flesh of his arm. "Please, Alex, let him go. He isn't worth it."

He dropped his fist slowly, releasing his grip on Campbell's coat at the same time. The man's legs buckled and folded beneath him and he sank into merciful oblivion.

Catherine collapsed against Alex's chest. Without thinking, she wrapped her arms around him and clung tightly, too weak to cry, too relieved to care about anything other than feeling the incredible tension drain from his body.

Deirdre, having not dared to move or breathe during the entire spectacle of violence, crumpled to her knees beside Aluinn MacKail and wept silently into her hands.

"I thought I told you to run and keep your head down."

Catherine stirred reluctantly, lifting her cheek away from the warmth of Alex's shoulder to look up at his face. The terrible flush of rage had faded, his features had lost the dreadful tautness, and his eyes . . . his eyes were deeper and bluer than any ocean she could imagine. She could easily give herself to those inky depths. Painlessly. Willingly. And somehow she knew if she did, she would feel safe, protected from anything ever harming her or frightening her again.

Alex was all too receptive to the message etched on her face, aware also of the fear that had caused it. The desperate longing he sensed within her carried him back in time to another similarily desperate plea — one he had wanted with all his heart and soul to honour, but in the end had failed. The pain of that failure hardened his heart and made him ease Catherine gently to arm's length. Neither one of them realized he had been clinging to her as urgently as she had clung to him, and the shock of separation was another jolt to his composure.

"We haven't much time," he said, avoiding her gaze. "Why don't you and Deirdre go to the stream and refresh yourselves. You will feel better."

Catherine looked down at the blood that was splashed on the silvered brocade of her skirt. Against her will, her eyes trailed over to where Campbell's body lay sprawled on the ground.

"Wh-what about him . . . them?"

Alex glanced coldly over his shoulder. "Let us hope, when their own men come across the bodies, they will delay to bury them. That will buy us a little extra time."

"Is he . . . is he alive?" she asked of Campbell. He was so still she feared the worst, but after a cursory examination, Alex let the body roll facedown again and pronounced the "bastard" still breathing.

Catherine shuddered at the memory of the battered face. "He could choke on his own blood. Isn't there something we could do?"

"You could let me finish what I started," Alex said harshly. "I'm sure he would not hesitate to do the same for any one of us if the positions were reversed."

The cruelty of his words drained whatever colour was lingering in Catherine's cheeks and she turned abruptly away, fighting the sourness of the nausea rising in her throat. Deirdre jumped to her feet and led her mistress past the grizzly tableau of death, then knealt with her beside the stream as wave after wave of sickness wracked her.

"You were a little insensitive, don't you think?" Aluinn observed quietly. "Especially after everything she's been through."

"She's tougher than she thinks. She'll survive."

"What about you? Exactly how tough do you think you have to be? Annie is dead, Alex. You can't bring her back and you can't keep punishing yourself for something that happened half a lifetime ago."

Resentment darkened Alex's complexion. "What the hell has any of this to do with Annie?"

"You tell me. You're the one who keeps breathing life back into her ghost every time you start letting yourself feel human. It isn't fair, Alex. Not to her, not to you."

"I loved her, Aluinn. And because I loved her, she died."

"I doubt if Annie would have seen it that way."

"Am I supposed to forget what happened? Or forget she ever existed?"

"Of course not — "

"Or should I ignore the fact that one of the animals who killed her is still sending his toy assassins after me to make sure I know *he* is still alive and well?"

"Is that why you have come back? To finish what you started with Malcolm Campbell?"

Alex cast a sidelong glance at Gordon Ross Campbell. "The God's truth — whether you choose to believe it or not — is that I bled Malcolm Campbell out of my system long ago. He bought his passage to hell fifteen years ago; my hastening him on the way won't make the flames any hotter." He paused and examined the scraped skin of his knuckles. "Mind you, I'm not saying I wouldn't oblige the bastard if he crawled out of his rat hole long enough for me to catch a whiff of him — but as to my going out and actively hunting him . . . no. That isn't why I've come back."

Aluinn sighed. "You may catch more than a whiff if what Iain . . . I mean, Campbell, said is true — that there are twenty men waiting in ambush for us on the other side of the river. Normally I would not find the odds particularly offensive, but at the moment, as I sit here slowly bleeding to death . . ." He turned a grim eye on the bodies. "I guess this more or less cancels any detour to Fort William?"

Alex took a breath and then, cursing freely, fetched a pouch containing powder and shot from beneath the driver's seat of the coach. Collecting the muskets and pistols from the scattered bodies, he handed some to Aluinn, who retained enough mobility to carefully load and prime each weapon; the rest he threw onto the floor of the coach. Next he unfastened the leather straps that held the trunks and cases on the boot and hauled them to the ground, unloading as much unnecessary weight as was possible.

"We have to risk all of us riding the coach down into the glen," Alex said as the two girls returned from the river. Catherine eyed the discarded trunks, but said nothing. She was still so pale, there were fine blue veins visible beneath the porcelain skin. "We will take it as slowly as we dare, but I must warn you, the going will not get any easier even after we reach flat land."

"You are worried about the man who got away?" Deirdre surmised.

Alex hesitated, debating whether or not to elaborate on the full extent of the dangers they faced on both sides of the Spean River. A glance into Deirdre's expressive brown eyes warned him against it. The maid knew about Campbell's men and had obviously said nothing to Catherine; the subtle plea was for him to respect her decision.

He nodded. "There was some mention made of a main encampment nearby. If he wasn't too badly wounded, he'll be returning with reinforcements."

"Help me up into the driver's box," Aluinn grunted, setting his teeth against the pain as he tried to stand. "You'll need a second pair of hands up there to control the brake."

"Surely *dead* weight will be of no help whatever," Deirdre said calmly. She squared her shoulders and turned her steady regard on Alexander Cameron. "I am not unfamiliar with driving a team, and I think, Mr. Cameron, your strength would be put to better use holding the brake."

Alex considered his options. Once again a soft voice and a soft pair of eyes were undermining his preconceptions. "Very well, Mistress O'Shea, you leave me little choice. If you are willing to take the reins, I will see to the rest."

Deirdre glanced at Catherine, who had not moved or spoken since leaving the riverbank. "Indeed, I would be more than willing to do anything within my power to speed my mistress and myself away from this accursed country, away from you." She looked Alex directly in the eye. "You, sir, ride with death on your shoulder and it does not make for pleasant company."

Chapter Ten

The descent from the bluff was slow and hair-raising. As the coach slipped and skidded on the broken sandstone of the road, the passengers were forced to cling to the seats and brace themselves as best they could while being tossed and tilted from one side to the next. Catherine, seated inside the precariously sloped coach, had the gruesome task of trying to keep Aluinn MacKail as steady as possible. Cameron had strapped thick wads of cotton over his wounds and belted them tightly to staunch the flow of blood, but there was no help for the pain caused by the constant jostling. MacKail lapsed into a state of semiconsciousness almost immediately, adding to Catherine's anxiety. She had never had a man die in her arms, never been witness to the dreadful deterioration that she saw now as his complexion changed from being simply pale to an ominous, ashen gray. She drew upon reserves she never knew she possessed to give her the necessary courage to remain calm throughout the involuntary groans and shivers of agony that chafed her nerves raw.

The inside of the coach was stifling, the air choked with dust. She could hear Cameron's husky baritone overhead, alternately shouting encouragement to the horses, and barking orders to Deirdre. The girl was undoubtedly terrified, for the voice she used to respond was shrill and brittle, as piercing on Catherine's wits as broken glass.

When they arrived in the basin of the valley, Cameron stopped only long enough to check on MacKail's condition — he was fully unconscious by then — and to allow the weak and trembling Deirdre to relinquish the reins and join Catherine inside the coach. The maid was as pale as MacKail, yet she relieved Catherine and assumed the burden of seeing to the wounded man's comfort. Cameron whipped the horses into high speed, veering east off the main road and traversing the grassy floor of the glen.

Aluinn's worsening condition was Alex's foremost concern — his friend had lost more blood than Alex thought was possible for a body to lose and still maintain a heartbeat. Taking the High Bridge that spanned the river Spean would have seen them on Cameron land in under an hour, and he cursed Gordon Ross Campbell's cunningness in blocking off the only viable route to Lochaber. Now they would have to circle far to the east and cross the river where it met the tributaries to Loch Lochy — a ten- to twenty-mile detour over trails that were never meant for elegantly spoked carriage wheels. The condition of the coach itself was his next priority. At the bottom of the hill he had noticed a crack in the rear axle. They carried no spare parts. If the crack deepened or broke through entirely, they would be left in a fine fix indeed.

The hours wore on with Alex calling infrequent halts to rest and water the flagging horses. They appeared to be suffering as much as their human counterparts; their glossy brown coats were crusted in a salty foam, their flanks quivered, and their mouths were worried raw around the bits. Only Shadow seemed unaffected. He cantered easily behind the coach, his coal-black head held high, his tail arched in a silken fan.

"You are ruining these poor animals," Catherine murmured dispiritedly as she watched Cameron water the loudly blowing team. "They were groomed to be nothing more than ornamentation. Must you drive them so hard?"

Alex stroked each velvet snout as he let them drink sparingly from a canvas bucket. She was right, of course. He was pushing too hard. The only other logical alternative deepened the frown on his forehead as he contemplated the eerie stillness of the forest closing them in on all sides.

They had been climbing steadily for the past hour, but the trees and bracken were so dense there was no way of judging how steep the mountains were or where the trail might be taking them.

"We only have about an hour or so of daylight left. Maybe it would be best for me to take Shadow and ride on ahead to find out exactly how far it is to the river. Do you think you could manage here on your own for a while?"

"On my own?" Catherine looked up with a start. She hadn't meant for him to take her observation so seriously.

"As I said, it wouldn't be for long. An hour at the most. Just until I find the river."

"Find it? You mean you don't know where it is? You don't know where *we* are?" She clasped her hands and drew a steadying breath. "Are you trying to tell me we are lost?"

"Temporarily misplaced. It has, after all, been a long time since I was in these hills."

The indignation and contempt he expected to see flush into her features did not materialize. Instead, she seemed to take the admission calmly, almost with a touch of dry humour.

"You cannot find your way out of a forest, yet you have the nerve to call yourself a spy?"

"As I recall, the label was affixed by you, not me."

"What would you call a man who poses as someone he isn't just to gain information for the enemy?"

"You still think of me as your enemy?"

Catherine trod lightly around the question. "I certainly do not consider you a friend."

The corner of Cameron's mouth pulled into a grin. His admiration for her courage under pressure soared even higher than his previous upward adjustment following the attack.

"Come now, you must admit your situation has been rather enlivened since we met. Think of the experiences you will have to tell your grandchildren."

"Being frightened half to death every other minute of the day," she recounted wryly, "being involved in a confrontation with armed soldiers and nearly being killed — not exactly bedtime stories. A further presumption is to suggest I will even live long enough to have *children*."

Alex's grin widened. "Madam, sheer obstinacy on your part will no doubt ensure you live to a very ripe old age."

Catherine did not share his optimism. "If you have no idea where we are, pray tell me how you presume to know where to look for the river?"

He whistled for Shadow. When the stallion danced up alongside him, he swung his broad frame into the saddle. "If I am not back within the hour, you will know I presumed wrong."

"Wait! Please!"

Alex reined in sharply. She ran up beside him and stretched out an ice-cold hand. Chance had placed them in one of the few pools of sunlight that filtered through the treetops, and the rays turned her hair, half out of the steel pins and trailing carelessly over her shoulders, into a drooping halo. Her skin was also illuminated, exposing the streaks of grime and spent tears that affected him nearly as deeply as the shock of feeling her hand on his thigh.

"Wh-what should we do if someone comes by?"

Alex stared, unable to stop himself from comparing the vulnerable woman who stood before him now to the haughty, condescending socialite who had commanded him to vacate her father's property. Instead of answering her question, he leaned over and angled her mouth up to his. He kissed her deeply, thoroughly, and when he released her, the fear in her eyes had been replaced by a different kind of distress.

"I won't be long," he promised.

"On your honour?" she breathed.

The faint, distant grin returned. "On my honour."

He urged the great stallion into a quick trot and within moments had vanished around a bend in the road. Catherine remained where she was, listening for the sounds of the fading hoofbeats until they had blended with the rustle of branches high overhead.

She raised her hand and pressed her fingertips to her lips. They still felt warm. In fact, her whole body felt suddenly warm and stirred by a confused array of emotions. On the one hand, she was coming more and more to appreciate his presence in her life, to rely upon the same heady aura of masculinity that had at first repulsed her. Conversely, the more she came to know about him, the more there was to guard against. He was still dangerous and unpredictable. He seemed able to quickly rationalize the charge of spying — had he as easily dismissed in his own mind the fact that he had kidnapped her and forced her into the life-threatening situations he took for granted? That he was capable of taking another human life was no longer a question in her mind. But was he a murderer? He would certainly have beaten Gordon Ross Campbell to death without a qualm if she had not stepped between them, but wouldn't any other man in his position do the same? Betrayal, deceit, and the spectre of death at the hands of the militiamen had set everyone's blood running hot — good Lord, she might have killed Campbell herself had her aim with the musket butt been truer.

Moreover, she had felt something totally unexpected as he held her in his arms afterward. There had been no mistaking the gentleness and compassion in his embrace. The desire to comfort her had been as genuine as his need for a moment's tender respite. She had felt that need as surely as she had glimpsed the hidden pain in the depths of his eyes before he had been able to conceal it again behind those formidable defenses of his.

Catherine sighed and gave the empty road a final glance before she walked back to the coach.

"Mistress Catherine?" Deirdre poked her head out of the window, her whisper startling Catherine into an urgent awareness of her full bladder. "I'm sorry, mistress, but I fear Mr. MacKail is taking a turn for the worse. His fever is climbing by the hour and there is no more water in the bucket to bathe him. Do you suppose we might be near a stream or a brook?"

Catherine scanned the fearsome woods. There could well be an army of bearded, greasy militiamen skulking behind those bushes and she would not know it. Despite the lack of any real breeze, twigs were mysteriously snapping, birds were arguing, and branches were shaking all around them. The thought of leaving the relative safety of the trail to forage for water was as appealing as the notion of picnicking in a crypt.

She curled her lip between her teeth and bit down so hard she tasted a warm spurt of blood. How could Cameron have done this? How could he have left them alone like this — lost and unprotected? His best — and probably only — friend in the world was slowly bleeding his life away: Didn't Cameron care?

What if someone *did* stumble across them? Two English-speaking women in a fancy English coach, lost in the heart of mountains that were supposedly overrun with bloodthirsty Jacobite rebels . . .

"Sweet merciful heaven!" she muttered disparagingly. "Could he not even have checked the water supply before he deserted us?"

"Deserted us?" Deirdre poked her head further out the window, blanching when she saw the stallion and its master were missing. "Mr. Cameron has left us?"

"He as much as admitted we are hopelessly lost,"

Catherine informed her. "He *thinks* he can find the river, which he *thinks* will lead us to safety."

"Oh," Deirdre sank back onto her seat. "Well then, we must believe him, mustn't we? And in the meantime . . . I do not mind going and looking for water if you would prefer to remain here and sit with Mr. MacKail."

Catherine declined both the advice and the offer with a scowl. She would scream if she had to sit in there alone with the cloying stench of blood and sweat.

"No," she decided. "I'll go. There must be a spring nearby, I can hear it. Give me something to collect it in. Something *small*. I have no intentions of giving myself blisters for the sake of a few mouthfuls of water."

Deirdre handed out a metal flask and a tin cup, the only two objects less cumbersome than the canvas bucket. She also handed out one of the loaded Highland dags Cameron had appropriated from the dead Watchmen.

Catherine tasted more blood trickling from her lip as she stared at the pistol.

"Perhaps you'll see a pheasant, mistress," Deirdre said lightly. "I'm ever so hungry."

Catherine smiled at the attempted levity and took the gun into hands that were somehow steadier for the knowledge that she was not alone in her fears.

"I shan't be long," she said, trying to echo Deirdre's nonchalance. "If that wretched bounder returns in the meantime, tell him we should like a fire. I shall try to find some marigold or purslane for tea. Something hot would do us all a world of good."

She set off in a direct line due west from the coach and followed the slope upward, picking her way carefully through the riotous growth of saplings and around the large clumps of bramble. She stopped every few yards to look over her shoulder at the coach, reassuring herself that no mysterious hand had lifted it off the road and banished her to the horror of her fantasies; she also wanted to listen and try to identify the source of the low burble of running water.

The mountains were undoubtedly riddled with creeks and natural springs, since Cameron had not seemed overly concerned about finding water.

Higher and higher she climbed and the stillness of the woods wrapped around her like a shroud. As chilly as it was, she could feel dampness across her brow and between her breasts, and when she stopped to catch her breath, she could no longer even catch a glimpse of the coach far below her. She was about to run back and abandon her quest when a distinctly liquid *blip* sounded to her right. She tramped hastily around a copse of junipers, and there it was: a tiny crack between two boulders from which spouted a crystal-clear ribbon of water. It collected in a shallow basin carved into the hard granite before spilling over the edge and running off into the moss-covered earth.

Catherine knelt wearily beside the small pool and set the gun, flask, and cup on the grass. She cupped her hands and splashed some of the cool water on her face and throat, letting it run in welcome trickles down the front of her bodice. She pushed back the soiled and limp lace of her cuffs and washed the grime from her hands and arms. She debated peeling down her stockings and soaking her aching feet but her conscience gently reminded her of the weak and feverish man waiting below.

As she turned to retrieve the flask, her heart ground to a thudding halt in her throat. A pair of coarsely shod feet stood mere inches from where her fingertips trembled. Above the feet were thick-hewn calves clad in diamond-patterned wool stockings that ended just below the bony knee. There was a span of a hand's width before the muscular thighs were concealed beneath the folds of a tartan kilt. A voluminous garment, it was wrapped about the waist and girted in pleats, with several yards left in the end to fling up and over the shoulder. Beneath the draped tartan was a sleeveless leather jerkin which emphasized the boldly muscular arms now crossed over the massive chest. Higher still, a beard black as coal and grizzly as wire framed a face as harsh and forbidding as a chunk of rock. Surmounting the whole was a woolen bonnet incongruously tilted at a jaunty angle over a pair of the coldest, greenest eyes Catherine had ever seen.

Her hands flew to her mouth and a scream bubbled from her lips. It was a rebel! She had not been imagining the phony birdcalls or the feeling that she had been watched every step of the climb from the road!

She paused to refill her lungs and in doing so glanced past the rebel's shoulder to where five . . . six . . . seven more ghoulish spectres were melting silently out of the trees.

For the second time that day, the second time in her young life, Catherine Augustine Ashbrooke slumped over in a dead faint.

When Alex had ridden away from the coach, his mind had not been on the forest or on the possible dangers the thick wall of greenery could camouflage. Instead, his thoughts were drowning in a pair of dark violet eyes, his senses were staggering under the lingering sensation in the pit of his belly which had a direct relationship to the brand left by a soft and searching pair of lips.

It was no wonder he did not see the score of armed men crouched on either side of the tract until Shadow had passed into their midst. When he did notice a flicker of movement, it was already too late. A gleaming semicircle of muskets had blocked the road ahead of him, a second flanking action had closed off any chance for a hasty retreat. More than one thumb reacted instantly on the steel hammers of their weapons as Alex started to reach for his pistol.

"I wouldna dae that, an I were ye," a harsh voice grated from the shadows.

Alex tracked the source and saw a giant of a Highlander leaning casually against a gnarled tree trunk. The tree was full grown and wide as a barrel, but the breadth of the man's chest dwarfed it by comparison. He stood well over six feet tall, his height aggrandized by a lion's mane of straw-coloured hair and a beard flowing past his brawny shoulders. His eyes were small and sharp, missing nothing as they shrewdly assessed both man and horse.

Alex was careful to keep his hands in plain view, and after his initial reaction, made no more sudden moves. Shadow stood as still as a black marble statue, his ears pricked forward, his flesh shivering as he awaited a command.

"Ye seem tae have strayed a ways frae hame, *Sassenach*," the Highlander spat derisively. His piercing gaze absorbed the rich brown velvet frock coat, the ruffled linen shirt, the expensively worked satin waistcoat and fitted breeches. "Ye look as though ye mout have a coin or two tae spare frae the insult. Were ye no' warned against ridin' these hills alane?"

"The only warning I received was to guard my back against a rebel ambush. A particularly amateurish clan raids these hills, or so I was told. A clan by the name of Cameron."

The distinctly metallic rasp of several more hammers locking into full cock sent the Highlander's hand up in a staying gesture.

"Ye've a strang lackin' in common sense, *Sassenach*. Ye should have heeded the advice given ye."

Moving cautiously, deliberately, Alex swung a leg over the cantle of his saddle and dismounted. "I rarely heed advice I don't ask for. Certainly not from any bastard named Campbell."

The Highlander straightened from the tree. His eyes flicked along Alex's clothing again, this time alerted to the stains of dried blood.

"Who are ye, *Sassenach*? An' what quarrel have ye wi' the Campbells?"

Alex smoothed a hand along Shadow's soft muzzle to set him at ease. "If you don't know the answer to either of those questions, Struan MacSorley, you deserve to spend the rest of your miserable life hiding in the forest."

The gigantic Scot took a step forward. "Ye've a tongue like a wasp as well. The sound o' it brangs tae mind a wild, surly pup I were o' a mind tae thrash now an' then f'ae bein' too big f'ae his breeks. That were a lang time ago, though. I hear tell he's grown soft an' sweet-smellin' now, an' pretty as a wee lassie.''

Alex advanced a step. ''Not too soft to bring a sour-breathed Lochaber boar to his knees . . . and whistle a tune while doing it.''

''Mayhap I'll let him try.'' MacSorley grinned. In the next breath he had spread his arms wide and clamped them around Alex's shoulders, pulling the willing man into a fear-some bearhug. ''Alasdair! Alasdair, by the Christ it's bonnie tae see ye! Where the devil have ye been? Lochiel's half mad wi' worry. He has men scourin' every glen an' glade frae Loch Lochy tae Glencoe!''

''We met some trouble on the road near the Spean. We were planning to come straight through, but . . . it's a long story and I've left a wounded man and two women a ways back along the road.''

The bushy eyebrows crushed together and the death grip relaxed from Alex's shoulders. ''God's truth, why did ye no' say so instead o' standin' here blatherin' like a fishwife! Who's the wounded mon?''

''Aluinn MacKail. He took a shot in the chest — ''

''Colin! Fetch the ponies, then take three men an' ride on ahead. Madach — keep half the men here wi' ye, the rest'll come wi' me. An' f'ae pity's sake, shy those guns awa' afore the *Camshroinaich Dubh* takes it in his heid as an insult an' scatters the lot o' ye 'cross the road!'' He paused and peered closely at Alex. ''Two *lassies* did ye say?''

''A *very* long story,'' Alex murmured, mounting Shadow again as a shaggy-haired garron was led up to MacSorley. ''But what news from Achnacarry? Other than my brother's lack of faith in me, is everyone well? And is it true what I've heard? *Has* there been a landing in the Hebrides?''

''Aye, laddie,'' MacSorley nodded sombrely. ''Wee bonnie Tearlach has come hame, or so he says.''

Alex rode in silence, alarmed by the confirmation, afraid

to ask the burly clansman what Lochiel's reaction had been or what, if anything, he planned to do if the Prince summoned an army.

There was no time to worry, however. Around the next bend in the road they came upon the coach and only two of its three passengers.

The roughly clad Highlander bent over quickly, almost, but not quite, catching Catherine before she struck the ground.

"Christ, but — " he swore in Gaelic. "The lassie's fain'ed. I ne'er touched her, she just fain'ed."

"She is becoming quite proficient at it," Alex said, hurrying forward. He went down on one bended knee and assured the bewildered clansman not to worry.

"Catherine?" He patted her cheek gently and chafed a limp wrist. "Catherine, can you hear me? You are all right, you are among friends. Catherine . . . ?"

Her head lolled and she came swimming back to consciousness. Her eyelids slitted open but it took her a moment or two to focus, to recognize the handsome features of the man leaning over her. Her eyes widened, her lips parted, and she flung herself up and into his arms.

"Alex! Oh Alex, you came back!"

"Of course I came back," he said gently, disconcerted by the bundle of softness he suddenly found himself comforting. "Didn't I promise I would?"

"Oh, yes, but — " she stopped and gaped past his shoulder. *They* were still there. She hadn't imagined the horde of bearded, kilted rebels. "Alex! Alex, have they caught you too?"

"Caught me?" He looked puzzled a moment, then smiled. "These are Cameron men, Catherine. My brother's men. They were sent to look for us — *have* been looking for us for a couple of days now. Are you feeling stronger? Do you think you can stand up?"

Suddenly aware of the two steely arms supporting her, and

of the way her own hands were clinging to his broad shoulders, Catherine said, "Oh. Yes. Yes, I can stand . . . I think."

Keeping a protective arm around her waist, Cameron helped her to her feet. She did not object. If anything, she leaned unabashedly against him, still unsure as to what to think of his so-called friends. They hardly seemed any cleaner or less dangerous than the kilted soldiers they had met earlier.

"Are you absolutely certain they are who they say they are?" she asked in a whisper. "After all, you did think Iain was your cousin."

"Yes, you *are* feeling better." Alex scowled down at her. "If so, we had best get moving while there is still some daylight left."

"Are we near the river? Did you find it?"

"It's just over the crest of this next hill. Don't worry, we are perfectly safe now. The coach will get you to Achnacarry in a couple of hours. I am going to go on ahead with some of the men, but you will be well protected. I'll leave — "

"No!" Catherine had kept her voice low up until then, but the shock of hearing that he planned to leave her alone again brought such a shrill cry to her lips some of the clansmen reached instinctively for their pistols. "No! *No!* You are *not* going to leave me with *anyone*! I do not *know* these men, I have no reason to *trust* these men . . . furthermore, I am tired of being frightened half to death and tired of being told what to do and where to go! I am not part of the baggage, damn you, I am your *wife*!"

Such a silence descended on the forest, it seemed as if not even the trees dared to rustle an interruption. Catherine did not immediately grasp the significance of Alex's hand reaching out suddenly to squeeze an imperative warning around her arm, nor did she see the hard, riveting stares that were being turned first on Alex, then on Catherine as she continued her exhausted tirade.

"I am your *wife*," she repeated. "However it may have

happened, or for however long I am forced to endure the indignity, *I am your wife*! Not a servant, not a child . . . *your wife*!"

More stunned expressions flowered among the clansmen. Many spoke only the Gaelic, but already those who understood the *Sassenach* tongue were hissing a translation of Catherine's fiery tirade.

The muscles in Alex's jaw worked furiously, as his eyes locked on Catherine's, boring into hers with a mixture of incredulity and fury. Slowly, with an even deeper chill of foreboding than she had felt walking into the forest alone, she realized her blunder. Until that very instant she had not seriously troubled herself as to how he planned to explain her presence to his family. She had never once considered their vows as legal or binding, nor had he — of that she was equally certain. But now . . . now she had verbally consummated their union before a score of his own clansmen!

"I'm sorry," she gasped through the ice-cold fingertips that flew to cover her lips. "I didn't know what I was saying. Perhaps if I explain — "

"You have done quite enough explaining for the time being," he snarled.

"But you must do something! You cannot let them think — "

"At the moment what they think is of no consequence. What I think, however, is that you should keep your mouth shut from here on in." The anger in his voice sliced clean through whatever threads remained of her composure, and she might have given way to the sudden flood of hot tears gathering on her lashes if not for the hand that clamped painfully around her upper arm. "And you are absolutely right: I don't dare leave you alone. Struan" — he angled his head slightly and faced the rawboned Highlander — "have you an extra horse?"

MacSorley was still in shock. "Eh? Oh, aye. Aye. One o' the lads can spare — "

"I . . . I think I would prefer to remain with the coach," Catherine hurriedly interrupted, "and stay with Deirdre."

"You are coming with me, dear *wife*," Alex's voice grated ominously. "And if you insist on arguing the matter, I would be more than willing to demonstrate how a Highlander disciplines a spouse who dares to speak out of turn."

Catherine drew back, not willing to challenge the dangerous gleam in his dark eyes or to test the edge in his voice.

Alex waited, glaring at her as if he fervently wished she *would* defy him. Closer to the truth, he wished he had never laid eyes on her, never been tempted to confront her in the garden that night or to win a startled admission from those lips and eyes. One more day — one more *hour* and he would have had her safely across High Bridge and on the road to Fort William. Damn the Argylemen. Damn Gordon Ross Campbell. And damn whatever it was that kept his blood at the boiling point and his common good sense at bay whenever Catherine Ashbrooke was within arm's reach!

He turned away abruptly, striding down the hill without waiting to see if she would follow. Surrounded as she was by the glowering circle of Cameron clansmen, Catherine had little choice. She could not believe so many things had gone so desperately wrong in so short a time. The attack, the killings, the treachery . . . one violent horror after another, and now this. She stumbled blindly down the hill, convinced her life could not possibly sink to a lower ebb.

She was wrong.

Chapter Eleven

Catherine rode the remaining miles to Achnacarry in utter despondency. Since Cameron had turned his back on her on the hillside, he had not spared a glance or a reassuring word in her direction. She could feel his anger deadening the air between them, and while she was prepared to accept the blame for her ill-timed slip of the tongue, it was unfair and unreasonable of him to treat her as if she had deliberately and spitefully entrapped him.

Far from being comforted by the presence of an armed escort, she found herself growing more and more leery of what lay ahead. She had not dared to envision what Achnacarry might look like or what kind of a reception she could hope to receive. Cameron had referred to his home as a castle, but so far, most of the structures she had seen peppering the land were nothing more than cramped, rancid-smelling stone cottages. Once or twice she had glimpsed the distant silhouette of battlements against a wind-blown sky, but the sight had been bleak and forbidding and brought to mind her father's tales of thick-tongued savages who lived, fought, and died for possession of their craggy mountain lairs. Ancient stone keeps, dungeons, ramparts . . . would Achnacarry be such a place? Would its inhabitants stare at her and sneer their contempt as did these silent, belligerent outriders?

Catherine was exhausted, confused, and frightened. She had not had a decent bath or a palatable meal since leaving Derby. The soiled, stained gown she wore was the only garment she possessed; she did not even have a cloak or shawl to ward off the evening dampness. One of the clansmen had grudgingly provided her with a coarse length of wool tartan which she wore wrapped about her shoulders and head like a peasant. Her fingers stung from the unaccustomed abuse of handling the stiff leather reins without gloves. Her hair was a yellow tangle, her nose red and dripping, her eyes swollen from the tears she had shed during the horrific afternoon and evening, and her body ached in places she had never been aware of before.

The sun had long since been swallowed behind the crust of blue-black mountains and long fingers of mist were creeping out of the shadows to burden the air with a fragrant dampness. The road they were taking skirted the banks of a loch and plunged and twisted around the shoreline like a coiling reptile. When there was nothing but the palest of pale blue light left smeared across the horizon, the tract emerged from the densely wooded hillside and Achnacarry Castle was suddenly before them.

Perched on an isthmus of land between two deep, inky lochs, the buff-coloured masonry stood out against the night sky like a ghostly chimera. The walls rose sheer from the edge of a bluff, the cold stone facings presenting a monstrous and deadly fortification nestled in a setting which was a perfect gem of tranquility. The castle itself consisted of huge square war towers capped by rust-hued turrets. Long ranges of rooms, each carefully designed and fitted one upon the other in tiers, were buttressed to the walls to form the upper stories, and surmounting the whole were tall ramparts, their parapets missing every other square of stone so that the sentries might look down over the surrounding countryside.

Catherine was suitably awestruck. Achnacarry Castle could easily have absorbed four Rosewood Halls within its boundaries and afford living space for a small town should the need for such defense ever arise.

The castle was approached along a well-packed road of earth and crushed stone, which because it was bordered with twin rows of elm trees, caused it to be called the "dark mile." On the one side was an orchard, scenting the air with the smell of budding fruit trees; on the other, water and the everpresent mist. The walls of Achnacarry, towering battlements from a distance, became even more impressive the closer they came, rising in places to a height of well over a hundred feet. The entrance was marked by two bright streaks of lantern light. Sandwiched between projecting stone turrets, the enormous black oak gates opened to a width equal to that of a large carriage. The gates were recessed and protected by a portcullis — a massive grille of wood and iron which could be dropped into place from its slot in the stonework at a moment's notice. Between the port and gate, the walls were slit at intervals, wide enough for men with muskets to worry any uninvited guests. As this portion of the road was now planked, their arrival was announced by the loud clacking of horses' hoofs.

Inside the main walls there were two large courtyards. A long range of lighted windows spanned the two like a bridge, with a vaulted stone undercroft forming a covered walkway beneath. The "bridge," Catherine later discovered, housed a long gallery and joined the two main wings of the castle. Stables occupied one full length of the first courtyard, alongside the block of rooms and chambers that comprised the old guardhouses. There were also servants' quarters and one of two huge buildings that contained a kitchen and laundry.

It was here, in this outer courtyard, that many of the clansmen separated from the group of riders and left

Catherine, Alexander Cameron, and the burly Struan Mac-Sorley to walk their horses through a second narrow gateway into the inner courtyard. Catherine had noticed many lights in the windows on every level, and at the echo of their horses' hoofs, the lights were blocked by the curious heads filling the spaces.

The second courtyard was measurably smaller, with a large stone well occupying its centre. Here was the principle entrance to the main living quarters as well as the chapel, the second range of kitchens, pantry, and smokehouse. Catherine could hear the excited murmur of voices before she had fully cleared the gateway and thus was not surprised to see a dozen or so people rushing out of the lighted doorway. The men all seemed to be bigger than life — tall and broad-chested, draped in swaths of tartan in crimsons, greens, and blues. The women were shouting and hailing their arrival with unabashed joy, their cries bringing forth more men, women, and children from doors located all around the courtyard.

Catherine had read stories about the Christians being led to the lions in the days of the Roman Empire — she was beginning to understand something of what they felt. Cameron had treated her with cold silence on the ride through the mountains, but now as he dismounted and was engulfed in a sea of waving arms and hearty hand-clasps, he all but forgot her. He was smiling, his eyes bright with unabashed pleasure and for the first time since their departure from Derby, the lines of tension around his mouth and eyes seemed to melt away. Hugged by men and women alike, he was passed from one deliriously happy group to another until he found himself before the main doorway.

A tall, elegantly lean man stood there patiently waiting for the excitement to run its course. Although his features were less angular than Alexander's and his colouring fair, in startling contrast to his brother's jet-black hair — there was no mistaking the family resemblance. There was also no mistaking his rank and station. He wore plaid woolen breeches patterned in crimson and black and a frock coat of hunting green, the cuffs and collar of which were heavily embroidered in gold thread. The lace at his throat was fine Castillian and spilled over a waistcoat that would have made a king raise his eyebrow in envy. Without hearing an introduction Catherine had no doubt this was Donald Cameron, The Cameron of Lochiel, and realizing this, she experienced an involuntary shudder of relief. He did not look like a mountain savage — the type of man who would hold her prisoner or ransom her as a hostage. He looked reasonable, rational, totally civilized in the midst of a world she had begun to believe was plunged into utter madness.

Slowly the swelling crowd fell silent and turned, one by one, to witness the reunion of the two brothers.

For a long moment, neither man moved, neither expression altering from the slight, crooked smiles and shining eyes.

"So then. Ye've come hame, have ye Alexander Cameron of Loch Eil," the laird said finally. "By all that's holy, we've missed ye nigh these long years."

The two men embraced, triggering a spontaneous eruption of cheers and laughter. When the wave of noise subsided somewhat, Donald Cameron raised his voice and addressed the crowd in Gaelic, which only caused a greater outpouring of enthusiasm. Alex, meanwhile, had turned to the slender, dark-haired woman who was standing quietly by Lochiel's side.

"Maura. You are still the most beautiful woman in all of Scotland."

Lady Cameron laughed and wept openly as Alex swept her into his arms. Two gangly, awkward youths were beckoned forward and introduced to their infamous uncle, but before any further formalities could be observed, a voracious roar reduced the crowd to quivering silence again. A shorter, rounder version of Donald Cameron exploded through the doorway and smothered Alex under a hearty embrace.

"Alasdair! Alasdair, be damned if ye're na the sicht f'ae

sore eyes! Stan' tae the light an gie us a leuk. By Christ . . .
he's the image of auld Ewen! Donal', leuk here. If he isna
Ewen Cameron born again, I'll set masel' doon here an' now
an' eat ma ain liver!''

''Ye've nae call tae waste the effort, Archibald
Cameron,'' came a cackle of a voice from behind them. ''It's
well enough alang eatin' itsel'.''

The stubby physician was elbowed aside by his wife — a
short firebrand of a woman who barely reached the height of
Alex's chest but whose hug very nearly lifted him off his feet.

''A fine welcome hame,'' she chided, glaring up at him
with a scowl. ''An' ye the least desairvin' o' the lot! A glib-
glabbet, educated man an' what dae ye send hame but a
miserable wee scratchet note once or twice the year.
Ungrateful swine, that's what ye are. If it were up tae me,
I'd send ye packin' again, na never mind.''

''Jeannie,'' Alex laughed. ''You haven't changed a bit.
Still the sharpest tongue in Lochaber.''

''Sharp enough tae cut ye doon a step or two,'' she warned,
thrusting a finger up under his nose. In response to the
threat, he gathered her into his arms and twirled her so hard
and fast her velvet skirts spread in a wide bell. ''Enough!
Enough ye daft fool! Put me doon afore I'm up tae seein' ma
supper again, puir as it were the fairst time roun'. ''

Alex set her aside and turned to Archibald again. ''You
know we met with some trouble on the road?''

''Aye, so the runner told us. We're ready an' waitin' on
ye. How bad off is young Aluinn?''

''Bad enough even before we had to rattle about in a coach
for six hours. He has lost a great deal of blood — ''

''A coach?'' Archibald interrupted. ''Were ye about
tellin' the whole world ye'd come hame?''

''It seems the world knew already,'' Alex said grimly and
started to briefly recount the treachery surrounding Gordon
Ross Campbell. He was halted before too long by the rising
ground swell of whispers and gestures that centred around

the tartan-wrapped figure still seated on her horse in the middle of the courtyard.

Catherine had been quite content to remain forgotten for the time being. She was plainly petrified at the very idea of dismounting, and as reasonable, rational and *civilized* as Alexander's brother appeared to be, she could not help but remember he commanded the loyalties and swords of a thousand or so clansmen who were blatantly less refined. Some of the men who had escorted them out of the forest were now circulating amongst the crowd milling in the yard, telling their own version of what had happened in full, glorious detail. The topic that earned the most attention caused the murmurs to grow in volume, to swell in disbelief until they washed over those standing in the main entryway.

"A wife?" Archibald's heavy jowls dropped in disbelief. "Saints presairve us! Ye've come hame wi' a wife?"

Without waiting for an answer or an explanation, the doctor barrelled his way through the crowd, his Gaelic greeting as broad as the grin that beamed from his face. Catherine did not understand a word of what he was saying; she only saw the short, stubby hands reaching up to snatch her out of the saddle.

"Don't touch me!" she cried, flinching back. "Don't you dare touch me!"

The doctor's wiry chestnut eyebrows flew upward, almost touching his hairline as Archibald, along with everyone else present, heard the cultured English accent.

Alex felt an angry, defensive flush seep into his face as one by one the startled and disbelieving stares focussed on him. Aluinn's words of warning flashed through his mind a heartbeat ahead of Jeannie Cameron's less than tactful gasp of shock.

"English?" she gaped. *"Ye've brung a Sassenach wife hame tae Achnacarry?"*

Whether it was an instinctive reaction to the contempt in Jeannie's voice, or an equally instinctive resentment over the fact that they seemed to think he should have sought their approval before selecting a bride, Alex did not stop to analyze as he turned from the stairs and walked back to where Catherine sat trembling with apprehension. His eyes were colder and bleaker than she had ever seen them, and his lips were pressed into a thin, uncompromising line.

He stopped beside her horse and without a word, reached up and clasped his hands about her waist. His gaze bored into hers as he lifted her down, the warning implicit: Say nothing. Do nothing. Just go along with it for now.

Catherine was not altogether certain her legs were strong enough to support her as Alex led her back through the silent crowd. Certain that the pounding in her chest could be heard all around the courtyard, she leaned heavily on his arm. When she was presented before Lochiel, she was breathing as if she had run a very long distance.

"Catherine . . . may I present my brother Donald Cameron, The Cameron of Lochiel. Donald, my . . . wife . . . Catherine."

Catherine heard the words dimly, through a tunnel hollow with fear. She was all too aware of the eyes that were on her, and of the collective breath that was being held as everyone waited to see how the Chief of Clan Cameron would react. She was also conscious of the familial trait of keen perception as the pale blue eyes studied her intently.

A slow and kindly smile spread over Lochiel's face as he raised one of her chafed hands to his lips. "A rare privilege indeed, Catherine. Ye've nae idea how long we've waited to see our brither happily wed, but then, wi' a lassie as lovely as ye, how could he have resisted?"

Catherine felt herself shrinking into an even deeper sense of mortification. She was hardly lovely at that precise moment; her hair was tumbled every which way around her shoulders, and she was cold and shivering, dangerously close to tears. Was he mocking her? If so, he was even more cruel and unconscionable than his renegade brother.

Lady Cameron was introduced next, and she extended her

hands with such genuinely warm affection, Catherine could barely contain the sob that caught in her throat.

"You must excuse our manners, dear," Maura said in a gentle voice. "We have all been anxiously awaiting Alexander's arrival and, well, naturally we should have supected he would not be able to resist adding a flourish. This is not to say we will easily forgive him; however — " she added with a smile, brushing Catherine's cheek with a kiss, "I'm so happy he brought you home to us. Welcome to Achnacarry."

Archibald had rejoined the group and was introduced next, along with his wife. Jeannie murmured a civil greeting, stopping short of saying welcome, but unwilling to ignore the warning look in Lochiel's eye. Sons, daughters, aunts, and uncles pushed forward out of a combination of curiosity and inbred Highland hospitality, the names and faces all seeming to blur together in Catherine's eyes after a few minutes.

"That is enough for now," Lady Cameron said firmly, stepping in to rescue Catherine before the numbers became unmanageable. "The rest of the formalities will have to wait until tomorrow, when both Alex and Catherine will have had a chance to rest. Jeannie — to the kitchens with you and see if there is some broth left from supper. Archibald — you had best finish your preparations in the surgery before you start celebrating. Aluinn MacKail will not want a foggy eye and an unsteady hand attending him. Donald — ?"

"Aye, love ye're right. There'll be plenty o' time on the morrow." He took Alex's arm and steered him to the door. "Yer old rooms in the west tower have been shaken out an' made fit f'ae a king . . . although . . . ye might want somethin' mair comfortable now."

"The tower is fine," Alex said firmly. "Catherine will not mind sleeping in the midst of a little history."

Catherine was appalled by the coldness in his voice. For a man who seemed to have no difficulty at any other time in reading her thoughts, could he not see she was as uncomfortable with the situation as he was?

"Come — " Maura slipped her arm around Catherine's waist and urged her into the warmth of the castle. "These past few hours must have been a nightmare for you. A hot bath and a fresh change of clothes will make you feel much better."

"I . . . I have nothing to change into," Catherine stammered. "We were forced to abandon my trunks."

Maura smiled. "In a household the size of this one, we should have no trouble outfitting you until our seamstresses can make up the loss. We have a storeroom full of silk and brocade and patterns fresh from Paris."

"Oh . . . but I couldn't possibly impose — "

"Nonsense. You are family now. What is ours is yours."

Any further thoughts of protesting were temporarily forgotten as Catherine stepped through the carved stone arch of the doorway. It was as if she had entered another century. The huge vaulted ceiling of the great hall rose up three full stories, its length occupying the whole of the west front of the courtyard. During the day it would be flooded with light from the large and lofty windows that spanned the length of the room, especially the enormous, floor-to-ceiling bay window, which looked out over the vista of mountains and lake. The bay was a recent renovation, as evidenced by the ornate plasterwork and firwood moldings. Having once served as the main living quarters for the whole family, the rest of the room was stark and functional. Further concessions to modern times were the wall coverings — tapestries alternated with large square panels of wood which had been carved to resemble rippled sheets of linen.

At the far end of the room, opposite the entrance, was a straight flight of stone stairs that led to the principal rooms and family apartments. Moving as if in a daze, Catherine kept pace with Maura, her head turning this way and that: to stare at a vast display of swords, axes, and medieval chain mail; to interpret a story or battle emblazoned on a meticulously woven arras; to mark the gloomily lit niches built into the twelve-foot-thick walls that had once served as sleeping chambers but now held artifacts and treasures. The floor was covered in oak strips, sanded, and polished to such a high gloss it reflected the arms and armour, the coloured standards and family crests. The great hall was aptly named; Catherine had seen none other like it.

Once up the stairs, she was taken along a hallway not quite as impressive in decoration but equally rich in panelling and smaller tapestries. She passed several minor passageways and entrances to stairwells and was afforded brief glimpses through open doors into the library, the dining hall, receiving room, and day room. They were all proportionately large and well furnished, and Catherine was struck again by the incredible size and substance of Achnacarry.

When they turned into the long gallery that bridged the two outer courtyards, Catherine drew to an abrupt halt. Between the many multipaned windows were hung lifesize oil paintings and, beneath each, clusters of miniatures representing members of that particular figure's immediate family. Even taken in perspective, it was an amazingly well-documented history of the entire Cameron ancestry.

Maura raised the candle she was carrying and aimed the brighter light at the portraits Catherine had stopped to study.

"This is John Cameron, Donald and Alex's father. He lives, at present, in Italy, with the court of King James."

Catherine was mildly surprised at the pride in Maura's voice. She vaguely recalled Alex mentioning his father, a staunch Jacobite who had been attainted after the 1715 rebellion and had chosen to share the exile of his Stuart monarch rather than swear an oath of allegiance to the Hanover king.

"Donald keeps in constant touch, naturally, and the clan makes a fine distinction between Old Lochiel and Young Lochiel, but . . . he's a stubborn old Scot, our father-in-law. He says he will not come home until a Scottish king sits upon the throne. He refuses any money Donald sends and lives in Italy like a common courtier rather than the Chief of Clan

Cameron. You would like him, I think. His sons share a good many of his qualities.''

Catherine studied the proud features more closely and found them as strong and uncompromising as his sons'. His cornflower blue eyes and chestnut hair had been passed down to Donald and Archibald, his massive shoulders and trim waist to Alexander. There was a miniature of a fourth son in the cluster beneath the portrait, one who shared the fair colouring but whose features were thin and sharp, almost unpleasant.

"John Cameron, of Fassefern," Maura explained. "He should be here by tomorrow; you will meet him then. He is . . . somewhat less strident in his politics."

"A bald disgrace, ye mean," Jeannie Cameron's voice declared. She had come up behind Catherine and Maura and was in the company of another petite, white-haired woman introduced simply as Auntie Rose.

"The Camerons are a very old clan," Maura continued, unfazed by the interruption. "The very first Cameron of Loch Eil was slain by Macbeth in 1020. He fought so bravely and so well that the king honoured him as being 'the fiercest of the fierce' — a motto the clan adopted and has kept ever since."

Catherine's gaze wandered to the second full-size portrait, the one that had originally caught her attention. The intensity in the probing blue-black eyes sent a shiver along her spine and gave her a chilling sense that the depiction was alive and breathing and poised to leap down off the canvas.

"Sir Ewen Cameron," Maura explained. "Your husband's grandfather."

"Grandfather? But I thought — "

Maura lifted the candle higher. "There is an incredible resemblance, isn't there? Even as a boy Alexander was mistaken for the son rather than the grandson, a fact the old rascal never denied in the company of beautiful young women. They are the only two of many generations of

Camerons to possess the black hair and eyes — a legacy from the dark gods, or so the stories go.''

''The dark gods?''

''Druids,'' Maura smiled. ''They either charm you or curse your life at birth, watch over you with a keen eye or laugh cruelly at each mistaken step. They certainly watched over Ewen. He was brash and arrogant, brave to the point of lunacy. He was the only Highland laird who dared refuse to submit to Cromwell's rule after King Charles was defeated back in 1649. He refused to take an oath of allegiance to a 'white-collared, cattle-lifting prelate' and even sent a demand to the new Parliament for remunerations, accusing the so-called New Model Army of destroying some of his fields and carrying away valuable livestock without paying for it.''

''What did Cromwell do?'' Catherine asked, well aware of the English reformer's swift and harsh justice for all rebels.

''He paid it. He also issued strict orders to his generals to stay clear of Cameron land.''

Catherine raised her eyebrows delicately and studied the darkly handsome face again.

''They were inseparable, Ewen and Alex,'' Maura added. ''I am surprised you have not heard all about him.''

''To be honest — '' Catherine set her jaw and turned to face Lady Cameron, the need to terminate the entire farce once and for all burning at the back of her throat. ''To be honest — '' The soft brown eyes were waiting expectantly, and Catherine's resolve faltered. ''We have not known each other very long; he has not told me very much about anything. I had no idea what to expect when we arrived and, well, frankly, I had imagined all manner of — ''

''Naked, bearded mountainmen?'' Maura's laugh was directed more at herself than at Catherine. ''I spent eight years in London, attending school. I know all too well the image most Englishmen have of Scotland and her people, and in some instances, it is well deserved. We are a proud and touchy breed, especially here in the Highlands where a man will draw his sword rather than shrug aside an insult. There are blood feuds that have carried on for centuries, some so long no one remembers the original cause."

"Like the Campbells and the Camerons?"

Maura drew back and for a moment looked as if she might drop the candle. But it only wavered in her hand, dripping hot wax over her fingers, which she did not seem to notice.

"I'm sorry," Catherine said quickly. "Did I say something wrong? I only asked because it was Campbell men who attacked us on the road today and a Campbell who seems bent on seeing Alexander hanged for murder."

This time Maura blanched. Her eyes flicked past Catherine's shoulder to the other two ladies, and she indicated by a shake of her head that they were not to say anything.

"Lady Cameron, I — "

"No, no you have not said anything wrong, dear. I was just not prepared . . . but of course, if Alexander has told you nothing about the family, you could not possibly be expected to know . . . to know that I am a Campbell."

"You?" As an image of the coarse, foul-breathed sergeant they had encountered earlier in the day flashed into Catherine's mind, she found it hard to make an association between him and the delicate, genteel Lady Cameron. Nor, from what she had begun to comprehend of clan warfare and blood feuds, should any member of an opposing clan have been allowed to set foot on the other's land and survive, let alone marry — and marry the clan chief! It was also disconcerting to realize one of Maura's relatives had fixed the price on Alexander Cameron's head, or had been directly responsible for the treachery of Gordon Ross Campbell.

There was simply too much going on that Catherine did not understand, too many complexities she did not *want* to understand. Her sense of isolation, her exhaustion came reeling down upon her with a vengeance and she raised a trembling hand to her forehead.

"Ye think tha's a shock, hen?" Auntie Rose muttered.

"Anyone tald me fifteen years back oor Alasdair would hae taken himsel' anither wife, I would hae called the mon a liar an' sent him tae the devil masel'. I still canna believe it. He kissed the dirk frae wee Annie MacSorley an' I canna believe he didna keep the oath."

Maura silenced the old woman in Gaelic, ignoring courtesy for the sake of expediency, but Catherine's weary mind had already absorbed and replayed the words.

Rose had said *another* wife, meaning . . . Alexander Cameron had been married before?

Catherine stared at Maura, then the elderly aunt. Rose was flushed and muttering to herself, and it occurred to Catherine then to wonder if part of the hostility she had sensed in the courtyard was not so much because Alex had returned with an English wife as it was that he had returned with any wife at all.

Chapter Twelve

Catherine slept eighteen hours through, waking at four o'clock the next afternoon without the slightest desire to rise from the heavenly comfort of the feather mattress. She lay in the huge catafalque bed and studied her surroundings with an acerbic eye.

Her first thought was that she was still asleep, immersed in a dream where she was playing the role of a medieval princess. The walls of her bedchamber certainly gave the impression of a castle tower: made of stone blocks, divided into large squares by heavy wood beams, they were bare, devoid of even the thinnest layer of plaster to seal the cracks — of which there were many. There were no curtains, no tapestries, no rugs of any size or thickness on the stone floor to alleviate the gloomy air. The keep was part of the original breastworks of the castle, dating back God knew how many centuries, and the only source of air or light in the ten-feet-thick walls was a long thin window corbelled out from the outer face of the stonework and elaborately molded with crumbling mortar tracery. A carved window seat ran the length of the window recess but did not boast a cushion or covering to blunt the stark surface.

To the left of the window was the entrance to a narrow newel staircase, hewn out of the stone, which led to a small chamber at the top of the turret. At one time the stairwell and chamber must have been kept secret, for there were niches in the wall where a bookcase or another such heavy piece of furniture had been hinged.

Apart from the antiquated bed — at least double the size of any Catherine had ever seen and seated on a wooden platform which raised it nearly five feet off the ground — the only other furnishings in the spartan chamber were a large armoire and dresser, a pair of boxlike dressing tables, and two deep, high-backed wing chairs. There was no fireplace, no immediate source of heat other than a small portable iron brazier that Maura had sent to the room during the night.

The room next to hers, however, was the fire-room, appropriately named for the predominance of a wall-to-wall, floor-to-ceiling fireplace that supplied heat for the three rooms located in the west tower. A brass and ebony bathtub was the only permanent fixture of the fire-room, and it was there where Catherine had soaked away the aches and pains, the weariness, the disillusionment, the horror of the day's events . . . . She had then consumed an emormous meal of hot soup, freshly baked bread, sliced meat, and cheese. Sated, and lulled by the heat of her bath, she had fallen into bed and was asleep before Maura and Auntie Rose could even draw the quilt over her.

Now she stretched and wriggled her toes, groaning inwardly at the luxury of clean sheets and a soft bed. It was the first time she had felt safe or comfortable since leaving Rosewood Hall, and the mere thought of stepping down onto the musty, damp, stone floor drove her deeper under the down-filled quilts.

"These were once Sir Ewen's rooms," Maura had explained last night. "He preferred the old charm, as he liked to call it. When he died, Alexander moved his belongings in here and claimed the tower as his own. He said he could look out the window in the evenings and see the old *gaisgach liath* — the gray warrior — roaming the shores of the loch.''

Lying in bed, Catherine wrinkled her nose disdainfully. She hadn't been impressed by the sentiment or the view. She was not particularly fond of heights and the tower seemed to be perched at the very edge of the spur of land. As to the jagged, mist-shrouded peaks beyond, she had had enough of mountains and landscapes and breathtaking tableaux to last a lifetime, thank you very much.

What she did want, and what she would probably not be able to get enough of over the next few days, was another bath. She had no idea how long she would be kept prisoner in this castle keep, or if the return journey to Derby would be as primitive or as miserable as the journey here, but she intended to make use of every opportunity for comfort while she had it. She could still feel a crawling sensation where the blood of their attackers had splashed on her skin, and worse still were the suggestions that her scalp was not entirely free of visitors.

A sudden spate of vigorous scratching sent her hopping out of the bed. She was wearing a loose cambric nightdress laced modestly high at her throat and fitted snugly to her wrists with a profusion of satin ribbons. She dragged at the heavy velvet robe that had been left for her use and was just tucking her feet into a pair of dainty silk slippers when she heard the bedroom door rasp open.

Standing in the entryway was a young woman Catherine had never seen before and certainly would have remembered if they had been introduced. Tall and slim, the visitor had the striking complexion of someone accustomed to sun and wind and fresh country air. Her long hair was lush with natural waves — titian red the colour was called — and streaked with bands of sun-bleached gold. Her eyes were large and almond-shaped, of no distinct colour but rather a shifting blend of green and gold and brown. She stood with her hands on her hips, a stance which had obviously been adapted to best display the astonishing fullness of her breasts.

"So. It's true then," the girl mused in broad Scots. "Alasdair has come hame wi' a bride."

Catherine made no immediate response as the girl came slowly into the room — undulated was a more apt description of the way her hips swayed side to side beneath the butternut wool skirt. She smiled, her eyes sparkling as she scanned the shapeless folds of cambric and velvet Catherine wore.

"Just a wee snip o' a thing, are ye na? Must be the English weather grows them small. Ma name is Lauren, tae save ye askin'. Lauren Cameron, cousin tae yer husban' Alasdair. I ken that makes me cousin tae ye as well . . . by marriage."

"How do you do," Catherine murmured uncertainly.

"I dae quite well, thank ye," the girl responded grinning. "Those are ma claythes ye're wearin': ma nightdress, ma robe, ma slippers. Maura asked me tae lend ye what ye needed till ye could replace what ye lost. I come by tae see if they fit."

"Thank you, they fit quite well. I appreciate your generosity."

"Mmm." The girl approached the foot of the bed and seemed amused to see only one side of the bedding rumpled. "Ye spent yer fairst night at Achnacarry *alane*?"

Catherine lowered her lashes. "I imagine Alex had a great deal to discuss with his brothers."

Lauren nodded. "Aye, so they did. I ken he kept company wi' Lochiel till well past midnight an' then later, when the coach arrived, he stayed wi' Archie an' helped sew up the holes in Aluinn MacKail's chest. Still an' all, ye'd think he would hae found the time f'ae a *visit*. The ghost of auld Sir Ewen could hae come an' snatched ye awa' durin' the night."

"Mr. MacKail . . . he is still alive?"

"O' course he's alive. He's a Cameron, is he na? A bit under the hedge, so tae speak, but still a Cameron. He an' I mout hae wed had he stayed in Scotland. Or mayhap Alasdair an' I. Camerons usually wed their ain kind."

Absorbing the snub, Catherine felt her cheeks grow warm as the catlike eyes watched and waited for a comment. When none was forthcoming, Lauren strolled along the foot of the bed, dragging her hand lazily over the quilt.

"Talk last night was all about ye an' Alasdair. Narry a one thought the *Camshroinaich Dubh* would marry again . . ." The hooded eyes narrowed. "Ye did know he was married afore?"

If I didn't, you certainly would have corrected the oversight, Catherine thought with growing irritation before replying, "Yes, I knew. To a local girl."

"Mind, they were only handfasted, but they acted like man an' wife all the same."

"Handfasted?"

"Aye. He spoke his vows wi' Annie MacSorley in secret, wi' only the stars above them an' the heather aneath them as witness. They would hae gone tae an altar the next spring, but . . . well, Annie died then, did she na?"

Fighting to keep her voice cool, her questions casual, Catherine picked up a brush and began running it through the tangled mass of her hair.

"MacSorley? Wasn't that the name of the tall blond man who rode in with us last night?"

"Aye, Struan MacSorley. Annie's brither." The feathery brows lifted delicately. "Now there's a mon would never leave his wife's bed empty. Big as a bull, accordin' tae Mary MacFarlane, an' as like tae ride his women all the blessed night long."

The brush came to an abrupt and startled standstill.

"I doubt he'd take tae a *Sassenach*, though. I doubt any but Alasdair would dae such a thing. Then again, he always was the one tae go against what was expected. It's the Auld One's bluid, ye see. There's a dark rumour says one o' Sir Ewen's wives had English bluid.''

Catherine laid the brush aside, careful not to let her expression betray her inner rage. Was this an example of Highland warmth and hospitality, or just *Cameron* sociability? The girl was insulting and crude, apparently bent on testing the newcomer's mettle.

Drawing on a dozen generations of aristocratic bloodlines, Catherine's smile signalled a frosty end to the conversation. ''I truly have enjoyed your quaint anecdotes, Mistress Cameron, but I mustn't keep you from your chores. Since you seem so interested in my bed, may I assume you have come to change the linens?''

Lauren's eyes sparkled green. The bitch! A laundress does she think me? Come to change the linens? Aye, mayhap what's *in* the linens if she isn't careful.

''In truth, I thought yer ain lass would hae done it by now . . . ach, but I forgot, she's awa' visitin' someone else's bed, is she no?''

''Someone else?'' Catherine demanded archly.

''Aye. She's been fawnin' over Aluinn MacKail like a lamb bleatin' over its mam's teat.''

Catherine's patience slipped another notch. ''Well I need her here. Where is Mr. MacKail's room?''

''North court,'' Lauren said, turning and strolling to the door. ''Ye'll never find it, but. I'm walkin' that way, I can tell her ye're in need, if ye like.''

''Thank you,'' Catherine said stiffly. ''You're too kind.''

Lauren paused at the door and glanced back over her shoulder, her eyes travelling from Catherine to the tousled bedding.

''Mayhap I'll come back f'ae the linens . . . when they've had some use.''

Lauren scowled thoughtfully as she descended the spiralling

stone staircase from the tower rooms. Well, if nothing else she had satisfied her curiosity as to what the Englishwoman looked like up close. She did not consider the white skin and pale hair particularly beautiful, nor did there seem to be much to the bitch's figure beneath the velvet robe. Men liked their women full-breasted and wild as field heather, not thin and vapid and blushing at every other turn of phrase. What on earth had Alasdair seen in her? Was it true he had gone soft living on the Continent?

He certainly hadn't looked soft. Lauren had arrived in the courtyard too late to see anything of the wife and only the disappearing shoulders of Alasdair Cameron as his brother led him into the great hall. Even in silhouette, however, those shoulders could never be called soft. He looked hard and conditioned, his muscles honed to perfection.

Curiosity had spurred her to follow them into the library. Abandoned by the other women, the mens' conversation over their whisky had been mainly business and politics. Lochiel had been anxious to hear from Alasdair about the conditions in England and Europe, the preparations — if any — for war. In turn, he answered Alasdair's questions about Prince Charles, confirming his arrival on the west coast of Scotland July 25, in the tiny inlet of Loch nan Uamn. Word had reached Achnacarry that a Cameron had been on board, acting as pilot to navigate the craft through the myriad islands, and Lochiel had felt sure it must be Alasdair. But no, the identity of the clansman — a distant cousin, Duncan Cameron — established him to be one of their father's loyal retainers. Knowing Alex was somewhere en route, Lochiel had used his concern about his brother as an excuse to politely refuse the Prince's request for an audience. Yet another summons had arrived that afternoon and again Lochiel had declined to answer, all too aware that if he did appear at Arisaig, it would seem he supported the idea of rebellion.

Already aware of Lochiel's problems and bored by politics, Lauren had listened to the voices without really hearing the words. Alasdair's voice, deep and mellow, had flowed down her spine like warm syrup and pooled in her loins so that the slightest movement had caused the pleasure to ripple through her body.

He had neatly avoided any mention of his wife — almost as if she hadn't existed until a few days before. But when talk turned to the events of the day and he described the encounter with the patrol, including the near success of Gordon Ross Campbell's plot to ambush them and take them to Inverary, Alasdair had given full credit to the *Sassenach* for saving the day.

However, now that Lauren had met the lass in person, she could plainly see the lie for what it was. Such a simpering, weak-kneed lily-mouse would hardly be capable of lifting a musket, much less swinging it with enough force to crack a man's head. No doubt Alasdair had been trying to protect his own honour by lending some of his to her. Heaven only knew why he should bother. Men took wives for all manner of reasons: money, prestige, power. Since Alasdair had been masquerading as an English peer for many years, it was only natural he should acquire the necessary camouflage, including a pale-skinned wife. But God's teeth! He was still a Cameron and his blood ran hot; the purple-eyed bitch could not possibly be adequate for his needs. Like as not she squealed and clamped her knees together in sheer fright if he dared to suggest more than a chaste peck on the cheek.

A man with those kinds of needs was exactly the type of man Lauren had been thriving upon ever since her breasts had grown large enough to attract more than a passing interest. The existence of Alasdair's wife would be merely an annoyance, and besides, it would give Lauren the greatest pleasure to see the *Sassenach* burn with humiliation.

Laughing at the image she had produced in her mind, Lauren moved out of the stairwell and started through the long gallery, so preoccupied with her thoughts that she ran headlong into a clansman crossing from the other side.

"Whoa there, lassie, where's the hurry? Have ye a bee up yer kirtle tae put ye in such a rush?"

Lauren smiled and smoothed her skirts as she gazed up at the coarsely handsome features of the captain of Lochiel's personal guard.

"Why Struan MacSorley. Damme if ye werena in ma mind not five minutes gone by."

"Only yer mind?" His grin broadened and his gaze dipped appreciatively to the cleft in her voluptuous breasts. "Can ye na think o' ither places ye'd rather have me?"

Lauren's breath quickened deliciously. She had been exchanging taunts and flirting with the yellow-maned giant ever since she had first heard the rumours of Alasdair Cameron's homecoming. Up until then — but for the exception of listening to Mary MacFarlane's whispered confidences about him — she had all but ignored his presence in the castle. He was, after all, only a bodyguard.

"I can think o' at least one ither place," she murmured, stepping up to the Highlander and pillowing her breasts against his broad chest. Her hand danced lightly over his kilted thigh and she felt the immediate response stirring lustily against her belly. "O' course, it depends on what ye're offerin' . . . an' who ye're offerin' tae share it wi'. I wouldna want tae be the cause o' breakin' wee Mary's heart. Ye are spoken f'ae are ye na?"

"I speak f'ae masel'," he said thickly. "I've nae claim on Mary an she's nae claim on me."

"What o' the bairn ye've put in her belly?"

"It were put there lang afore I ever spread ma kilt aneath her." MacSorley's big hands went around Lauren's waist to cup her buttocks and pull her closer. "But if ye're envious o' her condition, I'd be only too happy tae oblige."

"Envious o' a hedge-born brat? Thank ye, but no, I've better things planned f'ae ma future."

MacSorley took a last, lingering look down the front of her bodice before he released her. She was the devil in a skirt come to tempt him, and if not for the fact she was Lochiel's niece, he would have flung her over his shoulder and ended her games long ago. Then again, he had heard the stories about her, and if they were true, it was only a matter of time before she came tapping at his door.

He straightened and grinned disarmingly. "If ye grow weary o' the celebrations tonight, ye ken which door is mine?"

"Aye. The one wi' the path worn tae the bed?"

"Makes it easier tae find in the dark," he agreed blithely. "Just dinna go knockin' if ye find the latch bolted . . . unless ye fancy a pairty o' three."

"I never share," she purred seductively. "An' I've never met the mon who'd want tae share once I've taken him in hand."

With a parting flash of her amber eyes, Lauren brushed past him and continued along the gallery. She could feel him watching her all the way to the far end, and the knowledge of the condition she had left him in fixed a smile firmly on her face. It fixed a decision firm in her mind as well: She would have a man between her thighs before the day was through, but he would have jet-black hair and dark eyes . . .

"Sweet merciful heavens, where have you been?" Catherine demanded. "And how dare you leave me to fend for myself while you chase after that . . . that *criminal*!"

"I'm sorry, mistress," Deirdre said contritely. "But he is so dreadfully weak and . . . and I cannot help feeling responsible for him somehow."

"Responsible? What utter nonsense." In a bristling temper, Catherine paced to the window and back to the bed again. She glared at Deirdre, but the poor girl looked so worn and weary herself that the anger turned swiftly to concern. "You haven't slept a wink all night, have you?"

The dark brown eyes remained downcast. "I . . . think I did, mistress. Here and there."

Catherine chewed on her lip. "Well? How is he?"

"The doctor had to cauterize the wound to stop it bleeding. He hasn't wakened but once, in the middle of it all when it would have been far better for him to have remained unconscious. It took both Mr. Cameron and myself to hold him still so the doctor could work. I hope to never have to see a sight like that again, mistress. Never."

"Will he live?"

Deirdre raised her head and stared ahead with haunted eyes. "I don't know, mistress. The doctor said he is young enough and strong enough to see it through, but . . . he lost so much blood."

Catherine shuddered involuntarily and took Deirdre's hands into her own. "He'll survive, don't you worry about it. I have come to the conclusion these Highland louts are too mean to die; they will all live forever, if only to see us perish from frustration first."

Deirdre smiled faintly and, fearing she might burst into tears if the topic were not changed, she pointed to the scuffed portmanteau she had deposited by the door. "I managed to save some things from your baggage before it was taken off the coach. Your combs, brushes, bath salts . . ."

"Bath salts! Oh, Deirdre, you are a marvel. I swear the soap I used last night is the same vile concoction they would use to scrub pots. I should die for a *real* bath with *real* soap and *real* perfumes. I doubt I shall ever get the smell of blood and dirt off my skin — *not* that anyone cares, of course. Once again it seems we have been shoved into a corner and forgotten."

"I saw Mr. Cameron this morning," Deirdre said as Catherine began to rummage through the portmanteau. "He said he came by your room to speak with you, but you were still asleep."

"He was here?" Catherine straightened. "In this room?"

"He asked — and very nicely too, I must say — if we had everything we needed."

"He did, did he? A guilty conscience, no doubt. If not for

Lady Cameron I shouldn't doubt he would have left me sitting out in the courtyard all night long." She bent over the portmanteau again, muttering to herself, "I dare say if I had wild red hair and a thick Scottish brogue he would have been more attentive."

"He also asked me to inform you that the family will be dining at eight o'clock. I gather they have planned some sort of a celebration — "

"Celebration! What, pray tell, do I have to celebrate?"

Deirdre clasped her hands together nervously. "He said . . . he expects you to be dressed and ready to accompany him."

"*Dressed?* In what? He threw all of my clothes away and I will be damned if I will wear someone else's castoffs! I should sooner go as I am."

"An original idea," a husky baritone said from the doorway. "Although it might play havoc on the guests' digestion."

Catherine whirled around and scrambled to draw the edges of the red velvet robe closer about her. Alexander Cameron was leaning casually against the doorjamb, one of his infernal little cigars clamped between his teeth.

"Have you never heard of knocking on a lady's door before you enter?"

"Is there a lady present? Ah yes . . . Mistress O'Shea. Forgive me, I did not see you there."

Catherine seethed inwardly. "Deirdre . . . remind me to lock and bolt the door in the future."

"I have never cared much for locks," Cameron remarked conversationally. "Most of the time, in fact, when I run across one I am driven to kick it down just to see what it is I am not supposed to see."

"What do you want?" she demanded. "Why have you disturbed us?"

"Do I disturb you?" His grin broadened and he pushed away from the jamb. He walked into the room and cast a lazy eye at the bed. "You slept well, I trust? You certainly looked cozy enough — like a kitten all curled up around the pillows.''

He drew close enough for Catherine to smell the same harsh aroma on his breath that had nearly unseated her from the horse last night.

"You have been drinking," she said and wrinkled her nose in distaste.

"I have indeed, madam. Everyone from the smithy to the lowliest gillie has offered to share a toast to my new bride and wish me lifelong bliss and prosperity."

"Added to my hopes that you endure everlasting hellfire, you should have an interesting future, sir."

"Ahh, the sweet sentiments of marital euphoria. It is no wonder I have avoided the ensnarement for so long." He tossed a wry, whimsical smile in Deirdre's direction, earning a blush and a curbed giggle in response. A scathing glance from Catherine drew a hastily murmured apology and a quick retreat from the room. When she was gone, the hot violet gaze was concentrated on Cameron.

"*What* do you *want*?"

"What I want," he mused, casting a delinquent eye downward to rest on the tender swell of her breasts, "and what I can hope for are obviously two very different things . . . unless of course you feel inclined to join me in a few hours of relaxation before we prepare for our performance tonight?"

"What performance?" she asked warily.

"Why, that of the loving husband and wife, of course. The entire family is priming for the unholy inquisition; they have been sharpening their teeth all morning on vestal virgins. I trust you will be equal to the task?"

Catherine narrowed her eyes slowly. "You are more than drunk, sir, you are delirious if you think I have any intentions of continuing in this farcical charade. I do not intend to join you in any performance tonight — or any other night, for that matter. I shall remain in my room behind locked doors until such time as you see fit to honour your end of our agreement."

"Agreement, madam?"

"You promised to send me home if I co-operated."

"Ahh . . . *that* agreement. Yes, well, I shall certainly see what I can do."

"What do you mean, see what you can do?"

He stared thoughtfully at the glowing tip of his cigar and shrugged. "These things take time, you know. It could take weeks — "

"*Weeks!*"

"Months, even."

Catherine's jaw dropped. "But you promised! You gave Damien your word of honour!"

"I seem to recall some promises you made and then conveniently elected not to keep."

"Once," she gasped. "I tried to run away once! It was no more and no less than what you would have done had you been in my position. Since then, I have done everything you asked — *more* than what you have asked, or have you *conveniently* forgotten about Gordon Ross Campbell?"

"I haven't forgotten," he said lightly. "Self-preservation is a strong instinct in all of us; I'm sure you were glad to discover you could call upon it when it was needed."

Catherine backed up a step, turned away, then spun around again, the fury blazing from her eyes like darts of fire.

"Haven't you a single shred of common decency in your entire body? How can you expect me to attend something as . . . as frivolous and . . . and ludicrous as a dinner party after everything I have been through!"

"I have been through exactly the same things, madam, minus the luxury of a bath and twenty-four hours' sleep. And the longer you stand here arguing with me, the less likely it appears I shall get to indulge in either."

Catherine set her teeth on edge. "You can sleep until next year for all I care. I have no intentions of accompanying you anywhere. Not to dinner, not to breakfast . . . not *anywhere*!"

"You were the one who announced before God and man

that you were my wife," he reminded her evenly. "You were also the one who insisted on being treated accordingly — for however long we are forced to endure the indignity."

Catherine's cheeks coloured hotly at the bandying of her own words. "That was yesterday. Today I . . . I have a terrible headache."

"I am sure it will feel better when you have a solid meal."

"I am not hungry. I do not feel well enough to eat."

He arched a brow. "If you are ill, then it is my husbandly duty to remain here and offer you what comfort I can."

"I plan to go directly to bed."

His grin turned wolfish. "I have no objections to comforting you there."

Catherine clutched the edges of her robe tighter. "You are bovine and disgusting."

"And you, madam, are coming to dinner with me if I have to strip you and dress you myself . . . and we both know the consequences if you call my bluff."

"Get out," she hissed. "Get out of my room, get out of my sight at once or I swear I shall scream the roof down."

"Scream away. The walls are ten feet thick, the floors six. I doubt if any but the ghosts will hear you."

"If you force me to go down to supper with you, I will tell anyone who will listen how you kidnapped me and held me hostage, how you hid behind my skirts so that you and your fellow criminals could sneak back into the country like the true cowards you are."

He folded his arms across his chest and glowered down at her. "Is this before or after I tell them you are an English spy who duped me into marriage so you could come north and send detailed information back to your lieutenant of dragoons?"

"What?" The blood drained from her face, leaving it ashen. "No one will believe that, not for one moment."

"No?"

"They won't believe it because it isn't true!" she cried.

"Which part? That you tricked me into marrying you?"

"I did not trick you."

"But you were playing games that night in Derby, using me to make your lieutenant jealous, knowing full well there was a good possibility of him calling me out in a duel to assuage his wounded vanity."

"I didn't know — "

"Or perhaps you would care to deny that you tried, at every inn and posting house we stopped at, to leave a message in one form or another to help guide whoever might be following us?"

Catherine clutched at the velvet folds of her robe, her knuckles glowing white. He said it so casually, so coolly, mocking her even as he shattered whatever hopes she had that her family would not think she had simply vanished off the face of the earth.

"You knew?" she whispered brokenly. "Yet you said nothing?"

"It hardly seemed important. Annoying, perhaps, but not important. And it was a useful diversion: It kept you happy and out from under my skin by letting you believe you were so very clever."

The shock warmed her cheeks and in a movement so swift it caught him off balance, she swung her arm up and slapped him squarely across the face with the flat of her hand. His jaw remained angled to the one side for a full minute, and when he finally did turn slowly back to face her, a dull red imprint of her hand was staining his cheek, glowing through a paler mask of anger.

"By Christ, woman, you have more nerve than I would have accredited to you," His voice was laced with menace. "Far, far more than is healthy or wise to keep throwing at me."

"What would you have me do? Throw it under your feet to be trampled upon and ground into the dirt? Is that how you prefer your women: grovelling and spineless, so frightened of your bullying ways that they crumble to dust before you?''

Cameron flung his cigar to the floor and wrenched her forward into a crushing embrace. ''Since you ask, Mistress Ashbrooke, I like my women with fire and spirit. I like them blonde. I like them slender and willowy and soft in all the right places. I like them with eyes the colour of wildflowers and an insolent little pout of a mouth that begs to be kissed — kissed so thoroughly there isn't the breath or wit left for words.'' His mouth, warm and possessive, flavoured with the musky sweetness of whisky, came down on hers, forcing her lips apart in an intimacy greater than any she had known. His breath was hot and fierce against her skin, his tongue was bold and sensuously demanding, robbing her of the faintest ability to think or breathe or even to begin to know how to combat his towering strength. One of his hands twined itself around the web of golden hair, the long fingers cradling and caressing the nape of her neck. His other hand moved from her waist, skimming purposefully higher on her trembling body until it had intruded beneath the edge of her robe.

Catherine's groan echoed the sound that was torn harshly from his throat as his hand first stroked then engulfed the budding firmness of her breast. His fingers played across her flesh, circling and kneading the chilled peak of her nipple until it was pebble-hard and ruched with pleasure.

''Why don't we stop playing games, Catherine,'' he murmured thickly, his mouth spreading the flames to the slender arch of her throat. ''You want me to honour my promises. So be it. I will honour them . . . starting with the vows I made in your father's study: to take you as my lawfully wedded — and bedded — wife.''

''No,'' she gasped ''No . . . ''

''You keep saying no, Catherine, but your eyes and your body tell me something quite different.''

''No, please . . . ''

"I think you like being kissed, and I think you want more. Much more."

His lips captured the lobe of her ear and her knees buckled so that she was pressed deeper into his embrace. She was aware of the treacherous eagerness of her body as his fingers acknowledged the unwitting response and sought the knotted belt of her robe. She remembered — and fought the memories — of the night at the inn when she had stood naked and shivering in his arms. Then she had feared the shivering had not been entirely due to the soaking in the stream. Now she knew it for a certainty.

"Stop. Stop . . . please! I'll do anything you ask. I'll pretend to be anyone you want me to be only . . . please . . . *stop*!" The last word escaped as more of a sob as she felt the belt loosen and fall away. She kept her eyes squeezed tightly shut and her hands braced against his chest to continue the fight . . . knowing full well it was lost the instant his flesh touched hers again.

But he did not touch her again. He lowered his hands to his sides and stood looking down at the glossy crown of her head. If she had dared to raise her eyes she might have seen the self-disgust etched on the bronzed features. She might even have realized that he was fighting a similarly stunning weakness in his own body that another moment's contact would have shattered beyond his control. As Catherine fumbled to gather the edges of her robe together, he watched her intently, conscious of the ache that tightened his chest and throat at every breath.

"You will dress for dinner, madam," he said, forcing an indifference into his voice that he was far from feeling. "You will accompany me to dinner and you will be on your very best behaviour or — " He waited until the shimmering eyes tilted up to his. "Or I shall assume you have no further desire to see your England or your precious Lieutenant Garner again."

With the tears still bright along her lashes, Catherine squared her shoulders contemptuously. "Do you never tire of issuing your vile and inhuman threats?"

"Do you never tire of challenging me to deliver them?"

She took a deep breath. "You are indeed a loathsome creature, Mr. Cameron. You have no scruples, no morals, no faith, no conscience . . . not one single redeeming quality that should permit you to walk upright on two legs."

Alex stared a moment, then bowed deeply. "A man always appreciates knowing where he stands in a woman's estimation."

"You stand, sir, with one foot on the road to hell. I do not envy anyone who chooses to stand alongside you."

Alex paused on the threshold of the bedchamber and accustomed his eyes to the gloom. There was only one candle alight; the glow it shed barely filtered beyond the canopied bed. As he walked toward it, his thoughts were firmly, inexorably on Catherine Ashbrooke. He had sobered considerably since leaving her room, although there was no help for his blood, which continued to race and pound throughout his body, and no help for the lingering taste and scent of her that clung to his every pore. He had come close, closer than he even cared to think about, to simply throwing her across the bed and getting her out of his system once and for all. Was that the answer? Would the mere possession of her body shake this unnerving grip she had on him . . . or would it only make matters worse? Those eyes, that mouth . . . she defied him at every turn, baited him to do his worst, and by God, if he did not find some way to get her out of Scotland, out of sight and out of mind soon, he would . . .

He would what?

"Problems?"

Alex blinked, his fixation broken, and approached the bed. Looking down at the pale figure, he was surprised to see Aluinn's gray eyes sharp and clear, as free of congestion as if he had slept for days instead of a few hours.

"Problems? No, not really. Go back to sleep."

"Just how am I supposed to do that with you hovering over me like a carrion crow awaiting its next meal?"

Alex frowned. "All things considered, I should think you far too ill to be so witty."

"With Archie dispensing almost as much whisky as laudanum?" Aluinn shifted his weight on the pillows, wincing as he jarred the heavily bandaged shoulder. "He is threatening to have me dancing to the pipes by week's end, and frankly, I have no reason to doubt him."

"Seriously, how are you feeling? How is the arm?"

"Seriously? I feel as if a mountain dropped down on me. As for the arm, Archie took a good look at the damage — believe me, he did — and seems to think it shouldn't lay me up too long. The damned shoulder will be stiff for a while, but it will come back. Thank God it was the left side and not the right — I would hate to think my days of jousting with windmills were over."

Alex smiled and helped himself to a dram of whisky from the bottle beside the bed.

"No thanks," Aluinn said to the proffered glass. "But you look like you could have about twelve of those. Have you caught any sleep?"

"Some."

"You don't look too happy — certainly not for a man who has come back to the bosom of his family after half a lifetime away."

Alex sighed and raked a hand through his hair. "I am seriously beginning to think we would have been better off staying away."

Aluinn grinned knowingly. "Maura was in to see me earlier. She could hardly speak of anything but your lovely new wife. Should I say I told you so here, or should I wait a few minutes?"

"Wait. You'll undoubtedly find more causes to use it."

"There is more?"

"Glengarron. Struan MacSorley is all for forming a raiding party and going after what is left of Gordon Ross Campbell. You were right: I should have killed the bastard when I had him right there in my hands."

"What does Lochiel think?"

"He thinks like a clan chief. If there are any reprisals now, it could well blow the lid off the powder keg. He has sent for Glengarron's father. It will be up to Old Glengarron ultimately to decide what answer, if any, we will give for Iain's death, but it is my guess Donald will caution him to wait. He may get his chance to kill more Campbells than he ever dreamed of."

"That sounds like Lochiel is expecting the clans to rise for Prince Charles."

"I'm afraid my brother is caught with his breeches half-way down. If he pulls them up and buckles on his swordbelt, he keeps his dignity and his self-respect, but he has to bear the pain of knowing he has accomplished nothing. On the other hand, if he drops them all the way down, he's worried the relief could only be short-lived anyway. It is *my* considered opinion that the English want this rebellion almost more than Scotland does, if only to stake their claim in such a way as it can never be questioned again. Either way, we all lose."

"The eternal pessimist," Aluinn said dryly.

"The eternal fool, you mean. Was it so wrong to hope we could just come home and blend into the background somewhere?"

"You, my fine legendary friend? The *Camshroinaich Dubh* — the Dark Cameron — fade away with a wife and a brood of drooling kids?"

"It was just a thought," Alex scowled, realizing how mawkish and sentimental it sounded.

"Besides, if you fade away, who will fulfill the old prophesy?"

Alex dragged his thoughts back from the west tower with an effort. "What? What prophesy?"

"The ravens will drink their fill of Campbell blood three times off the top of Clach Mhor," Aluinn quoted. "They have already drunk twice because of you. Why do you think the Duke of Argyle is in such a frenzy?"

"I'd almost forgotten that old fishwife's curse."

"So had I until Maura reminded me of it today. Rumour has it the Duke wakes up out of a sound sleep, frothing at the mouth because he swears he has seen you standing over his bed with a dripping *clai'mór.*"

"If nothing else, then, I've killed his peace of mind. If he chooses to believe the two-hundred-year-old ravings of a lunatic, who am I to enlighten him?"

"Allow me to enlighten you, in that case. Something else Maura told me: Gordon Ross Campbell is Malcolm Campbell's bastard son."

"His *son*?"

"Sort of changes the perspective a little, doesn't it?"

"It sort of makes me feel as if the curse is on me, not them," Alex muttered.

"Imagine what they will make of your not killing him when you had both reason and opportunity. Malcolm will take it as a gauntlet thrown at his feet."

"Let him take it as he will, and pray to God he doesn't cross my path again, not him and not his bastard son." Alex stared at his empty glass and swore. "That's two mistakes I've made out of a blind sense of Christian charity."

"Two?"

Alex thought of Hamilton Garner and the corner of his mouth pulled down. "Maybe I'm just getting old and soft. I should have aimed my sword true, squeezed my hands tighter . . . and taken my peace of mind when it first tempted me."

Aluinn had no doubt the solution to the riddle lay somewhere in the events of the past few weeks, and no doubt at all that the root of the problem had long blonde hair and violet eyes.

"What are you going to do about Catherine?" he asked quietly. "I am loathe to dwell on the obvious, but you are going to have to do something one way or the other, and soon."

"I wasn't aware there was an 'other.' "

"Isn't there?"

The silence stretched, broken only by the faint ticking of a clock somewhere in the shadows.

"You only think you can read my mind, old friend," Alex said. "And this time, you're dead wrong."

Aluinn leaned back and half closed his eyes. The candle-light was not kind to the smears of fatigue under his eyes or the tautness around his mouth. "Dead wrong, eh? If you say so."

"I say so. Even if it were possible . . ."

"Yes?"

"It would never work."

"Why? Because you are infallible as well as legendary? Because you expect everyone to have the same thickness of armour around their hearts as you do?"

A tic shivered in Alex's cheek. "You don't understand."

"You are right, friend. I don't understand. For fifteen years you have been killing yourself on the inside, and I don't understand."

"Aluinn, for Christ's sake — " Alex was forestalled by the sudden creaking of the door on its hinges. As he turned, the look on his face was so shockingly stripped of defenses it sent Deirdre's hand fluttering up to her throat.

"I'm sorry," she whispered. "I did not mean to intrude."

"No intrusion," Aluinn said quickly. "Please, come in."

"Yes," Alex agreed, "please do. I was just about to leave anyway. Aluinn . . . I'll look in on you later; try to get some sleep."

"You too," Aluinn replied, but Alex had already disappeared into the blackness of the hallway. Deirdre continued to stand partway in the gloom, as if she were debating the wisdom of being there at all. She had not thought MacKail would be awake, certainly not lucid enough to hold his own in a conversation with Alexander Cameron.

"I . . . I mustn't stay," she stammered and backed toward the hall. "I've left Mistress Catherine in her bath and — "

"Wait! Please don't go."

She halted, poised on the black edge of shadow.

"Deirdre?"

She curled her lip between her teeth and chewed anxiously. "I thought you would be asleep. I only came to see if . . . if you wanted for anything before I went upstairs to my mistress. In a household the size of this one, I'm surprised there are so few servants about."

"Actually" — his eyes darted to the nightstand — "I am a little thirsty, if you wouldn't mind."

Deirdre debated with herself another long moment before she moved slowly toward the side of the bed. The glass, she saw, was within easy reach of his uninjured arm, as was the pitcher of water.

Her eyes carefully downcast, she reached for the jug.

"I confess I am a little surprised that you would care one way or another for my well-being. Pleasantly surprised, to be sure, but still . . ."

"I was only waiting for a chance to . . . to thank you properly for what you did yesterday."

"What *I* did? As I understand it, I should be the one thanking you for keeping me from bleeding to death."

"It would not have been necessary if you hadn't thrown yourself after that brute who tried to snatch me off my feet."

"Oh." Aluinn remembered and smiled. "I suppose you do deserve a scolding at that, for not staying on the ground where I put you in the first place."

She bridled, "I am not one to cower behind coach wheels, thank you very much. Eight brothers I have, and not a one able to pull my hair or knock me down in a fair fight."

"I can believe that," he mused, rubbing his jaw. "You have a damned good left hook, as I recall."

She warmed under his smile, then, remembering the glass she was holding, offered it to him, uncomfortably aware of the tremors in her hand. Even worse, the gray eyes stared at her until she thought her fingers would lose all sensation.

"Do you want the water or not?" she asked tartly.

"I want it," he said and closed his grip around the glass and her hand together. Deirdre balked at the contact but he would not relinquish his hold.

"Will you sit with me for a while?"

She flushed and extricated her hand from beneath the lean, warm fingers. "I musn't. My mistress is waiting for me — "

"Please. Just for a few minutes."

The tip of her tongue slid nervously across her lower lip. "Well, I . . . I suppose it couldn't hurt . . . a few minutes more."

Aluinn smiled and leaned back, sipping at the cool water. The effort seemed to drain his reserves of strength and he closed his eyes.

With his long lashes cloaking the seriousness in the gray eyes and his sand-coloured hair flung haphazardly across his brow, Deirdre thought Aluinn MacKail looked more of a boy than a man full grown. His tanned skin was smooth and stretched evenly over high Celtic cheekbones. A faint stubble of fair beard covered the angular jaw and led down to a reddish-gold cloud of hair that exploded across his chest. The muscles beneath were hard, the skin supple, with bands of precisely molded sinew narrowing to a trim waist and flat belly. Below that, below the line of the blanket, it was left to her imagination to surmise what might be seen there, but Deirdre had no difficulty envisioning the long legs, steely with muscle, furred with the same fine coppery hairs as his wrists and forearms.

With eight brothers she had thought herself immune to the mysteries of a man's body, but the one lying before her was so overpoweringly masculine, it made her forget everything she had seen or learned. She could no longer believe, however remotely, that he was evil — dangerous perhaps, but not evil. And not a cold-blooded murderer. Not him, and not Alexander Cameron.

"What did you mean when you said he had been killing himself on the inside for the past fifteen years?"

The gray eyes opened slowly.

"I was not meaning to eavesdrop," she said hastily, "but I was fully through the door before I realized . . . I mean, before I could do anything about it. I am not the kind who listens at keyholes and then spreads the gossip thick as jam in every ear I find. You needn't look at me that way, and you needn't tell me anything more if you feel you have to keep it so secret. It's just that . . . well, it might help if one or both of you stopped treating everyone like they were your enemies."

"Alex is a very private man. He does not find it easy to offer up his trust; nor do I, for that matter. Nor do you."

Deirdre lowered her eyes. "You have not given anyone any reason to trust you. You have forced my mistress to compromise herself. You have dragged us both half the length of Britain against our wills. You very nearly were the cause of getting us both killed yesterday, and goodness knows what might happen between here and our finding our way home again — *if* we are ever allowed to go home again."

"Alex gave his word, and I have never known him to break it. If he has promised to send you and your mistress home, and if you still want to go, he will see that you get there."

"If we still want to go?" she asked softly.

"People change their minds."

"Not my mistress. She has it firm in her mind that Mr. Cameron is a spy and a murderer and so far he's done nothing to defend himself on either charge."

Aluinn studied her pale features. "Tell me something: If you went back to Derby tomorrow, and if Lord Ashbrooke asked you what you saw and heard while you were travelling through Scotland — would you tell him?"

"Of course I would. It's my duty, both as a loyal servant to my mistress and as a loyal servant to my king."

"King George?"

The brown eyes sparkled. "He is my sovereign."

"What if you believed your sovereign to be unjustly exiled in Italy? What if you believed King James Stuart to be the rightful king of England and Scotland — and please" — he said, holding up his hand to ward off the protest forming on her lips — "I do not want to argue politics or semantics or who is right and who is wrong. I just want you to offer me a straight and honest answer to the question. Walk in our shoes for ten seconds. If you believed James Stuart to be your king; if your family had fought and died for that same belief, would you look upon Alex and me as spies simply because we rode through England with our eyes and ears open?"

Deirdre's gaze held his. "I . . . under those circumstances, I probably would not, but . . ."

"Yes?"

"But a change of shoes cannot explain away a charge of murder."

"No. It can't." Aluinn hesitated, but something in her eyes made him want to make her understand. "You are absolutely right. There is a charge of murder hanging over Alex's head — two murders, in fact — a charge he will probably carry with him to his grave if Argyle has anything to say about it."

"*Two* murders?"

"The count would have been three but for a small fluke of nature: The third bastard survived."

Lacing her hands tightly on her lap, Deirdre said, "You sound almost proud of it."

"I am. I only wish I had been there with him at the time." A cold, hard edge crept into his voice. "I would have made sure there had been no flukes of nature to get in the way."

Deirdre flinched inwardly. She was trying to understand, she truly was. But not only was he admitting to the murders, he was condoning them.

"It happened the week of Donald and Maura's wedding. She is a Campbell; her father and the Duke are cousins. She met Donald while on a tour of France, and even though I'm sure they both did their damnedest to prevent it, they fell in love.

"I should interject here that the Campbells and the Camerons have been snapping at each other's hindquarters for generations. Lochaber is a nice rich plum of land The Campbell would dearly love to absorb into his own territory, but since our clan has always been blessed with either warriors or diplomats for chiefs, the glen has remained in Cameron possession. It is not an unusual situation. Blood feuds are an integral part of the Highlands, and without them we would just be another little nation of warring tribes, probably invaded and conquered long ago by the English. But with our uniquely savage traits, we have made quite a formidable name for ourselves and managed to keep our borders relatively inviolate.

"At any rate, the wedding took place as planned, here at Achnacarry. As a gesture of goodwill, a large party of Campbells were invited — oil on troubled waters, more or less — including Maura's cousins from Argyle: Dughall, Colin, and Malcolm Campbell."

Aluinn paused, his features darkening as the memories crowded back. "The ceremony went smoothly. Maura's father, Sir John Campbell of Auchenbreck had by then become genuinely fond of Donald and was actually supporting the union in hopes of making peace between the two clans. Argyle did not see it that way, of course. He took it as a personal affront, especially since he had previously chosen Dughall Campbell for Maura's groom. Have I managed to totally confuse you yet?"

Deirdre unconsciously moved closer to the bed. "Who is this Duke of Argyle? He sounds very important."

"He is unquestionably the most powerful Hanover chieftain in Scotland. He personally commanded the army that all but finished it for the Jacobites in 1715 at Dunblain. He is power-hungry, land-hungry, and not above a fair amount of cheating, scheming, and back-stabbing to get what he wants — the prime ministership of Scotland when and if it comes completely under English rule.''

"He does not sound like a very nice man," Deirdre understated.

"He isn't . . . and wasn't. I expect his displeasure over Maura's defection was communicated to the Campbell brothers; the tension was so thick in the air that day it made your ears ring. Yet for a while, they seemed to be behaving. They filled their bellies with food and ale, they sang, they danced, they even flirted with Cameron women.''

Again Aluinn drew a long, painful pause, as if, in the retelling, he was also reliving the past events.

"Alex was in love, as are most healthy seventeen-year-old young cocks. Annie MacSorley was slim and fair, as shy and unprepossessing as a rose in bud. Half the countryside was in love with her, myself included, but it was Alex who won her. They were completely smitten, as much in love as any two people have a right to be. They had been handfasted the previous winter and planned to marry in the church later that summer — '' The words backed up in his throat and he faltered. "Perhaps they should not have waited or have been so secretive about it. Or perhaps we just should have found some reason to keep Alex away from the wedding, knowing how much he and Dughall Campbell loathed each other. At any rate, the real trouble started when Alex and Annie slipped away from the celebrations to steal a few moments of privacy. The Campbell brothers saw them and followed.

"To make an ugly story short, they managed to sneak up on the lovers in the stables. They saw a chance for some crude fun and knocked Alex around just enough to leave him semiconscious while they took turns with Annie. One of them — I don't know who, got a little too rough and slammed her head against the stone wall. Alex was nearly insane by then and somehow broke free of his bindings. He grabbed a sword and attacked, killing the youngest — Colin — on the first pass. The other two fought back and . . . frankly, I do not know how he did it, but when the bodies were discovered a while later, Dughall had been gutted stem to stern and Malcolm . . . well, it would have been a greater mercy at the time for someone to have finished him off. Alex was himself more dead than alive, acting like a wild wounded animal, not letting anyone near him or Annie. She died in his arms.

"The Campbells naturally claimed the ambush had been staged. All of them at the wedding swore they had seen Annie flirting with the boys and finally luring them into the stables where Alex was waiting to attack."

"Did no one take Mr. Cameron's side?" Deirdre asked in a shocked whisper.

"The entire clan was willing to put their swords with his; we would have gladly taken on the Campbells, the militia, the whole government at a nod from Lochiel. Donald agonized for weeks over what to do. Argyle had declared it murder and demanded a warrant be issued for Alex's arrest. There was no possibility of a fair trial. To refuse to surrender him or to call the clan to arms to protect him would have laid the Camerons open to military discipline. Finally, knowing it was the only way to save Alex's life and avoid a bloody clan war, Lochiel sent him to France, to be with his father, Old Lochiel."

"But . . . he wasn't guilty of murder. That was so unfair."

"Unfair," Aluinn agreed with a wry, weary smile. "And for the first ten years or so Alex expended most of his energy hating the world. He threw himself into every battle, every skirmish, every war he could find on the Continent, and when he ran out of enemies to fight there, he took himself across the ocean to the colonies where there were plenty of Indians to oblige his thirst for blood."

"You have stayed with him all these years?"

His smile softened further. "We were raised like brothers, treated like brothers — it seemed the natural thing to do. Mind you, it did become a rather poignant test of friendship when the Duke put a price on his head and we were pressed to dodge assassins everywhere we went. I have a few scars I would prefer not to remember coming by and a nightmare or two that still chase me into a cold sweat. On the whole, though, we have managed to come through it with both feet on the ground.''

''The pair of you do seem to be indestructible,'' Deirdre conceded. ''I should think an army of you Cameron men could conquer the world, never mind England.''

''Why Mistress O'Shea,'' he murmured, ''that sounds suspiciously like a compliment. Does this mean I have almost convinced you we are neither brutes nor beaters of innocent women?''

She shielded the expression in her eyes behind the thick dark lashes. ''I never truly thought you were either.''

''Never? Not even that night at the inn?''

''You hadn't ought to have grabbed me. I don't like being grabbed.''

''I shall endeavor to remember that,'' he said and reached forward, his hand gently cradling the side of her neck. Against her instinctive resistance, he drew her to him until her mouth was a breath away from his. He felt a shudder ripple through her, then another. A soft moan parted her lips as his hand tightened and his fingers raked up into the silky brown hair. The kiss was long and impassioned, full of trust and honesty — two qualities which had always been sorely lacking in the courtesans and gaily uninhibited women he was accustomed to winning into his bed. She tasted sweet — so very sweet and innocent, like someone blind to all faults and transgressions, someone who could offer her heart with no conditions, no pretenses.

He released her slowly, reluctantly, noting that even his pain seemed to have been alleviated by her touch.

Deirdre brushed her fingertips across her lips and blushed self-consciously.

''You should not have done that, sir,'' she whispered.

''There are a good many things I should not have done in my life,'' he answered sincerely. ''That was not one of them. And my name is not sir, it is Aluinn. Al-oo-in. You have to twist the tongue around the middle part, it's the Gaelic word for — ''

''For beautiful,'' she said on a rush. ''Yes, I know.''

The gray eyes gleamed as they held hers and for the moment their world was nothing more than the cocoon of pale yellow candlelight enclosing them.

''I . . . I must go,'' she said softly. ''I have been neglecting my mistress terribly.''

''Will you come back? Will you come back and sit with me when you can?''

The question raised two bright spots of crimson on her cheeks and Aluinn thought to himself: My God, but she is lovely. Born to a king instead of a gameskeeper, she would have slain half the hearts of Europe.

''Will you?'' he asked again.

''I-if you wish me to, sir,'' she murmured.

''Aluinn,'' he reminded her gently. ''And I do wish you to. Very much.''

Chapter Thirteen

Wary of the wintry frost that emanated from her mistress, Deirdre worked quickly and diligently to shape Catherine's long golden mass of curls into a reasonably artful presentation. Her task was severely hampered by her subject's sudden pacings from one end of the room to the other, by an impatient hand flinging finished sets of curls into disorder, by twists and turns that nearly tore the combs and pins out of the poor girl's nerveless hands.

The toilet accomplished, Catherine stood broodingly silent as Deirdre fetched a borrowed chemise and pantalets and, then assisted her into snowy-white stockings and lace garters. She sucked in her tummy by rote and braced herself against a bedpost while the heavily boned corset was girded tightly about her midsection. Deirdre hauled on the laces, squeezing as much of Catherine's waistline up into her chest as was humanly possible, shaping her torso into an unnatural but highly prized funnel so narrow at the waist it could be spanned by two large hands. To contrast the trimness, wire panniers formed like baskets were positioned over each hip, held in place with satin tapes and covered by three billowing layers of petticoats. Still gasping from the enforced pressure around her ribs, Catherine rounded on the bed with a curse that made the Irish girl look up in surprise.

"Do you see what she had the nerve, the utter *gall* to loan me?"

"Beg pardon, mistress? She?"

"That Scottish virago," Catherine railed and glared down at the voluminous folds of silk spread on the coverlet. "Have you ever, in your life, seen me wear green? *Green*, dammit! She did it deliberately, I know she did!"

Deirdre was bewildered. She had assumed Catherine's temper was the result of her earlier confrontation with Alexander Cameron. While it was not her place to do so, Deirdre had been agonizing over whether or not to share the truth with her — the truth Aluinn MacKail had so painfully revealed. She knew her mistress was not nearly as cold and unfeeling as she purported to be. Indeed, she was just as vulnerable and just as determined to guard herself against that vulnerability as was Cameron. Perhaps if she knew the truth . . . perhaps if they *both* knew the truth . . .

"It is six months out of style," Catherine muttered, pulling and tugging the skirt into place. "And I am certain I saw a gravy stain on the bodice . . . *good God*!"

Deirdre was momentarily distracted from her thoughts as she joined her mistress in staring at the shocking expanse of pale flesh left bare by the plunging neckline. Very little remained for the imagination, whereas a great deal was left to chance. Her breasts sat like two half moons, propped and plumped in such a way as to make viewing her toes impossible. Moreover, if not for the delicate ruff of lace that edged her chemise, more than a hint of each nipple would challenge propriety at every move.

Catherine steadied herself and walked to the mirror.

"Perhaps a shawl, mistress," Deirdre suggested, hurrying

after her, but Catherine held up a hand, her expression solemn as she studied her image in the gilded surface.

Her first thought was that she looked like one of the preened and painted courtesans who frequented the royal court and vied for the paid attentions of lewd, gout-ridden ministers. Her second was that she could have commanded the interest of the king himself. Although the gown was green — a colour she normally avoided like the flux — it was an unusually soft shade, a mignonette which not only seemed to emphasize the translucence of her complexion, but drew attention to the soft shimmer of silver-blonde hair.

"Will you be wanting the shawl, mistress?" Deirdre inquired.

Catherine opened her mouth to reply in the affirmative, but a movement in the reflection of the mirror caught her eye and her gaze was redirected to the figure who loomed suddenly in the doorway. For a moment she almost did not recognize her own "husband."

Since their arrival at Achnacarry, Cameron had elected to retain the English style of clothing — the plain frock coat, dark breeches, stark white shirt and neckcloth, an embroidered waistcoat as the only splash of flamboyance. For this, his first formal dinner at home, he had been provided with a short, richly shaded frock coat of sky-blue velvet. The sleeves were turned back almost to the elbow, the cuffs trimmed with wide gold braid and scalloped over the gathered white ruff of lace at his wrists. The coat was left open over a gold-and-royal striped waistcoat which buttoned high to the throat and seated a dazzling white, multi-tiered jabot. From his waist he wore a length of scarlet-and-black tartan, pleated into a kilt and held in place with a polished leather belt. The end of the tartan was brought up and draped across one shoulder, pinned to the coat with an enormous silver brooch studded with topazes. His calves were encased in scarlet-and-black wool stockings; his jet-black hair had been molded into curls at his temples with the remainder tied back in a neat queue.

Even the most grudging appraisal would term him magnificent; he looked as if he could stand atop a mountain and command the sun to rise and fall at will.

Despite the change in his appearance, the eyes remained the same. Black and bold, they roved over Catherine's figure, leaving her with the distinct impression that her own summation of her appearance had been too kind.

"You might want to take Deirdre up on the suggestion of a shawl," he said politely. "The dining room is apt to be chilly."

"In that case — " Catherine retorted, ignoring the filigreed shawl and snatching up an ivory fan, "if I turn blue, someone is bound to take pity on me and send me back to my room."

Alex felt a steady, low hammering within his chest and had to force himself to step aside as she swept regally past him into the hallway. He looked at Deirdre but she only averted her eyes in embarrassment.

Not a single word was exchanged through the twisting, turning descent from the tower. The only sound along vaulted stone corridors was their footsteps — his firm and regulated to keep pace with her smaller, softer taps. It was only when they stood outside the main receiving room, guided there by the sound of laughter and clinking glasses, that Catherine's nerve faltered and she held back.

Cameron's hand was there instantly, tucked beneath her elbow, propelling her forward.

"Don't worry," he said out of the side of his mouth. "We Camerons have pretty well forsaken the rite of offering up live sacrifices to the dark gods . . . I think."

They entered a room full of glittering candlelight and splashes of brightly hued tartan. Almost immediately, at their appearance, all conversation ground to a halt, and one by one the heads swivelled and stared at the couple in the doorway. Catherine felt the first flood of colour in her cheeks recede, only to rise again, darker and deeper, as she realized that because of their curiosity about the Englishwoman, most of the attention was on her.

Archibald and Donald Cameron stood together by the huge marble fireplace, their heads bent in conversation with a third man, soon to be introduced as John Cameron of Fassefern. Catherine recognized his face from the miniature in the gallery and decided he was the least attractive and the least appealing of the Cameron men. They were dressed similarly to Alex in pleated tartan and lustrous velvet and satin.

The women were elegantly gowned in silks and brocades, laying to rest yet another of Catherine's preconceived notions that Highland women would still regard Elizabethan bombazine and Norse braids as the height of fashion. And despite her prior reservations, there were several décolletages equally as shocking as her own. Lauren Cameron, for one — Catherine's feline instincts had sought her out at once — dared not bend over so much as an inch, for the added strain would surely send her popping out of her bodice. Catherine felt a measure of her old self-esteem return as she saw the amber-flecked eyes narrow with resentment. She had indeed been hoping Catherine would draw attention, but certainly not the admiring whispers and pleased nods that were circulating around the room now.

The familiar feeling of silent combat with another female bolstered Catherine's confidence even more, so that when Lochiel and Lady Cameron crossed the room to greet them, she was able to return their smiles and even execute a graceful curtsy.

"I hope we have not kept everyone waiting," Alex said, trying not to notice the shine of tears in Donald's eyes. He had made the right choice by wearing the clan tartan, and he could feel his own pride reflected in the faces around him.

"Welcome hame, brither," Lochiel rasped, his voice thick with emotion as he grasped Alex by the shoulders. "This is as it should be, by God. The Camerons. Together again, strong an' united. Let no man, king, or government step between us again!''

A round of passionate 'ayes' swelled to the roof timbers. From somewhere, two goblets appeared and were thrust into Alex and Catherine's hands.

''The Camerons!'' Donald toasted and raised his glass.

''The Camerons!'' the family and guests responded, and as one they tilted their glasses and tossed back the golden liquor in a single swallow.

Catherine, acutely aware of the eyes watching every move she made, drained her glass as she had seen the other women do and was feeling quite proud of herself . . . until the liquid ball of fire plunged down her throat and sucked the air from her lungs with such a vengeance her knees collapsed. Unable to breathe through the flames, she grabbed frantically for Alex's arm and would have fallen had someone not cried out to catch her.

''Oh dear.'' Maura's face came swimming before her. ''Who gave her the whisky?''

''Wisna me,'' Jeannie declared at once, looking as innocent as a cat with feathers clinging to its chin.

''The poor child has probably never had anything stronger than canary wine. Someone fetch some water, quickly.''

''Here, gie her this.'' Auntie rose pushed a crystal goblet into Maura's hand. ''Ye canna gie her plain water, it'll only bring the *uisque* back up again. A wee dram o' claret, that'll dae it. Just a wee sip tae cool the throat.''

''A small sip,'' Maura cautioned as she held the goblet to Catherine's lips. Thankfully the remedy worked; the sweet red wine doused the embers in her throat and returned some of the sensation to her mouth and tongue.

''My Lord,'' she gasped. ''What was that?''

''Only the finest *uisque baugh* in all the Heelands, lassie,'' Archibald Cameron boasted proudly. ''A mon can drink ten pints an' still stan' tae piss in the mornin'. Gangs aff like a cannon when ye mix it wi' the black powder. That's how ye test the virtue o' prime *uisque:* Mix it wi' gunpowder, light it, an' if it disna explode, it's na warth the spit tae swally it. Aye, an' may God strike me deid, Donal' has lost near a score o' stillmen over the years — been blown clean tae hell an' gaun wi'out even a footprint ahind tae tell the story."

"Footprint me arse," Jeannie scowled. "I'd as like tae mix a wee bit o' gunpowder up yer kilt an' see what like the virtue is there."

Lochiel cleared his throat pointedly and smiled. "Well now, I believe we are all present, an' I f'ae one have the appetite o' ten men."

He raised his hand in a signal to someone out in the hallway, and the seams of Alex's coat suffered another moment of stress as Catherine reacted to what appeared to be the screech of a tortured animal. Looking quickly around she was confronted by the innocent sight of a piper filling his instrument with air. As soon as it was inflated, the raw screeching assumed a clean and distinct wail, one that was no less fearsome in substance but was at least recognizable as music.

"The pipes are inviting us to dinner," Cameron murmured in her ear.

"Inviting? It sounds as if they are trying to frighten us away."

"That was the original intent of the *piob'rachd* — the clan marching song — to throw terror into the hearts and souls of the enemy. Ten pipers playing at the head of a column of clansmen can do as much damage to an adversary's nerves as a battalion of artillery."

Catherine did not doubt it.

"And this is a cheerful tune they're playing," he added.

She looked up and nearly returned the smile in the blue-black eyes. But then Donald was beside her, offering his arm, escorting her out of the receiving room at the head of a solemn procession that followed the piper along the hall and down the short flight of stairs to the great hall. A transformation had taken place in the spacious room. Two long oak tables had been set up to accommodate the large party of family and friends. The smaller of the two was mounted on the foot-high dais that ran the width of the bay window, while the second table ran at right angles and stretched the length of the hall, with seating for nearly fifty children, aunts, uncles, cousins, and guests who had gathered to share the homecoming.

One by one the deep-chested, long-winded Scots rose to offer toasts or speeches or recount various historic moments of the clan's past. Many of the speeches were incomprehensible to Catherine, for they were delivered in rousing Gaelic with much gesturing and shouting. She had been seated on Donald's right, with Archibald on her other side and John Cameron's wife, Elspeth, opposite her. A short, stout gentleman addressed only as Keppoch sat between Elspeth and Jeannie Cameron, and across from him was Auntie Rose. Lady Cameron was seated well along at the far end of the table, with Alex positioned on her right and his brother John to her left. By leaning forward ever so slightly and peering through the tines of a candelabra, Catherine could frame almost all of Alexander's face. A small flick of the eye and she had an exasperatingly full view of Lauren Cameron, who had somehow managed to win the seat next to Alex.

When the speeches drew to an end, more pipes heralded the arrival of the first course of the meal. The dish was unfamiliar to Catherine but proved to be a delectably creamy soup of lentils and potatoes playing host to chunks of tender pink salmon. There immediately followed platters of roast duck drowning in a rich butter sauce, potato scones browned and crisped in bacon fat, mutton pies smothered in gravy, puddings, sausages, and crusty pastry shells stuffed with spiced venison and pork. Various wines accompanied each course, and due to the diligence of Dr. Cameron, Catherine never found her glass wanting. By the time she had allowed for a sampling of everything, she was regretting the effort Deirdre had expended lacing her into her clothes.

"Ach, so ye like oor Heeland victuals, dae ye lassie?"

Keppoch caught her eye and winked. "Aye, I were in London a time ago. Foun' the townsfolk too purse-proud tae make but ane sauce, an' that they poored on everythin'. Aye, the English hae a hunnerd opinions, but only the ane sauce."

Catherine sipped her wine and glanced absently along the table, but the old gentleman would not be put off.

"Aye, they come up here an' tell us wha' fine silver an' gold they hae. I once't bade ma clansmen stan' roun' the table, each wi' a taper in their hans, an' demanded tae be shown a finer lot o' candlesticks in all the lan'. That's wha' should matter tae a laird — tae count his wealth by the number o' stout lads he has willin' tae walk intae battle ahind him. Nae gold, nae silver. *Men!*" He paused and a sharp eye drilled into Lochiel. "Ye may hae need o' such wealth afore too lang, Donal'. It willna take a kick in the heid f'ae Argyle tae ken wee Alasdair has come hame."

"Aye." Lochiel nodded. "I've already warned The MacDonald an' The MacNachtan tae be on the watch. Nae doubt Campbell will have the hounds out, sniffin' the trail."

"Squint-eyed bastards," Jeannie declared to no one in particular and helped herself to more wine. "High time someone shot the lot o' them."

"Mayhap someone will, hen," Auntie Rose said sagely. "Mayhap soon."

"Aye — " Jeannie brightened for a moment. "The Prince has called f'ae an army, an' when he gets it, ye'll see, he'll put all the vermin in their places."

"Whisht, woman," Archibald commanded. "Hald yer tongue."

"I'll nae hald ma tongue!" she countered indignantly. "There's far too much haldin' o' tongues already!"

"We will not hold council at the dinner table," Maura said firmly. "Nor will we have any arguments."

"There isna any call tae argue," Jeannie insisted. "The Prince has summoned the chiefs tae meet wi' him, an' they have tae go. *They have tae go!*" She glared directly at Lochiel.

"They canna say they dinna *want* tae go, an' they canna send an auld daft cow tae dae their talkin' f'ae them — "

"Jeannie!" Archibald barked. "Mind who yer talkin' tae!"

"No," Lochiel held up his hand. "Let her speak."

"Aye, I'll speak. F'ae every man, woman, an' bairn who lost a kinsman in the last rebellion, I'll speak. Yer faither wouldna tairn his back on a Stuart. Yer faither wouldna stall an' delay an' question this an' that, like as tae send the puir wee lad cringin' into the groun' wi' shame."

Lochiel pushed his plate away. "Ma loyalty tae King Jamie has never been at question, nor ma respect f'ae his son. Have I not worked all these long years tae find some way tae bring them both hame again?"

"Wi' *words*," Jeannie spat. "Ye canna fight the *Sassenachs* wi' words!"

"We could if they had yer breath ahind them," Archibald roared. "Now hald yer silence, dragon, afore ye send *me* cringin' tae the groun' wi' shame."

"*Me* shame *you*?" Jeannie's eyes bulged with the challenge. "You who rode tae Arisaig wi' yer tail tucked up atween yer legs where yer manhood should ha' been? You who tald the Prince he wouldna find a hame here an' tae go back tae France?"

"I tald him the bald truth, woman! I tald him we couldna form an army wi' naught but a han'ful o' rusted *clai'mórs* an' a few score matchlocks."

"Bluid an' courage will form an army," Jeannie persisted.

"Aye," Archibald nodded heatedly. "The bluid o' Scotland's youth an' the courage o' fools."

Jeannie surged forward in her chair and for a moment Catherine thought the tiny woman was going to fling herself across the table and physically attack her husband. Catherine was already shocked by the very notion of a woman daring to be so outspoken in front of friends and neighbours as well as family. No one else seemed too outraged by the impropriety; they sipped their wine or picked at their sweetcakes as if it was a commonday occurrence.

"Dinna listen tae any o' this, Donald," John Cameron drawled, sucking a piece of meat from his teeth. "Ye've made the wisest decision, an' now ye must stand by it. Ye always said there could be no uprisin' against the Hanover government unless we had solid support from France. The Prince knew that. He knew it afore he came, an' yet he came anyway, wi'out the support he promised ye in return. Since he didna keep his pledge tae Scotland, it stands Scotland shouldna be bound by a pledge tae him."

"I am bound by ma honour tae King Jamie," Lochiel said with quiet intensity. "If he was tae command me tae fight, I would — tae the death if need be an' glad f'ae it."

"Exactly." John Cameron leaned forward. "But it isna yer king askin' ye tae pledge yer hame, yer family, the lives o' a thousand bonnie men! It's that wee upstart o' a pup who had to sneak out o' Europe himsel' wi'out his faither's permission, because he knew full well it wouldna come. He's naught but a lad o' four an' twenty! What does he know o' fightin' an' dyin'? He's but drunk on the romance an' the sweet smell o' power!"

"Aye, he's young an' he's drunk on pride an' glory, an' perhaps if I were young an' hot-bluided maself, I wouldna find so much fault in what he has done."

"God's bluid!" Fassefern looked around in dismay. "Ye talk as if ye admire the fool f'ae what he's done . . . f'ae what he wants tae do! There's never been an army invaded English soil in the past six hundred years! Even if — miracle o' miracles — it did, who would provision it? The Royal Navy is a thousand ships strong. Unless they all mutiny against the Hanover government at once, they'll seal these bluidy isles off tighter than a whore's garter an' wait till we all choke on our pride."

"Aye," Lochiel mused, having heard all the arguments before. "We would need King Louis' navy to distract them."

"His navy?" Keppoch guffawed. "We would need his army too, tae show us how tae fight wi' cannon an' musket, na *clai'mór* an' targe. We need trained sojers tae lairn us the ways o' the English army, leaders tae gie us discipline. Christ knows we hae the heart an' courage tae carry the fight tae the streets o' London, if need be, but wi' an army o' crofters an' shepherds, who'll keep them frae worryin' after their hames an' crops after a few harsh months o' war?"

Archibald refilled his glass, topping up Catherine's as he did so. "An' then there's our ain clans willin' tae tairn their backs or their swords against us. The Lord President himsel', Duncan Forbes, is offerin' commissions in the Hanover army. He's bribin' guid men tae denounce King Jamie an' take up the black cockade. Ye ken The Mac-Dugal? He were given back the lands an' title taken awa' in the '15, an' in exchange, he has pledged tae keep tae his hame at Dunstaffnage Castle; he an' all his clansmen."

"The MacDugal has taken his Judas gold an' f'ae that will hae tae live wi' his conscience," Keppoch declared. "It's the ithers, the anes we dinna know about an' willna know about until it's too late."

"MacLeod," Jeannie spat derisively. "I tald ye that bastard couldna be trusted. I tald ye he would ne'er hald tae his word. He smiles through his arse, that ane does. Thank the Christ he has ane bairn no' afraid o' his ain shadow."

"Young Andrew MacLeod? Aye, he'll keep his vow tae the Stuarts, but on his ain, wi'out his faither tae gie the order, it will be like a single bee leavin' the hive. A single sting instead o' thousans."

"Well it could be thousands too," Lochiel sighed. "If The MacKenzie o' Seaforth follows MacLeod, or The Ross or The Grant. The MacIntosh controls three thousand in Clan Chattan alone, an' if he accepts the commission Forbes has offered him . . . "

"If he takes it," Keppoch predicted, "he'll split the great Clan o' the Cats in two. The Farquharsons will ne'er follow an order tae fight against us, nor will The MacBean or The

MacGillivray; they would break their clans awa' frae Clan Chattan fairst.''

"Angus Moy is very conscious o' his responsibilities as The MacIntosh. He would never deliberately pit one clan against anither, one clansman against anither.''

"Responsibilities!'' Jeannie Cameron nearly choked over the word. "A clan's responsibility is tae their chief, an' the chief's responsibility is tae the kirk — tae Scotland — nae the ither way roun'!''

"Despite the way it seems,'' Lochiel countered evenly, "Angus Moy has no great love f'ae the English government. His uncle was attainted f'ae joinin' the fairst rebellion an' his faither was killed in the fightin'!''

"Aye, rest his soul, a braver mon ne'er fought. But it were also his uncle who was ane o' the fairst tae agree tae disarm his clan after the bluidy defeat in order tae save his lands an' title. One o' the fairst tae swear allegiance tae the German king an' break his life's pledge tae his rightful sovereign! There were many a clansman cursed him f'ae that, many who still dae an' willna folly a Hanover chief though he threaten tae burn a cross on their very flesh!''

"What I dinna ken,'' Keppoch interjected in a calmer voice, "is why these lairds think they'll be treated any kinder this time if they support German George. They canna hae forgotten how every clan — Whig or Jacobite — was treated after the Grand Rebellion. It didna matter if a clan fought wi' or against The Stuart, they were all ordered tae disarm. They were all stripped o' their weepons an' powers, all treated like bairns, wi' contempt an' mistrust . . . it willna be any different now.''

"The majority o' the clan chiefs know that,'' Lochiel agreed. "They dinna want tae see this country torn apart any more than you or I. Nor do they want tae force any man tae take up arms in a cause they dinna believe in.''

"Crofters have nae beliefs,'' Jeannie roared. "They're bound by bluid tae dae as their chief commands. Tell a shepherd he can make up his ain mind an' he'll run an' hide wi' his flock! *James Francis Stuart is the rightful heir tae the throne o' Scotland:* that's all a true Scot needs tae know. As f'ae Duncan Squint-Eyed Forbes, someone should have fed a musket doon his throat years ago, connivin' against his ain kind!''

"The English would only have appointed another man in his place,'' Donald said patiently. ''An' whether ye approve his methods or no', he wants peace in the kirk as badly as we do. He disna want tae see brither fightin' brither, Highlander fightin' Highlander. He knows, as do we all, that a war wi' England now means the end o' any chance we might yet have o' a free an' independant Parliament in Scotland.''

"We may have lost that chance the minute the Prince set foot on Scottish soil,'' Alex pointed out softly, having held his silence until now. ''If he stays, or if he manages to convince even a handful of clans to form up behind him, it will be all the excuse England needs to cross our borders in strength. Parliament has already voted to reinforce the garrisons at Fort George and Fort William. I saw evidence that half of England is mobilizing its militia . . . the other half have never stood down from the alert caused by that fiasco last February when the Prince nearly drowned himself in the Channel.''

"The Prince promises us there is an army o' Englishmen waitin' tae join us.''

"If so, I did not see them,'' Alex said dryly. ''What I did see was an army of fanatics warning the common people of the swarms of naked, bloodthirsty cavemen who will be pouring down out of the mountains to rape their women and sacrifice their children to the druids.'' The ebony eyes flickered to the silent figure beside Lochiel. ''You will never convince them we want only to be left alone to live in peace. You will never convince them that we shouldn't be conquered and civilized as it suits them.''

Catherine warmed, imagining all eyes at the table were on her. How dare they sit and talk around and through her as if she were not there. How dare they talk of rebellion so openly, discuss treason so freely, bandy the words loyalty and honour about the table as if she had left hers behind at the border! Arrogant braggards the lot of them. How dare they even dream they could challenge the might of King George's armies.

"The Prince has clans already," Archibald was saying with a morose frown. "Clanranald, Glenaladale, Kinlochmoidart . . . they've all fallen f'ae the laddie's charm. Aye, an' a grand charm it is, brither. He has his faither's face, the Stuart eyes. He leuks intae yer soul an' seems tae twist it right oot through yer throat. Ye were wise tae send me in yer place tae answer his summons, Donal'."

"Ma mind is firm on where I stand, where the Camerons stand. This I have told him an' I will not change."

"Then dinna go within a mile o' him," Archibald ordered blithely, "for I ken ye better than ye ken yersel', an' if this Stuart prince once sets eyes on ye, he'll have ye weepin' an' gratin' an' dain whate'er it is it pleases him tae have ye dae."

Lochiel frowned. "It would please me, brither, tae share a dram o' that wine ye seem tae be hoardin' tae yerself. Have ye finished the ither already?"

Archibald chuckled good-naturedly and the topic slid painlessly into less volatile areas. Catherine stole a glance along the table. Alex seemed to be lost in thought; at any rate he was staring at his wine glass, tracing patterns on the surface of the crystal. Beside him, Lauren Cameron was purring away, her eyes fairly devouring the broad shoulders, the lean jaw, the long, tapered fingers. He seemed not to notice the scrutiny he was coming under, but Catherine doubted it. If anything, he was probably enjoying it immensely, encouraging it even by the very fact of ignoring it.

What was going on in that unpredictable, unreadable mind of his? she wondered. Had anyone ever been close enough to the man to be able to read his thoughts or understand his moods? Had anyone ever *wanted* to understand him? Each time she thought she had found a flicker of tenderness, he proved her wrong. He baited her, played with her emotions, teased her unmercifully, used his vile threats to —

Without warning, his thick black lashes lifted and he was looking directly along the table and into Catherine's eyes, his mouth curving into a faint smile, as if he had somehow intercepted her musings.

Catherine's flush was deep and instantaneous as she flinched quickly back in her chair and stared straight ahead. He was the devil. He had to be. Maura had spoken of dark gods and druids; perhaps there was more to it than simple superstition.

She reached hastily for her wine goblet and drank the contents in a single rush. Although Archibald was engrossed in conversation with Keppoch, he barely drew a pause to refill Catherine's glass as well as his own. The wine had calmed the sudden fluctuation in her heartbeat, and she emptied the second glass with equal determination, hoping to work the same miracle on her burning cheeks.

Druids indeed! He was mortal and human just like any other man. He bled, did he not? He ate and slept and . . . and no doubt had soiled his dresses when he was a babe, just like anyone else.

What were they on about now? She concentrated all of her powers on Lochiel's mouth — it was moving and sounds were coming forth, but for the life of her she could hear nothing over the annoying hum that was building around her.

Invade England! How she wished Hamilton Garner was here in his fine scarlet tunic and white breeches! He would show them all how laughable their plotting and debating was, how useless their speculations. A handful of blustery Jacobites would not even make it as far as the River Tweed unmolested.

Hamilton!

Where was he now? Had he recovered from his wound?

Had something terrible happened — infection, fever, or worse? He surely would have come after her if he had been able, for there was no question of him abandoning her to the likes of Alexander Cameron. And *Damien*! Had something happened to Damien? Why had he not been on the road behind them? She had indeed left markers, scratched messages, given clues as to which direction Cameron was taking . . . the canny Scot could not have found them all. Why had there been no sign of pursuit?

It was too late, she decided glumly. She was irretrievably trapped in this medieval mountain fortress. The inhabitants — some of them anyway — might be friendly enough, she supposed, but she was nonetheless the intruder here. The stranger. The foreigner. The *Sassenach*! She would be watched wherever she went, whatever she did. If rescue did not come soon, or if Cameron refused to let her go, she would have to find some way to accomplish an escape on her own — but how?

It just was not fair! She was not prepared to cope with everything that had been thrust upon her — the bloodshed, the violence, the strange wild ways of the Highlanders. She wanted to go home. She wanted to wake up in her own bed at Rosewood Hall and find this had all been a horrible nightmare.

"Are ye feelin' poorly, lass?"

Lochiel touched her arm lightly and Catherine's head jerked up, her vision blurred behind a stinging-hot veil of tears.

"I . . . I'm fine. Really. I was just . . ."

"Aye, ye're tired lass, an' wi' good reason. I'm surprised ye insisted on comin' down f'ae dinner. We told Alex tae leave ye be."

"She would not hear of it," Alex said, his voice coming from over Catherine's shoulder. He leaned down to help her to her feet.

"I'm fine," she insisted. "I am just a little tired."

"Of course you are," said Maura, standing immediately. "How thoughtless of us to keep you here so long. Alexander, you must see her into bed at once."

Catherine heard the command and stumbled slightly against her husband's arm. He was bidding good evening to his brothers and their wives, and his arm was like a steel band around her waist, holding her steady, offering unseen support as he steered her along the great hall and up the flight of stone steps.

"You do not have to leave with me," Catherine protested, trying unsuccessfully to wrestle his arm away from her waist. "I would not want to be accused of taking you away from your precious family."

"How very considerate of you," he murmured. "And I may just return after I make sure you get where you are going."

"Are you implying" — she stopped abruptly, swaying — "that I am not in my proper senses?"

Alexander smiled despite himself. Her eyes were dark, the centres so dilated there was only a thin halo of violet surrounding them. Her complexion was dusted pink, and her breasts were fluttering against the confines of her bodice like trapped birds longing to fly free. He had partaken liberally himself at the dinner table and his blood was not as cool as it should have been — not if he had to resist the lure of those fiery eyes and that soft white flesh very long.

"I should have warned you the wine was nearly as potent as the whisky. My brother Archibald oversees the making of it."

Catherine detached his arm from her waist and squared her shoulders. "You, sir, make far too many presumptions. If anything, I found the Burgundy weak and lacking in body, its effects disappointing."

"Disappointing? In that case, perhaps it has just been your father's fine gin you have been missing since we left Derby, not your gallant lieutenant?"

"Vile," she hissed and with a flounce of her wide skirts,

she marched ahead, making only one wrong turn before she located the gallery leading to the west tower. Cameron lagged behind, smoking one of his cigars as he trailed her through the corridors and up the stone corkscrew staircase.

Her bedchamber was in darkness save for a single beam of blue-white moonlight that streamed through the window. Catherine stood in its path, silhouetted by the soft shimmering glaze of silver.

"Deirdre? *Deirdre?* Sweet Mother of God, where is that girl?"

"Anything I can help you with?" Cameron asked from the doorway. His features were in shadow, his broad frame lit from behind by a candle somewhere out in the landing. The blood pounded into Catherine's temples as she saw the tip of ash on his cigar glow brightly for a moment then fade again.

"You can snuff out that dreadful black weed and light one of the candles," she said sharply. He gave no indication he was about to oblige either request until she sighed and added a grudging, "Please."

"Certainly." He went back out onto the landing and returned with the taper from the wall sconce. He touched the flame to the candle on the dresser and another beside the bed, then set the taper in an empty stand.

"Thank you," she said as civilly as she could manage.

"You're welcome. And thank *you.*"

"For what?"

"For tonight. For behaving as if everything was as it should be. I can appreciate how difficult it must have been for you to sit through the dinner conversation without once speaking your mind."

Catherine regarded him suspiciously, uncertain as to whether she had just been insulted or complimented.

"And despite my earlier reservations — " he added, pausing to let his eyes drift downward along the sweep of pale green silk, "I believe you managed to win me the envy of every warm-blooded male in attendance."

Catherine held her silence. Compliments? Flattery? What was he up to? Their afternoon confrontation still bristled in the foreground of her mind; she had walked blithely into his verbal trap then, and was determined not to do it again.

"Thank you for escorting me up the stairs," she said stiffly. "Now, if you have no objections, I am very tired."

"Are you certain you can . . . manage everything else on your own?"

Catherine felt the dark eyes probe the curves of her bodice and she fought an unexpected urge to bait him into admitting she had earned more than the envy of his family members. It was there in his eyes: regret that he had not carried through his threats earlier in the day, had not taken advantage of her defenselessness. No doubt he was also wondering, speculating on just how much effort would be required now to coax her from the window to the bed.

"I assure you, Mr. Cameron," she said icily, "I am quite able to tend to myself from here on in. I *have* undressed myself on occasion."

He shrugged and smiled lopsidedly. "I was only trying to be friendly. If you change your mind, or if you need me for . . . well, for anything at all, I am right across the hall."

Friendly? she thought. A tarantula would have a better grasp of the meaning of the word. Aloud, she mimicked his dry tone. "If I change my mind, sir, I shall fling myself out the window and let the wind undress me."

He paused on his way to the door and grinned. "An ingenious solution, madam. Perhaps a tad melodramatic, but then I have often admired your vivid imagination. Good night."

Alexander was still smiling to himself as he walked into his own small chamber and closed the door. The girl had a certain spark to her, there was no denying. She constantly managed to get under his skin, to rouse more than just his anger in these verbal jousts. Too much more and he could not be held accountable for his actions. He had come damned close that afternoon. *Damned* close. He had felt slightly off balance ever since.

The hell of it was, he still could not pinpoint what it was about her that attracted him. They were as opposite in character as a man and woman could be. She was spoiled, proud, haughty. She provoked him deliberately, repeatedly, smug in the belief that she was above anything so base and repulsive as desire. Yet there were times — coming more and more frequently — when the icy facade showed cracks. When he sensed she just needed to be taken into someone's arms and held.

Someone's?

His?

No. In spite of Aluinn's rose-tinted view of the world, there was just too much to overcome. The pain, the memories . . . they were too strong, the guilt too near the surface even after all these years. Annie MacSorley might still be alive if not for him. She certainly would not have suffered degradation and pain at the hands of the Campbells if they had not been able to use her love as the ultimate weapon against him. He never wanted to place himself or anyone else in such a position again. Emotion was a weakness he just could not afford.

Suddenly Alex's body ached, and his head drummed with a vengeance. His good intentions had been thwarted at every turn, and so far he had not had an opportunity to enjoy more than a cursory wash or an hour's catnap since his arrival at Achnacarry. A steaming hot bath. A tall glass of brandy. A soft mattress and twenty-four hours of sleep . . . Heaven.

He sighed and turned from the door, but had only progressed a few steps into the room before he drew up short again.

She was lying on the bed, curled there in a pool of tousled lace petticoats. Her hair was spread in a gleaming red billow around her shoulders, accentuating the whiteness of her bared arms. Her corset had been removed, leaving only a slippery wisp of silk to cling to her breasts in a way that was far more enticing than naked flesh could have been. Her shoes and stockings were tossed in a casual heap at the foot of the bed and her petticoats allowed to ride deliberately high above the slender calves.

Seeing where his gaze was temporarily stalled, Lauren Cameron bent her knee slightly so that the skirt of her petticoat was displaced further, luring the eye higher along the shapely white thigh.

With an effort, Alex lifted his eyes first to her face, then over to the night table, where a partially full bottle of whisky stood.

Lauren smiled and drained the last few drops from her glass. "Shall I pour ye a wee dram? Ye look as though ye need it."

Alex watched her pour the whisky and, like a cat, curl her legs beneath her to rise up on her knees, her arm outstretched toward him. He moved forward and took the glass, conscious of the way her fingers lingered on his.

"I suppose it would be timely at this point for me to ask what you are doing in my room . . . in my bed?"

She pursed her lips and her eyes feasted openly on the aggressive breadth of hard, muscular chest and shoulders. "Why, I wouldna want tae be accused o' refusin' ma ain cousin's invitation. A fine welcome hame that would be."

"Invitation?"

"Mair'n the one, I think," she purred, shifting closer to the edge of the bed. "Although it's hard tae keep track when it's yer yer eyes dain the talkin'."

"If I gave you the wrong impression at dinner this evening, I'm sorry. You are a beautiful woman, Lauren. I apologize for looking, but that is all I was doing: looking."

"Mmm." Lauren raised both her hands to the silver and topaz brooch that held the length of tartan draped over his shoulder. She unpinned it and let both the clasp and the wool fall to the floor.

"I am a married man," he reminded her quietly.

"Aye, married. But sleepin' in separate rooms, separate beds? An odd way f'ae husban' an' wife tae behave, is it na?"

Alex glanced downward. Her hands had not been idle. The pearly buttons of his waistcoat had been unfastened, the ends of his jabot unwound and flung onto the floor. Her fingertips slid up the fine linen of his shirt and began loosening the ties at his throat.

"O' course, we could just talk," she suggested with a sigh, the tip of her tongue leaving a hint of moisture on her lips, "if that is what ye truly want tae dae."

"What I truly want — " His eyes dropped unwittingly to the voluptuous expanse of firm white flesh that still clung stubbornly to the silk chemise. The nipples jutted out like ripe berries, lusciously dark beneath the fabric. "What I truly want is to get some sleep. I haven't had much in the past few days."

Lauren sidled even closer, ostensibly to enable her to peel away the heavy velvet of his coat and assist him out of the brocade waistcoat. She worked his shirt open to a point below his ribs, and as she leaned back her hands found their way onto the plane of his chest. Her fingers spread wide in the thick black hairs and her lips parted as if the sensation was too much to bear. The sultry eyes lifted slowly to his and Alex felt himself drawn into the smoldering flecks of green and gold and hazel. It would be one way to prove that Catherine Ashbrooke meant nothing to him, he reasoned. A way to prove it was only the tension and the excitement of returning home that was stirring his blood, not the lure of silver-blonde hair and pleading violet eyes.

Sensing a victory, Lauren lowered her head. She bared the dusky island of his nipple and closed her lips around it, making warm, wet circles over the sensitive flesh with her tongue. Alex grasped her by the shoulders just as the silk of her chemise decided to sigh free of her breasts. She pressed them unabashedly against his torso, moaning throatily as the heat of contact sent a rush of anticipation spurting into her loins.

"I don't think you want to be doing this," he advised in a low voice, his own body reacting involuntarily to the feel of her warm and eager flesh.

"I ken exactly what I want tae dae, Alasdair," Lauren whispered brokenly, her mouth carrying the assault higher to the boldly defined hollow of his breastbone. "Ye've nae idea how long it's been since a *real* mon took me in his airms. Hold me, Alasdair. *Hold* me."

With an urgent whimper she pulled his mouth down to meet hers. Her body moved against him, breasts, belly, and thighs all joining in the conspiracy to undermine him. There was no hesitation, no shy apprehension as her tongue darted and probed between his lips, taking command of the kiss in a way that brought Alex's senses crashing back down around him.

He tightened his hands around her shoulders and forcibly thrust her to arm's length. The glassy eyes looked mildly startled as they stared up at him. Her bare breasts rose and fell on laboured breaths, their whiteness gleaming under a sheen of perspiration.

"What's wrong?" she asked on a gasp. "Why have ye stopped?"

"It isn't difficult to stop something that hasn't started yet."

Her hands, quick and deft as hummingbird wings, descended to the pleated folds of his kilt. "Has it na?"

"Lauren," he said, prying her hands away gently, "I am extremely tired. I am also somewhat drunk or I would have turned you over my knee and sent you packing ten minutes ago."

"But ye didna," Lauren said with a sly smile. "An' ye canna tell me ye have a warmer bed tae lie in this night. Ye look tae me like a mon in need, Alasdair. *I* need, too. I need a mon can take me awa' frae this place. Ye dinna belong here, Alasdair, ye dinna fit the sights or the smells. Ye'll never be happy, no' wi' this ruin o' a castle, no' wi' yer simperin' *Sassenach* wife.''

''I think I've heard about enough — ''

Lauren was not daunted. ''D'ye know what they dae o' a night here, Alasdair? D'ye know what ye've come hame tae? They sit about the fire each an' every night an' talk of auld times, of kings long forgotten an' glories long deid. They live in the past, all o' them. They spoke the night o' bluid an' courage like as if the glens were full o' both — but they're wrong! The kirk is full o' crofters an' bandy-legged shepherds who've never seen a broadsword, much less raised one in battle. Run wi' me, Alasdair, afore it's too late. Take me awa' frae here.'' Her eyes sparkled and her hands wrestled free of his grip to stroke brazenly between his thighs. ''Ye'll no' regret it, I promise ye.''

Alex did not answer. Instead he walked away from the bed and crossed to the tall armoire that held his few articles of clothing. He fished in the gloomy interior and found a small leather case, then opened it and extracted a fresh cigar.

He closed the armoire door and walked back to the bed, his eyes cold and dark as he saw Lauren slide expectantly toward him.

''You found your way here without any difficulty. I assume you can find your way out again.''

Lauren froze on the rumpled sheets, her eyes narrowing as she watched him pick up the whisky bottle and stalk toward the chamber door.

''Where are ye gaun?'' she demanded in disbelief, the shock flowing redly into her cheeks.

''I am going, mistress, to indulge in the sinful but very safe pleasure of a bath. When I come back, if you are still in my bed, I will not be quite so polite in ejecting you.''

Lauren's hands gathered into fists, her nails digging into the folds of bedding. Two glaring blotches of colour painted her cheeks, and her mouth compressed into a thin white smear.

"Bastard!" she spat. "There's nae mon alive tairned me out o' his bed! Nae mon alive would dare!"

Alex looked back over his shoulder just in time to duck as an empty glass came sailing past his ear. It crashed against the stone wall and a tiny fragment ricocheted off his wrist, slashing a thread of a scratch in the skin.

"Good night to you, too," he murmured dryly, and without another glance, he exited the room.

The faint sound of breaking glass took Catherine's attention away from the window, where, seated on the cold stone bench, she had been gazing listlessly out at the night vista. Finding her knees suddenly much in need of support, she had taken a seat soon after Alexander's departure. She had not moved in the intervening minutes but had stared glumly out at the black velvet sky without really seeing the loch or the mountains or the swollen, glistening beauty of the Highland moon.

Sighing, she began to pull her hair out of its stiff coils, dropping the steel pins carelessly beside her, uncaring as to whether they landed on the window seat or the floor. When her hair was loose and flowing around her shoulders, she stood and reached around for the laces that held her bodice bound so rigidly in place. Her movements were so sorely restricted that after a few feeble tugs she had to lower her arms and wait for the blood to flow into her fingers again.

On the third attempt — one away from tearfully executing her threat to launch herself through the window — she succeeded in slipping the knot and unwrapping the layer of shiny green silk. Another minor struggle with more laces and the relief was palpable as the pressure of the whalebone corset was released from her aching ribs. She groaned aloud as the heinous instrument of torture was flung aside, and she spent several moments massaging her flesh and relishing the ability to breathe deeply again.

Leaving a trail of cast-off petticoats, wire panniers,

chemise, stockings, and slippers, she groped through the rack of borrowed garments until she found the cambric nightdress. The giddy effects of the wine had abated and her temples throbbed; she sought out the china basin to splash some cool water on her face and found both the bowl and pitcher empty.

"Oh Deirdre . . ." Her shoulders slumped wearily and her lips mouthed a silent oath.

Snatching up the offending pitcher, she padded barefoot to the door. The circular landing outside her room was dark, and the door across the way closed, emitting only a thin blade of light along the lower edge. She tiptoed across the cold floor and listened to the silence, failing to detect any noise or movement from within. It *would* be just like him to return to the party belowstairs. No doubt he had some unfinished business to tend to — business in the guise of flaming red hair and gold-flecked eyes. Catherine knew the type well enough: a seductive little harlot with loose morals and even looser undergarments. There had been no mistaking the gleam in the narrowed cat eyes or the intentions announced plainly by each sway of the shapely hips.

"What do I care?" Catherine asked herself irritably. "Good riddance. They deserve each other."

She crossed to the fire-room and, pushing the door wide, took several angry steps into the room before she realized she was not alone. Alexander Cameron was there, relaxing in the brass bathtub, his eyes closed as he savoured the wall of steam rising around him. In one hand he nursed a half-filled glass of whisky, in the other, a fresh cigar. The huge cast-iron pots that were kept filled and suspended over the fire were sitting empty on the hearth.

Catherine dared not move, dared not breathe. The door had made no sound on its rope hinges, and her bare feet had issued no alert to her presence. But even as she hesitated, poised to fly back to safety, the ebony crescents of his lashes were raised slowly, warily. Fully expecting to see Lauren Cameron standing there armed with her bruised vanity and perhaps a weapon or two of more substantial consequence, Alex was mildly taken aback to see Catherine, scantily clad and clutching a porcelain pitcher to her bosom as if it were her heart sprung from her chest.

He lowered his cigar and checked the flow of resentment that infused his bloodstream. Two beautiful women in a highly provocative state of dishevelment presenting themselves before him in less than a ten-minute span . . . if he did not know better, he would declare it a conspiracy!

"If you have come in here with the intentions of interrupting my bath, I give you fair warning of violence. I have waited the whole blessed day long for these few minutes of privacy and will relinquish them for nothing less calamitous than an earthquake or flood." He shifted slightly, sending more wisps of steam into the air as he leaned back and closed his eyes again. "On the other hand, if you would care to join me — "

"*What?*"

The whiteness of his teeth flashed in a grin as he lifted his glass. "In a drink, of course. There should be another glass around" — he waved the cigar absently — "somewhere."

"No," she said on a sigh. "I do not wish to join you in a drink."

"Mmmm." He exhaled a cloud of smoke "You're absolutely right. You have had quite enough already."

Catherine gripped the pitcher closer, the temptation to throw it almost too much to bear. "I thought you were going back downstairs."

"The idea of a hot bath and cool sheets appealed to me more."

"Cool sheets? I should have thought you could have done better for yourself tonight, what with all the attention being oozed on you at dinner."

The dark eyes opened.

Catherine moved closer to the heat of the fire, blithely unaware that the brightness behind her rendered the cambric nightdress all but invisible.

"Do I detect a confrontation in the air, madam? If so, be so kind as to fetch the bottle down from the mantel."

She studied the heaviness of his eyes for a moment and frowned. "I would as soon say what I have to say to you while you are sober, if you don't mind."

"I don't mind at all, but if you want me to *hear* anything you have to say, I suggest you move away from that fire: The view from here is extremely distracting."

Catherine glanced down, then stepped quickly to the side of the hearth.

"Thank you," he murmured. "Now what is it you wish to discuss so earnestly?"

Catherine set the pitcher aside and clasped her hands in front. "I do not wish to *discuss* anything. I insist on knowing exactly when you plan to honour your word and send me home."

A smile creased his mouth. "You insist, do you?"

"Yes," she said quietly. "I insist. You gave your word not only to me, but to my brother as well. You promised to send me home as soon as we reached your Archberry safely. Well, we are here and we are reasonably safe . . . although for how long is a matter of conjecture, what with all this talk of rebellion and crusading princelings."

Cameron delayed a response long enough to draw deeply on his cigar. "It might please you to know Donald thinks I have exhibited an extremely poor sense of responsibility by bringing a new wife to the Highlands at this time — a new English wife at that. He did not put it into so many words, of course, for he is far too much of a gentleman to do so, but he does have an uncanny way of saying a great deal by saying nothing at all. In other words — " He waylaid an interruption by raising his hand. "Even if you were my wife and we were passionately . . . or should I say *desperately*, infatuated with one another, there would be little argument or opposition to my sending you packing back to Derby until the troubles are resolved one way or the other."

"Is this a roundabout way of saying you plan to leave

everyone with the impression we are still married . . . even after I am gone?''

"The thought did occur to me," he admitted. "It would certainly remove the need for any painful explanations."

Catherine watched him reach out and tap the ash from his cigar. His hair was wet and clung to his neck in glistening black curls. The firelight gilded his upper torso, burnishing and polishing his flesh beneath the forest of curling black hairs. She had forgotten — or perhaps just refused to remember — the virile perfection of his chest and shoulders, the leanness of his waist and hips, the long powerful legs that could carry him through the graceful steps of a waltz as easily as they could execute the deadly steps of a sword fight.

He was a frightening and dangerous man, full of contrasts, full of surprises. The thread separating the savagery from the compassion was fine indeed, yet if she could appeal to his logic, and at the same time keep a rein on her own emotions, perhaps he would be more obliging.

Catherine moistened her lips. "When?"

He ignored her, ignored the question, and she felt the tension increase.

"If you haven't the time or the inclination to deliver me to the border yourself, at least let me send for Damien. He will be worried sick by now, and I'm sure he would as soon come to fetch me himself as trust my safety to strangers."

"Are you forgetting the patrol we met on the road?"

"Of course I am not forgetting. How *could* I forget? I shall carry the horror of that single day with me the rest of my life!"

"What makes you think your brother would fare any better?"

"I . . . don't understand."

"Come now, Mistress Ashbrooke. You may not understand Gaelic, but surely you grasped the drift of what the sergeant and his men had in mind for us? A stupid Englishman and his wife . . . a little fun and entertainment to wile away the afternoon. After they finished robbing, raping, and killing, they would have blamed the ambush on the rebels — popular scapegoats these days, I'm told.''

Catherine paled. ''Damien and . . . and Hamilton will come and fetch me. Hamilton will bring a regiment of dragoons with him if necessary!''

''I have no doubt that man would start a war if necessary, and take the greatest pleasure in doing so. But your fiancé's misguided ardour is not my biggest concern.'' He rolled the cigar between his long, tanned fingers. ''Just out of curiosity, has it occurred to you yet that your name and description, everything about you, is probably known by now by every Campbell, every Watchman, every militiaman and English soldier garrisoned between here and the Tweed? Even if your brother managed to make it through — and that is a very big 'if' — what makes you think either one of you would make it out of the first glen alive? Do you understand what I am telling you . . . *Mrs. Alexander Cameron*? I would imagine the Duke of Argyle and his kinsmen break out in rashes just thinking of what they could do if you were to fall into their hands.''

Catherine stared at him aghast. The blood had drained from her face, her eyes were round and unnaturally bright.

''Then why?'' she cried softly. ''Why did you bring me here if you knew . . . if you even *suspected* there would be a chance I could be trapped here?''

His dark eyes avoided hers — possibly the first time they had done so.

''To be quite honest, I have been asking myself that same question since we left Derby.''

Catherine recoiled from the unexpected huskiness of his voice. It was another trap, another ploy to make him seem human, to unsettle her, to throw her off guard.

''And?'' she demanded shrilly. ''Did you manage to come up with an answer?''

He took a deep breath. ''No. No answer.''

''No answer,'' she whispered. ''You just took it upon yourself to play god? You ruin my life, ruin any chance I might have had for happiness in this miserable world, and then . . . and then you have the arrogance to sit there and . . .'' She backed slowly toward the door, her eyes blinded behind a rush of tears. "Oh, you are cruel and heartless. You bully people and use them thoughtlessly; you prey upon their weakness then throw it in their faces time and again for the pleasure of your own base amusement. You ridicule my feelings for Hamilton Garner because you know you are incapable of experiencing or even understanding the purity of such an emotion. You are cold and empty and I pity you. You would not understand any emotion, least of all love, regardless if it stood up and slapped you in the face! Loving *you* sir, would be a curse I would wish on no other living soul, friend or enemy, for it would indeed be a desperate and fruitless undertaking!''

Cameron moved suddenly. Through a film of startled tears, she saw him rise up out of the water, saw him step out of the bath and stride toward her, his body shedding moisture in sparkling sheets. She whirled and groped for the exit, but he was right behind her. His hand shot out and slammed the door, his body crowding hers against the wall so that she had nowhere to turn, nowhere to run. She cringed against the cold stone, her face buried in her hands, her entire body cowering before the expected brutality.

He stood behind her, his feet braced wide apart, his arms held rigid by his sides. She could feel the heat of his body, smell the moisture of the bath water steaming from his skin. The impression of hard male flesh was boldly stamped on her mind, shocking her to the very core, and when she felt his hands close firmly around her upper arms, it was like a fork of lightning jolting along her spine. Her limbs were useless, too numb to offer any resistance as he slowly, inexorably turned her around to face him. Her belly flooded with liquid fear as she glimpsed the rage in the narrowed eyes; it spread and swooped lower as the mirthless lips curved into a smile.

"So. You find me cruel and heartless, do you? Cold and lacking any emotions?'' His voice chilled the nape of her neck and sprayed her arms with gooseflesh. "Well, Mistress Ashbrooke, it might interest you to know how absolutely correct you are in your analysis. Furthermore, it has taken a considerable effort over the years to achieve such a high level of immunity — an immunity which does not come without its faults, which I am also freely willing to admit. You, on the other hand — "

"Let me go," she gasped and twisted her head in a wild, frantic motion, one that was gravely impaired by the sudden pressure of his steely fingers beneath her chin.

"You, on the other hand, admit to nothing," he continued. "You have the body and passions of a woman, yet you are afraid to see them for what they are. You have strength and courage — enough to make a man wonder why you would persist in playing the role of a spoiled, petulant child. I told you this afternoon, madam — I *warned* you in the plainest terms possible that I was tired of playing games. I also warned you of the consequences should you choose to test me any further."

"Let . . . go of me." The throaty whisper was barely audible. Not so the soft and animal-like moan that broke from her lips as he shifted forward enough for her to feel the threat rising in his body.

"P-please," she gasped. "Don't — "

His hands cradled either side of her neck, angling her mouth up to his.

"Y-you gave your word not to h-hurt me!"

"I have no intentions of hurting you," he murmured. "And my promise was not to *force* you to do anything you did not want to do."

"I . . . I don't want you to do this . . ."

"I don't believe you," he said quietly and his lips brushed her temple. They roved slowly, deliberately, along the verge of her hairline to capture the delicate pink curve of her earlobe, remained there a moment, then sought the rapidly beating pulse below.

"Oh no . . . please . . ."

Catherine swallowed hard and used her fists to push against him, but her hands were trapped against his chest, pinned there by a powerful wall of muscle. The feel of his hot, sleek flesh prompted another cry, so that when his search progressed her lips were parted and vulnerable to his assault. His hands kept her face upturned to his, his mouth held hers hostage. His tongue lashed at hers with a single-minded possessiveness that produced another moan — more of a whimper this time as she realized her nails had ceased their mindless clawing and had curled into the springing black hairs. Aware of the subtle change, Alex drew her even closer, molding his body, his mouth to hers so that each bold thrust of his tongue evoked stunningly sharp reverberations deep in her loins. The kiss became the centre of her consciousness, all she knew or felt, yet she fought the rising tempest of emotion — fought it, cursed it, craved it.

His hands moved downward, stroking, smoothing a path of icy thrills along the quivering outline of her body. His thumbs brushed over her breasts, his palms engulfed the tender spheres and found the nipples hard and straining, aching with a need that etched itself plainly on his skin. With his mouth still slanted over hers, he began to unfasten the chaste row of satin ribbons that bound the neckline of her gown. Catherine was helpless to forestall him. She tried to push him away, but the effort was halfhearted. There was not strength enough left in her arms to deter him, no command on earth that could keep her hands from spreading across the heated surface of his chest. She had fought his power in the garden at Rosewood Hall and lost. She had fought it at Wakefield and she had fought it through eight interminable days and nights of travel. She could fight it no more.

He slipped the bows one by one until the cambric lay open to her waist. When his hand eased the fabric aside, Catherine tore her mouth free from his on a gasp of unholy pleasure. The blood in her veins turned to quicksilver, her legs were useless beneath her, and if not for the arm that knowingly curved around her waist to support her, she would surely have melted to the floor.

When he heard her shivered cry, his black eyes flicked briefly up to hers, but what he saw there was not enough to stop him from lowering his head and closing his lips around the ruched, insolent peak of her nipple. Catherine's body jerked; her lips formed a moist rigid *O*. Her hands, moving of their own accord, climbed to his shoulders, then higher, until they were grasping thick handfuls of the gleaming black waves of hair. Her neck arched back as his lips suckled and led her through a series of shuddering inner explosions. She was hardly aware of him stripping away the rest of the cambric, pushing it down over the rounded softness of her hips.

Reeling with the effects of this new intoxication, she scarcely saw him sink down onto his knees before her, his hands bracing her, opening her for his pleasure. She could not watch, dared not conceive of the dark head lowering to her again, of his mouth blazing an outrageous path into the junction of her thighs. She wanted to cry out for him to stop, but when the probing hot wetness found her, ravished her, scattered what remained of her senses to the four winds, she had neither the words nor the desire to discourage him. It was an unheard-of violation, a sinful tease of forthcoming delights, and she suffered the erotic torment until a sob sent her trembling to her knees. Slipping down beside him she shamelessly dragged his mouth back to hers, her lips matching his in eagerness, her tongue as bold and greedy to know the taste and feel of him.

Their bodies came together, their movements hauntingly reproduced in the shadows that danced and writhed across the walls. Catherine revelled in the heat of his limbs twining with hers, she marvelled at the iron strength of his flesh, the devouring hunger of his lips as they roved everywhere, sampled every sweet hollow and curve. A thousand bright slivers of anticipation welcomed his hands as they spread her limbs and she felt him settle purposefully between her thighs. Her hands clutched the bulging muscles of his upper arms.

Her eyes opened wide . . . wider as the incredibly hard slide of flesh began to furrow into her — stretching, tearing, impaling, as if he meant to split her in two. Her limbs tensed involuntarily and for a long moment, her passion was overshadowed with the anguish of doubt.

Alex twisted his fingers into the golden spill of her hair and forced her to look up into his face, into eyes that no longer burned with rage or arrogance but with an entirely new emotion, naked and raw, more utterly devastating than the awesome, straining hunger in his body. Catherine saw it and her heart soared. Her hands moved, driven by the wisdom of instinct to smooth down the corded muscles of his back until they settled over the carved marble of his flanks. Her fingertips were cool and trembling, their invitation as tentative as the sob of assent on her lips.

Alex lowered his mouth to hers. The kiss was restrained and unhurried; he seemed content to wait until the shy undulations of her body became a bolder demand for unity. Gently he held her, gently he braced her and pushed against the valiant barrier until the last vestige of her resistance tore inwardly. Her eyes squeezed shut over an explosion of orange and red sparks; her mouth broke free with a groan of disbelief and she felt him continue past the bright slice of pain, thrusting determinedly forward until her innermost soul throbbed and ached with the shock of initiation.

An instant, no more, and the pain subsided.

An instant more and a smothered gasp acknowledged the warm, swollen presence that marked the end of one identity and the beginning of another.

He began to move within her, slowly, firmly, introducing her to the moist, sensual friction of flesh on flesh. Her hands, she discovered, were still poised on the molded iron sinews of his hips and she left them in place, lightly riding the gauged and deliberate pelvic thrusts.

His hands stroked the satiny curves of her body, guiding her limbs wider, coaxing them higher, encouraging her to join in the languid rhythm. She tried to choke back the unbidden cries of pleasure each measured movement produced, but it was impossible, and when he abandoned a wet and tingling nipple to arch his torso above her, she thought she had never seen anything so beautiful as the gleaming, sculpted perfection of his bronzed muscles. Her eyes moved lower and she saw how her hands grasped him, how her body arched and writhed and strained to pull him deeper as he kept thrusting . . . thrusting . . .

Now not even the commanding power of his obsidian eyes could hold her. Her head thrashed side to side, fanning her hair in a fine-spun web beneath them. Her nails ribboned his flesh with tiny white scratches and she began to shiver, to quake uncontrollably as a mindless urgency overtook her, an urgency born of blood and fire and consuming desire. His hands were there to lift her and support her as his thrusts came harder, deeper, faster. She sobbed raggedly as she neared the edge of some incredible precipice and her long slender legs twined frantically around his, fusing their bodies together as she rushed headlong over the brink of erupting passion.

She was not aware of crying out his name, but Alex was. He heard it through a crimson mist of pleasure that drenched him, clouded his senses to everything but the lithe, supple body shuddering violently beneath him. Each muscle, each nerve, each scorched vein screamed for release, yet he forced himself to wait, to resist the lure of the pulsating velvet sheath until the spasms grew so intense they robbed him of both reason and sanity. He plunged his hands beneath her hips and thrust himself as deep as life and breath would take him, and as one they soared beyond rapture into the brilliantly lit realm of ecstasy.

Lauren Cameron pressed herself against the rough stone wall, her eyes closed, her cheeks flushed, her fists clenching and unclenching as hatred seethed green and evil within her. Her feet had become rooted to the floor, her nerves singed raw as she listened to the choked cries of unimaginable joy coming from the other side of the fire-room door.

How dare he humiliate her like this! How dare he scorn and dismiss her, then run straight into the arms of his *Sassenach* wife!

Lauren had *not* mistaken the glances and half smiles he had cast sidelong at her throughout the evening. She had *not* imagined the pressure of his thigh leaning against hers or the riveting suggestiveness in the long, tapered fingers as they had stroked and caressed the curved sides of his wine goblet. These actions had been deliberate — as deliberate and unnerving as the knowing glimmer in his eyes each time they sought her reaction. Her reaction? She had felt naked during the better part of the meal.

Not invite her? He had practically raped her right there at the dinner table! What game was he playing? What game were they both playing — he the stalwart and untarnished husband, she the prim and virginal bride so quick with her blushes of modesty. Yet at a moment's notice they were sprawled on the floor, naked and grappling together like dogs in heat.

Lauren had heard them arguing, had heard the door slam and the anger intensify. Then what: Submission? Compliance? Eagerness? Perhaps he had boasted about Lauren's visit, used it to rouse the yellow-haired bitch into a jealous rage. Perhaps the whole thing — the glances, the touches, the subtle innuendo throughout the evening had all been staged for that purpose!

Lauren backed slowly away from the door, fury darkening in her eyes. No man used her in such a way. She was no man's vehicle for winning the attentions of another woman . . . not unless she willed it to be so!

She whirled around and descended the stone spiral with no thought or care for the sound her leather heels made on the steps. Flushed and wild-eyed, she paused at the bottom and glanced along the darkened corridor, but it was deserted. The candles were dim and shed little light on the gloom, and for that she was momentarily thankful. She had thrown her clothes on in haste and anger, not troubling herself with laces or bows, and she was in no mood for making explanations to anyone who might stumble upon her in the hall.

Rape, she thought blackly. I could always say he raped me before he crossed the hall and obliged his simpering wife.

No. That story was only good the one time. A second, similar incident would not only fall under suspicion, but would cast doubt on the first. And if the first charge were questioned, Lochiel might begin to wonder if he had hung an innocent man, and if indeed that man had ever stolen the gold and jewels that had been found among his possessions. The blame might then shift onto Lauren's shoulders — where it rightfully belonged — and her years of careful planning and scheming might crash down around her shoulders like a house of cards.

She hated this place. Hated Achnacarry with its oppressive stone walls; hated the mountains and the isolation and the primitive mentality of a land dominated by loutish warlords and chest-beating zealots. There was another world out there waiting for her, a world infinitely more suited to her talents and desires. She craved a life of gaiety and bright lights, of exquisite gowns and handsome lovers only too eager to part with their gold and favours.

Orphaned when she was twelve years old, Lauren had been sent to Achnacarry — banished, as she liked to think of it — to live under the guardianship of her great-aunt, Rose Cameron. Born and raised in Edinburgh, the sudden isolation had been almost as great a shock to the young girl as her appearance had been to the Cameron household. Anticipating a shy and refined lass barely out of bibs and aprons, they had been surprised to greet, instead, a developing beauty with a mind and will of her own. Coming from a distant branch of the family, they had had no way of knowing the upbringing or lifestyle Lauren had been subjected to. They were ignorant of her father's criminal history and blithely unaware that her mother had owned and run one of the most profitable brothels in the city. A Cameron was a Cameron, regardless of her sly disposition and despite the fact that within the first month of her arrival, Lauren was the cause of a bloody, jealous dispute between Lochiel's two eldest sons.

A thin, malicious smile drew out the corners of her mouth as Lauren hurried along the corridor. What fools men were, young or old. How truly weak they were in spite of all the brawn and bluster. A few scant inches of moist pink flesh could undermine the best of them, could reduce the most fearsome warrior into a quivering mass of uncertainty. In the beginning such power had excited and intrigued her. The bolder the conquest, the higher her aspirations and, coincidentally, the greater her own pleasure. She had been even quicker to appreciate the material benefits that could be earned through a particularly enthusiastic demonstration of her skills, and over the years she had amassed an impressive nestegg of gold and silver coins.

It would have been far more impressive had young Gregor MacGregor not fallen prey to his passions while aiding her in an ill-conceived attempt to run away two years ago. When they were caught, not only was his kilt loosened and his body firmly engaged in acts of joyous depravity, but his saddle was weighed down with rings, bracelets, and coins extracted from Lochiel's family chest . . . Lauren had been left no recourse but to smash a rock against the side of his head and scream for deliverance. Her performance had been flawless and convincing. Her aim had been faultless as well, for the lad never did regain his full senses, and tempers had been stirred to such a peak no one troubled to stay the noose long enough to hear his defense.

Unfortunately, the nestegg of her own painstakingly gathered coins could not be separated from the pouch before it was returned to Lochiel, who in turn blithely locked it away in his strong-room again. Lauren was cleared of any taint of treachery in the alleged theft and kidnapping, but was then faced with the prospect of searching out a new means of financing her liberation. Twice, in her sixteenth and seventeenth years, Lochiel had ventured to arrange a suitable marriage for her, and both times Lauren had appealed successfully to her great-aunt and Lady Cameron for reprieve. Marrying any Highlander, rich or poor, would have sealed her fate for all time.

So she remained at Achnacarry, discouraged by the minor setback in her plans but far from daunted. There were still some who suspected she had not been entirely innocent in the MacGregor incident, and for that reason her actions required an inordinate amount of discretion — which was why she had avoided liaisons with men like Struan MacSorley. He was lusty and virile, yes, and she had spent many a restless night wondering how it would feel to be driven to ecstasy on the wings of his sheer brute strength, but he was also fiercely possessive. He was not the type of man likely to keep an affair secret, nor was he the type to dally overlong with a niece of Lochiel's and not feel bound to do the honourable thing. Lochiel would be only too happy to see his old friend wed again; Struan had been without a wife for nearly three years now.

All of that was rendered inconsequential when the first rumours of Alexander Cameron's homecoming began to circulate.

Lauren had, naturally, heard all the stories centring around the black-haired, black-eyed renegade who was the *Camshroinaich Dubh*. She had stood for hours in front of the portrait of Sir Ewen Cameron and knew without a doubt that the grandson was exactly the type of man who would suit her needs perfectly. He was a soldier of fortune, a man who had spent half his lifetime in cities like Paris, Rome, Madrid . . . ! He would not be content to ramble about the decaying walls of a medieval castle. Bored with the peace and tranquility, he would soon be drawn into the jaws of adventure again, and when he left this miserable formation of rock and mortar, he would have no qualms about taking someone along who shared his hunger for excitement.

In the days and hours prior to his arrival, when the tension within the castle walls was as taut as a bowstring, Lauren had been beside herself with anxiety. She paced the battlements as often as the guards searching for some sign of activity in the surrounding forest. Scores of clansmen had been sent out to scour the countryside, on guard against any possible interference from either the militia or rival clansmen. She spent every spare moment ingratiating herself with the Cameron women, running errands for them, coddling their loathesome brats, sitting through hour after grating hour of trite conversation, advice, lectures . . .

And then the dam had burst. A clansman had galloped into the courtyard shouting the news at the top of his voice. The *Camshroinaich Dubh* was less than five miles away — he would be at Achnacarry within the hour!

There had been no mention of a wife. Not ever. The entire family had been stunned to learn not only of her existence, but of her nationality. Alexander Cameron, a man who had almost singlehandedly started a war between the Hanoverian Campbells and dozens of enraged and sympathetic Jacobite clans, had come home with a pinch-lipped, stiff-backed Englishwoman who fairly reeked of Georgite decadence. Her presence at Achnacarry was an insult, a slap in the face to every clansman old enough to remember the arrogance of the English victors after The Fifteen and every clansman young or old whose pride stung at the thought of their rightful chief, Old Lochiel, forced to live the life of an exile in Europe.

It was not that Lauren gave a damn one way or the other about politics or that she felt any loyalty to anyone other than herself. She had simply considered Alexander Cameron to be her future benefactor, her means of freeing herself from the strangehold of anonymity. The obvious amusement he had taken in humiliating her tonight did nothing to deter her from her original goal; if anything, she was more determined than ever to leave Achnacarry, leave every last Cameron behind in the dust. There was more than one way to achieve that end. She simply had to rethink her strategy, reroute her energies, so to speak.

Lauren hurried along the gloomy corridor until she came to a narrow stairwell frequented mainly by the servants. She slipped into the entry and glided soundlessly down into the bowels of the castle, pausing now and then to listen for footsteps. She ran the length of the vaulted stone undercroft, passing various storerooms where grain and foodstuffs were hoarded and great hogsheads of whisky and ale were left to age undisturbed. At the northernmost end she turned up a well-worn flight of steps that fed tributaries to the pantry and kitchens, the courtyard and stables, and, of immediate interest to Lauren, the guardhouse.

She went unerringly to the third door from the stairwell and tested the latch cautiously. It was not locked, and, taking a deep breath, she eased the door open and slipped inside. The room was dark, the only light coming from a high slitted window that looked out over the courtyard. She gave her eyes a few moments to adjust to the heavy shadow, then walked softly toward the cot in the corner. He was lying there, one arm folded comfortably beneath his head as a pillow, the other tucked under the single layer of woolen blanket he wore.

Lauren paused, her pulse beginning to quicken, her limbs trembling under a rush of sweet-hot sensitivity. Her breasts felt sheathed in ice, the nipples so tight within their silk prison they throbbed with an agony of pleasure.

"Ye should know better than tae creep up on a mon when he's asleep," a low voice murmured from the cot. "It's that dark ye could have a dirk atween yer eyes afore they'd finished blinkin'."

Lauren savoured the tension for a moment before acknowledging the voice. "Ye werena at the pairty the night, Struan MacSorley."

"I prefair tae celebrate in ma ain fashion," he said, and Lauren's gaze was drawn to where a bold stirring was visibly reshaping the folds of the blanket. The blood flushed sluggishly into her belly, swirling there until the heat became almost unbearable.

She lifted her hands slowly and began shrugging the already loosened halves of her bodice and sleeves off her arms. "An' would ye be cravin' company . . . or would ye prefair tae celebrate alane?"

MacSorley's eyes followed the movement of her hands as they peeled away the modest layer of her chemise and left only a sheer wisp of silk clinging to the ripe and swollen mounds of her breasts. The dusky peaks were proudly defined, straining against the fabric with an impatience that sent a scalding spurt of hunger into his loins. The blanket stirred again and Lauren sent the delicate tip of her tongue around her lips to moisten them.

She reached down and casually lifted the corner of the blanket, skinning it back inch by solemn inch. Her breath dried in her throat as she bared the hard, flat plane of his belly, the coarse cable of reddish-gold hair that whorled down past his navel and furrowed into the junction of his thighs. Her eyes widened appreciatively and she did not even notice the grin that welcomed her bold stare. His body was truly awe-inspiring, his dark and weathered skin stretched over muscles proportioned for a Samson.

Lauren set her teeth against a violent shudder as she felt one of his huge, calloused hands skim up beneath her petticoat and without preamble delve greedily into the moist nest of curls. Lauren gasped and trembled against the pressure, which only invited the blunt-tipped fingers to deeper intimacy. Lauren crumpled slowly to her knees beside the cot, her mouth agape, her hands clutching his broad shoulders for support. With a growl of satisfaction he tore the silken shield away from her breasts and feasted on the voluptuous bounty, his hard body beginning to quiver with an intensity Lauren might have found amusing if not for the shattering distraction of her own needs. Her cries were real, her passion genuine. She gave herself completely to the pleasures of the night, knowing that by morning she would be stronger for it, thinking more clearly, whereas Struan MacSorley would be thinking not at all. And a man incapable of thinking clearly made mistakes, believed the unbelievable, abandoned the most steadfast convictions.

MacSorley had been Alexander Cameron's friend once, almost a brother by marriage. He could not be feeling too comfortable with the idea of a *Sassenach* taking his dead sister's place in Alasdair's affections. Perhaps he was downright displeased. If that was the case, Lauren would know it by morning. And knowing it, she would not only do her skillful best to acquire an obsessive new lover, she would also win a potentially useful ally.

Chapter Fourteen

Catherine drifted back to reality slowly, her arms locked tightly around a bunched feather bolster. She stretched slowly and lazily, inwardly noting each pleasurably bruised muscle. Her body tingled with a new awareness. She felt young and healthy and alive, wanting to take back every sour, accusing word she had ever said to anyone in her lifetime and replace them all with laughter and smiles.

She opened her eyes and stared at the canopy overhead. She was in her bedchamber, ensconced in a nest of fat cozy blankets. She could not remember precisely how she had come to be here. Her last vague recollection was of curling sleepily and contentedly against Alexander Cameron's warm body, of feeling his arms enfold her and hold her close as if she had left him as utterly depleted as he had left her . . . yet not enough to let her go.

The thought produced such a flooding of immodest guilt to her cheeks that she sank below the line of the covers until only her eyes and the pink tip of her nose were left exposed.

What on earth had come over her last night? What had come over the pair of them — cavorting like debauched lovers, first on the hearth in the fire-room, and then when the fire died and the air had become chilled, he had carried her into the huge feather bed where their shameless behaviour had continued. What would he think of her in the harsh light of day? So prim and proper and righteous until now . . . sweet merciful heaven, the things he had done to her body! The things she allowed — no, begged him to keep doing! Eighteen years of propriety, of striving to learn to be the perfect, cool hostess and wife . . . in one night it had all been tossed through a hole in the wind, never to be reclaimed.

It never should have happened, the prickling voice of her conscience hissed. *You should have stopped him.*

"I did not exactly encourage him," she whispered.

Didn't you? What do you call parading around in a flimsy nightdress before a naked man?

"I did not know he was naked — "

How else does one bathe?

"I certainly did not know he was bathing!" Catherine insisted.

Well, when you found him and saw what he was doing, why did you not run back to your chamber and bolt the door?

Catherine chewed her lower lip in agitation. It was a logical question deserving a logical answer and, indeed, had that not been her first impulse — to turn and flee?

But you didn't. You stood there and defied him again, knowing — knowing, I say — what his reaction would be.

Catherine had no rebuttal, no defense. There *was* no defense; her actions had been utterly irresponsible, unconscionable . . . just plain *foolish*. She was *weak*, in body and in spirit. So much for the lofty Miss Catherine Augustine Ashbrooke who thought herself above such base instincts. So much for her righteous contempt for her mother's actions — hadn't Lady Caroline said it was in her blood to make the *best* of the situation? *What* was in her blood, though? The ability to crave and feel passion, obviously, but was there nothing more? Last night she had become a woman, yet she felt more childlike, more helpless than ever before, floundering in a sea of new doubts.

Might I also remind you that last night put a quick and easy annulment to rest along with your virginity.

Catherine groaned and buried her head in the pillow, but the little voice persisted, turning tart with sarcasm.

Lieutenant Garner will not be pleased. He had reserved the honour for himself — would have had the honour had you simply refused your father and left Rosewood Hall on your own. You could have been Mrs. Hamilton Garner by now.

Somehow, the thought of waking up naked and dishevelled in Hamilton Garner's bed did not cause nearly the intensity of blush it should have. Nor did the thought of lying in his arms rouse quite the same kind of stirring in her loins as Alex had. The two men were totally opposite, in character and in form. Hamilton was . . . well, smooth. In every sense of the word. Polished. As if he were a statue or a figure to be admired daily, and every last detail had to be just so: every hair placed just right, every fingernail a clean white crescent. She could not imagine him with a stubble of beard showing or a stray piece of lint on his tunic sleeve, whereas Alexander . . . She quite believed he was capable of tumbling her in a muddy field if the mood came upon him — and making them both wildly happy in the process.

Catherine covered her face with her hands and sank even deeper under the covers. How could she even think of such things? How could she even dare to compare Hamilton Garner's precision to the strong, brooding animal-like qualities of Alexander Cameron?

Where was he anyway?

Catherine sat up and glared at the empty side of the bed. Surely he knew she would wake up feeling confused and guilt-ridden. Surely he would have something to say to her, even if it was only —

"Good morning."

The quietly spoken salutation cut through the silence with

such unexpected force that Catherine gasped and clutched the blankets to her bosom. Alexander was standing in the doorway, a small tray balanced easily in his hand. She had been so absorbed in her own thoughts she had not heard him enter. He was fully dressed, wearing breeches and a plain white shirt, giving the impression he had been awake for some time. His hair was combed but carelessly swept back into a queue. His jaw was clean-shaven, his eyes clear and piercing and showing no sign of fatigue or guilt. In fact, he looked so refreshed and so obviously satisfied with himself that Catherine allowed her conscience to answer for her.

"We must be waking on different mornings. I see nothing good about this one so far."

A half smile tugged at his mouth. "I was beginning to think we might waken on different mornings at that. It is past two o'clock in the afternoon."

"Two — " Catherine forgot herself and pushed upright. "In the afternoon? But why wasn't I wakened sooner? What must everyone be thinking of me?"

Alex shrugged easily. "They are undoubtedly thinking you endured a long and dangerous journey over the last two weeks. You wouldn't raise any eyebrows if you failed to make an appearance for another two weeks."

"You made the same trip. I doubt if anyone expects you to lounge about all day."

His smile turned wry. "Men are expected to eat, sleep, and think on their feet, didn't you know?"

"Women are able to eat and sleep and think on their feet just as well as men. Probably better, since we are also expected to feed, clothe and provide for their comforts on top of everything else."

On the word "provide" the blanket slipped completely to reveal the two perfect moons of her breasts. Alex's gaze fell involuntarily. For his part, he was treading very carefully through these first few minutes. He had steeled himself out on the landing for the initial confrontation but had no means of preparing himself for the slippery cascade of long golden hair or the smooth marble-white shoulders or the thrusting pertness of the rose-tipped breasts. His senses were already finely tuned to the lingering, musky scent of their lovemaking; at the sight of the temptingly bared flesh it was all he could do to maintain the balance of the tray.

As she hastened to cover herself, he cleared his throat savagely and set the tray on the night stand. "I thought you might be a little hungry. I managed to scare up some tea for you and fresh hot biscuits. I did not bring too much in case you were still asleep, but if you like, I can send Deirdre to the pantry for something more substantial."

The violet eyes flicked to the door in some surprise. "Deirdre? Good heavens, yes. I should have thought she would have wakened me hours ago."

Alex felt her eyes turn to him as he crossed to the window. "Actually, she was here earlier. She came into the room this morning and . . . well, that was what woke me. I guess she thought it best not to return until she was sent for."

Catherine's fingers clenched around the blanket and her eyes grew as round as medallions.

"She saw us? You and I . . . *together*?"

"My fault," he admitted with some chagrin. "I had every good intention of tucking you into bed and retiring to my own room across the hall, but . . ."

Catherine remembered. He had carried her from the fireroom and set her on the bed, but somewhere between drawing the covers over her and brushing back the flown wisps of her hair, he had succumbed to the urge to kiss her again and . . . before either of them knew it . . .

At least he is being civil, she thought as the colour ebbed and flowed in her cheeks. He could as easily have been clumsy and belligerent, or worse — casual and stand-offish. Instead he appeared to be almost as uncomfortable with their new status as she was.

"It never should have happened," she remarked, her voice whisper soft.

"My fault again. Entirely. You had a little too much to

drink and it gave you a little too much false courage, which I, rather shamelessly, took advantage of. To be quite honest, I probably had more than my share of the dinner wine as well, and I guess the temptation . . . twice in one day . . . was more than I could handle. I am sorry.''

"You were not *entirely* to blame,'' she conceded guiltily. "You did not force me to drink the wine, nor did you force me to . . . do anything else against my will.''

Alex turned his head and she was struck by the completely incongruous thought that he should always stand in a partially sunlit window. The light bleached his shirt almost transparent, made his hair gleam like molten metal, his eyes burn a deep, dark sapphire blue.

"Whether you had been willing or not last night,'' he said evenly. "I doubt very much if I would have stopped. Do you understand what I am saying? That it was an act of pure selfishness on my part and you are right: It never should have happened.''

Catherine laced her fingers tightly on her lap. She kept her eyes deliberately downcast, although she was aware of every movement, every sound from the window. For some reason the warmth that had suffused her since wakening had given way to a hollow chill. She knew, suddenly, what he was leading up to, why he *was* being so civil and understanding. She also knew, or at least suspected very deeply, that he hoped her pride would step in to prevent any further humiliation.

"Last night you told me it would be impossible for me to leave Achnacarry.'' Somehow she managed to keep her voice nonchalant. "I trust that was also the wine speaking?''

"It will be difficult, not impossible.'' (Was that relief she detected?) "There has always been a thriving business along the coast smuggling contraband in and out of the country.''

She smiled softly. "Am I considered contraband?''

"At the moment, very much so. And I am afraid it is the only way to absolutely guarantee your safe passage home.''

There it was: the final rejection. She was so accustomed to being the one to *do* the rejecting, it left her a little bemused.

"Home," she murmured. "Yes indeed. Father will undoubtedly rant and rave; Mother will . . ." She hesitated and lifted her thick, honey-coloured lashes only to find he was watching her, studying her face with eyes that were as cool and distant as the snow-capped mountain peaks.

"Yes? You were saying?"

"Nothing." She quickly lowered her lashes again. "It doesn't matter. I am sure I can manage them."

A glimmer of brightness in Alex's eyes faded and died away. "Well, then, I shall see what I can arrange. I have to go to the coast for a few days anyway — "

"You are going away?"

He turned to stare out the window again. "Donald received another message this morning from the Prince. It stated in no uncertain terms that the royal regent would consider it a direct affront to himself and to his father if The Cameron of Lochiel does not meet with him in person."

"Your brother is going to meet with Prince Charles?"

A nerve shivered high in Alex's cheek. "You can see why this is not the best of times for me to introduce any new complications into the family?"

So now I am a complication as well, she thought. Aloud she asked, "How long will you be gone?"

"I hope for only a few days. A week at the most. I imagine there is a good deal of diplomacy involved in refusing a prince his royal due. At any rate, you will be quite safe here as long as you remember to stay inside the castle walls. No more riding through the woods alone. Campbell's men may still be in the vicinity, and I would lay odds young Gordon Ross would dearly love to meet with you in a clearing somewhere."

He allowed the subtle warning to sink in a moment, then added, "If you would care to write a letter to Damien, I'll see it leaves on the first available ship. You can advise him of the arrangements I am making. I'll add my own note to let him know the exact date of departure and point of arrival when I learn them.''

''I imagine it will be an expensive way to remove me from underfoot.''

Alex frowned and his dark eyebrows crushed together in a single black slash. He studied the soft oval face, noting the eyes that refused to meet his and stared adamantly at the bedpost. There were two unrelenting blooms of colour high on her cheeks, like the flush of a fever, and the slender white fingers were curled tightly around the folds of the quilt, holding it like a shield to guard her nakedness. She looked so very small and fragile in the old warrior's bed, and he was battling a strong urge to cross the few steps that were separating them. He ached to gather her into his arms and wipe away the hurt and confusion she was suffering, but to do so would only compound the host of errors he had committed last night. Her emotions were too raw; she was not thinking clearly. When she came to her senses she would be grateful he had listened to his head, not his heart.

He looked down at his hands, disturbed by his inability to stop them from shaking. He balled them into fists and held them rigidly by his sides.

''Actually, I have been giving the matter a good deal of thought. Since Raefer Montgomery ceased to exist in Wakefield, why not take it one step further and kill him off completely? His death would give you the perfect excuse for returning home . . . the bereaved widow, et cetera, et cetera.''

''Widow?'' she whispered.

''You would hardly be expected to mourn overlong, having only known the poor fellow a short time. Naturally there would be a considerable estate to . . . shall we say, blunt the residual scandal somewhat.''

''I don't want your money,'' she said angrily. ''I don't want anything else from you.''

''A noble sentiment, but when your feet are dancing on

English soil again you might have second thoughts. I will leave the details to you . . . a tragic accident on the streets of London, a headfirst tumble into the River Thames. I will include a second letter to Damien giving him power of attorney and a new will.''

''You do not have to do this,'' she said with a shiver.

''Yes,'' he said quietly, ''I do. It is little enough, considering . . .'' He saw the bright shimmer of tears welling in her eyes and he brusquely changed the topic. ''Well, I'll see what I can do about rounding Deirdre up for you. If you like, I will also make your excuses to Donald and Maura so you will not be disturbed for the rest of the day. The entire castle is in an uproar anyway, what with Donald's decision to leave first thing in the morning.''

''Will I see you before you go?''

Alex hedged. ''You can just give the letter to Deirdre. She will deliver it to me before we leave.''

Catherine nodded, accepting this final rebuff with as much grace as she could muster. He walked to the door of the bedchamber and paused there a moment, looking as if he might say something more, but then he was gone and the door was shutting firmly behind him. Only then did Catherine look away from the bedpost. She did not see anything, however, for her eyes were glazed behind a thick shroud of hot, bitter tears.

Chapter Fifteen

Alexander Cameron stamped his feet to ease the tension, cupped his hands around his mouth and blew a hoary breath to warm his fingers. The dawn was beginning to lift the gloom, to give shape and substance to the stone and mortar. Clouds of mist, tinted the yellowish hue of goats' milk, rolled over the walls of Achnacarry Castle and dripped onto the cobbled courtyard in a steady drizzle. It had rained during the night and there were puddles everywhere. The cold seemed to soak through his heavy layers of clothing to scratch icy fingers up and down his spine.

Alex wore the *breacan an fheile* — the belted plaid kilt common to Highlanders winter and summer. He was well armed — two steel-butted dags were belted to his waist, and his sabre was strapped into place on his saddle, easily within reach, as was a flintlock musket. He was not alone in the courtyard. A cacophony of horses' hoofs rang out on the stones, competing with the efforts of the clan pipers to inspire the assembly of men into some sort of order. The lights had blazed from the castle windows all night long as hasty preparations were completed for Lochiel's departure. Hardly anyone had slept, and now hardly a single window was empty of the dark silhouettes of excited onlookers.

The mist, low and thick, blotted out most of the upper stories — not that any one particular face could have been distinguished from another, even if that one particular face were the only one surrounded by long blonde hair. Besides, the windows in the west tower faced the opposite direction . . .

Catherine had barely slept a wink all night long. She had tossed and turned in the huge empty bed, alternately climbing down to pace back and forth to the door, and staring unseeing out into the rainy night from an uncomfortable perch on the stone window seat. She had not seen Alexander since his visit to the room that afternoon. She had written her letter to Damien, and Deirdre had delivered it as instructed, but the slim hope she had fostered that he would still stop by to see her, even for a moment, faded with the last of the midnight blackness. She knew Lochiel's party was leaving at dawn and she spent most of her anxious hours debating whether or not she should find her way down to the courtyard to be on hand when they departed. As Alex's wife, surely her presence would be expected. As his "complication," however, she feared his resentment at such a presumption. She did not know what to do, how to feel, how to act anymore. One night . . . one single, reckless night, and her world had been overturned.

She spent the hours thinking of home, of Derby and Rosewood Hall, of Damien and Harriet . . . even of Hamilton Garner. But they had all become detached somehow, as if they had been part of a life she had lived years, not mere weeks ago.

What would Damien do when he received the letter? He would be relieved to hear she was safe and coming home, but would he also be able to read between the lines and know something had happened between her and Alexander Cameron? He had admitted befriending the man who had called himself Raefer Montgomery — what had he said? "The name might have changed, but not the character of the man." He had obviously liked and trusted Raefer Montgomery, and as his lawyer he would have been privy to information concerning not only his business assets, but his life as well. Was there something *she* should be reading between the lines? Something she had missed in their relationship? Something out of focus about that night in Wakefield? Something not right about Damien's . . . *performance?*

Catherine was not permitted to finish the thought. A soft tapping on the bedchamber door announced the arrival of Deirdre, who seemed surprised to find Catherine awake and sitting by the window.

"Shall I bring you up a cup of chocolate, mistress? Or perhaps a cup of tea? It is a dreadful, dreary morning, is it not?"

Catherine turned toward the window. The mist formed an opaque wall she could not see through, but she imagined the loch below and the jagged beauty of the mountains. If she tried very hard, she could see a horseman riding along the crest of the hill, his black cape flowing behind him, a giant black stallion prancing beneath him . . .

Go to him. The harm is done, what more could happen from a simple farewell?

"Pardon? What did you say?"

Deirdre frowned. "I asked if you wanted your meal up here or if you intended to join Lady Cameron and the others."

"Oh." She delayed a direct answer. "How is Mr. MacKail this morning?"

"Angry as a mule with a burr caught in its saddle. He actually tried to get up out of bed to join the others, daft man. Dr. Archibald had to pour a whole vial of laudanum down his throat to stop him. I don't suppose it helps, his room being directly over the courtyard and all."

Catherine pricked to attention. "Can you see anything from there? I mean, the fog is so thick . . ."

"Oh yes, mistress. His is a small room only a story above the ground. You cannot see across the yard, but you can see quite clearly into it. And they are making ever so much noise."

Deirdre saw the look on her mistress's face and ventured to add, "Mr. MacKail is sound asleep now. He would never know you were there if you wanted to take a peek from his window."

"I . . . I don't know. I — "

"After all, it is rather an important errand they are setting out on. A bit of history in the making, I should think, riding out to see the Stuart prince." Seeing Catherine's further indecision, she took up the velvet robe and carried it to the window seat. "We would have to hurry if we're not to miss them."

MacKail's room, as it turned out, was not very far, and the window was, as Deirdre had said, directly above the courtyard. The dripping fog had enveloped everything in a light haze, but there was enough activity below to keep the mists swirling and clear large patches at a time.

Impervious to the rain, Donald Cameron stood near the center of the yard, dressed with all the pomp and splendour befitting an influential Highland chief. He wore plaid woolen trews, not the kilt; his hair was tied back with a black silk ribbon and covered by a bonnet trimmed with the eagle feather that marked his rank. His jacket and waistcoat were tartan, as was the voluminous length of plaid draped regally over his shoulder. Each was a different pattern and colour so that he glowed crimson, black, yellow, and green from head to toe.

Surrounding him, awaiting the order to form and march, were a dozen personal servants, several pipers, the clan bard, who would record every word of the momentous occasion, and no less than sixty heavily armed clansmen led by the lion-maned giant Struan MacSorley. Catherine did not envy Lochiel and his entourage their trip over hazardous mountain passes and rocky gorges in this weather. The rain, if anything, showed signs of turning into a full-fledged storm, and the lingering effects could well hang over their heads for the entire journey.

On the other hand, like Deirdre, Catherine could admit to some curiosity over the man they were riding to meet. She had heard all the stories about the Stuart prince — how handsome he was, how witty, how charming. She could not help but feel a little sorry for him, having gathered over the last few days that with Lochiel's refusal to join any forthcoming rebellion, the Prince had little hope of convincing any of the other important clans to join him. Another cruel twist of fate to add to the doomed Stuart history. Was there ever a royal family so plagued by misfortune? Catherine mused. James I of Scotland had been murdered, James II killed by a bursting cannon, James III slain in a rebellion of his own nobles led by his son. James IV had fallen in battle at Floddenfield, James V had died of shame after the army he led at Solway ran from the field. Mary, Queen of Scots, had been forced to flee her country and her throne and had sought sanctuary with her cousin Elizabeth, only to be considered a threat to the English throne and imprisoned for nineteen years before being executed. Her son, named heir by the childless Elizabeth, ruled both England and Scotland after the Union of the Crowns in 1603, but, arrogant and despotic, he believed in the divine right of kings to rule as they saw fit. His beliefs were passed on to his son, Charles I, who not only endeavoured to strip Parliament of its powers, but attempted to control the church through his own appointed bishops. To the Puritans of the Church of England, this seemed to be a step back toward the papacy they had rid themselves of in the reign of Henry VIII. Parliament sided with the Puritans, and by 1642 England was embroiled in a civil war. Charles was defeated and his head eventually rolled the way of this grandmother's.

Following eleven years of parliamentary rule under

Cromwell, the monarchy was restored and Charles II crowned king. The restoration brought back the Stuarts, but also, upon Charles's death, a Roman Catholic king in his brother, James II, who again tried to strip Parliament of its powers and to reconcile England to the Church of Rome. In desperation, the leading politicians asked William of Orange, then married to James's Protestant daughter, Mary, to come to England and wrest the throne in his wife's name. The invasion of the Orangeman sent James II fleeing to France and set William and Mary on the throne to rule jointly. During their reign, Parliament not only enforced the signing of the Bill of Rights to guarantee their own powers then and in the future, but passed the Act of Succession, which decreed all future monarchs had to be of the Protestant faith.

During his daughter's reign, James II died in exile. Louis XIV of France was quick to recognize his son, the thirteen-year-old James Francis Stuart, as rightful king of England, as much to stir up old hostilities as to win an ally in the exiled youth and his court. In 1702 the English throne was again bereft of an heir, but the government ignored James's claim in favour of Mary's sister, Anne.

In 1707, after the Act of Union officially disolved the Scottish Parliament in favour of one ruling body of government, those clans who had been adamantly opposed to the imposition of English laws had turned to James Francis in the hopes of restoring not only the Stuart monarchy but Scottish independence. The attempt failed and James retreated to France again, but a spark had been lit in the Highlands, and while it flickered and showed little strength in the next seven years, it continued to burn deeper and deeper as more and more of the Scots' way of life was eroded.

James was shunned yet again in 1713, when Queen Anne died without an heir, and Parliament looked across the Channel to a descendant of James I's Protestant daughter, who ruled the state of Hanover in Germany. In 1714 the elector of Hanover was crowned George I, and in 1715

James Francis Stuart made his most successful bid to date to reclaim the throne.

It was probably true, Catherine reflected, that the people of England would have preferred the son of James II to the doughty, fifty-four-year-old foreigner who spoke no English and made no secret of the fact that he cared more for Hanover than for England. But James Francis Stuart was Catholic and adamantly refused to appease Parliament by converting to the Protestant faith. Moreover, he had already shown his preference for his Scottish blood, a burr which undoubtedly scratched the righteous hides of the political leaders of the time.

But where the English could see the logic in offering the crown to a foreigner, the Scots only saw it as a further insult to the long and regal line of Stuart kings. Religion aside, they preferred to have one of their own occupying the throne, and in 1715, ten thousand loyal Jacobites lined the field at Sheriffmuir to face the army of King George. Catherine's father and uncles, including her Uncle Lawrence, had joined the neighbouring gentry in support of the Hanover claim and had fought in that great bloody battle, but had it really been fought to decide a king's fate, Catherine wondered now, or had it been a declaration of superiority? England was master of the sea, boasting an empire of colonies in America, the West Indies, and India. Could it have afforded to allow the comparatively small nation of bristling Scotsmen to gain the upper hand, regardless of whether their cause was legitimate or not? Could it afford to do so now?

Catherine knew the answer, just as she was beginning to understand why Alexander Cameron had come back home after so many years away. It had nothing to do with politics, certainly nothing to do with religion. It had everything to do with family, with pride, with his identity and self-respect as a Scot and a man.

As to who was right and who was wrong, whose claim was legitimate and whose in contention, Catherine did not know.

Well schooled in her father's prejudices and beliefs, she had been content up until now to recite them blindly and had never troubled herself to question whether there was as much wrong on both sides as there was right.

You are beginning to sound as if you hold some sympathy for these rebels, her conscience warned silkily. *That could be dangerous. Very dangerous indeed.*

Catherine ignored the little voice and leaned forward to press her forehead to the window. She had caught sight of a familiar form striding through the wisps of fog, and her eyes followed him now, her mind completely blank of any other thoughts. He was dressed like everyone else, in a woolen kilt and short frock coat. A sword hung in a scabbard at his side and she could see the twin butts of a brace of pistols riding comfortably in a belt slung about his waist. His head was uncovered, the shock of ebony hair curling against his temples and throat in the dampness. Stopping by Shadow's side, he began to check the tension of the cinches, and the stallion's elongated, graceful head turned, nudging him affectionately on the arm. Alex smiled and murmured something in the velvet ear before producing a juicy red apple from within the folds of his tartan.

As Shadow munched contentedly, Cameron's gaze strayed upward toward the multitude of windows facing into the courtyard. Catherine flinched back, even though she knew he could not possibly see her through the rain and haze, and instead focussed on a poignant moment shared by Lochiel and Maura. His hand was pressed tenderly to her cheek and they were exchanging soft smiles, unmindful of the milling, bustling confusion that surrounded them. Their moment together was shattered by Archibald, who burst into the courtyard with the subtlety of a small hurricane.

The doctor had wanted to go to Arisaig again, to protect his brother's sensibilities, or so he claimed, but Donald had stood firm. Judging by Archibald's piqued expression as he went from group to group checking things that had already been checked a dozen times before, his resentment at being left behind would undoubtedly spill over into the week ahead. Jeannie Cameron was close on his heels, waving and gesturing, spreading words of encouragement and advice as thick as treacle.

After a final word with Maura, Lochiel mounted his dapple-gray stallion, the signal for the horsemen to do likewise. As half the party was mounted, half on foot their progress would be slow and cumbersome. The pipers filled their chanters and struck up a lively marching tune, the chords swelling and echoing off the wet stone walls.

Alex drew his horse in line next to Struan MacSorley and bent an ear to hear him over the furious skirling of the pipes. There was a bright flash of titian red and Lauren ran out from the crowd gathered around the rim of the yard. She stopped between the two men, pouting at them with her hands on her hips, and Alex, laughing, accepted the invitation and leaned over, aiming a friendly kiss toward her cheek. Pulling back at the last moment Lauren flung her arms around his neck, redirecting his lips to land fully over hers.

Catherine, watching from the window, felt something deep in her belly twist and curl into a tight knot. He was doing nothing to end the shocking display; if anything, he seemed to be enjoying it immensely.

Struan roared with amusement and leaned down himself, scooping an arm around Lauren's waist and lifting her into his saddle as if she weighed a mere nothing. With her eyes still bright and her lips still parted and moist from Alex's kiss, her face was turned toward Struan's and his mouth plunged down over hers. The hand around her waist slid boldly up to fondle a breast while she squealed delightedly and made a halfhearted effort to break free.

Catherine backed away from the window. The tightness in her stomach had spread up to constrict the muscles around her heart. Last night she had willed Alexander Cameron into Lauren's arms with haughty contempt. Somehow she did not feel so haughty now, knowing that when she was gone and out of the way, Lauren — or someone else like her — would undoubtedly be eager to fill Catherine's place in Alexander's bed.

She was suddenly tired. So very tired. She glanced over at the sleeping Aluinn MacKail and felt a rush of envy. She would sleep, yes, but the hours would be filled with the memory of hot, sleek flesh, of hands sharing their power and their tenderness, of lips so bold her body ached just thinking of where they had been, what incredible sensations they had roused.

Catherine knew she had to put those memories behind her. She would need all of her strength, all of her concentration to face the ordeals that were sure to lie waiting for her at Rosewood Hall. She would have to resign herself to the reality that she was no longer Catherine Augustine Ashbrooke, most sought-after heiress in three counties. She was Catherine Ashbrooke Montgomery, and widow or no widow, the damage to her reputation had been a *fait accompli* the moment she had ridden away from Rosewood Hall. Had she herself not always been among the first to laugh and gossip with relish over the merest hint of scandal involving any of her peers? Had she not regarded it as a solemn duty to destroy a rival's reputation, however flimsy the evidence of misconduct might have been against her? In her case, there would be no shortage of former victims absolutely drooling for a chance at revenge. Two weeks . . . two *hours* in the company of a man like Alexander Cameron would have sealed her fate in stone.

There was nothing she could do about it. Her only defense was stupidity: She had defied Cameron at every turn. She had challenged his authority, she had flaunted herself before him at the party, and she had deliberately poked and prodded his unstable temperament time and time again. She had acted childishly and with a naïveté that in hindsight she could only regard with wonder. Add to the list ignorance, stubbornness, conceit, duplicity . . . all of the qualities Cameron had accused her of possessing from the outset. He was so clever. Why then, could he not see the doubts that were tearing her apart?

"It isn't fair," she whispered. "It just isn't fair."

"Eh? Ye want some air?"

Catherine looked around, startled by the sound of Auntie Rose's voice so close by her ear. Even more startling was the fact that she was seated before the fire in the family retiring room, that she had been totally immersed in her own misery for the umpteenth time since Lochiel's departure from the castle three days earlier.

"Ye're warm, hen," Rose said solicitously. "Aye, ye've been sittin' here lang enough tae roast yer cheeks a rare shade o' pink."

Maura glanced up from her needlepoint. "Would you care for another cup of chocolate, or perhaps some wine?"

"Chocolate?" Rose's button nose wrinkled in disdain. "Bah! Devil's brew, that. Pour us oot a wee dram o' *uisque*, there's a guid lassie. Dae mair guid f'ae the soul than all the sweet brown coo's water in the world."

Grateful for the opportunity to stretch her legs, Catherine set her own square of neglected needlework on the arm of the chair and crossed to the sideboard. She glanced askance in Jeannie's direction, but the doctor's wife was sound asleep in a chair by the window, her mouth quivering open on each rattled breath.

"Some o' us dinna have the stamina," Rose declared cheerfully and bent her snowy head to the length of lace she was tatting.

Catherine smiled and unstoppered the decanter, but before she could pour out a glassful her gaze was attracted to the bright square of light showing through the high, narrow window. It had rained the first two days and nights of Lochiel's absence. As strong and well fortified as Achnacarry was, the damp had found its way through the doors and windows, rendering most of the rooms — especially those in the more ancient sections — cold, musty, and unfriendly. To-day, even though the clouds seemed to have lifted temporarily and the fire was hot and crackling, Catherine's mood seemed determined to continue its downward slide.

"Pour some f'ae yersel', hen," Rose ordered. "It'll dae ye nae harm on a foul day such as this."

"Lady Cameron?"

"No, thank you, dear. I still have some wine." Her glass from the noon meal sat on the table by her elbow, the contents not diminished by more than a mouthful over the past hour.

"Aye, love, aye." Jeannie snorted herself awake. "I'll have a wee ane. Ma throat's dry as an auld sock."

"Nae wonder f'ae tha'," Rose commented. "Ye've snorked enough air this past hour tae pipe us all the way tae Glas'gy."

Catherine delivered their glasses but did not resume her seat. "I think perhaps I shall take a walk outside while the sky is deciding what to do."

"Quickest way tae rot yer lungs, hen," Rose cautioned.

"Nonsense." Maura laid her embroidery aside. "I feel like a little fresh air myself — assuming you would not mind the company?"

"Not at all." Catherine found herself growing genuinely fond of Donald's wife. It had been at Lady Cameron's insistence that she leave the dreary loneliness of her room and join the others for meals, the afternoons of sewing, and the evenings of casual conversation. Her discomfort had quickly been eased when she realized the gossip revolved mainly around harvests and sheep shearing, the children's tribulations and education — everyday problems concerning everything from pending marriages to the market price of wool. Normal and civilized. There was the expected amount of discussion surrounding the Prince's presence in Scotland but, oddly enough, not nearly as much as had filled the parlour conversations in Derby. For Catherine, who had assumed all of Scotland was frothing at the mouth in anticipation of swarming south and invading England, it came as an unsettling revelation to know that so many advocated peace. They were not all warmongers and savage barbarians. In many ways, their lives were more serene, more civilized, less pretentious than those she had witnessed in Derby and London.

She thought of the dandies in their tight fawn breeches, stiff neckcloths, wigs, and pomades, and compared them to the Cameron clansmen who had gathered to celebrate Alexander's homecoming. Their clothing was drastically different to be sure; there was hardly a frock coat, neckcloth, or scented handkerchief among the lot. But their smiles were genuine, their laughter honest. The Cameron family had shown no reluctance or lasting hostility in welcoming Catherine among them. Would Sir Alfred or any of his influential, socially prominent, *civilized* friends have reacted in the same fashion had she introduced a black-haired, kilted Scottish renegade to the table at Rosewood Hall?

More likely than not he would have been shot out of hand and his body fed to the hounds.

Catherine sighed and drew the borrowed wool shawl closer around her shoulders. She and Maura had exited the castle by a small Judas gate and were strolling along the gravelled path of the formal gardens. The air was drenched with the sweet fragrance of rhododendrons and azaleas. Briar roses and heartsease grew in riots behind neatly trimmed hedgerows, the flower heads drooping with the weight of the recent rains. Rooks and curlews wisely kept to their shelter beneath the arbours, but the sound of their quarrelling was an incessant as the patter of dew dripping off the branches at each quiver of breeze.

Catherine stooped to pluck a rose, one that was pure white with just a blush of creamy pink in the centre, and noticed the two clansmen following at a discreet distance. Their eyes were not on the two women, but on the surrounding border of forest, the sloping shoreline, the hills in the distance.

"You get used to them," Maura said casually. "You even appreciate them sometimes when you have an armload of berries or fruit."

I doubt if I would ever get used to bodyguards, Catherine thought, and was about to turn away when one of the men glanced her way and smiled. With a start she recognized Aluinn MacKail.

His wound, according to Deirdre, was healing remarkably well, with equal credit going to Archibald's doctoring skills and the Scotman's own determination. Twice in the past two days she had seen him wandering the halls of the castle, and while he never remained overlong in their company, he joined the ladies each night for their evening meal. He appeared to be a particular favorite of Rose and Jeannie, being cavalier enough to laugh at their bad jokes, roguish enough to embellish their good ones. His manners were impeccable. He could pluck flattery out of the air and bestow it on the least suspecting person with hardly more effort than a quick, easy smile.

Catherine could scarcely fault Deirdre for falling completely under his spell. He was handsome, charming. He had proved on the journey north that he could be attentive and considerate to everyone regardless of their station in life. He had also proved, however, that he was capable of extreme, cold violence. Even if they had not witnessed his abilities in the attack at the River Spean, the reality of his having spent the past fifteen years in Alexander Cameron's company told far more about his character than two brief weeks of acquaintance could reveal.

His loyalty to Alexander was unquestionable. Had some of that silent diligence shifted to Catherine during Alex's absence? Why else would he be out in the cold and the damp, assuming the menial task of guardian?

"This was always one of my favourite retreats." Maura drew Catherine's attention to an ornate octagonal summerhouse positioned in the centre of the garden, with gravel pathways radiating outward like the spokes of a wheel. "When it seems the whole world is conspiring against me, I come here and just sit. It is very peaceful, so very pretty in the sunlight." She laughed as she glanced up at the dirty banks of clouds gathering overhead. "Unfortunately, I see the weather as well as the world is conspiring against us today."

"I cannot imagine you troubled or needing solace from the world," Catherine said shyly.

"When you have four children pulling at your skirts at the one time and a husband raging about like a fifth child in a tantrum, I shall remind you you said that."

Catherine's smile faded and she lowered her thick lashes. She was not quick enough, however and Maura reached out to touch her arm gently.

"What is it, dear? Is something troubling you?"

Catherine studied the rose in her hand. She wanted very much to confide in someone, to pour out all of her doubts and fears . . . but she simply did not know how or where to begin.

"Men can be such strange creatures at times," Maura said, guessing at the cause of Catherine's crestfallen mood. "Strong, domineering, so unbending at times it makes you want to take them by the throat and scream. Yet at other times they are so childlike — lost and groping for a few words of reassurance. That can make you angry, too, unreasonably so sometimes, especially if you happen to be feeling lost and lonely yourself."

Catherine swallowed hard and tried to contain the wavering sheen of tears.

"The Cameron men," Maura continued, "are particularly stubborn and strong-willed. A curse of their bloodlines, I believe. There isn't a one of them who you could say had a true grasp of the word compromise, certainly not if it applies to their own behaviour."

"Donald seems very loving and gentle."

"Donald? Yes, he is. Loving and gentle. But there are times when the sheer strength of his love frightens me half to death."

"How can love be frightening?"

"When it consumes you. When it blinds you to all other

considerations. When you can no longer distinguish right from wrong, love becomes a terrible weapon and it can destroy you as easily as it can save you.''

Catherine pondered the words carefully then sighed. ''I don't think I would ever want to be that much in love.''

''My dear, you do not have a choice. Sometimes it just happens, whether you want it to or not, whether it makes sense or not, whether it makes you happy or not. And believe me, the harder you fight it, the harder you fall. Donald Cameron of Lochiel was the last human being on this earth I wanted to find myself in love with. I was raised *knowing* all Cameron men were heartless and despicable and that all their women wore black and conjured spells over iron cauldrons. Heaven only knows what Donald thought of us Campbells. You cannot begin to imagine the shock waves that tore through both clans when we announced our intention to marry. But I fought it as long as I could, I truly did. I refused to see him, refused to think about him, threw myself wholeheartedly into a courtship with another man — a more suitable fiancé, naturally, but Donald was always there, standing between us. I thought if I could just get him out of my system — '' She halted and her eyes took on a faraway look. ''I agreed to meet with him one last time. I listened to what he had to say. We argued. I presented all the logical, sensible reasons why the union simply could not work . . . and . . . he touched me. That's all he did, he just touched me. Here, on the cheek — '' She pressed her fingertips over the faint blush, and her smile blossomed with the memory. ''I knew then I would die if he ever took his hand away.''

Catherine remembered the scene she had witnessed in the courtyard prior to Lochiel's departure. He had laid his hand on Maura's cheek and she had kissed his palm in a way that suggested she felt the same way now as she had all those years ago. Not a showy gesture, by any means. Not as brassy and demeaning as Lauren Cameron's display.

Thinking of Lauren and of courtships brought another memory to the foreground.

"Who was Anne MacSorley?"

"What?" Lady Cameron was startled out of her reverie.

"I know she was Struan MacSorley's sister, and I gather she and Alexander were betrothed at one time — "

"Handfasted," Maura whispered, and it seemed to Catherine as if her complexion had drained of all colour and texture. "But I should not be the one to tell you about her — "

"Please." Catherine took Maura's hands into her own, her expression so earnest, Maura's heart wrenched in sympathy. "I am trying so hard to understand . . . to understand *him*."

Maura nodded slowly. "Perhaps we both need to talk about it. I've tried to block it from my mind so long . . . we all have. But if Alexander is to have any peace here, we must all learn to put the ghosts to rest. Dear Lord, but I wish Donald were here. I have a feeling we are both going to need the support of a strong pair of arms before we are through . . ."

Thirty miles to the west, at that precise moment, Donald Cameron was having much the same thought. He wished Maura was by his side. She was his strength, his weakness, his logic, his compassion.

It had taken the slow-moving train the full three days to reach the coast, passing through the luscious green glens of Lochaber and Rannoch, climbing and snaking its way around fairy-tale gorges, ravines and waterfalls only to approach a desolate and wind-ridden coastline that was a smuggler's paradise. In one of the small, rarely frequented inlets, the Prince's ship, *DuTeillay*, lay at anchor, a modest three-masted brigantine, much abused by the seas and offering the barest of comforts to her royal passenger.

Lochiel's party had been stopped twice in the descent to the harbour; once by an armed band of MacDonald clansmen whose chief had assumed the monumental responsibility of protecting the Prince; once by a dour-faced, belligerent Highland laird who had himself been summoned for an interview with Charles Edward Stuart.

"Aye, he's a likable enough laddie, Donal'," the old man had said. "A Stuart through an' through. He'll have the royal crest tatooed on yer arse afore ye even ken there's summit up yer kilt."

Donald's frown — it had not left his brow since they had ridden away from Achnacarry — grew darker as he studied Hugh MacDonald's wizened features. Glengarry was an old warrior, an old friend and strong ally of the Camerons. His loyalty to the Jacobite cause, like Donald's, had never been in question, but like The Cameron's, it was also tempered by reason.

"Glencoe has been an' gone," Glengarry continued wearily. "Aye, an' his kinsman, MacDonald of Scotus. We've all tald him the same thing: go hame. The time's nae guid. Aye, we can fight in the mountains an' we can raid oor neighbours tae the south, but it willna be shepherds an' yellow-hearted merchants waitin' ayont the Tweed f'ae us. T'will be German George's artillery an' stiff-backed scarlet troops."

"Does he bring any encouraging word from France?"

Glengarry screwed up his face. "He brings wha' he wants tae bring. Nae troops, nae weepons, nae gold — just a blind eye an' a swelled heart, an', truth be tald, I canna fault the lad f'ae tha'. There's little enough faith in the world as it is."

"Has there been any word from The MacLeod or The MacDugal?"

The old man leaned sideways and spat noisily onto the ground. "They didna trouble themsel's tae reply tae the fairst two letters wee Tearlach sent them. Thaird time it were young Clanranald himsel' teuk the summons tae Skye, an' he come back wi' a message f'ae the bonnie laddie tellin' him since he came wi' nae troops, nae supplies, an' nae money, he shouldna be surprised tae find nae army waitin' f'ae him."

Lochiel felt a crushing confirmation of his worst fears.

MacLeod and MacDugal had been two of the most outspoken Jacobite chiefs, bragging about how many men they could bring into the field to support a Stuart uprising. With them both reneging so openly it meant others of less conscience would not hesitate to follow, placing the greater burden of responsibility on Lochiel and his fellow moderates.

"There are mair'n a few guid men waitin' tae see how ye call it, Donal', afore they commit their ain minds ane way or t'ither. Dinna lead them wrang. Dinna choose in haste or we all suffer f'ae it. If ye believe we can fight an' win, so be it; we're wi' ye. If ye dinna think we hae a whore's prayer in saintdom, then we willna think any the less f'ae yer courage in sayin' it's so. I'm an auld mon, a foolish mon who dreams o' a Scottish king on a Scottish throne. I'd pledge ma soul tae the devil just tae see the *Sassenach* bastards driven back ayont the borther where they belang."

Donald's heart had been leaden as he watched Glengarry and his small entourage ride away. If every laird in Scotland felt the same way, if that was all they were being asked to fight for — a free and independant Scotland — how different the circumstances might be! There were thirty thousand fighting men in the Highlands. United behind that single purpose, they could form an impenetrable wall across the border that no English king in his proper senses would dare challenge.

But that was not the Stuart dream. They wanted all of it: Scotland and England united under one monarch. It was an unrealistic goal and the one that was doing the most harm to the Prince's cause. And in the eyes of the English it was also the single most condemning factor, one that would unite all of England against them.

Glengarry had said a dozen lesser chiefs had eagerly pledged their support already, but only — Lochiel suspected unkindly — because they knew their numbers would not influence the greater scheme of things one way or the other. It was an unfair judgement, for their homes and lands and responsibilities were taken every bit as seriously as his own, but the harsh reality was that these same lairds could pledge perhaps two hundred fighting men. And two hundred fighting men out of thirty thousand simply did not tip the scales. As chief of the Camerons, hé controlled the lives and destinies of five thousand men women and children. He could not enter into any commitment lightly, even though it galled him to think that someone, somewhere, might see his caution as cowardice, his efforts at diplomacy merely a ruse to ingratiate himself with the Hanover government.

"Ahh, Maura, ye were right," he whispered. "All those years ago, ye were right, ma love."

Alexander leaned forward and Lochiel waved his hand in a dismissing gesture.

" 'Tis naught. I was just rememberin' somethin' Maura told me on our weddin' night. She said we Highlanders possess the pride of lions. Like lions, we have nae fear tae temper our actions, only pride tae govern them."

Stubborn Scottish pride, Catherine thought and dragged the stiff horsehair brush through her hair so furiously the strands crackled and flew about in a spray of sparks. Why had he not told her the truth behind the murder charges? Why had he not explained the reasons for his exile and the subsequent persecution by the Campbells that necessitated assuming a disguise? The story of Anne MacSorley's death had stunned Catherine. Where she had once feared to discover Alexander Cameron's human qualities, she now knew he was not only human, but deeply scarred and terribly vulnerable.

Snatches of conversations, arguments came back to haunt her. The wretchedly caustic voice of her conscience, so newly awakened, gleefully took advantage of her new flood of guilty feelings and reminded her of each insult she had hurled, each accusation she had spat, each occasion when she had called him cruel or cold-blooded or incapable of expressing an emotion. Cruel? Without emotion? He had killed two men for the love of a woman, accepted banishment from his home, his family for the sake of averting a bloody clan war, and then tried his utmost to exorcise the demons that haunted him by throwing himself into every reckless, dangerous enterprise he could find.

Catherine sighed and stared at her reflection. It was too late. What good did any of this compassionate insight do her now? Nothing had changed. The same pride that had kept him silent before would continue to keep him silent, even though he might be suffering the same tearing doubts as she was having.

Why don't you just admit you are in love with him?

Catherine's eyes widened in shock. "No . . . !"

Oh, I think you are. And I think you have been fighting it for some time now . . . since the moment you met him.

"Don't be ridiculous. There is no such foolery as love at first sight. For all I know, there is no such thing as love. Certainly not for me. Certainly not with him."

Two of a kind?

"Two complete opposites. He has told me that often enough."

People say all manner of things in anger . . . or self-defense. And as virginal as you may have been in body, you must know his actions were not those of a man who simply craved a night of pleasure.

"No!" Catherine pushed away from the dressing table and paced to the window. "Love has to be more than just . . . actions."

The storm that had been threatening earlier was lashing across the land in full force; the heavens cracked wide with lightning, the thunder rolled over the castle battlements like a muted cannonade. Trees were bent, whipped in half by the wind's fury. The surface of the loch was churned white and bubbling with the driven rain.

"Besides," Catherine insisted quietly, "if he . . . feels anything for me, why is he sending me away? Why would he not ask me to stay, or suggest we try this marriage for real?"

Pride, Catherine. Or perhaps he just doesn't know how you feel.

"How *I* feel?"

A jagged white fork of lightning streaked across the night sky, strafing the crust of mountains, illuminating the landscape, and causing the ground, the castle foundations to shudder with the impact. Catherine unlatched the windowpanes and flung them wide, lifting her face to the icy pinpricks of rain and wind.

Could you do it? Could you give up the parties, the seasons at court, the social prestige . . . even the simpler things, like new ribbons for your hair whenever the fancy took you? Could you forfeit all of it for a chance to share the life of a man like Alexander Cameron?

''I . . . I don't know if I'm strong enough — ''

You can be strong enough if you want him badly enough. It isn't only his pride standing in the way, you know.

Catherine opened her eyes and stared out at the raging storm. The front of her dress was soaked, her hair wet and plastered to her skin.

''If I thought . . . if I dared believe . . .''

Believe it, Catherine. Tell him . . . before it is too late.

''Too late? What do you mean too late?''

There was no answer. There was only a sudden bright flare of lightning — so bright she had to throw her hand up to shield her eyes. It left an image seared on her mind of the same littered battlefield she had glimpsed once before. Standing alone, surrounded by a sea of clashing swords, was the same tall warrior, only now, as he turned toward Catherine, she could see his face. There was no mistaking the square, rugged jaw or the blazing ebony eyes, no way to warn him of the glittering ring of steel closing in around him as he raised his fists and the bloody talons of his fingers clawed skyward . . .

Chapter Sixteen

It seemed to take an eternity to dispense with the formalities. Lochiel had been welcomed into the crowded great cabin of the *DuTeillay* with the enthusiasm accorded a long-lost relative. The Prince and his staff of seven advisers who had embarked with him from France had lavished food and drink on the Cameron chief and half a dozen envoys from neighbouring clans, all of whom were charmed and disarmed by his humble graciousness.

Charles Edward Stuart was the perfect host. He had deliberately dressed to downplay his heritage, wearing plain black breeches and a coat of cheap broadcloth. His shirt and stock were made of cambric, not very clean; his wig was sparsely curled and fit poorly over the pale copper hair beneath. He was a handsome man, a fact which added to the romantic aura surrounding him, at least where the Jacobite ladies were concerned. His eyes were large and expressive, his nose thin and prominent, his mouth as prettily shaped as a woman's. There was a calmness about him, an assuredness unhampered by his youth or inexperience. It was the assuredness of royalty, of knowing his cause was right and just and that there could be, should be, no possible argument against it.

He was also a very clever prince, playing with the emotions and sentiments of his guests as if they were instruments to be finely tuned before a performance. The opening chords were struck without warning, without preamble, shortly before midnight.

"Now that you have toasted your loyalty to my father's cause, my faithful Lochiel, perhaps you will tell us what manner of support you bring us from the beautiful glens of Lochaber."

One by one the voices around the dining table fell silent and the earnest faces turned toward Donald Cameron. Even Alex, who had been aware of the subtle manipulation of the conversations all through the evening, looked to his brother to see if the experienced statesman had been expecting the trap to be sprung. Here, after all, was a prince born to the royal house to which Lochiel had pledged eternal allegiance. This same royal prince had embarked against all odds, armed only with the might of his personal convictions and the hope of persuading — or shaming — his father's loyal subjects into a holy crusade.

Alex had to admire the young man's audacity. The dinner had been sumptuous, the wine had flowed like water, and now the regent planned to serve himself along with a hefty side dish of sentiment for dessert.

Lochiel set his empty wine glass on the table and waved away a servant who rushed over to refill it. "Perhaps, Yer Highness, ye could tell us fairst what support we might expect from yer cousin King Louis, an' when it might arrive."

The Prince's smile did not waver. "As you know, my father's cause has the full support of the French government. Even as we speak, the king is conferring with his ministers to finalize the plans for a full-scale invasion of England, to be co-ordinated, naturally, with our army's march south."

A rousing cheer was prompted by one of his advisers, the Reverend George Kelly, a tactful attempt to forestall identifying exactly which army the Prince was referring to. Alex glanced along the table, firm in his opinion of their host's poor choice of companions. Kelly was thin-lipped and bald as an eagle, with the same predatory instincts. The Irishman, O'Sullivan, boasted some military experience but discreetly avoided giving any but the vaguest references to specific battles fought. Sir Thomas Sheridan was seventy years old and had been Charles's classroom tutor. William Murray, the exiled Marquis of Tullibardine, was so crippled by the gout he could not walk unsupported. Aeneas MacDonald was a Paris banker whose only function as far as Alex could deduce was to enlist the aid of his elder brother, the chief of Kinlochmoidart. Francis Strickland was the sole Englishman, a Roman Catholic from Westmoreland whose family had always been loyal to the Stuarts. At the moment both he and the seventh member of the elite group, Sir John MacDonald, appeared to be more interested in the quality of the claret than the conversation.

These were the men closest to the Prince, the men who had vowed to see him claim the throne of England in his father's name. Of the seven, O'Sullivan seemed to be the slipperiest, exchanging frequent glances with the Prince and prompting him with either a nod or a shake of the head.

Alex lowered his gaze and wiped at the beads of sweat that had formed on the outside of his tankard. He could not say anything. Protocol demanded his silence but inwardly he screamed for Donald to be on his guard.

"I am glad the French are sendin' troops," Lochiel continued. "We can well use their trainin' an' experience tae organize our ain efforts."

"As I said, the king of France will need assurances that we have an army willing to support my father's holy cause."

"Which ye canna raise, Highness, wi'out some show of assistance from France. An army needs swords an' muskets, lead f'ae shot, an' gunpowder — "

"The cargo bay of this ship is full of muskets and broadswords," the Prince interrupted hastily. "Bought on my own initiative."

"Aye, but a broadsword canna stop a cannonball," Lochiel said gently, "an' the English army has cannon by the score. We have but a few rusted weapons an' none who ken how tae fire them."

"Men can be taught."

"Aye, they can be taught, but learning requires practice, an' we have neither the powder nor the shot tae waste."

The Prince surged to his feet, ignoring a glared warning from O'Sullivan. "Were you or were you not chief instigator of the committee formed to entreat my father to return to Scotland?"

"I was on the committee," Lochiel agreed easily. "I still am, so far as I know, an' will be until we find a realistic way tae bring King James hame."

"You doubt my sincerity in this venture, sir?" the Prince inquired stiffly.

"On the contrary, I find ye a remarkable young man. Furthermair, I believe if anyone could lead an army tae victory in Scotland, it could be you."

The Prince flushed and sank slowly back into his chair. "Then why do you hesitate — you who have the power to sway half the clans in the Highlands to our favour . . . why?"

"The men's hearts are wi' ye, Highness, but their heids — " Lochiel threw his hands up in a gesture of helplessness. "After that calamity last year — "

"Surely you cannot hold me to blame for that?" Charles demanded, his lips pressing into a thin white line. "We had twenty-two ships bulging to the seams with men, guns, and supplies . . . all of it collected through *my* persistence."

"Aye, an' half of it lost through French incompetence."

"The fleet encountered a storm in the Channel — "

"Which should have been expected by anyone addled enough tae attempt the crossin' in February. I ken yer hands were tied; ye had no choice but tae sail when the French decided they were ready to sail . . . but, by the Christ . . . the Royal Navy knew tae the day, the hour, the minute when the fairst ship sailed an' where it was bound.''

"There are spies in every conflict," O'Sullivan decried wanly, spreading his hands in a placating manner, which only caused Lochiel's anger to snap.

"Aye, there are spies. Ours tell us the French have as yet made na move tae send help. In fact, they tell us the king's ministers are so deid against any further involvement they have drawn the treasury purse strings shut.''

Two red splotches stained the Prince's cheeks as he stood again. With a visible effort, he forced himself to remain calm, to turn from the table and pace the length of the cabin until he stood near the multipaned gallery windows. Light from a brass lantern poured over his head and shoulders, bathing him in a halo that could not have been more unnerving had the effect been staged.

"We must not bicker among ourselves," he said tautly. "Indeed, we must not quarrel, especially over an incident which occurred better than a year ago. The main thing to remember was that we set sail then with seven thousand French troops. There are at least that many waiting to embark again at the first word of our army marching south.''

Lochiel steadied himself, astounded by the regent's refusal to admit he had entered into this present endeavour without the slightest proof of solid support from either avenue.

"Highness — " He laid his hands carefully on the table. "There will be nae army marchin' south. At the most ye could raise two, three thousan' men, but it still couldna be called an army, for ye'd have nae weapons, nae food, nae money tae pay them — "

"Would we have their loyalty?" the young man asked quietly.

Lochiel's face flushed. "I can speak only f'ae maself an' in that ye have ma most passionate loyalty. But loyalty canna buy guns. Loyalty canna grow men out o' the ground tae fill the ranks o' an army.''

"We were led to believe we could rely upon twenty, thirty thousand faithful Highlanders."

"Then ye were poorly advised, Sire. A damned sight mair poorly advised than even the English garrisons posted here. They can tell ye tae within ten men how many each clan could put into the field, how well they would be armed, an' behind whose standard they would march."

"I have heard the rumours, sir, that our cause has suffered grave losses to the lure of Hanover gold," the Prince said, glancing back over his shoulder. "Still others remain silent, too ashamed, I must surmise, to acknowledge their king's plea. Others have had to be cajoled to come down out of their mountain lairs and hiding places to appease me with their patronizing bromides." He paused, watching the colour deepen in Donald's cheeks. "I tell you now, I will not be patronized. I will not be swayed by cowards and nay-sayers. The time is right to strike, and to strike hard! The main bulk of the English army is across the Channel fighting in Flanders. The few regular troops who remain are not sufficient to withstand a Highland army, regardless of whether it is but one-tenth the promised strength.

"All we need, gentlemen," he said, addressing his rhetoric to the rapt and silent group, "is a single victory to prove to the whole country that we are committed to our cause. All of our friends who have doubted us would come forward; all the foreign aid we might need would pour into our borders. Gentlemen" — he squared his shoulders and faced them fully so that the dazzling light from the lantern spilled over his countenance, making it appear to glow from within — "this is my home. These are my Highlands as much as they are yours. The blood of my ancestors stains the soil beneath my feet and their voices cry to me through the glens and mountains. I will not go back to France in defeat again. I will stay and fight to restore honour to my father's name though not another single man has the courage to stand by my side!"

A sickening wave of humiliation drained the blood from Donald Cameron's face, yet he still groped for threads of reason. "Aye, Highness, perhaps ye should remain in the kirk. Perhaps, wi' time an' care, ye can win over yer detractors, prove tae them ye are indeed committed tae victory. In the meantime, I would pairsonally guarantee yer safety — "

"My safety? You think I care one wit for my safety? And would you have me skulking from cave to cottage to avoid the hounds the English would undoubtedly set after me while we waited for an army formed out of pity to grow around me? No, my good Lochiel. I will, indeed, stay in Scotland, and I will, indeed, walk these glorious hills, but not as a criminal, not as a thief in the night, not as a begger seeking alms. In a few days, with the few friends I have, I will erect the royal standard of the House of Stuart and proclaim to the people of Britain that Charles Stuart has come home to claim the crown of his ancestors — to win it or to perish, if need be, in the attempt."

A round of furtive glances was exchanged around the table. Only one pair of dark, midnight-blue eyes did not waver from the ashen face they had been watching throughout the Prince's impassioned speech. There were tears in Donald's eyes, and small half circles of blood cut into the flesh of his hands where his fingernails had dug.

Slowly, lowering his gaze, the Prince looked directly at Donald. "You say I have your loyalty, Lochiel, and so I believed, or else why would I have been drawn so relentlessly to these shores? You and my other faithful Highlanders filled me with hope, with the heart to keep on even though man and nature pitted their fury against me. *My* Highlanders: We share the same blood, the same courage, the same quest for honour . . . or so I thought."

The golden head tilted up again, angling the angelic face into the full shine of the light. "I would force no man to stand by my side if he lacks the faith to do so. Lochiel may stay at home if he finds he has so little hope for me and my cause. There he may learn the fate of his prince from the newspapers . . . and perhaps offer a toast or two in our favour? Surely it would be little enough to ask?"

Donald Cameron stared unblinkingly at the gilded prince. Then, he rose slowly from his chair, his body rigid and trembling, the tears falling in two shiny streaks down his cheeks. Through a sluggish wave of helplessness, Alex heard his brother's voice break the crystaline silence. "No, by God. I will not keep tae ma hame while ma prince fights alane f'ae ma king . . . nor will any man over whom nature or fortune has given me power."

There was more, but Alex did not hear it. He found himself thinking, irrationally, of an avalanche he had witnessed once. One small step had sent half a mountain exploding down upon an unsuspecting village. He had the same feeling now, that he was poised to take that one small step, and if he did, the only way to go was down . . . .

Chapter Seventeen

The storms that had plagued the skies over Achnacarry finally
dissipated, and on the fifth morning of Lochiel's absence
from the castle, the sun made an appearance over the
horizon. The mists were reluctant to leave the coves and inlets of the loch, and the forests rained dew for another full
day before they too relinquished the dampness and steamed
themselves dry. Catherine took long walks in the garden and
along the shoreline. She ventured bravely into the woods
with Deirdre and her shadow of silent guards to pick wild
berries, and while there discovered a narrow stream looping
its way through the saplings, its waters flashing silver with
salmon.

She startled Aluinn MacKail one morning by joining him
unexpectedly in the courtyard and requesting to be allowed
to accompany him on one of his rides. After a brief debate
and a longer delay to arm a small escort, they rode up into
the hills, where she was afforded a breathtaking overview of
the castle, the loch, the seemingly endless rolling sweep of

Highlands. Seeing the appreciation in her eyes, Aluinn told her some of the Cameron history. He pointed out the ruins of an ancient keep nearby and filled her imagination with stories of past battles and feuds. He spoke of Alexander and hinted at a misspent youth but never broached the subject of his exile and Catherine did not give any inclination that she knew. By the end of the morning, they were both relaxed and laughing and she felt somehow that she had gained an important ally should she have need of one.

As the days stretched into a week, so, too, did Catherine's patience stretch to the breaking point. She was still wracked with doubts, confused by what she was feeling, but as bad as it was suffering alone, she suspected her turmoil would only increase when and if her husband ever returned. To that end, she rehearsed whole speeches and thought of countless arguments to present both for and against the idea of her remaining at Achnacarry. She walked the gardens tirelessly, one turn convincing her she was a fool to even entertain the notion of staying in Scotland, the next convincing her she would be a fool to leave. Always at the back of her mind was the very real possibility that she was debating with herself needlessly. Alexander Cameron was as stubborn as he was proud. If he had already made up his mind to send her away — and had she not badgered and insisted repeatedly he do just that — no amount of rationalizing would budge him. Also at the back of her mind was the recollection of his telling her he had a distinct and everlasting aversion to marriage. What made her think a single night of passion had changed his opinion? He must have spent many similar nights with many other women over the years. Perhaps she *was* reading far too much into a few murmured phrases, a too-soft caress, an undisguised tremor. Perhaps it was nothing more than what he had so bluntly told her the next morning — a matter of too much temptation stretched out over too long a time. Would he have stopped or wouldn't he? Was it a simple case of lust or was it something else?

Dear God, she simply did not know anymore. There were

no storms to affect her senses now, no providential bolts of lightning to frighten her into seeing something that was not there. What had seemed so clear then was, in the stark reality of daylight, a confused and hopeless situation. He did not want her. He could not possibly love her. Perhaps she should go home, if only to get away from the mystic beauty of the mountains and the treacherously hypnotic effects of heather and peat smoke. Would she be so willing to cast her lot to the wind if she found herself back at the River Spean, confronted by a dozen armed, filthy militiamen?

The answer was a resounding no. She would die of sheer terror if she had to endure what lay beyond these thick stone walls and fortifications. She *was* soft and she *was* pampered, and she honestly did not know if she wanted to change, or if she could change.

Catherine sighed and kicked at a tuft of weed. Always sure of herself in the past, she now felt mired in doubt and confusion. She wanted to stay. She wanted to go. For the first time in her life she wanted someone to tell her what to do, but even the obscure little voice of her conscience remained stubbornly silent.

"Cow piss," Rose announced, startling Catherine into almost spilling her tea. "Take ma advice, hen, a wee tot o' cow piss an' vinegar each mornin' an' yer bairns'll all be laddies. I ken. I've had six o' ma ain."

"Cow piss me arse," Jeannie countered derisively. "All that'll gie ye is a sour belly an' nae much mair. Beetroot jelly. That's wha' ma mither tald me, an' all *twelve* o' ma bairns are laddies. Ye take a wee dram an 'muckle it on his nether part just afore — "

An abrupt roar of laughter interrupted the dissertation and Catherine glanced gratefully toward the door of the retiring room. Archibald Cameron poked his head into the room and thundered for their attention, as if the trembling walls had not already alerted them to his presence.

He swung an arm wide in a sweepingly flamboyant gesture and stood aside as two tartan-clad, bedraggled figures who had obviously ridden long and hard through the night and morning walked past him into the room. Catherine's heart needed but a second to flutter with recognition.

"Alex," she whispered.

The dark eyes found her immediately, but any greeting he might have offered was drowned in a swell of anxious voices.

"Alex! Struan!" Maura grasped each man's arm in welcome. "Thank God you are back with us safely. We've been hearing all manner of rumours — "

"What has been happening at Arisaig — ?"

"Did ye see the Prince? Did ye speak wi' him — ?"

"Where is Donald — ?"

Alex held up his hands to staunch the flow of questions. "Donald is a day or so behind us, nothing to worry about. Struan and I came ahead with a few of the men . . ." His voice trailed away and his gaze strayed back to Catherine.

Drinks were thrust into their hands and both men were ushered closer to the fire. They were relieved of their heavy sword belts, bonnets, and plaids, questioned as to the last time they had eaten. Both men looked exhausted. Struan's glorious mane of hair was stringy and limp, his beard thick with the dust and grime of travelling. Alex fared no better. His hair stuck to his neck and brow; his jaw was blue-black with several days' growth of stubble. His eyes, normally so clear and piercing, were heavy with weariness, ringed with dark purple smears.

"Ye leuk like hell, brither," Archibald announced with his usual aplomb. "Has the war started wi'out us?"

He had asked the question half jokingly, but at the look on Alex's face, Archibald's jowly smile faded and the light in the pale blue eyes became bright with alarm.

"Oot wi' it, lads," he said sombrely. "What news frae Arisaig?"

"The clans meet ten days from now at Glenfinnan. The

Prince plans to raise the Stuart standard and proclaim himself regent in his father's absence."

Jeannie let off a hoot of excitement and executed a quick little jig before Archie glared her into silence.

"A gathering of the clans?" Aluinn asked quietly. "Who will join?"

Alex drew a deep breath and stared at the untouched glass of whisky in his hand "Clanranald and Kinlochmoidart are already arming; Glenaladale and most of his MacDonalds; Keppoch, and Glencoe of course — "

"Keppoch? But he would never commit unless . . ."

"Unless the Camerons were committed," Alex concluded grimly. "The same holds for the Stewarts of Appin, the MacLeans, Glengarry, the Grants, the Frasers . . ."

"They have all pledged?" Aluinn asked in horror.

"They will all have to search their own consciences and make their own decision now that the gauntlet is thrown." Alex downed his whisky in a single swallow and set his teeth through a shudder. "Donald did everything but get down on his knees to beg the Prince to return to France, or at least to wait for a better time, but . . ."

"How is he?" Maura asked.

"Donald? Oddly enough, I think he's relieved that the waiting, the arguing, the endless debating is over. It was his decision to make and he made it, committing himself one hundred percent."

"Everything?"

Alex knew what she was asking. There were lairds who had agreed — and more who would agree — to send half the clan under a son or a brother to fight for the Stuarts and thereby honour their oath of allegiance to the exiled king. The other half would secretly pledge for Hanover to ensure that, regardless of the outcome, their titles and estates would be protected. But Donald would no more consider dividing his loyalties as he would give half an oath.

"Refill yer mon's glass, hen," Rose whispered in Catherine's ear, loud enough to draw the dark eyes toward her again. Catherine was suddenly aware of how she must look. She had spent the morning taking a leisurely walk along the shore. Her hair was scattered every which way from the glossy blonde braid braid that hung down her back. She raised a hand to smooth the tendrils back from her face, but there were too many and his eyes were too sharp. Her flush deepened and spread down her throat. Her ability to move, to think, to speak had deserted her in the shock of being in Alex's presence again. Her heart was pounding so loudly, she had scarcely heard a word he had said.

Rose prodded her again and she walked haltingly forward. She was aware of his eyes on her all the way; the heat from them coiled through her loins like a silken ribbon.

She somehow carried the bottle without dropping it to where he stood, but it was all she could do to lift the decanter and rattle it against the edge of his glass. Alex raised a hand and steadied it.

"Have you been well?"

"Yes," she whispered. "Quite well, thank you."

Alex tightened his grip on the glass, fighting a desire to reach out and stroke the soft white curve of her cheek. He had tried not to think of her too often over the past week, and for the most part had been successful. Only when he closed his eyes did his willpower fail him. If he had hoped to exorcise her from his blood that night, or sought to use the week away from her to regain his perspective, there, too, he had failed miserably. Even now he was drowning, floundering in the perfume of her hair and skin, and if she did not stop looking at him in that way —

"Alasdair! Struan!" Lauren Cameron came running into the room, skidding to a halt in a breathless swirl of flying red hair, yellow skirts, and excited laughter. "I've just haird the news! Is it true? Is cousin Donald raisin' the clan f'ae Prince Charlie?"

"Aye, mistress," Struan said, filling his massive chest proudly. "Lochiel has pledged the Camerons tae fight f'ae King Jamie."

Her eyes lingering on Alex's face a moment longer than they should have, Lauren smiled to acknowledge Struan's remark. "When? When are we marchin' tae meet Prince Charlie?"

"As soon as Donal' retairns, he'll tell us all aboot it," Archibald said. "Nae sense workin' yer jaws tae a flap till then. By the Christ, this calls f'ae a toast. Aye, there's a bonnie wife. Fill ma glass, Jeannie, then fill all the rest."

Catherine refrained, as did Maura. Alex joined the toast in silence, then returned his glass to the tray.

"If no one objects, I've lived in these clothes for a week now — half that time in the pouring rain. Struan, I thank you for your company. Aluinn — can I speak to you out in the hallway for a few minutes?"

Catherine watched Alex lead MacKail out of the room, then was distracted by Maura clapping her hands for order in the mild pandemonium of voices. Luncheon, she suggested, should be delayed by an hour or so to give the men a chance to freshen up. Lauren was dispatched to find the cook and inform her of the change; Struan MacSorley, after a hastily murmured excuse, followed a few minutes later.

Catherine was still standing by the mantel when she noticed Aluinn come back into the room alone. The smoky gray eyes held hers for a moment before he joined Archie by the sideboard.

Catherine's legs moved of their own accord, carrying her out of the room and along the quiet sunlit hallway. She told herself she was only going to change her own clothes and brush her hair into some semblance of order, but as she climbed the stairs to the west tower, her footsteps lagged and she had to firmly grip the carved stone banister for support to the top.

The doors to all three rooms were closed, and she thought of a game she had seen played at a country fairground with walnut shells and a dried pea. The gamester had hidden the pea under one of the shells and taken penny bets from the onlookers, who tried to guess where it had ended up.

She had no excuse to enter the room across the landing from her own, nor did she want to confront Alex if he was in the bathtub again. She would go into her bedchamber and leave the door ajar. That way, if he wanted to see her or speak to her, he would know where she was.

Resigned to the wisdom of her strategy, she entered her room and adjusted the width of the door opening twice before she was satisfied. The single narrow window at the end of its recessed bay did little to alleviate the gloom of the vaultlike chamber, and she crossed to the dressing table and had begun to unwind the long blonde plait before she realized Alex was standing in the bay, his broad frame slashing the beam of sunlight into hazy, dust-laden streamers. She stared at his reflection in the mirror, her hands frozen on the separated strands of hair.

He moved, distorting the foggy beams of light further as he walked the length of the recess and leaned casually on the stone casement.

"Don't let me interrupt you," Alex said.

Catherine forced her hands to move, to resume the process of combing out the braid.

"Aluinn tells me you've been venturing outside the castle."

"He took me riding, yes. I was beginning to feel like a prisoner."

He frowned slightly. "Has anyone said anything or done anything to — ?"

"Oh no," she said quickly. "No. I just meant . . . I mean, the walls were beginning to close in on me a little, I guess. No, everyone has been very . . . accommodating."

He pursed his lips and looked down at his hands. "Archie seems to think there is Scottish blood in you somewhere. He is quite taken with you."

"I . . . rather like him too. He is — " She groped for an appropriate phrase and failed to find one.

"A bit unorthodox?"

"He is a very fine doctor. He has worked a minor miracle on Mr. MacKail's shoulder."

"He should be good — he was trained in Edinburgh and graduated at the head of his class."

"Archibald?" She could not keep the incredulity out of her voice, and he smiled.

"Every family has an eccentric or two hiding away in a closet. In our case, we have Archibald."

"And Jeannie," she murmured, matching his shadow of a smile.

"Ahh yes, Jeannie. She is another matter entirely. Good solid farm stock, not the least impressed by the Cameron name or position. She would be as happy stomping around in a sod *clachan* as she would be living in Holyrood House."

Catherine glanced surreptitiously at him in the mirror's reflection. Oddly enough, his week's absence had sharpened her perceptions about him and she could hear the faint depression in his voice, see it in the bend of his shoulders. He was more upset, more shaken by his brother Donald's capitulation than he let on; the conversation had so far been trite, the casual small talk not at all in character. He seemed almost . . . lost.

To cover her own nervousness, Catherine took up the hairbrush and began dragging it through the length of her hair, smoothing the tangles, taming the heavy cascade into a sleek ripple over her shoulders.

"Your letter to Damien got away safely," he said after a moment. "We managed to find a ship that was just leaving . . ."

Their eyes met in the mirror and there was a breathless little silence between them. He thought how lovely she looked standing there, her face dusted pink, her hair bright and flowing around her shoulders. Even the plain cotton dress she wore took on a certain elegance for simply being graced with her form. Looking at him, Catherine no longer saw the man who had kidnapped her, frightened her half to death, and introduced her to horrors she had never dreamed existed. She saw a very vulnerable man who had survived his own private hell and emerged strong and vital and on his guard against any further possible damage to the heart that beat so formidably within that chest. If she could steal but a portion of that strength, a small part of that heart . . .

"One of the reasons we left Arisaig ahead of Donald," he was saying, "was to make a detour down along the coast to meet with a smuggler Struan knows quite well. After a deal of haggling and a few threats on both sides, we managed to arrange passage for you and Deirdre as far as Blackpool."

The brush faltered for the span of a few quick heartbeats. "When?"

"The end of the week. Saturday." His voice was strained, so low she almost could not hear the words. Her face paled and her fingers turned icy around the brush.

"I see."

"Under the circumstances, it is the smartest, safest route to take. Naturally there are risks travelling by sea, but — " Catherine laid the brush aside and his gaze followed her warily as she moved away from the dressing table. "But the captain assured me he pays the coastal revenuers an exorbitant sum to keep them looking the other way."

"Will you be taking me?"

"To the coast, yes. After that, you will be well protected, don't worry."

Catherine remained remarkably cool, commendably calm as she joined him before the window recess.

"And you?" she asked, her hand toying absently with the laces that crisscrossed over her bodice. "What will you do now that your brother has decided to go to war?"

He was silent, his body immobile, his arms taut with the knowledge that they could reach out and touch her.

"I am a Cameron. I cannot turn my back on that fact regardless of my personal feelings. Sometimes . . ." His voice trailed off and his eyes fell involuntarily to where her hand lingered over the dusky cleft of her breasts. "Sometimes there are larger issues than a man's private convictions."

She turned from the window and looked directly up into the clear indigo eyes. His expression was stony but her senses were absorbing very different undercurrents. She let them flow over her, suffusing her body with a subtle tension that was more arousing than any physical act of touching or caressing. The blood flushed through her limbs, her loins, her belly. She swayed slightly with a dizzying rush of heightened awareness and knew beyond a doubt he was fighting the same raw urges. As she watched, a thin white line formed around his mouth and a pulse began to beat in his temple — the same temple scarred from his duel with Hamilton Garner.

She stepped deliberately closer, bringing the ripe, sweet musk of her woman's body tantalizingly near. Alex felt her eyes plumbing the depths of his with a defiance that made his every nerve stand on end.

"I am a Cameron too," she reminded him. "You made me one."

"Catherine, I don't think — " She stepped closer — close enough that the heat of her body paralyzed him. His fingers clamped a rigid warning around her arm but she ignored it. She raised her hand and curled it around his neck while the other pressed softly against the front of his shirt. The contact intensified the ache in his loins and stretched his willpower dangerously.

"You don't know what you're doing," he began, but he felt her breasts cushion enticingly against his chest and he saw the bright violet shine of desire defy him to pull away. His lips parted, intending to offer a final warning, but with a soft rushing breath, her mouth was there, moist and supple, sweeter than anything he had imagined or remembered. The pink tip of her tongue flicked between his lips, teasing him, taunting him in a way he himself had taught her. The hand at the nape of his neck moved higher, forcing him to bend, entreating him to capitulate.

With a deep-throated groan his fingers sank into the glossy mass of her hair, crushing her to him. He cast aside all of his good intentions, his honourable resolutions, his firm and supposedly unshakeable determination not to further enmesh himself in a dilemma that could have no happy solution . . . and he kissed her. He kissed her with lips that were bruisingly hard, he held her in arms that trembled like those of a schoolboy. The rasp of new beard on his chin chafed her tender skin but Catherine did not seem to notice. She flung her arms around his neck and responded with an eagerness that flamed his need beyond all reason.

Alex lifted her and carried her to the bed, his hands tearing at her clothing almost before he had set her down. He bared her breasts and his mouth plundered each straining peak, tasting, remembering, unleashing an urgency as great and ungovernable as his own. His hands abandoned her, but only for as long as it took to release the yards of pleated tartan from around his waist. When they returned it was to press her down onto the bedding, to feverishly brush aside the remaining barriers of her clothing and thrust himself as deeply as sense and passion would allow.

A cry was shocked from his throat as the pleasure gripped him instantly. The hunger that had haunted his every unguarded thought engulfed him, driving him to a possession that was willful and forceful. He tried to hold himself back, knowing it was too soon . . . too soon . . . but Catherine sensed his weakness, shared it as she drew him deeper, held him tighter, and felt the hot torrent of his ecstasy surge and erupt within her. She writhed with the joy of it, clawing her hands into his flesh, into the bunched muscles of his back and shoulders as he shuddered again and again. Blindly, convulsively, she arched herself higher, opened herself wider so that his life force throbbed and pulsed at the very heart of her soul.

Her name was on his lips as he shook the last of the mighty spasms free and collapsed, gasping, atop her. Catherine lay absolutely still, stunned and splintered with wonder. She raised her hand and combed her trembling fingers through the waves of raven hair, her skin tingling in a wash of utter contentment as she felt his lips move against her throat. Reluctantly, he slipped into an exhausted sleep, but his arm remained fast about her waist and his head stayed pillowed between the soft mounds of her breasts.

Catherine drifted back from a dreamless slumber some time later. She and Alex were still curled together, although their positions had changed; her head was now nestled in the curve of his shoulder, one of her legs lying carelessly across his. She raised her head slowly, tentatively, but he did not stir except to release a deep and contented breath. It occurred to her that she had never seen him sleep before — in fact she had often wondered if he slept at all. How different he looked! Gone were the brooding lines of worry, gone the stern set to his jaw. The thick black crescents of his lashes lay like fallen wings on his cheeks, and his hair, swept back from his forehead, looked like black paint against the whiteness of the sheets.

In their haste to reach the bed, neither had completely disrobed. Catherine still wore her chemise and bodice, although both were loose and gaping open over her breasts. Her skirt had been discarded, but his impatience had only allowed him to push her petticoats above her hips and free one slender leg from the pantaloons. Alex still wore his shirt, the linen spread open across the breadth of his chest and shoved up beneath his arms.

Her eyes wandered lower and she stared. Despite their previous night of passion, when she had been left with the distinct impression there could be no possible secret or mystery yet to discover, she realized she had never seen a man's naked body in the full, uncompromising light of day. By candlelight, or by firelight, her modesty had been greatly spared. There was no such vestige of charity now, and her cheeks flushed a hot, bright crimson as she studied the sleeping male form, measured and charted it as an artist might who was about to transfer the bold contours to canvas.

Aside from the sheer physical presence of Alexander Cameron, there were harsher realities revealed by the daylight. Dozens of scars, both fine and wide, threaded their way across the hard surface of his flesh. The thigh cut by Hamilton Garner's sword bore an older welt, the skin shiny and pulled flat over the surrounding tissue. His ribs, his arms, even his belly wore the telltale signs of the life he had led in his fifteen-year absence from Achnacarry.

The love in her heart swelled to epic proportions and she could not resist stealing a tender kiss from the wide, full lips. She carefully disentangled herself from the circle of his arms and left him to sleep, deciding she would make his excuses to the family and bring him a tray of food later.

Moving quietly so as not to disturb him, she slipped her skirt back on over her petticoats and repaired the froth of confusion he had made of her chemise and blouse. A quick glance at the mirror told her she would never to able to offer conversation as an alibi for their prolonged absence, and she worked a few minutes with a brush and comb to restore a modicum of propriety. Inwardly, she did not care if the whole world knew what she and Alexander had been doing in the tousled arena of the bedchamber. Nor did she feel the least shamed or embarrassed that she had practically seduced him into her bed. If there were any lingering doubts as to how she felt about herself or her husband, they were gone, and that was all she knew or cared about.

She had claimed to love Hamilton Garner, but that love had been as phony and pretentious as the rest of her sorry existence. Her heart had never beaten wildly out of control at his approach, her skin had never prickled at the sound of his voice, her bones had never seemed to melt from within at his touch. All these happened, and happened with shocking intensity, whenever Alexander Cameron was near her — even from that first moment when she had laid eyes upon him in the clearing. She could no longer deny it or question the logic of it: She was in love. Honestly, completely, painfully in love. And such a sweet pain it was! Sweet and all-encompassing, from the tenderness between her thighs to the ache within her heart. She would gladly forsake anything to hold on to this feeling. She would willingly live in a little sod cottage if he asked it of her, and if he was there to share it with her.

She finished her repairs and was walking softly to the door when she saw Alex raise a hand and rake the hair back from his temple.

"Catherine?" His voice was slurred, heavy with fatigue.

"Go back to sleep," she whispered and crossed to the bed. She pulled the quilt over his body and, on a sudden impulse, leaned down and kissed him squarely on the mouth.

The dark eyes showed surprise . . . and pleasure.

"What was that for?"

"You seem to thrive on challenges, sir," she said and straightened from the bed. "Here, then, is a new one for you: I love you, Alexander Cameron. More than common sense or decency should allow. Your strength frightens me, and your stubbornness angers me, and I believe you to be a truly dangerous threat to a woman's inbred gentility. But there you have it. And unless you are prepared to give me several honest and convincing reasons why I should do otherwise, I intend to remain here at Achnacarry as your wife, as your lover, if you will have me, as the mother of your sons, of which — please dear God — there will be many."

His eyes widened and he started to push himself upright, but Catherine was already half out the door. She heard him call out but she dared not stop or go back. She had said it and she meant it and it was up to him now whether they used the smuggler's ship to send out a second explanatory letter to Damien or a bound, gagged, and screaming Catherine Ashbrooke Cameron.

Her heart was pounding and her hands were shaking as she ran though the long gallery and down the narrow secondary corridor that bypassed the family apartments and opened into the courtyard. She slowed down and tried to calm herself. She walked through the gates and out into the garden, following her usual path down to the tranquil solitude of the shoreline.

When she was into the small band of trees that edged the shore, she heard footsteps running quickly up behind her. She took a deep breath to brace herself for the inevitable arguments, and turned stoically to confront her husband. But it was not Alex who came to a grinning halt behind her. It was not Alex who reached out his arms to her, and it was not Alex who clamped a brutal hand over her mouth to stifle her scream of horror.

Alex cursed as he threw back the quilt and swung his long legs over the side of the bed. A wife! A lover! A mother, goddammit! Where had all that come from?

"Catherine!"

His roar died away with no results as he hastily spread the six yards of tartan on the floor and began pleating and folding it until the length was reduced to five feet. His mind replayed Catherine's departing speech word by word as he muttered to himself about the inconsistency of women. She loved him, did she? Didn't she know there was a war about to break out? Didn't she know her position here in the Highlands could only get worse, not better, regardless of whatever support and protection his own immediate family might afford?

What the hell had happened during his absence?

When the plaid was folded, Alex lay down on it so that the lower edge was level with his knees. He wrapped it around his half-naked body, securing it about his waist with the leather belt, then sprang to his feet, flinging the surplus wool over his shoulder as he bolted out the door.

She loved him! Of all the stupid, untimely . . .

He ran through the gallery and checked several of the main rooms before a startled servant reported seeing her walking into the garden.

He was not entirely blameless, he realized as he pushed

through the wrought-iron outer gate to the garden. He never should have touched her. He should have cut off his hands first before surrendering to the tempting allure of her body. He never should have kissed her. He never should have looked into those bottomless eyes of hers and fancied seeing a plea there . . . a plea to be taken and held and loved.

His footsteps slowed on the path.

So he had bedded her, what of it? He had bedded dozens of women over the years, some equally as taxing on the patience as Mistress Catherine Ashbrooke. What made her different? What separated her from the rest? Why the devil had he married her when he could easily have slipped away into the night as Damien had pleaded with him to do? Why had he gone to her room today? He had wanted her too badly, needed her, truth be known, in ways he did not even want to think about . . . and hadn't thought about until just now.

A wife? A lover? Not since Annie's death had he allowed such thoughts to enter his mind.

Annie. There was the real hell of it. He could hardly remember her face anymore, aside from the impression of sweetness and sunshine. When he tried, all he could see was Catherine dancing under the glitter of candlelight at Rosewood Hall or Catherine leaning away from that first kiss under the moonlight, her lips parted and moist, her eyes searching his for the answer to the tremors they had both felt.

Aluinn had said it was time to let the ghosts rest. Perhaps he was right.

"Catherine?"

He listened for a reply but there was only the furious chatter of birds echoing in the trees somewhere off to his left. He ignored the irritating little prickle at the nape of his neck and listened to his heart instead. It was beating against his breastbone, thudding inside his ribcage, demanding to be heard. He had kept it prisoner too long, denied it softness and tenderness and trust . . .

"Catherine?"

The breeze snatched his voice and ran ahead with it into the strand of trees. He saw the shine of the falling sunlight on the water of the loch, and he pictured Catherine sitting there, prim and stiff with rebelliousness, waiting no doubt for him to present all his righteous arguments as to why he should send her away and why she should go.

He paused at the edge of the garden and plucked a snow-white briar rose from the side of the path.

A wife, a lover, a mother for his sons . . .

Alex stopped. This time the uneasiness at the back of his neck was too insistent to ignore. He stared hard into the trees on either side of the path and tried to determine what it was that was out of order, but he could see nothing. He could hear nothing but the faint lapping of water against the shore . . . the incessant screaming of the birds . . .

His hand fell to his waist and he gaped down in shock as he realized he had been so distracted in his haste to dress and chase after Catherine, he had neglected to bring along a weapon of any kind — something that had become as instinctive to him as eating or breathing during the past fifteen years. And looking down, he saw something else: a bright patch of colour where there should only have been the drab brown and green of the hedgerow.

Alex clutched the dainty satin slipper in his fist, and again his eyes bored into the maze of trees and rolling hollows. There was no movement, no sound. He pushed aside the bushes that bordered the path and almost missed it: a long, shiny thread of silver-blonde hair.

"Catherine," he grated under his breath.

There was more — freshly turned earth, the clear imprint of boots, and evidence of the struggle that had taken place before they had managed to quiet her. Alex ran back along the path, shouting the alarm to the guards on the castle battlements before he had even cleared the trees.

Struan MacSorley was just pacing himself toward the final moments of sexual rapture when he heard the alarm sound in the courtyard. His eyes bulged wide and he sucked in an enormous breath as he caught Lauren midstroke and tossed her summarily off his thighs. She gasped and scrambled blindly to reseat herself, but he was already off the cot, unmindful of his nudity or his glaring tumescence as he took up his sword and flung himself out the door.

He was back less than a minute later.

"What is it?" she cried. "What is wrong?"

"Get yersel' dressed an' out o' here," he snapped. "There's Campbells on the land."

"Campbells? At Achnacarry? But how — ?"

"Are ye deaf, woman?" he roared, flinging himself down on his spread tartan and rising seconds later fully clad. "I said get dressed. They'll be wantin' tae count heids in the great hall, an' yers had best be among them — wi' all yer claythes *on*."

Lauren glanced down along her flushed and gleaming body. "Surely they havna come tae attack the castle? An' how did they get so far onto Cameron land?"

"The point is no' tae let them get off again — and no' wi' Alasdair's wife."

"The *Sassenach*? They've taken the *Sassenach*?"

"Aye."

Lauren sank back against the wall, her eyes glittering, her mouth shadowing the excitement that raced through her body. She could scarcely believe the deed had come about, and so swiftly!

"Gie us a wee kiss f'ae luck, lass," MacSorley growled, scooping her into the circle of his arm. He was about to promise a finish to what they had begun but halted when he noticed the malicious smile. "Here now, why d'ye look so pleased wi' yersel'?"

"Pleased?" she gasped. "I'm nae *pleased*, Struan MacSorley. But I'll nae lie by sayin' I'm sorry it was her they took. Truth be out, would ye rather it be the *Sassenach* bitch gaun or Lady Maura? Or one o' the ithers? Or mayhap even me?"

"The *Sassenach* is still a Cameron," Struan said with a frown, his loyalties obviously in conflict.

"How much o' a Cameron, but? She keeps tae hersel' all

the day long. She has naught tae dae wi' anyone else, ither than tae peer down her long English nose an' laugh ahind our backs. Why, she thought I were a laundress fairst day she were here, an' told me so tae ma face. Laundress, hah! She only wanted tae be left alane so her an' her clarty-breeked maid could plot an' steal ahind our backs.''

''Plot an' steal? What are ye blatherin' on about now?''

''I've haird them talkin', God's truth. She never wanted tae come tae Achnacarry; she were brung against her will.''

Struan's eyes narrowed and his hand pinched so tightly around her flesh she shuddered with the pain. ''If ye have somethin' tae say, say it, damn ye.''

''She didna want tae come tae Achnacarry,'' Lauren repeated tersely. ''She has neither a love f'ae Scotland nor a love f'ae Alasdair. She keeps a separate bed an' bars the door at night. An' I haird her, clear as a bell in June, say she had a proper fiancé back in England. A sojer! A lieutenant in the dragoons! An' she threatened tae send f'ae him, tae send f'ae her sojer an' his whole regiment if Alasdair didna send her hame!''

Struan's beard split in an ugly scowl. ''Ye're speakin' through yer teeth, woman. Why would he bring her here an' call her his wife if it werena the truth?''

''I dinna ken the answers, Struan, only the questions. Were I you, I'd be askin' them too. I'd be askin' how the so-jers knew tae find them by the river Spean. A patrol wouldna attack wi'out a signal o' some kind. An' why did the *Sassenach* stop Alasdair frae killin' Gordon Ross Campbell? I mout even go so far as tae ask how the Campbells knew she'd be alane in the gairden an' how they were able tae take her wi'out a sound in full daylight.''

''I dinna like what ye're sayin,'' Struan hissed, his breath ragged with disbelief.

He relaxed his grip and stepped back from the cot, his every instinct fighting to deny the ring of truth in her words. How could he deny it? Had he and Alex not spent the better part of three days negotiating passage back to England for the lass and her maid? Struan had not questioned his reasons and no explanations had been offered, but Alex had seemed almost relieved when the arrangements had been finalized . . . as if he could not wait to get his "bride" out of Scotland. Yet that first day on the hillside, when the lass had fainted and he had revived her, the look on Alasdair's face had not been the look of a man eager to dispose of a burden . . . nor had the one on hers expressed any longing to escape.

Something was not right, Struan admitted, but just what that was . . .

"What is it?" Lauren asked in a whisper, her eyes intent on Struan's changing expressions. "Are ye thinkin' on Annie, yer ain sweet sister deid these many years? Are ye thinkin' on what she would make o' such a shamelss bed o' lies?"

"I'm thinkin," he said evenly, "that ye'll wish it were ye an' no' the *Sassenach* stolen by the Campbells if I hear ye've breathed one word o' this tae anyone else. *Anyone*, d'ye hear me?"

"Aye, Struan, I hear ye." Rising onto her knees, she pressed her moist, imploring lips against his. "Struan. Struan . . . dinna be angry wi' me. I couldna bear it if ye were angry wi' me f'ae speakin' the fear that was in ma hairt."

His eyes lost some of their hard glaze and his hands clamped around her arms again, this time lifting her so that her mouth was crushed brutally against his. She clawed her fingers into his shoulders, partly a reaction to the renewed pain of his embrace, partly because of the promised violence in his lips.

"Ye will be careful, will ye na?" she cried softly. "If it *is* a trap . . ."

"If it's a trap, it will be sprung on the one who laid it. Now, get dressed. Lady Maura will be needin' ye."

Lauren watched him snatch up his blue woolen bonnet and set it on a slouching angle over the straw-coloured hair. Without a glance, he left her, his angry steps fading away on the stone. She released a long, drawn breath and massaged the tender flesh of her upper arms, knowing there would be dark, ugly bruises left behind as a further warning. She did not particularly appreciate a lover with an unpredictable temper. A violent passion was one thing, *threats* of violence a different matter altogether.

Deep in thought, she dressed and slipped out of the guard-house unnoticed. Instead of following instructions and making her way to the great hall, she veered toward the dingy, sooty structure that housed the castle smithy. There was no one working over the furnace, no clang of hammer on anvil, and she moved on quiet feet through to the small chamber in the rear.

He was there, asleep in a curled fetal position, an empty jug of whisky cradled in his arms. Lauren stared at the thin, bony frame of the man and a shudder of revulsion washed through her. She could scarcely believe she had let him crawl over her body or that she had allied herself with such a vile, foul-smelling excuse for a human being. But it had been a necessary evil. Doobie Logan was the lowest form of life imaginable to a Highlander: a clansman who informed on his own kin to their enemies. Logan was paid, and paid well, by the Campbells to keep them abreast of the comings and goings at Achnacarry. Lauren had discovered his treachery purely by accident yet had kept his secret to herself on the chance it could be of use to her some day.

Indeed, she had used him, but not without paying the exorbitant price he had demanded as proof of her loyalty as a fellow conspirator. Her skin still shrank when she thought of him straddling her, forcing her to join him in acts of such depravity she had scrubbed her body raw afterward.

Lauren approached the snoring figure and her hand crept stealthily beneath her skirt. She experienced a cool shiver of anticipation, almost sexual in nature, as she withdrew a wickedly sharp dirk from its hidden sheath and plunged it deeply, repeatedly, between the jutting plates of his shoulder blades.

Catherine regained consciousness by way of a jarring series of loose-jointed bumps that caused the already formidable pain in her temples to explode into agony. She was on horseback, supported roughly on the saddle by a bare-armed, barrel-chested Highlander who smelled abominably of old sweat and rotten teeth. The garron they shared was one of the short, stout ponies common to the mountainous region, but the animal's sure-footed attack of the path they were on was no consolation for the view of the steep and jagged cliff they were circumventing.

There were three of them, one riding ahead, one behind. There was very little light left in the sky to see by, only the sunset hues of pink and gold which distorted the shadows and made the ground they covered seem more ominous than it really was. The features of the man who rode in the lead were already distorted, but not by the shadows so much as by Alex's fists, which had already done the job at their last encounter. Catherine had never thought of Gordon Ross Campbell as being a particularly handsome man, although in a lean, shifty way he might have appealed to some women. Now, however, his nose was flattened across the bridge and his eyes sunken in dark hollows. He had not shaved in many days — possibly because of the gouges, cuts and scratches that still showed angrily through the dirty stubble. When he talked he moved his lips very little. They were still puffed and scabbed, and Campbell had learned to be self-conscious about his row of broken, cracked teeth. Whatever youth he had possessed, or pretended to possess, had vanished. She would not have recognized him in the garden had it not been for the hatred blazing from the cold blue eyes.

The shock of seeing him at Achnacarry, of recognizing

him, of realizing she had dashed out of the castle without troubling to wait for her usual shadow of guards, had delayed the scream long enough for Campbell's hand to clamp viciously over her mouth and smother it completely.

Catherine had kicked and squirmed, her nails had torn at the flesh of his forearms, but he had simply dragged her through the hedge and whistled softly to the two other men lurking behind the trees. One of them carried a large burlap sack; seeing it Catherine had bitten the flesh of Campbell's palm so hard her mouth had filled with blood, but he had only grunted and brought his other fist down against the side of her head — once to break the hold of her teeth, a second time to knock her soundly unconscious.

They were moving very fast, with no thought to spare for their captive's comfort. They all rode with one hand on the reins, another on the muskets that swung easily by their hips.

Who they were was apparent, where they were taking her was a matter of conjecture, and what they planned to do with her was something she did not care to speculate on. Obviously someone had been watching the castle and knew Lochiel and most of his men were away. They had waited and watched and she had presented the perfect target for a quick raid — something she had been warned about but never really thought could happen, certainly not so close to the castle itself. The whole thing seemed bizarre, out of a nightmare, not to mention a different century.

The shiver of pure terror that coursed through Catherine's body did not go unnoticed by her captor. He shouted something to Gordon Ross Campbell in Gaelic, and at the first reasonably wide ledge in the hazardous trail they were following the young Campbell called a brief halt. He drew his horse alongside Catherine and she tensed inwardly at the sight of his battered, broken face.

"Where are you taking me?" she demanded. "Why are you doing this?"

Campbell grinned evilly. "Why Mrs. Cameron, I thought

ye were a wee smart bitch — smart enough tae ken it isna ye we want, but yer husban'. Where we're takin' ye is of nae concern ither than ye behave well enough tae live tae see it.''

"He won't let you get away with this," she hissed. "Alex will come after you."

"Aye, I'm hopin' he does. I'm countin' on him followin' us all the way tae Inverary, where there's a hangman's noose waitin' f'ae him.''

"And ten thousand gold crowns waiting for you?" she asked derisively.

"That'll sweeten the pot some, aye," he admitted. "So will ye, an' it'll be a fine choice indeed tae make whither I sell ye back tae The Cameron or back tae Lord Ashbrooke . . . an' in what condition. But here . . . I thought ye werena opposed tae the idea o' collectin' the reward yersel' at ane time?" He narrowed his eyes and let them slide down to the firm thrust of her breasts. "Mayhap, if ye're nice tae me, I wouldna mind sparin' a few coins in yer favour.''

"I would sooner be nice to a ground slug," she said coldly. "As for your coins and what you can do with them — ''

He laughed suddenly and leaned forward. He grabbed a fistful of her hair and dragged her forward, jerking her head painfully to one side. Her cry of pain opened her lips to the revolting feel of his mouth sucking wetly over hers and she gagged. She brought her fists up and tried to beat him away, but the man holding her chuckled lustily and captured her wrists in one hand while the other clamped around her breast and squeezed.

Campbell released her with another husky laugh. "God's teeth, ye're a worthy hellcat tae tame. Aye, an' mayhap I'll take up the task afore the night is through.''

The third rider edged closer, muttering something under his breath, and Catherine did not need a translation of the words to know he was bidding for a turn with the *Sassenach*. Campbell's eyes were on Catherine's face as he laughed a rejoinder, but before anything could be decided their amusement was cut short by the sound of hoofbeats on the mountain path.

"It looks like they joined up wi' someone here," MacSorley grunted, pointing to the impressions on the cold ground. "Fifteen, twenny men in all."

He straightened and cast the light of the torch around the ledge, waiting calmly for Alexander Cameron to decide their next move. It had taken nearly three-quarters of an hour to assemble a dozen well-armed men and retrace the kidnapping from the garden to the hills beyond where the Campbells' horses had been tethered. By then the dusk was well upon them, and more precious time had slipped past as they were forced to move slowly and carefully so as not to lose the tracks among the many well-worn trails that wound through the mountains. It would have been even worse if not for the heavy rains that had washed away all but the most recent signs of traffic.

"Twenty men, you say?" Alex murmured.

"Coincidence?" Aluinn stood beside him, his features illuminated by the flickering light of the torch. He had insisted on accompanying Alex and the hunting party, and although he refused to show any signs of discomfort or fatigue, his shoulder felt like a small torch burning all on its own.

"I stopped believing in coincidences a long time ago," Alex said grimly. "Campbell said he had twenty men waiting across the Spean. *Goddammit!*"

"Don't crucify yourself. *I* had the same opportunity to kill him and didn't."

Alex was not appeased. "For every five minutes we lose verifying their tracks, they gain fifteen on us. We'll never catch them this way."

"They're smart," Aluinn agreed. "They know where they're going and they're not taking any chances by using a trail we could identify and circle ahead. Struan — you know the lie of the land better than anyone . . . any ideas?"

"Aye, I ken the land," MacSorley said after a lengthy

pause. Lengthy enough to earn inquisitive glances from both men.

"And?"

Struan contemplated the features of the man who had won and claimed to cherish forever the love of his sister Annie. It had been many years since Struan had caught the two of them together, naked as the day they had come into the world, clasped to one another in a tangle of writhing limbs, oblivious to everything but the glorious give and take of lovemaking. Struan had drawn his knife with every intention of gelding the strappingly handsome Alexander Cameron despite the fact that he was Lochiel's brother. Alex had faced him calmly. He had defused the giant with a simple honest admission of his love for Annie, his respect for MacSorley's skill with a blade, and a true hope that he would not have to kill his future brother-in-law in order to prove his sincerity. Kill MacSorley? The pup had been tall and lanky, half his weight soaking wet, yet — as he had demonstrated less than a year later — capable of making up in determination what he lacked in stamina.

Since then, of course, a hard life had provided the power and presence to make him any man's equal. There was still the quiet intensity in the eyes and the deceptive looseness in his stance, but the brashness of youth was gone. Gone also was the wild, killing passion that had governed his actions after Annie's death — was it a result of maturity or had Lauren Cameron's bitter accusations had some foundation?

"I ken the land," MacSorley said again. "Enough tae ken that what we've covered has been the easiest. I wisna sure till the past hour, but ye asket me, I'd be willin' tae stake ma life on they're gonny cut through the mountains at Hell's Gate."

"At night? They'd never make it!"

"Fast as they're gaun, they'll be in the glen wi' an hour or two tae spare afore dawn. Slow as we're gaun, they'll be through the pass an' dug in f'ae as fine an ambush as a hunnerd clansmen couldna survive."

"Is there no other way over that ridge?"

Even though it was dark and nothing much was visible in the night sky, all three men turned to stare up at the formidable wall of blackness.

It was Struan who broke the silence, again weighing his words carefully. "Nae man could fault ye f'ae dain as much as ye have already tae try an' catch the lassie back."

Alex's eyes narrowed as he slowly turned to stare at Mac-Sorley. "Are you suggesting we give up and turn back?"

The big man shrugged. "She's *Sassenach*; the Campbells willna harm her. Furthermair, I'm after knowin' ye spent the better part o' the past four days arrangin' a way tae send her hame tae England. Seems tae me ye could save yersel' a purseful o' gold by lettin' the Campbells dae it f'ae ye."

Alexander's expression was unreadable in the wavering light of the torch. He appeared to hesitate, to start to turn away, but only a few degrees — the better to channel all of his strength and fury into the fist he drove upward into Struan's bearded jaw. The bigger man staggered back a step, his head twisting violently to one side as the flesh of his cheek was nearly sliced through by his teeth. His response was instinctive. His left arm lashed out to block a second punch while his right delivered a crushing blow to Alex's midsection. The frustration he had been harbouring, the anger he had been feeling over his doubts and misgivings exploded on a curse, and Struan's voice roared in vibrating waves from one rock to the next.

"Jesus!" Aluinn tried to step between them but was unexpectedly held back by two of the Cameron clansmen.

Struan and Alex grappled in the shadows, their movements lost to the gloom but clearly defined by the impacting thud of fists on flesh. The torch was brought forward but the shapes and actions were only rendered more grotesque, more disjointed. Grunts and curses punctuated the scuffle of feet; muted groans and the hiss of escaping breaths marked a bruised belly or a brutally struck diaphragm. The smell of sweat and rage steamed the air, the sound of blood-slickened punches finally stirred the other men into responding to Aluinn's shouts.

It took three men to hold Alex in abeyance, four to counter the incredible blood lust of Struan's fury.

"Goddammit!" A frankly astounded Aluinn MacKail stepped into the swirl of disturbed dust and commanded silence. "What the bloody hell are the two of you trying to prove? Struan — ? Alex — ?"

Alexander strained against the men who were pinning his arms and spat out a bloodied chip of a tooth along with a curse aimed at MacSorley's ancestry.

Struan surged forward, dragging his keepers with him as if they were weightless.

"I said *enough*!" Aluinn withdrew his pistol. "The next bastard who moves is going to earn an ounce of lead for his troubles!"

The men tested their restraints a moment longer before grudgingly giving way.

"Now then — Struan: You seem to have something on your mind. Would you care to say it in plainer terms we can all understand?"

"There are cairtain things need explainin' — "

"Explanations!" Alex erupted savagely. "I don't owe you or anyone else explanations!"

"*Alex!* Leash that goddamned pride for ten seconds and hear what he has to say!" Aluinn's brow beaded with sweat. He had no idea what could possibly be causing Struan's animosity — surely not Annie! Not after all these years! "Struan, you want explanations? For what?"

"The *Sassenach* didna want tae come tae Achnacarry; her husban' spent half the week an' half a thousan' in gold tryin' tae ship her out o' Scotland again. We're out here in the middle o' the night walkin' smack f'ae a trap that couldna be set nor sprung wi'out help frae somewheres . . ." He paused and his chest heaved with restrained emotions. "It has tae be asked, and it has tae be answered: Is the lass yer wife or na?

Is she a Cameron . . . or has she gone willingly wi' the Campbells?''

The complete unexpectedness of the questions and the underlying implications drained the remaining fight from Alex's body. "Struan, for the love of — "

"Answer him, Alex," Aluinn said abruptly, his voice as stern and level as his gaze. He saw the question in Alex's eyes as they turned to him, but he could also see, where Alex could not, the taut expressions on the faces of the other watchful clansmen. "Answer him," he said again, softer this time. "Unless you are not sure of the truth yourself."

Alex's dark eyes turned to Struan. "Catherine and I were married three weeks ago in Derby, and you are right, she did not want to come to Scotland. For that matter, she did not want to marry me, nor I her, but we were forced by circumstances to oblige." He paused and wiped at a trickle of blood leaking from his cut lip. "In the beginning she only thought I was a bastard. Then, when she found out who I really was and where I was headed . . . well, it seemed the lesser of two evils to take her along and travel openly as Lord and Lady Englishman. Somewhere along the way — and I'm damned if I know where or why or even how — we stopped fighting one another. We still have a lot of prejudices to overcome, and I will admit that right up until this afternoon, I wasn't sure it would be worth the effort. I wasn't even sure it would be possible."

He stopped and frowned, his thoughts stumbling and struggling for clarity. "But when I saw her today . . . and held her . . . and heard her telling *me* she was a Cameron now — " He looked up from his bloodied, scraped hands. "A part of me came back to life, a part I had thought I buried fifteen years ago. I loved Annie, Struan. I would gladly have given my own life to save hers or bring her back. But I couldn't. And she'll never come back. And now I can't stand by and let anything happen to Catherine, not even if I have to fight my way to Argyle myself."

MacSorley's eyes had not wavered from Alex's face since he had started speaking; they did not waver now as he stepped slowly forward and grasped Alex's arm. "I ken what ye're sayin' lad, an' it's mair than I need or desairve tae hear. We'll stop the bastards an' get yer lassie back. An' ye'll nae have tae fight yer way tae Inverary alane either, nae while there's breath left in this miserable body."

Alex reinforced the gesture of friendship by clasping his hands to MacSorley's arms. "Then you *do* know of another way across the mountains?"

"Aye." MacSorley grinned. "I ken a way only the goats are daft enough tae use, an' then only when the devil has their balls atween his teeth."

Alex saw the other clansmen exchange nervous glances. The desolate range of mountains they were approaching were shrouded in superstition, believed to have been thrown together on a day when the Creator had been in a rage. Hell's Gate, aptly named for its sheer drops and torturously steep corries, was the only pass Alex knew of within a five-mile stretch in either direction.

"Can you take us through by night?"

"Better at night," Struan said guilelessly, "Then ye canna see where ye're gaun. Mind, f'ae his trouble, the madman who takes it will be waitin' on the ither side o' hell when the Campbells ride through."

Alex glanced at Aluinn, who only shrugged noncommitally and stared down at the pistol he still held in his hand.

"All right. We'll do it," Alex said. Suspecting there would be men who would not be especially eager to take additional risk, he suggested several volunteers might remain on the Campbells' trail, hopefully getting close enough to them by morning to keep them looking over their shoulders and not ahead.

But there were no such volunteers forthcoming. In the end, four men had to be selected to press on in the pursuit. Struan's choices seemed random, but a careful scrutiny

would have revealed the four men to be those with the largest
families and most number of dependents.

Catherine was faint from cold and terror. The trail they were
following had deteriorated to hardly more than a sheep track
and descended into a narrow gorge devoid of any living thing
as far as she could ascertain in the weak torchlight. Even the
sturdy little horses balked at the sight of the bleached
skeletons of trees leering out of the darkness, the sharp pro-
jections of rock that suddenly thrust forth from the shadows.
Catherine even thought she detected a genuine sigh of relief
from the man whose horse she shared when Gordon Ross
Campbell gave the signal to dismount.

The animals were staked around the stump of a gnarled
old tree but remained saddled for an emergency. The torches
were doused, the rations limited to a couple of rock-hard
biscuits and a mouthful of water. No one thought to provide
Catherine with a blanket or a length of tartan. Her body
ached from an untold number of bruises, and her temples
throbbed with an appalling rhythm all their own. She gingerly tested the lump on the side of her head, just above her
ear, where Campbell's fist had silenced her, and found the
skin broken, her hair and cheek crusted with dried blood.

The moon was a crescent-shaped sliver hanging over the
top of the mountain like a scythe. Stars bloomed by the
millions, but the light they shed did little to alleviate the
sinister landscape. She was glad she could not see where they
were. And as she edged her way around a large boulder, she
hoped the Argylemen were as blinded by the darkness and as
disoriented as she was.

The stone scraped her wrists and the ground was gravelled
with sharp pebbles that cut into the bare soles of her feet. She
kept moving, kept sliding along the boulder, moving away
from the gutteral snatches of conversation. Catherine's hope
of a speedy rescue had died when the three men had joined
forces with a larger body on the hillside. Even if Alex were

within reach, what could he do against so many? There were barely any clansmen of fighting age left at Achnacarry — the most experienced were with Lochiel. But even if he had a hundred with him, how could he follow in the pitch blackness?

Catherine reached the end of the boulder and groped at the darkness beyond. She kept her eyes and ears trained on the nearby voices, and her panic flared as she distinguished Gordon Ross Campbell's voice above the others. He was asking for her, demanding the prisoner be brought to him; it would only be a matter of moments before her absence was discovered.

Catherine leaned farther out, but her hand found nothing but air. She heard the scratch of tinder on flint and she knew a torch was being lit; she had seconds, fractions of seconds, to hide herself away in one of the fissures that riddled the walls of the gorge. Taking a desperate risk, she turned and ran into the blackness, her arms outstretched, her eyes opened so wide the lids felt stretched to the point of tearing. Her hand smashed into stone and the pain brought a choked cry to her lips, but she forced it back and scraped her way along to yet another niche in the rock. This one was narrower and tore the fabric of her sleeves; the cold stone teeth bit into her tender flesh. Her skirt snagged on a hooked outcrop and she felt it rip just as her forward foot slid over the rock and hurled her headlong into a black void.

The pass Struan led them to was not much more than a crevice slashed between two mighty spirals of twisted and overlapping rock that rose hundreds of feet into the air above them. The entrance was covered with brambles and thorn bushes so that in daylight, from more than a score of paces away, it would appear to be a solid, sheer cliff of stone. As it was, in the darkness, it took MacSorley nearly an hour to hack his way through the undergrowth and locate the opening.

The chasm was just wide enough to accommodate the breadth of a horse's flanks. Shadow, by far the largest of the animals, balked at the entrance, his nostrils dilated, his muscles quivering with undisguised fear. Alex stroked the gleaming neck and soothed the stallion as best he could, but even he had to fight back a strong and intense revulsion to the idea of entering the black maw. Struan's torch threw ghostly illumination on the slime-covered rock overhead; the air became thick with smoke and made the men's eyes water until the ceiling lifted and a draft sucked the fumes upward. Then there came a more terrifying assault on the senses: Thousands of bats began to screech and scream and stir the air with a frenzy of stinging wings.

Alex kept Shadow moving forward, kept his eyes fastened on the bright flare of Struan's torch. His knees were scraped raw on the walls of stone, and he did not want to think of what might happen should the torches fail or the horses become stuck or the mountains shift suddenly and crush the jaws of the trap closed. His eyes were burning from the smoke and his ears rang from the high-pitched shrilling of the bats. He did not turn around to see if the next man in line was faring any better, for his own nerves would not bear too much more pressure before they snapped and screamed as loudly as the bats.

Fifty yards into the bowels of the mountain, a chilled, wailing wind forced each rider to lower his head to protect his eyes from flying bits of dirt and grit. The flames of the torches streaked straight back and Alex followed Struan's example and held his tartan up to protect the light. Each man involuntarily found himself holding his breath. There was a distinct clamminess to the skin and an uncontrollable smothering sensation that forced the acrid taste of bile into each dry throat.

One hundred yards . . . two hundred yards, and the men's brains began to feel as if they might explode from their skulls. Two of the four torches had been snuffed, and the men shouted back and forth, encouraging each other and the petrified animals.

Three hundred yards into the chasm the walls began to relent. The howling of the wind stopped as abruptly as it had begun, although any exposed skin still felt stung and whipped raw. Alex wiped the streaming moisture from his eyes and saw that they had entered a chamber of sorts, an oval cavern hollowed out of the rock, twenty feet across by perhaps forty feet in length. In the middle was a still, glasslike pool of water; huddled around the rim was a silent audience of gruesomely emaciated stone pillars, some so life-like in size and shape they appeared to shuffle uncomfortably in the glow of the torch. Some boasted faces hewn out of the rock, grizzly distortions of half-rotted noses and sunken eye sockets.

"A hellish sight, is it na?" Struan whispered. "Legend tells these are the men tairned tae stone by the gods f'ae their lack o' courage."

Alex glanced at MacSorley and was mildly surprised to see the same beads of moisture shining on the wide brow as he felt on his own.

"Hellish indeed. How do we get out of here?"

There were cracks in the walls of the cavern every few feet, none of them seeming wide enough to afford an exit.

Struan relit the blackened torches and grinned easily as he led the way toward one of the fissures on the far side of the pool. As he passed between two of the stalagmites, he reached out and patted one of them on what might have been an incredibly well endowed bosom.

"Take heed o' Beulah the Bitch if ye ever need come this way again. Mind ye gie her a wee pap on the teat f'ae lettin' ye go through. She'll remember if ye dinna an' she'll switch the stones on ye out o' spite."

Alex had no reservations about leaning over and caressing

the rough stone breast. Each man in line did likewise until the last one was swallowed into the vastness of the mountain again.

Chapter Eighteen

When the sun poked its bloodshot eye over the horizon, the Cameron clansmen were in position at the southern exit of Hell's Gate. They had ridden most of the night, but true to MacSorley's promise, they were settled into a perfect ambuscade where the Campbells would least expect to find them. Alexander, Aluinn, and MacSorley waited out the dawn at the mouth of the pass, keeping a close eye on the distant column of men as they coaxed their reluctant animals up the treacherously steep slope. The Campbell encampment at the base of the mountain had been invisible in the darkness — obviously they had ordered no fires lit — but as the sky began to leak colour onto the landscape, the tiny figures moving among the rock and bracken became distinguishable. The gorge, heavily pocketed with mist, revealed most of its secrets to the watching eyes above. They saw, for instance, when two men rode swiftly into the camp at daybreak. It had to be assumed they were the rear guards and, further, that they had seen the men MacSorley had ordered to maintain the pursuit, for within minutes fresh guards were sent out at a gallop while the rest of the men mounted and began creeping their way up the mountainside.

Alex stared at each horse and rider as they moved closer and noted the bright splash of yellow hair at almost the same instant as Aluinn MacKail's finger jabbed out over the boulder they were crouched behind.

"There," he hissed. "Right in the middle."

"I see her," Alex murmured, inwardly cursing that because of Gordon Ross Campbell's innate sense of caution she had been placed well back in the column. Yet the relief he expected to feel on seeing Catherine alive and relatively safe did not materialize. Instead he felt an annoying, itching sensation at the back of his neck, as if there was something more down there he should be seeing but was not. The itch grew and spread as the minutes passed by and the threat came closer; his nerves tautened and his instincts screamed. He had to set his teeth on edge to keep from roaring out his agitation.

He glanced at MacSorley and saw that Struan had stiffened as well, like a bloodhound scenting fresh game. What was it? What was it they both sensed but could not identify? Something was out there, something deadly and dangerous and evil. He had ignored his instincts once already, with horrific results. He would not ignore them again.

"Good God," Aluinn whispered.

Alex saw him. Second in line in the column, sitting fat and squat on a pony whose back and belly sagged from the bulk of the man. Half of his face looked human enough beneath the cocked blue bonnet, but the other half had the texture and appearance of lava spewed from some demonic volcano, left to cool around the distorted crater of an eyeless socket. His nose was a misshapen mass of darkly pigmented skin, split with spidery red veins. His hair was greasy and parted around a diagonal welt of a scar that ran from the crown of his head to the hollow of his throat. His arms were so thick they were held away from the trunk of his body; his legs were like tree stumps, the flesh as scarred and ridged as bark where it showed between the hem of his kilt and the top of his hose.

"Where the bloody Christ did he come from?" Aluinn asked tersely.

Alex felt the recognition press against his throat, constricting his windpipe, mottling his face a dull, angry crimson. A wave of hatred, black and glutinous, boiled up from some hidden depth of his soul, flushing through his blood and cramping the muscles in his belly and thighs.

"Malcolm Campbell." The name was uttered through taut white lips. "I should have known. He never would have trusted such an enterprise to another man, bastard son or not."

As if Campbell had heard the words spoken, he jerked on the reins of his horse and called an abrupt halt to the column. The single reptilian eye narrowed, almost disappearing into the porous folds of skin.

He's picked up the scent too, Alex thought with malicious pleasure. He's feeling it crawl along his skin, but he doesn't know what it is.

Below, Gordon Ross Campbell edged his horse alongside his father.

"Summit smells wrong here," Malcolm snarled, his voice like the sound of two marble slabs grinding together.

Gordon Ross studied the formidably steep summits of the surrounding rim of mountains but sensed nothing but the desolation of the barren rocks.

"Are ye cairtain there's nae ither way roun'?" Campbell demanded.

"No' unless a man sprouts wings an' flies," Gordon Ross said confidently. "Besides, they canna be in two places the same time."

Malcolm Campbell kept his eye trained on the shadows and corries. His men had reported seeing the Cameron trackers closing on their heels — a remarkable feat all things considered. Perhaps it was just the sweet taste of revenge setting his glands to spurting saliva around his mouth. Perhaps it was just the anticipation of finally confronting his hated enemy after all these years that had the sweat squeaking between the leather of his saddle and his bare thighs.

The great *Camshroinaich Dubh* was within his grasp at last. A legend — *faugh*! He, Malcolm Campbell would be the legend before this day was through. He was already a minor miracle, having survived a wound that should have killed any other mere mortal. Hadn't he been given up for dead by his own people? Cameron's sword had hacked the flesh from the bone, tearing half his face away and severing the muscles from the left side of his chest. A clansman had roughly stitched the flaps of gristle back as a courtesy to his family, but they had dug three graves, carved three names into the stone cairn laid to mark his fallen brothers, Colin and Dughall. Through it all, through the shock and the infections, through the weeks of fever and delirium, only one thought had kept Malcolm Campbell alive: Revenge. He had nurtured that same hatred, that same desire for retribution in his son, and together, by God, they had done it. Before the day was through, they would have their prize. They would have the head of the *Camshroinaich Dubh* and the fear of every Cameron who had ever dared raise his voice in disdain!

From more than a quarter of a mile away, Alex thought he detected a smile on the cruel, twisted lips. MacSorley touched him on the shoulder, beckoning him away from the entrance of the pass, and the three men raced back through the gully to where their horses were staked. They galloped down the rutted slope, stopping several hundred yards beyond a wide avenue carved into the rock and scrub. It was the perfect spot for an ambush. Where the trail cut through the rocks and stunted trees, it was just wide enough for two men to ride abreast, while the banks on either side were chest-high and covered with a wild hedgerow tall enough to conceal a man. The overall gloom, if the sun obliged by delaying its entry into the world behind the slow-moving bank of cloud overhead, would make discovery unlikely until the full troop of Campbell's men had passed into the avenue.

Knowing this was undoubtedly the place Malcolm Campbell would have chosen to set up his own ambush, Alex took a particularly primitive delight in the loading and priming of his steel-butted flintlock pistols. Aluinn was beside him, gently massaging his stiffened shoulder, the calm gray eyes watching without comment as paper cartridges were torn open and measures of black powder poured into each barrel. The actions of the long, lean fingers were steady and precise — almost loving — as if the man tamping down the wadding and balls knew exactly where each solid round of lead shot would be placed.

"There are twenty of them," MacKail remarked dryly. "Eight of us."

"Fair odds," Struan interjected wanly from behind, "considerin' they're Campbells an' we're Camerons."

Aluinn crooked an eyebrow. "Still, it wouldn't hurt to make every shot count during the first few seconds of surprise."

Struan nodded grimly. "Aye, there are those desairvin' o' a quick an' painless death. Ithers have a deal o' accountin' tae dae."

Alex stared at the battered face, knowing there were similar bruises discolouring his own features.

"Malcolm Campbell is still mine," he said quietly. "I am holding you to your bond."

MacSorley's eyes narrowed. It had nearly killed him fifteen years ago to pledge on his honour not to hunt Malcolm Campbell down like the animal he was and finish the job Alexander had started. A score of times he had drunk to the bottom of a whisky jug and staggered off in search of vengeance, and a score of times he had sobered and turned back. Making that pledge had been the only means of coaxing Alex to relinquish the cold and lifeless body of Anne MacSorley after a ten-hour vigil that had bordered on madness.

"Aye." Struan nodded. "I made ye that promise. He's yers. But I'll be directly ahind ye lad, tae be sure he disna cheat Auld Hornie again."

"Fair enough. Aluinn — " He turned to MacKail. "As soon as the first man falls, they'll be pointing their guns at Catherine."

Aluinn nodded. "I'll get to her first, don't worry."

"Aye," Struan grunted. "An' I'll be directly up *yer* arse as well, count on it."

A shrill whistle from the lookout warned the men of Campbell's entry into the pass.

Forcing his mind to go completely blank, Alex ducked into position behind a wall of greenery. He placed his musket beside him on the rocks and checked to make sure his sword was strapped securely about his waist. Then he stood waiting, both pistols held before him, cocked and ready. Out of the corner of his eye he could see the other clansmen crouching into their placements, not a muscle or hair twitching to betray their presence. Every instinct was tuned to the stillness of the air, every breath was held lest a rising puff of steam reveal them.

The first of the riders entered the cloistered avenue, the slow plodding hoofbeats echoing off the hard ground. Alex raised both pistols. He waited until the flanks of the lead horses were directly in line with his barrels before he leaped to his feet and discharged both weapons point-blank into the startled faces of the Campbell clansmen.

They were not the faces he expected to see, but Alex did not stop to question the whereabouts of Malcolm or Gordon Ross Campbell. He flung the empty pistols aside and snatched up his musket, remembering to suck in his breath and brace himself for the tremendous recoil of the Highland firing piece. The cloud of smoke from the exploding powder stung him blind for a few precious seconds, but by then he had also discarded the musket and was unsheathing his sword from its scabbard.

His face set, his body moving with the supple precision of a bullwhip, Alex sprang forward, his throat vibrating with a battle cry as old and savage as his Highland ancestry. All along the curve of the avenue, the shouted *cath-ghairm* was echoed as his men flung themselves out of the cover of the bushes and met their enemies head-on. The first volley of gunshots had been effective — ten Campbell clansmen lay either dead or dying beneath the panicked frenzy of horses' hoofs. From the rear of the avenue, high on the rocks, came one of Struan's surprises: a steady stream of wickedly barbed arrows that proved to be deadly efficient in adding to the carnage of writhing bodies and thrashing horses.

Alex slashed his sword across the saddle of the first man in line, cleanly severing an arm at the elbow. The man's sword, with his hand still gripped around the hilt, flew off into the rocks, spattering them red with blood and tissue. A second slash went to MacSorley's aid, relieving his attacker of his pistol and his life.

"I see ye've nae forgotten how tae fight!" MacSorley roared, baring his teeth in a fearsome snarl as he meted out equal punishment to another Argyleman. "But I'd nae be worryin' so much on ma back as yer ain!"

Alex whirled and lunged out of the way only moments before a terrified horse charged past him. He had barely regained his balance when a second animal thundered toward him, this one driven by a screaming, sword-wielding Campbell. He ducked as the blade hacked down in an arc across his shoulders and was never certain if it was his own sword that brought the man crashing to the ground or the well-placed arrow that skewered cleanly through the man's throat.

Alex dashed a hand across his brow to keep the sweat from rolling into his eyes as he vaulted over two bodies. No more than two minutes had passed since the first shots had been fired, but already the ground was red with blood, the air choked with dust and acrid smoke. Horses were rearing and blocking the laneway, their screams adding to the confusion as they reacted to the smell of fear and death.

Catherine, still trapped in the middle of the column, felt the arms of her captor go limp as a carefully placed shot tore away the back of his skull. As he slumped forward, she pushed him to the side to free the saddle, but his foot caught in the stirrup and he hung grotesquely over her thigh. She was too terrified to think about what she was doing as she leaned over and began to tug and pry at the stuck foot. It would not budge and the dead weight was beginning to pull her off balance when a pair of lean hands came to her rescue. Aluinn freed the foot and shoved the body off the pony, but before he could give Catherine more than a brief smile of reassurance, she was screaming a warning to him of a new threat over his shoulder.

Aluinn spun around like a dancer, his sabre flashing as he brought it up to block a thrust from Gordon Ross Campbell's broadsword. Campbell's blow was deflected with a sharp ringing of steel, but as his weapon was much heavier than Aluinn's, he lost valuable seconds during the recovery and by then it was too late. Aluinn regained his balance, pivoted lightly on the balls of his feet, and sliced the blade across the younger man's arched throat.

Catherine's horse shied from the spray of warm blood, and she scrambled to hold on to the reins, to keep her seat as he reared and pawed the air. A hoof flayed wildly in Aluinn's direction and he turned headlong into the danger just as a foreleg glanced off his wounded shoulder. His lips drew back over a raw scream of pain and he staggered to his knees.

Catherine wheeled the horse around and let go of the reins, slipping to the ground seconds before the animal bolted into the clashing melee of swords. She ran to Aluinn's side but he was beyond movement, beyond feeling or knowing anything apart from the shattering agony of his shoulder. He did not feel the slender arms circle his chest and try to lever him to his feet; he did not see her whirl away or hear her strangled cry as a pair of trunklike arms reached down and dragged her onto the back of yet another short, stout animal.

Malcolm Campbell wrapped his arm tightly around her waist, holding fast to the reins in the same hand while his other one thrust the snout of a pistol sharply up beneath the curve of her chin. His first thought was to kill her, but he knew the moment he did so, he would have no protection from the stinging flights of arrows or the lashing swords. As he watched the last of his men fall to the ground beneath Cameron swords, anger burned through his veins like acid. Images flashed in disjointed sequences across his memory — a stable turned from one moment to the next into a bloody battleground; his brothers Colin and Dughall split open and leaking viscera onto the straw; his own wounds, the first time he had dared look into a mirrored glass . . .

"It's over, Campbell! Let the woman go!"

Malcolm Campbell whirled in the direction of the hated voice. It was him — the black-eyed devil responsible for his pain, his disfigurement, his *humiliation*!

"Cameron, ye bastard!" he screamed. "I'll kill her! So help me Christ, I'll kill her here where ye can watch her brains fly up tae feed the bluidy ravens!"

Catherine squeezed her eyes shut as she felt the nose of the pistol gouge deeper into her throat. She had a hand clawed around his forearm, but it was like trying to scratch stone. Her other hand groped instinctively for support on the saddle, knowing a slip on her part would only further Campbell's cause. Her fingers struck cold metal and it took a moment for her to absorb and identify the shape. It was the hilt of a dirk he wore tucked into the top of his hose.

"Let her go," Alex repeated evenly. "This is between you and me. It always has been."

"If that's so, then yer men'll listen when ye tell them tae put their weapons doon an' move awa'."

One by one the Cameron men looked from the last seated Campbell to Alexander's taut white face . . . and one by one they laid their swords aside and backed slowly away from the crimson slaughterhouse before them. Campbell watched them, alert for any sudden movement, and then his single rat eye flicked down to where the body of his son lay sprawled and still twitching on the blood-slicked ground.

"Ye've added tae the price ye'll pay, Cameron," he grated. "Ye've added tae it twofold."

The ebony eyes did not waver from Campbell's face. Ignoring the snarled threat, Alex directed his voice, soft and low, toward the pale and trembling figure of his wife.

"It's all right, Catherine. Don't be afraid."

Catherine opened her eyes but her head was tilted at an angle that allowed only a view straight up into the sky. The clouds were drifting away from the sun. In a few moments it would burst free. She wrapped her fingers around the hilt of the dirk and prayed the sunlight would blind her to whatever pain she was sure was about to come.

Campbell sat poised on the saddle, every muscle and nerve tensed to explode. Fifteen years of hatred and frustration welled from the depths of his soul and set his finger trembling against the trigger. But before he took his just due, he wanted Cameron to suffer. He wanted the bastard to *remember*.

"I gie ye credit f'ae yer taste in lassies, Cameron," he hissed. "This ane were as sweet an' soft as the ither. Aye. Sweet an' wet an bonnie enough tae satisfy most o' ma men, though I foun' I had tae take her twice afore she stopped squirmin' lang enough tae enjoy it. See the bruises an' cuts? A rare hellcat she is."

Catherine tried to scream out against the lie, but she could not manage more than a dry gasp past the terrible, viselike pressure stretching into her throat.

Grinning as he saw Alex's face blanch a sickly gray, Campbell nudged his heels into the garron's flanks, easing the animal away from the avenue and back up the hillside.

Alex followed, step by rigid step, his hand clenched around the hilt of his sword so tightly the veins rose along his forearm like snakes.

Campbell waited until the last possible second, luring his enemy far enough away from his men so that his escape would be only a matter of a few galloped strides into the mouth of the pass. When he judged Alex's position and patience to be at their limit, he brought the pistol down from Catherine's neck and swung it toward him.

At the same instant, the sun broke from behind the foaming white clouds and Catherine jerked her hand up, bringing the sharp little stiletto with it. Alex saw her hand move, and the cold shock of seeing the dirk clutched in her fist, coupled with the colder shock of realizing the extent of the sacrifice she was prepared to make, brought forth a violent roar of fury from his throat. He launched himself forward just as Campbell brought the gun down and pulled the trigger.

The horse reared as the gun discharged inches from his ear. Catherine slipped further back in the saddle, and her hand was startled from its driven path, long enough for her to see Campbell fling the empty gun to the ground and kick the horse in the direction of the pass. His arm was still around her waist and she slashed at it frantically with the knife. She heard a loud curse explode in her ear and the next thing she knew, she was being shoved to one side and thrown to the ground.

Unencumbered by Catherine's weight, the horse responded to Campbell's furious commands and galloped up the hill, but before they had covered more than ten paces, an arrow struck the animal's neck, just behind the hard bone of the skull. Horse and rider went down hard in a crash of flailing legs; Campbell was thrown clear and did not attempt to stop his fall but rolled with it so that he was on his feet and running as the next arrow ricocheted harmlessly off the rocks beside him. He retrieved his broadsword and threw himself into the mouth of Hell's Gate, mindful of the pounding steps pursuing him into the gloomy chasm.

Crouched low and using every fibre of speed and muscle in his powerful legs, Alex hurled himself through the air like a human catapult. He caught Campbell by the shoulders and together they slammed into the jagged face of the stone wall. Alex's arm was scraped of surface flesh as Campbell's bulk trapped him momentarily against the rock and he felt the sickening tear of muscle and tendon. Campbell wasted no effort on niceties; he raised his sword and charged, roaring obscenities as he aimed a cutting slash intended to part Alex's head from his shoulders.

Cameron lunged to one side with a hair's breadth to spare as the steel blade missed and rang loudly on the cold stone. He avoided a second deadly windmilling slash and was forced to retreat out into the sunlight, only then discovering he had lost hold of his sabre in the mad charge. Campbell came after him, his broadsword clenched in both hairy fists.

Something came stinging through the air and landed inches from Alex's foot. He heard a bellow from over his shoulder and recognized the five-foot length of blooded steel Struan MacSorley had sent to his aid. Grasping the broadsword, he pulled it free of the ground, raised it with barely enough time to block against the jarring impact of a strike. There was no finesse, no grace involved in duelling with the heavy weapons; power and brute strength were more important than agile footwork, and a man drunk on the scent of blood was far more dangerous than a man adept at parry and thrust. Alex had forgotten more than he cared to admit about the tremendous weight and momentum of the Highland weapon, and he paid for his ignorance with two successive slices across his ribs and shoulder.

Sensing the weakness in his adversary, Campbell grinned malevolently and advanced in a killing frenzy, the edge of his blade seeking an arm, a thigh, the exposed belly, the neck . . .

Alex staggered back from the force of the attack, his breath laboured and dry, burning along his throat, scorching into his lungs. He felt the sword slip in his hands, twisted loose on a wrenching blow that left his fingers and arm numb from the recoil. He grasped the hilt in both hands and swung with all his might, but Campbell had seen the move and dodged to avoid it. Steel scraped on steel as their blades crossed, and for a long moment the two men stood eye to eye, the muscles in their arms bulging, their sweat and blood splashing each other's face.

In a sudden downward plunge, Alex canted his blade forward, breaking the tension in Campbell's wrists and at the same time locking the edge of his adversary's sword against the ornate scrollwork of his own basket hilt. He brought his blade down and turned it inward, feeling it bite hard flesh as he dragged it up against the straining muscle of Campbell's inner thigh. He heard Campbell scream and felt the hot spurt of blood as the artery was severed. Releasing his hold on the broadsword, he let it fall to the ground and his hand went to the dagger sheathed at his waist. He thrust it high and deep, stabbing through sinew and tissue to rupture the stubbornly beating muscle of Campbell's heart.

Dimly, he was aware of a loud clang as Campbell's sword followed his own to the ground. Campbell slumped forward, his single eye gaping in outraged disbelief as he stared down at the handle of the knife protruding from his chest. His hands clawed upward and curled around Alex's throat, but there was no strength left in the fingers to do more than draw two bloody scratches down the side of Cameron's neck.

Alex supported the horrendous weight of his enemy for another moment before he shrugged the body aside. He stood over it a few moments more, his chest heaving, his hands red and dripping, until a cry from behind made him tear his eyes away and turn to catch the slender body that came running up the slope toward him. Catherine threw herself into his outstretched arms, weeping his name and sobbing a great wet patch onto the front of his shirt.

"It's over," he murmured at length. "It's all over."

"I was so frightened you wouldn't come," she gasped and buried her head deeper into his shoulder.

"Wouldn't come?" His hands cradled her head and tilted her face up to his. She met his questioning gaze through a fresh flood of hot tears.

"I . . . I thought perhaps you . . . you would not want me back," she whispered.

He stared at her a moment then bent his head forward. He wrapped his long arms around her and held her close while his lips moved against her temple.

"Well, now you know better," he said simply, and his mouth pressed firmly, decisively over hers.

Aluinn came up beside them and glanced silently down at

the still figure lying on the sun-spilled rock. He was holding his shoulder and gently massaging the wounded flesh, but when he looked up at Alex and Catherine a smile broke through the gray mask of pain. "It's about bloody time you two acted like man and wife."

"She's stubborn, for a *Sassenach*," Alex mused.

"And he's an obstinate, arrogant Scotsman," Catherine responded, her voice muffled against his throat.

"You will hear no arguments from me," Aluinn said. "On either count."

Both men sobered and looked down at the splayed form of Malcolm Campbell.

"All these years," Alex said. "I've carried his face with me all these years."

"Aye." Aluinn tipped his head up and narrowed his eyes against the dazzle of sunlight. The lofty, windswept vista that surrounded them was too regal a setting for such grizzly business. He noticed then a scarred, skeletal tree as old as time itself standing alone some distance down the slope. On its spread branches sat hundreds, perhaps thousands, of black-winged ravens, silently watchful, awaiting their bloody reward. A chill shuddered over the surface of Aluinn's skin as he remembered that one of the peaks forming Hell's Gate was also known as Clach Mhor.

. . . The ravens will drink their fill of Campbell blood three times off the top of Clach Mhor . . .

The prophesy had come true. First Colin, then Dughall . . . now Malcolm.

"Why don't we get out of here?" MacKail suggested, shaking his hand to rid it of the blood trickling down his arm. He had not stopped to assess his wounds before now; no one had.

Alex, by far the most seriously injured, lifted Catherine gently in his arms and carried her, despite her protests, down the slope to where the horses were tethered. He placed her on Shadow's back and climbed painfully up behind her, then rearranged his tartan so that they were both wrapped within the warm cocoon.

"Alex?"

He pressed his lips into the golden crown of her hair. "Hush, don't talk. There is a tiny hamlet a few miles down the glen and — "

"He did not touch me. None of them did." The wide violet eyes sought his. "He only said it to make you angry, to goad you into making a mistake. I earned these bruises and cuts trying to run away last night. I didn't get very far. I slipped and I think I must have fallen halfway down the mountain before I stopped . . . Why are you laughing?"

"You are a deal of trouble, you know. One of these days a man will be clever enough to tie you hand and foot before trusting you on your own."

A flicker of a challenge sparkled in her eyes. "Will that someone be you, my lord?"

"I believe I have other methods in mind for keeping you in one place," he said and kissed her gently on the lips.

The farmhouse Alex took her to was small and primitive, huddled in the lee of an imposing overhang of rock. The structure was stone and thatch, windowless aside from a single square cut in the mortar to allow ventilation. The floor was dirt, the fireplace large and smoky and hung one end to the next with assorted pots, cauldrons, and dried meats. The family, recognizing Alexander Cameron instantly, set about preparing food and drink, boiling vast quantities of water, tending each of the wounded men in turn until every last cut was bathed and wrapped in bandages. A bathtub was an unheard-of luxury in the glen, but Catherine was given strong soap and plenty of warmed water. Her torn dress was replaced with one of simple homespun many times repaired but obviously the best the family had to offer.

Word of the *Camshroinaich Dubh*'s presence spread and

within the hour, men and women were arriving at the cottage door with baskets of food, bread, ale — whatever they could spare. The clansmen who had won such a resounding victory over the Campbells were offered lodgings for the night, and as dusk began to settle over the valley, fires were lit and crocks of whisky opened to celebrate the triumph.

Catherine slept through the afternoon and most of the evening. She wakened briefly each time she felt Alexander's presence in the room with her, but fear anxiety, shock, and trauma exacted their toll, and she could do little more than acknowledge his concern with a weary sigh.

Alex allowed the crofter's wife to tend to his own wounds only after the rest of his men had been seen to, and only after he had been assured Catherine was resting comfortably. He bore a wealth of cuts on his body, a nasty gash across his cheek where Campbell's sword had sought to relieve him of an eye, and a multitude of bruises in varying shades and sizes that earned him a long lecture in muttered Gaelic.

"Thank you, Old Mother, I'll be fine."

"Ye'll be deid, ye dinna get some sleep," she pronounced belligerently.

"Aye, I will do," he promised and his dark eyes wandered to the slender form already asleep on the straw-filled ticking.

"Alane," the old denizen declared. She was reed-thin and if she stretched, she might possibly stand level with Alex's waist. She was ageless, toothless, and had a tongue as sharp as an executioner's blade. "The puir wee lamb's exhausted, she disna need ye climbin' all over her wi' yer lusty thoughts."

Alex was permitted no defense, no denials as a bony finger was thrust toward the hearth to indicate where he could spread his tartan.

"Mayhap when she wakens an' when the thoughts come frae her, ye can gie her a wee cuddle, no' afore."

Alex demurred gallantly, but before he could give way to the overwhelming weariness that gripped him, he went out of doors and spoke to Aluinn and Struan MacSorley for nearly an hour. When he returned, he checked on Catherine one last time before spreading his tartan and falling into a deep, well-deserved sleep.

Chapter Nineteen

Catherine woke with a start and for several panic-filled minutes did not know where she was. She heard the crackle of flames in the fireplace and smelled the musky sweetness of burning peat, but it was only when she saw the outline of the old woman bending over to stir the contents of one of the large iron pots that she remembered.

She was safe. The horror was over. Alex had rescued her, had ended the nightmare, and had admitted to wanting her back — a declaration that almost made the terror of the past twenty-four hours worthwhile.

Catherine stretched carefully, testing the aches and pains that flared along her body. She did not know how long she had been asleep or whether it was day or night. The door to the cottage was closed and a rag hung over the single window, but she thought she could see tiny particles of light winking through the cloth.

"Excuse me?" With one hand she pushed herself carefully into a sitting position, while with the other she held the thin blanket modestly high to cover her nakedness. "I beg your pardon, mistress?"

The old woman looked up from the fire.

"My . . . husband. Is he nearby?"

The crofter's wife frowned and said something unintelligible.

"Mr. Cameron," Catherine tried again. "Is Mr. Cameron nearby?"

"Aye, aye. *Camshroinaich.*" The woman beamed and patted her shrunken breast, confirming herself to be of the clan. She bowed her head to the fire again, babbling away to herself in Gaelic.

"Oh dear," Catherine muttered. She gathered the blanket around her shoulders and climbed up off the pallet. The woman glanced over and the volume of what she was saying increased, but Catherine only shrugged helplessly and pointed to the door.

"I just want to speak to him. Actually, I . . . I just want to see him."

The woman clamped her gums together and jutted her chin out in a gesture of disapproval as she watched Catherine take short, stiff steps to the door. It was held closed by a crude wooden latch, and as she drew it aside, the door swung outward. Catherine raised a hand instantly to protect her eyes from the flash of bright sunlight; it blinded her for some few seconds, as did the sight of clean blue sky overhead and brilliant green foothills. The air was crisp and clear, filled with the sounds of insects buzzing, cattle lowing, and children playing somewhere off in the distance.

It was such a different and welcome scene to what she had wakened to the previous morning, she felt tears spring into her eyes. She let them flow unchecked and could not have moved from the spot had she wanted to, not even when the three men seated beside the narrow sluice of a stream stopped their conversation to turn and stare at her.

Alex got up immediately from his seat on a tree stump and walked up the gentle slope to the cottage. Seeing her tears and the shimmering heather of her eyes, he said nothing; he simply took her into his arms and held her until the last of the tremors had faded from her body.

"Has anyone told you you are an exceptionally lovely woman?" he asked softly. "Even when your eyes are running and your nose is red."

Catherine sniffled and smiled through the shine of tears. "And you, sir, have a most unpleasant habit of not being around when I wake up in a strange place."

"Ahh, married life," he murmured. "The nagging begins."

Unmindful of the eyes watching them, Catherine rose on tiptoe and kissed him purposefully on the lips. She raised her hands to his shoulders, carrying the edges of the blanket with her so that her slim and naked body was pressed urgently to his. She felt his quick intake and smiled inwardly as his arms moved unhesitatingly to draw her even closer. His lips were warm and hungry, his eyes dark and, for once, clearly readable in their intentions.

Their gazes locked, he murmured something in Gaelic to the old woman, and Catherine heard a chuckled response. The crofter's wife brushed past them, cackling with feigned disapproval as Alex scooped Catherine into his arms and carried her inside.

The firelight cast a soft pinkish glow on their bodies, the heat from the flames was strong enough to reach into their corner and keep the drafts from chilling their damp flesh. Catherine moaned huskily as her hands slipped on his gleaming muscles; she shuddered and bowed her head over the vast plane of his chest, letting her hair sway and drag across his skin. Her mouth reached greedily for the hard bud of his nipple, and she sampled it with slow, swirling probes of her tongue. His hands were on her hips and she felt him rise up beneath her, his flesh seeking her moist sheath even as she teasingly wriggled away. She slid lower on his body, her fingers tunnelling through the luxuriant mat of black hairs on his chest. Her lips roved shamelessly onto the flat surface of his belly and her teeth nipped playfully at the descending bands of steely muscles.

For two days they had rarely left the cottage. Alexander seemed almost desperate to make up for lost time, for the squandered days and nights when they had fought instead of loved. From the quiet comfort of walking hand in hand through the dusk to the stretching, thrusting power of his body bringing hers to incredible heights of ecstasy, Catherine was kept in continual awe of her husband, discovering facets to him she had not known existed. But however idyllic her newfound love, she suffered under no illusions. There were still a good many secrets and mysteries surrounding Alexander Cameron, and certainly he would not change overnight into someone who could bare his innermost feelings to scrutiny. Neither could she. But with time she could break through that formidable wall he had built around his emotions, of that she was sure. Already, almost hour by hour, she was coming to know and interpret each glance, each special half smile, each moment of exquisite stillness that preluded the urgent hunger in his body.

Catherine felt his urgency now as her lips moved lower and the mighty body tensed beneath a volley of tender, erotic caresses. It was her pleasure to feel him curl every one of his ten fingers into her hair, to hear him shiver her name free on a disbelieving breath, to cause him to suffer the rapturous agony until he could no longer bear it. With a deep and heartfelt oath, he drew her mouth back up to his and rolled with her, silencing her throaty laugh with one powerful thrust after another until she felt herself growing faint from the thrill of it.

His groan was harsh, torn from his chest, as she turned to quicksilver, growing hotter and hotter, tauter and more insistent with each vaunted stroke. He could feel the passion ripping through her, feel it squeeze around him and share a single bright spark of perfect fusion before he was plunged headlong into a whirlpool of colliding sensations.

They clung together, rocking gently in their mutual wonderment as the last of the shimmering vibrations dissipated. Their limbs remained entwined possessively; their lips gradually relinquished contact as they collapsed limply on the rough ticking. Catherine was panting lightly into his shoulder, the flutter of her lashes brushing against his neck. Her body glowed and throbbed within his arms, the musk of her skin soaking his senses like an exotic perfume, and he felt the unaccustomed prick of tears behind his eyes.

She was so lovely. So young. So untouched by the harsher realities of life — and yet time and again she seemed determined to prove he was the innocent, the more naïve of the two. He had thought her weak and willful, yet she had saved their lives at the Spean bridge. He had thought her pampered and temperamental, yet there were untapped reserves of strength and courage in the slender body. She had remained brave and levelheaded during the Campbells' flight into the mountains, and by God — he tightened his arms and his body ached with love for her — she had almost sacrificed herself so that he could end once and for all time the nightmare that was Malcolm Campbell. All that, and she could forgive him his ignorance and stupidity. She could tolerate his pride and stubbornness and defy him to love her. He wished he could take her and run with her, run far away from the troubles of the world and find a niche of fairy-tale happiness somewhere where she would never be hurt or frightened again.

Catherine traced her fingertips lightly over the armoured muscles that sculptured his chest. His heart thundered beneath, and she was content in the knowledge that at least a small part of it belonged wholly to her.

"I never really loved Hamilton, you know," she whispered softly.

"I know." He stroked a hand through the silky length of her hair. "I would have killed him if I thought you did."

Catherine propped her chin on her fist and studied him intently. "How did you know? I mean . . . how did you know this would happen?"

The dark eyes narrowed as they drank in her naked beauty. "I could be clever here and say I knew it the moment I took you in my arms and kissed you in the garden. And thinking back, that was probably the precise moment that did us both in. Where did you learn to kiss like that?"

"I was about to ask you the same question."

"I have led a sullied and tarnished life these past long years — or haven't you been listening to what you have been telling me all these weeks?"

"People — " She paused and bit her lip, trying to recall a note of wisdom she had heard somewhere. "People say all manner of things in anger . . . or self-defense."

"Ahh, but in this case, you were not far off the mark. I am stubborn and pigheaded, arrogant and conceited. I have made a career out of searching for the hard life, of putting my anger and my selfishness before all else."

"True," she said with amazing alacrity. "And so you should not strive for sainthood."

The dark eyes narrowed further. "You should also know I have had a dozen mistresses over the years — few of whom would have a kind word to say in my defense. I am a bastard to live with, a man who has spent thirty-two years avoiding any kind of commitment, even to myself. I have never pictured myself in a domestic situation, never wanted to be held accountable for another human life."

"I suppose you dislike children and kick small dogs?"

"I abhor children and kick animals of any size if the mood comes upon me."

"Then it will be enough, I think, if you can reconcile yourself to the fact that you have a wife now."

"A wife I did not ask for," he reminded her, "but won in a duel."

She inched higher on his chest and let her thigh slide pointedly over the top of his. "You may have won me in a duel, my lord, but I am no mere possession to be placed on a shelf and forgotten. Take heed as well that I will not endure any further confessions of past misdeeds — especially those concerning female persuasion."

Alex eased his lips free after a long, leisurely kiss and gazed deeply into the sparkling violet of her eyes. Why could he not have stumbled upon Catherine Ashbrooke six months, a year ago? So much wasted time . . . He would have liked six months to try to tame her, to be tamed . . .

"Why are you smiling?" she demanded.

"Can a man in love with his wife not smile?"

A shiver raced through Catherine's body and caused her to draw a tremulous breath. Her chin quivered and her lashes fluttered down.

"What is it? What is wrong?"

"Nothing," she whispered.

He tucked a finger beneath her chin and waited until she looked up.

"It's just . . . you have never said it right out before."

He took a deep breath and drew her forward. "Words and I often trip over each other, you must have guessed that by now."

She nodded and his fingers stroked the curve of her cheek. His mouth covered hers, his tongue content to wait until a soft cry invited, then encouraged a deep, searching unity. The scent of him, the feel of him, the taste of him filled her senses, sent them reeling, spinning out of control even as the words echoed in her mind and made her body flush with pride. He loved her! *He loved her!*

He caught her shoulders and pulled her beneath him, his hand twining itself in the long strands of her hair and forcing her head to arch gently back so that he could lavish the creamy smooth flesh with honeyed kisses. He cradled her breast, reshaping the pliant mound to fit his palm, and his mouth was there, plundering the swollen nipple for his enjoyment. Her lips parted and she leaned brazenly into the assault, a gasp welcoming his greedy fingers as they curved into the thatch of golden down, into flesh as warm and sleek as satin. Deftly, skillfully he stroked the silken petals and she melted against him, losing herself to the icy rushes of sensual gratification.

The joining that followed was swift and tumultuous, and Catherine revelled in the knowledge that they gave and received equal pleasure.

"Catherine . . . ?" His breath was hot against her throat, his lips like those of a man long starved of such shattering passions. "Do you believe that I love you?"

"Oh yes . . . yes . . ." She curled her body against his, her heart brimming with love, her flesh still flaming where he had touched it.

"And if I asked you to do something for me, would you do it without question, without argument?"

"I thought I just did," she murmured with a smile.

"Just because you have proven yourself to be a wanton at heart, young lady, do not try to lay the blame at my feet."

"You are completely innocent in my corruption?" she asked sardonically.

"Completely."

"You have no idea where I came by such . . . presumptions?"

"The skills you have acquired have left me frankly astounded."

"But pleased?"

"Euphoric," he admitted, earning another sigh as she nestled her head deeper into his shoulder. He allowed the mood of gentle bantering to fade away before he repeated his question.

"Without argument? You are not going to ask me to endear myself to someone who is beyond endearment — " She thought of Lauren Cameron, whom they had discussed from opposing viewpoints over the past two days. "Or perhaps tell me for the thousandth time I mustn't wander anywhere without a regiment of bodyguards? Believe me, you will hear no arguments on that point. I shall probably remain locked tight within the castle walls until I am old and shrivelled and of no use to anyone — and quite happily too, I might add.''

"Catherine — '' He folded his arms around her gently. "I'm not taking you back to Achnacarry.''

"Not taking me back? Where are we going?''

For a brief, blissful moment Catherine thought he was going to say he was taking her away — far away — from Scotland, from England, from anything that might threaten to destroy the joy she had found within his arms. In the next heartbeat she knew that was not possible. He had already told her he would stand by his brother's decision to join the fomenting rebellion. He had pledged his word, his honour, and she knew him well enough to realize he would never break such a bond to his family, not when he had travelled all these miles, endured such risks and dangers just so that he could stand by their side. And if that was the case, if he was not proposing to run away with her . . .

"Oh no. No! No, Alex . . . *you cannot mean to send me away!*''

"Catherine — '' His arms prevented her from jerking up and away from him. "Catherine, listen to me.''

"No! I *won't* listen! And I won't go. You cannot make me go!''

"I can and I will," he said evenly. "We are a two-hour ride from the coast. The ship I made arrangements for you to sail on should be docking sometime before midnight and leaving again within a few hours. You are going to be on it.''

"No. No. No. *Nooo!*''

"Catherine! Goddammit! Will you stop squirming and listen to me? Don't you know there is going to be a war?''

"I don't care. I'm your *wife*!'' She twisted frantically to break out of his grip, but he only wrestled her flat on the mattress and pinned her down with the weight of his body.

"Yes, you are my wife. And I would be a pretty damn

poor husband if I did not do everything in my power to see that you were safe.''

"I will be safe at Achnacarry — "

"A castle is only as strong as the men who guard the walls — and there will be precious few men left behind to do so. Donald has pledged to raise every clansman who can bear arms. Catherine, don't you understand? Clans will be fighting against one another; boundaries, territories, laws will cease to exist.''

"I don't care. I . . . I'm not afraid. And I don't see Donald sending Maura away, or Archibald sending Jeannie to safety.''

"They have lived with blood and violence all their lives. They know what to expect and they can accept it.''

"Tell *me* what to expect and I will accept it too. Haven't I just proved I can survive the worst life has to offer?''

"Catherine — '' His voice became softer and more desperate. "I never wanted you to prove anything to me. I don't ever want you to have to prove anything to me again, only that you trust me enough to know this is what is best for you. I want you to be safe. I want to know you are safe and warm and protected — ''

"Please,'' she sobbed, and her hands trembled against his cheeks, "please don't send me away, Alex. Please . . . *please . . .*''

Alex lowered his mouth to hers. He kissed her with all the tenderness and passion it was within his power to impart, and when the kiss ended, his weakness was so acute he knew he dared not look into her eyes or the resolve he had been building so carefully over the past few hours would desert him completely. He laid his head between her breasts and prayed to feel her arms close around him. One last time. Just one last time. Dear God, he did not want to lose her now, he did not want to send her away or let her out of his sight for even an instant . . . but he knew it was what he must do. He had to save her at all costs, even if it meant destroying her love for him.

Catherine stared unseeing at the thatched roof over their heads. All of the joy, the peace, the contentment she had been feeling, and learning to feel, vanished, leaving her hollow and empty. He was going to do it. He was going to send her away, then go off to fight a war, possibly to die —

"You knew all along it would come to this, didn't you?" she asked tautly. "Why didn't you tell me? Why did you let me think, let me believe . . . let me *hope* you loved me enough that it didn't matter who or what I was?"

He frowned and raised his head.

"That's it, isn't it? It's because I'm English, because I am an embarrassment to the great Clan Cameron?"

"Your being English has nothing to do with my decision," he said evenly, "and you know it."

"As of this moment, I do not know anything anymore. I only know you are sending me out of your life without giving me a real chance to try to belong in it."

"Catherine, it's the wrong time — "

"Yes. Yes, I understand all about your valued sense of timing," she interrupted. "It is a convenient excuse to use when it suits your needs. Yesterday and today you needed time to prove you were capable of feeling and acting like a human being — a caring, compassionate, loving human being. Tomorrow and the days, weeks after that, you'll be going off to play at war, and the only needs you will have then are the need to kill, maim, and brutalize — all in the name of family honour. Well, thank you, perhaps you are right. Perhaps I shouldn't be here to see you degenerate into something less than a man."

She pushed away from him and swung her legs over the side of the pallet. He did not try to stop her, not even when he saw how badly she was shaking as she reached for her clothing. He watched her slip her arms into the cheap cotton chemise, and he longed to stay her hand from lacing it closed over the delicate whiteness of her breasts. She stepped into the single petticoat and drew it snug about her waist, then shrugged the plain homespun dress over her shoulders, thankful that the practical peasant style fastened in front and that she had no need to ask for his assistance.

And yet Alex could not resist standing behind her, placing his hands on her shoulders, and smoothing the tousled weight of her hair.

"I love you, Catherine. I know you are angry with me now, and you may not believe it absolutely, but I do love you. What is more, I swear on that love — and on my life — that I will come for you as soon as I possibly can."

The slender back remained like a solid, impenetrable wall before him; her hands continued to lace the bodice of her dress as if she had not heard — or did not choose to hear.

The impending sense of loss drove him to lean forward and place his lips tenderly over a fading bruise that marred the slender column of her neck. He turned away to dress, so ridden by his own inner turmoil he did not see the terrible shudder that swept through her body and sent her nails gouging into the flesh above her heart.

Catherine stood on the beach watching the last of the longboats being loaded with contraband. Highland wool was at a premium in Europe, along with the heady amber spirits distilled and taken for granted in nearly every castle and bothy in the kirk. Incoming goods reflected the suspicions of intrepid businessmen and merchants: gunpowder, flint, lead, and weaponry of all kinds would command exorbitant prices in the months ahead.

The captain of the *Curlew* was a short, wiry bristle of a man who appeared to have gone through most of his life without ever having laid a hand to soap and water. Blackpool, she had been informed in no uncertain terms, was not one of his regular stops, but as a personal favour to The Cameron of Lochiel, he would set her ashore in a small inlet he knew of about four miles downcurrent from the city. From there, two of Alexander's most trusted men would accompany her into the city, stay long enough to arrange a coach and escort to Derby, then find their way back across the border again. Catherine recognized one of the men from the group who had rescued her from the clutches of Malcolm Campbell. The other was Aluinn MacKail.

Part of the reason for their delay in the shepherd's glen became apparent when Struan MacSorley reappeared after a two-day absence. He rode at the head of a sizable column of armed clansmen whom he had collected from Achnacarry. Lochiel had returned to the castle and was already making preparations for raising the clan. Struan carried with him a packet of letters, hastily written, from Maura, Donald, and surprisingly enough, Archibald Cameron. They wished Catherine a safe journey and a quick return to Achnacarry.

Also in tow amongst the burly clansmen, was Deirdre O'Shea, loyal to her mistress even though she paled noticeably each time she glanced in Aluinn MacKail's direction.

Catherine blinked to keep the tears back as she looked up at the hazy rift of moonlight breaking through the clouds overhead. A crisp, salty breeze cooled her cheeks and stirred the sand underfoot into tiny whirling dervishes. She was wrapped in a broad swath of tartan that kept out all but the most persistent drafts, and yet she shivered. Her mind brimmed with pictures and images, yet she thought of nothing; no voices echoed in her head, no words of reassurance or condemnation.

"It's time," Alex said softly, startling her, for she had not heard his footsteps in the sand.

She looked up and saw his face in surprisingly sharp detail: his eyes, his nose, his wide and sensual mouth, the truant locks of black hair that insisted on curling forward on his brow . . .

"You will give Maura and Jeannie my fondest regards?" she began. "And your brothers, your Aunt Rose . . . ? You will tell them this wasn't my idea?"

"If you want me to, I will."

She bit down on the fleshy pulp of her lip and gazed out

over the water. The waves were clear and carved with foaming backwash, glittering under the moonlight as they ran up on the shore and slipped back again.

"Ironic, is it not, how I should have pleaded so hard for you to send me home, and now that you are . . ." Her voice faltered. He reached out a hand but she saw the movement and flinched out of range. "Please don't. I never was very strong when you touched me . . . but then, you knew that, didn't you? You relished that particular little hold over me; used it rather shamelessly too, I dare say."

He could hear the brittleness in her voice, see it in the rigid way she held her body.

"The captain tells me the winds are fair. You should have clear sailing between here and England."

"Assuming the revenuers do not interfere. But then, what new adventures could a battle at sea provide over and above what I have already experienced thus far? It would seem tame by comparison."

"The captain is skillful. I doubt you will even see another ship on the horizon."

Their eyes locked for the span of a brief strained silence before Catherine looked to the sea again.

"Yes indeed, the little man looks anxious to be away. I should not delay him any longer."

"Catherine — " His voice was thick and low, the sound shivered across the nape of her neck. She did not turn to face him again but stared steadfastly out across the water so as not to let him see the tears collecting along her lashes. She would not let him see her cry. If it was the last thing she did on this accursed shore, she would keep the shreds of her pride intact.

A rolled, sealed, and beribboned set of documents was pressed into her hand.

"The letters I promised you," he said softly. "The choice as to whether you return to Derby a wife or a widow is yours. In any event, these papers will give you legal access to the accounts . . . or the estate . . . of Raefer Montgomery. Aluinn has copies of everything; he will send them on to London.''

''I told you once before I did not want your money.''

''Then safeguard it for me. This also — '' He took her hand and she felt something cold and hard glide onto her finger. A ring?

''It belonged to Sir Ewen's wife, and before that, his mother, and so on back a couple of generations. I had almost forgotten about it until Maura reminded me it had been a bequest for my wife.''

''It . . . should stay at Achnacarry,'' she whispered.

''It should stay exactly where it is.''

Catherine averted her face from a particularly cutting gust of wind and found herself looking up into her husband's dark eyes. The ache in her chest grew until the pressure threatened to smother her, and without another word she turned and stumbled toward the two pots of burning tar that marked the landing area for the longboats. Deirdre was already seated in the bow, her hands clasped around the portmanteau she had guarded ever since leaving Derby.

Feeling the water crawl up the sand and lick at the hem of her skirts, Catherine braced herself for the final farewells. The expressions on the faces of Aluinn MacKail and Struan MacSorley were grim and uncomfortable, the latter looking as if he wanted to grasp two heads and knock them together.

''I am sorry to have been the cause of so much trouble, and I do appreciate everything that has been done for me. I . . . I cannot honestly say I wish your venture well, but I do wish you personal success . . . and safety.'' She moistened her lips and cast a final glance along the craggy shoreline. She had been less than a month away from Derby, yet she felt as if she had aged by a score of years. Sights she would never forget had been forged onto her memory: Did the moon ever balance so brightly in the sky over Rosewood Hall as it had over the ancient battlements of Achnacarry Castle? Was the mist as eerie and secretive, the grass as green, the moorlands as pungent with heather and moss? True, she had spent the most frightening days of her life in

Scotland, but she had also found happiness and meaning . . . and love.

The captain cleared his throat impatiently, prompting Catherine to turn her back on the shore and step into the longboat. Alex stood rock-still his face expressionless, his fists balled down by his sides. Aluinn regarded him with an impotent frustration, knowing there was nothing he could say or do to change Alex's mind or make the parting easier.

"I'll take good care of her," he promised and clasped a hand around Alex's arm.

Catherine nodded, but before he released Aluinn's grip, he reached beneath his coat and withdrew a slim, sealed letter.

"When you arrive in Blackpool, give this to Deirdre. Ask her, in your most cavalier manner, if she would pass it on to Damien for me. You may assure her the contents are purely personal — a simple request from me to my brother-in-law."

"I'll see she delivers it." He stepped into the longboat as the oarsmen prepared to shove it into the surf. He tossed a wave of his hand in Struan's direction and as an afterthought shouted, "Don't start the war without me."

"Bah! We'll hae it fought an' won by the time ye find yer way back!" MacSorley declared and returned the wave as the little boat cut into a shallow trough of water.

Alexander remained on the glittering shore, his broad frame bathed in the bluish moonlight, his hair whipping in the salt air. His gaze stayed locked on the bobbing craft until it was absorbed into the black shadow of the waiting *Curlew*. Within minutes the sheets of wide canvas were unfurled on her two tall masts, swelling and curling forward eagerly as they filled with the stiff breeze. The ship glided soundlessly out of the narrow inlet, bending her bow gracefully into the larger waves beyond the jagged point of land. By morning they would be clear of the most dangerous stretch of water and out into the open sea-lanes. Three days, four at the most, and they should be close off Blackpool.

"I will come for you Catherine," Alexander whispered. "I swear I will come for you, though hell stands between us."

The wind snatched the vow and flung it to the heavens as he turned away from the water's edge, his convictions pounding solidly in his chest. But it would be many months before he would find himself on the road to Derby, and then not as a husband seeking to reclaim his wife, but as a soldier in the Highland army seeking to reclaim a throne for his king.